Golden Image

by

Henry Bendow

Grosvenor House
Publishing Limited

All rights reserved
Copyright © Henry Miller, 2009

Henry Miller is hereby identified as author of this
work in accordance with Section 77 of the Copyright, Designs
and Patents Act 1988

The book cover picture is copyright to KHM, Wien

This book is published by
Grosvenor House Publishing Ltd
28-30 High Street, Guildford, Surrey, GU1 3HY.
www.grosvenorhousepublishing.co.uk

This book is sold subject to the conditions that it shall not, by way of
trade or otherwise, be lent, resold, hired out or otherwise circulated
without the author's or publisher's prior consent in any form of binding or
cover other than that in which it is published and
without a similar condition including this condition being imposed
on the subsequent purchaser.

A CIP record for this book
is available from the British Library

ISBN 978-1-907211-08-9

They spoke to the King Nebuchadnezzar,

"Oh King live forever. Thou, Oh King, hast made a decree, that every man that shall hear the sound of the flute shall fall down and worship the golden image...."

Daniel 3:9 & 10

Content

Prologue	1
Part I: The Reluctant Flute Player	3
Part II: The Craftsman	29
Part III: The Killer	75
Part IV: The Prisoner	181
Part V: The Frenchman	323
Part VI: The Man on the Pisa Road	481
Afterword	566
Acknowledgements	567
Author's note and Bibliography	568

Prologue

Benvenuto Cellini was both the friend and enemy of Cardinals, Popes and Kings. He lived and worked in humble shops and palaces. He was exiled, thrown into prison and became a fugitive when he escaped. He took part in a great battle, and, in violent times, when life was cheap, he brawled, fought and quarrelled, and was himself responsible for several killings.

But he was also a sculptor, whose works grace great museums around the world, and above all, was the greatest goldsmith ever known, and against whom the works of other goldsmiths are still measured.

His bust stands in the middle of the Ponte Vecchio, the centre of the jewellery trade, in his native city of Florence.

He was born on All Saints' Day, November 1st 1500 to Elisabetta and Giovanni Cellini.

Giovanni was an architect - an unsuccessful architect - because he had gone into the profession very unwillingly at his father's insistence. He had wanted to be a musician, and regarded every minute he spent at his drawing board and away from his cornet as being totally wasted. Eventually his employer, Lorenzo de' Medici, dismissed him for neglecting his work, and he was forced to eke out a living by designing lifting gear for builders and making the beautiful picture frames inlaid with silver and ivory that were then in vogue.

Giovanni was also the leader of the Signory orchestra, and his ambition was that his older son should become a great flute player. Putting completely out of his own mind his identical arguments with his own father, he totally ignored the fact that Benvenuto wanted no such thing. From his early childhood, Benvenuto had only ever wanted to be a goldsmith.

Elisabetta's role in the family was to try to come between her obstinate husband and her equally headstrong son in the constant quarrels about the boy's future.

But for his son, Giovanni would now be completely forgotten.

And in spite of all his protestations, Benvenuto was, on occasions, and very reluctantly, a flute player......

Part I: The Reluctant Flute Player

-1-

The five prisoners shuffled slowly down the corridor leading to the courtroom, prompted by pushes in the small of the back from the guards.

Led by the police corporal, Benvenuto Cellini helped his younger brother, Cecchino, on whose head was a blood stained bandage. Cecchino's face was pale, his eyes were slightly glazed, and dizziness made him stagger slightly.

Close behind were three of the di Ferranti's. Carlo, his head also bandaged, as was his arm, limped along, supported on one side by his brother and on the other by his cousin, who was himself nursing a badly swollen right hand in the fold of his doublet.

As the party approached a wooden bench, Benvenuto's father, Giovanni, stood up. He had been there since early morning, waiting to see his sons who had been locked up all night.

"Cecchino! My God! What's happened to your head? Are you alright? Benvenuto, how did you get him into this trouble?"

The Corporal roughly shoved Giovanni back on to the bench. "No talking to the prisoners; prisoners will remain silent," he ordered.

"He got into trouble on his own," Benvenuto retorted angrily. "I saved him from these murdering whore's sons."

The Corporal turned on Benvenuto with an upraised fist. "I said 'shut up'!" he shouted. "Wait here."

They had reached a door at the end of the passageway. The Corporal went inside the room, leaving the door slightly ajar. Giovanni again stood up and made as if to approach his sons, but one of the soldiers quickly stepped in front of him, holding up his hand to silence the older man, but did nothing to make him go back to his seat.

Straining to listen through the crack in the door, Benvenuto and his father could hear the Corporal making his report.

"Fighting...sword....daggers...di Ferranti wounded.... Cecchino Cellini....hit by stone...unconscious. Informer says older Cellini boy came later....protecting his brother...."

Benvenuto stole a glance at his father's face. He saw a thin shabby man in his late fifties, whose hair had receded in a half-moon from his forehead, but with bushy eyebrows that accentuated his deeply sunken eyes and bony cheeks. The collar of his tunic was far too big for his scraggy neck, and his clothes hung loosely from his rounded shoulders as if they belonged to someone else.

Giovanni's normal expression was a mixture of worry and bewilderment. This time he had begun by being angry, but as he listened to the snatches of what the Corporal was saying, Giovanni's look had changed first to misery and then to pride. Risking a further reprimand from the guard, he mouthed the word, "Sorry" to his son.

Benvenuto sniffed and turned his head aside.

At that moment the door opened wide. The corporal came out and looked at Giovanni with some surprise, and pointed to the bench again, but then relented.

"Oh, what the hell! They want you inside, too." He jerked his head indicating that everyone should go in.

Giovanni entered the room, and Benvenuto, with Cecchino still leaning on his arm, followed hesitatingly. As he did so, Carlo di Ferranti accidentally stepped on his heel.

Benvenuto, fists clenched, turned to protest, but the Corporal hissed through the corner of his mouth, "Stop it, sonny! You're in enough trouble as it is."

The door crashed shut behind the little group, and ominously, one of the two soldiers shot the massive bolt, sheathed his sword, and stood in front of the door, arms folded. His companion also sheathed his sword and leaned against the whitewashed wall.

There was a heavy carved table in some dark wood, behind which stood eight high-backed chairs covered in faded red brocade. This was the Courtroom of "Gli Otto", ("The Eight"), the Magistrates who administered the Criminal Law in Florence. Only two of the chairs were occupied.

The Corporal lined the prisoners in front of the table: Benvenuto, Cecchino and their father to the left and the di Ferranti's to the right. The Corporal stood between them and Benvenuto noticed for the first time that half a dozen lengths of thin rope were hanging from his belt. Just the sort of thing to tie convicts hands with!

Benvenuto glanced around the room. In the centre of the wall was the inevitable crucifix. To one side of it was a painting of the head of St. John on a silver dish, being presented, staring eyes, and blood and all to Herod. On the other side of the crucifix was a dream-like painting of the Avenging Angel, sword held over his head in both hands, ready to strike at a kneeling prisoner whose chained hands were upraised in a plea for mercy.

The message of both paintings was quite clear to Benvenuto, who suddenly felt very nervous.

The only light in the room came from a row of windows high in the same wall behind the Magistrates. Shafts of sunlight shone through, straight into the prisoners' eyes, forcing them to stand looking down at the floor, shuffling their feet in little jerky movements, while specks of dust and fluff danced in the air. To the side of the Magistrates' table was another little square one, at which a small, mouse-like man sat. Benvenuto took him to be the Clerk, as before him were some sheets of paper, an ink horn, pens and a sand sifter to blot the ink.

He was dressed in a grubby, stained brown robe, tied at the waist with a piece of frayed cord. His bony bare ankles, showing over the tops of his sandals were black with grime. He had a greasy skull cap on the back of his bald head.

He had been picking his nose with his thumb as the little group entered the room. Once everyone was in place to the Corporal's satisfaction, he looked up at them with pale, watery eyes, wiped his fingers on his beard and said in a thin voice, "Your names?"

He wrote them down, and then seemed to lose interest in the whole proceedings as he began to gnaw on his thumb nail, stopping to look at his handiwork from time to time.

One of the Magistrates began to speak.

"The charges are making an affray, wounding, and causing a breach of the peace." He paused and looked along the row of prisoners and then said, almost conversationally, to Giovanni, "Signor Cellini, we've already had all the details of what happened, and we'll never find out who started it....."

"He did!" Cecchino and Carlo di Ferranti said simultaneously, pointing at the other.

"Corporal," the Magistrate said, "is that a truncheon I see hanging from your belt?"

"Yes, your Excellency."

"Well, next time a prisoner interrupts, just hit him with it. Don't wait for orders."

The Magistrate turned to Giovanni. "You see what I mean? Each one always blames the other. Now I personally assume that the one who's hurt the least is the one who started it. In this case, that's your son, Cecchino, but I can't really believe that a fourteen year old boy would really start a fight with a man six years older and over a foot taller. So you see, we just don't know."

"He's a good boy," Giovanni said.

"I never had one in front of me who wasn't, according to his parents," retorted the Magistrate. "Now look, I'm not surprised to have the di Ferranti's here. Hardly a week goes by when I don't have to deal with one of the clan. One day one of them will do something I can hang him for, and then maybe they'll stop. But your sons? Why? I hear your oldest boy is always fist fighting. But this time, apparently, he wasn't to blame even though he did most of the damage." He turned to Benvenuto. "What's all this fighting about, boy?"

"It's his fault, not mine," Benvenuto replied, jerking his head in the direction of his father.

"It's his name," Giovanni explained.

"Cellini?"

"No, 'Benvenuto'. People make jokes about it, so he fights them."

"So would you," said Benvenuto, risking the Corporal's truncheon. "Every time you meet someone new, they say the same thing, 'Benvenuto - you're welcome', and expect you to think it's funny."

"It doesn't seem much to get annoyed about to me."

"It's not you it's happening to all the time," Benvenuto said, truculently.

"You call me 'Your Excellency', and you keep a respectful tone in your voice," the Magistrate reminded him. Benvenuto bit his lip.

"Messer Cellini, what made you pick a name like that? Why wasn't the name of one of the Blessed Saints good enough?"

"My wife and I had been married for twenty-three years. We - she - didn't have children easily. We lost twin boys at birth. Then we had a daughter, Cosa. Then, a long time later she fell pregnant again. We were sure it was another girl. All the signs said so. So did the fortune-teller and the midwife."

Giovanni told the story in disjointed sentences. "She was in labour for hours. The neighbours kept coming in. They kept giving me wine to drink. When he was born, I was drunk. Then the midwife told me it was a boy, and I couldn't believe it. I just kept saying 'E Benvenuto', 'he's welcome, he's welcome', over and over again."

"And then they brought the priest round to baptize him in case he died like the others." Giovanni wiped a tear from his eye. "When the priest asked what the boy's name was, all I could say was 'Benvenuto'."

The two magistrates exchanged puzzled glances. The second one took up the questioning. "Tell me, Signor Cellini, what profession is the older boy going to follow?"

"Musician." "Goldsmith," Giovanni and Benvenuto said simultaneously.

There was a moment's pause, and then Benvenuto continued angrily, obviously repeating a much rehearsed argument, "He wanted to be a musician, but his father, Grandfather Cristofano, wanted him to be an architect, just like he was. Now that my father is the head of the Signory band, he wants me to be a flute player. Why is it," Benvenuto continued plaintively, "that fathers always try to make their sons do what they weren't able to do themselves?"

The Magistrate ignored the outburst. "What about your younger son? What's he going to be?"

"A lawyer." "A soldier," Giovanni and Cecchino said together.

The Magistrate suppressed a smile. "How long has Benvenuto wanted to be a goldsmith?"

"Since he was a child," Giovanni replied. "The ungrateful boy! He's right. When I was his age, my father made me study mathematics, physics and drawing. I would have given anything to be allowed to devote myself to music. Did he thank me? No! He spent all his spare time and some of the time he should have been at school hanging around those dirty little workshops at Orsanmichele."

"I wasn't hanging around," Benvenuto said, indignantly. "How many times have I got to tell you? First I ran errands and did the sweeping up, and then they started teaching me how to do things."

"A goldsmith. What is a goldsmith?" Giovanni asked contemptuously. "Nothing but a shopkeeper." He managed to inject a note of scorn into the word. "A shopkeeper. Bowing and scraping to his customers. 'Does this fine piece please the Madonna? Will his Lordship condescend to tell me what his wishes are? What? He wants to kick my arse? Certainly. Allow me to grovel on the floor to make it easier'."

"That will do!" the Corporal interjected. "You will also be respectful to their Excellencies!"

The first magistrate resumed the questioning. "If he's so set on being a goldsmith, why don't you let him? It's just as artistic, if that's what you want, as being a musician. It's an honest trade."

Giovanni was rapidly getting the feeling that he was the one who was on trial. "I did. I apprenticed him to Michelangelo of Pinzi di Monte."

"Yes," Benvenuto retorted bitterly, "and then he took me away again. 'It's because I love you, my darling son. I just can't bear to live without seeing you every day'." Benvenuto gave a cruel imitation of his father's reedy voice. "What he really wanted was for me to stay at home and play my flute."

"So what did he do?" Giovanni appealed to the magistrates, "He ran away and apprenticed himself to Marcone the goldsmith. He stayed away for a whole year. In the end I agreed to pay Marcone something towards his wages so that at least he would spend more time learning his trade than sweeping the floor and running errands."

"Was he a good apprentice?"

"Yes," Giovanni admitted reluctantly.

"Good?" Benvenuto boasted. "Both my employers said they never had a worker like me. Not even Bandinello's own son, Baccio. I can beat gold into leaf. I can make gold plates. I can use all the tools: saws, augers and punches. And I can etch with **Acqua Regis** - Royal Water - that's sulphuric acid and nitric acid mixed. It's called 'royal' because it is the only thing that will dissolve gold," Benvenuto explained.

"Very interesting," the Magistrate said in a tone that indicated that it was not. "Let's get back to last night's fight."

"I was on my way back from the goldsmith's shop where I work. Look, he gave me this as my week's wages." Benvenuto produced a tiny pellet of gold that that he had melted down from filings swept from the workbench. Not much fell on the floor: the workers pinned their leather aprons to the bench to catch any stray specks of gold. The nugget was worth perhaps the same as a small silver coin.

The Magistrate took it between thumb and forefinger, squinted at it, and gave it to his clerk.

"That will pay your fine."

"Fine?" Benvenuto protested. "Why should I be fined? I didn't do anything, except save my brother from being murdered!"

"Corporal!" the Magistrate said menacingly, and Benvenuto subsided.

"It's not often we get a defendant here with real gold in his pocket. You di Ferranti's," the Magistrate addressed them directly for the first time, "you're nothing but trouble. The whole wretched family. The three of you are all banished from Florence - to the South. Let me see - yes, to Arezzo, for six months. If you come back earlier than that, I promise you that you'll see the inside of the dirtiest, dampest dungeon I can find.

"But now, as for you two Cellini's," the Chief Magistrate continued, "don't think we're taken in by your story either. We know your reputation too. If there's a fight anywhere, somehow one or other of you seems to be in it. Now maybe you started this one, and maybe you didn't, but we think you could do with a lesson too. So, we're going to give you one. Just to make up for all the times that you didn't get caught.

You are both also banished from Florence for six months. It's for your own good, because otherwise the rest of the di Ferranti's will nail you to the nearest wall when they catch you. Benvenuto Cellini - you can go back to Pinza and work for Bandinello if you want to." He smiled at Benvenuto benignly, and winked.

"I can come back in six months?" A pause then, Benvenuto added reluctantly, "Your Excellency?"

"Yes, you can, and when you do, you know what? You'll be welcome!" The Magistrate's smile turned into a broad grin and Benvenuto at the age of sixteen began the first of the several exiles he was to suffer in his life.

-2-

The "welcome home" party that Elisabetta Cellini gave for her two sons, six months to the day after their sentences had begun did not, in the end, turn out to be a success.

"Mama, the food's all gone. We've been working since before daylight, and they've eaten it in no time at all!" Benvenuto's sister, Cosa, was close to tears.

"That shows how much they enjoyed it. Now shush! I think your father's going to say something."

Somewhat unsteadily Giovanni got to his feet. Kicking his stool to one side, he leaned against the wall of the courtyard of his house and stared, owlishly, for a few moments at Benvenuto's uncles and aunts and the handful of neighbours seated at two long tables. These were now covered with a litter of dirty crockery and the remnants of the meal, on which the flies were now beginning to feast.

Giovanni made a sweeping gesture with his hand, slopping wine from his goblet over his wrist.

"My dear friends....," he began.

"He's no friend of mine," one of his brothers-in-law muttered to his neighbour. His wife dug him sharply in the ribs with her elbow.

Giovanni had not heard the interruption. "I need not tell you how delighted my beloved wife and I are to have our sons with us again....."

"But you're going to, just the same," said his brother-in-law, a little louder this time. Giovanni's sister kicked him on the ankle, while Benvenuto and Cecchino squirmed with embarrassment.

"......and I'm not going to make a long speech...."

Everyone cheered. "....however, I do have an announcement to make. It's too early to make any final decision about Cecchino's future...."

Benvenuto squeezed his brother's arm. "It looks like you're not going to have to be a lawyer after all," he whispered.

"....but," Giovanni continued, "I have been able to do something for Benvenuto's career. I have discussed it with Cardinal de' Medici."

His brother-in-law could not contain himself any longer and jumped up from his chair.

"You? And Cardinal de' Medici? Since when has his Eminence been your adviser?"

The normally mild-mannered Giovanni turned on his tormentor.

"Listen, Rudolfo Caprietto, I may not have as much money as you, but don't forget it was the dowry my father gave you when you married my sister that set you up in business!"

Caprietto stared round him, and allowed his wife to drag him down to his seat by his sleeve, while hissing the word "Porco!" at him. The guest sitting on his other side ostentatiously moved his chair away, and the others averted their eyes.

Giovanni turned to Benvenuto. "The Cardinal has decided you shall go to Bologna. To study." He paused for dramatic effect. "To study music."

"Never!" Benvenuto was on his feet, white with rage. "Can't you get it into your head? I don't want to be a musician! I want to be - I already am - a Goldsmith."

"Silence!" Giovanni ordered. "When the Cardinal tells you to go to Bologna, you go. And when he says you will study music, you will study music! One day Cardinal de' Medici is likely to be Pope. What makes you think a boy not yet seventeen years old can argue with him? Who do you think you are?"

"Who am I? I am Benvenuto Cellini, and I am going to be the greatest goldsmith the world has ever known. I'll tell you this. Cardinal or Pope, one day he'll be paying me more for one piece of my work than he'll pay you in wages for your whole lifetime."

Benvenuto ran out of the courtyard into the street, pausing only to yell through the bars of the gate, "And I'll tell you something else! People will remember me long after Cardinal de' Medici - and you - are dead, buried and forgotten."

- 3 -

Of course Benvenuto did go to Bologna. He had no choice. As his father had pointed out, boys of seventeen do not disobey Cardinals, and despite his protestations, he really did not mind the opportunity of travelling such a distance. At a time when a man could live and die without leaving the town where he was born, or going further than the next village, this chance to go as far as forty-five miles was really "seeing the world".

He only stayed away for as long as he thought it would take for the Cardinal to forget all about him. He came home after about six months without forewarning his parents.

His father was not in the house, and one of a neighbour's children was sent to look for him. In the meantime, Benvenuto sat at the kitchen table greedily spooning mouthfuls of soup and bolting down chunks of his mother's warm, fresh bread. In-between gulps, he tried to tell his mother and sister what he had been doing.

"I went to work for a goldsmith."

His mother wrung her hands. "Benvenuto! You were supposed to study music!"

"Oh, I did that too," he said scornfully. "I had a lesson every day. Well, nearly every day. But you've got no idea what it was like in the shop. Not just sweeping up and fixing the tools. I not only helped the craftsmen, I actually made things myself. I even made a goblet for father."

"Show me," Cosa squealed.

"Not yet. Father should see it first."

"Is it made of real gold?"

"Of course not," Benvenuto said with a little smile. "I couldn't afford that - nor even silver. I made it out of pewter, but at least you can see what I can do already, and I've only just started. I can take gold rods and turn them into rings and bracelets. I can even turn rods of gold into wire for gold braid or filigree work."

"I never thought about that before," Elisabetta said, "I suppose someone does have to do it. How do they get the gold wire?"

Benvenuto was delighted that, at last, one of his parents was taking an interest in his work. "You have a big pair of pliers attached to a thick leather strap and you grip one end of the rod in that and using a big wheel to tighten the strap, you pull the rod through a lot of holes, each smaller than the other. It's just like the Rack in a torture chamber!"

Elisabetta shuddered and crossed herself against the Evil Eye, so Benvenuto decided he had better change the subject a little.

"And you should see the stones, all beautiful and glittering. Diamonds, rubies, emeralds, sapphires, blue lapis lazuli, dark red garnets, yellow topazes, pale blue beryls and aquamarines, and purple amethysts. White, cream, grey and black pearls. Every colour, shape and size that you can think of!"

"You know," he said, "despite all of that, it's the gold that I really love working with."

"How so?" Elisabetta asked.

"It never rusts or tarnishes. It's tremendously strong and yet it's so soft you can make it into any shape you like. Working with it, it's like - it's like - **creating**. And do you know, I've even learned to paint and bake it so that the enamel sets without cracks or bumps!"

Cosa rushed over and threw her arms round her brother. "Oh Benvenuto! You're so clever! Isn't he mama?"

Elisabetta smiled and blew a kiss across the room, while Benvenuto blushed and cleared his throat with a little cough.

"Look Cosa, do you see my ring?" He showed her a small signet ring he had made for himself which he was wearing on his little finger. "The gold from this was once in a gold ring given to King Solomon by the Queen of Sheba."

"Ooh! Was it really? Let me look!"

Benvenuto laughed. "No, of course it wasn't, silly! Although it might have been. You never know. That's the whole thing about gold: you can use it over and over again. One day a coin, the next a vase, and then a candlestick or a brooch."

Elisabetta and Cosa just stood looking at him, each beaming with pride.

"When I've finished learning all I have to know, I'm going to make things that are so beautiful that no one will want to melt them down," he vowed. "They'll last forever, and in a thousand years time people will say, 'Benvenuto Cellini made that'."

Giovanni hurried home to see his son, accompanied by his former pupil, Piero Malcesine, who was now his chief assistant at the orchestra.

Benvenuto embraced his father warmly, but gave Piero only a perfunctory nod of recognition. Benvenuto suspected that his being sent to Bologna was Piero's idea. Piero wanted to get rid of a rival for the future leadership of the Signory Orchestra, which was the last thing in the world that Benvenuto wanted.

Giovanni could not contain his impatience. "Have you been practising your music? Have you been studying composing and orchestration? Let me hear you!"

Benvenuto reluctantly produced his flute and played the most difficult piece he knew. Giovanni applauded and turned to Piero. "I don't care what anyone says, I'll make him the greatest musician in the whole of Florence - in the whole World!"

Piero shook his head. "He's not bad, but nothing more than a gifted amateur. Benvenuto will get far more out of being a goldsmith than by playing a flute."

Seeing Benvenuto nod in agreement, Giovanni turned on Piero.

"I knew it! I knew it! It's you who's been poisoning the boy's mind against me all these years. I taught you all the music you know and you want to stop me teaching my own son. It's you who talked him out of studying music."

Still spluttering with rage, and jabbing his finger at Piero with every word, Giovanni thrust his face close to Piero's. "You're jealous! That's what it is. You're jealous because you know he can be better than you - or even me. You'll be punished. You'll see. Not in years, not in months, but in weeks. You'll lose everything you have. Starting with your job; today!"

Hearing this curse, Cosa's hand flew to her mouth, but Piero just laughed. "Maestro, old age has made you soft in the head. I won't lose anything! On the contrary, I and my sons will finish up supporting you and yours."

This was too much for Giovanni. He uttered a second curse. "Your miserable sons support my clever, rich sons? Never, never, never! It will be your children who will come begging from mine!"

He flung open the street door. Piero walked out without another word, and Giovanni slammed it shut.

"Now, my dear son, pick up your flute again, and you and I will play a duet for your mother."

―∞―

Less than a month later, Piero, who was having a cellar built under his house, was standing on the ground floor with some of his friends and was telling them about his quarrel with Giovanni.

".... and then the silly old fool said I would lose everything. Can you imagine it? My family have been merchants for generations; I can buy and sell him fifty thousand times over and he says I will lose everything."

To emphasise the point, he raised his knee, slapped his thigh, and stamped his foot. The weakened floor collapsed and he fell through into the basement, breaking both legs.

Piero contracted gangrene as a result of the accident, and died a few days later.

—⚎—

No one doubted that Piero's death was as a result of Giovanni's curse - least of all Benvenuto. In fact it made him distinctly nervous. Obviously there was more to his nondescript father than he had previously given him credit for. The terrible fate that he had brought down on Piero just for arguing with him - and arguing about music of all things - clearly showed that his father's lips were very close to the ear of God - or Satan!

Benvenuto had no wish to end up with two broken legs, or even worse, as a result of his never-ending disagreement with his father about music, but on the other hand, he certainly had no intention of wasting his time twittering away on that damned flute either!

To cap it all, he had just had another scene with Giovanni. This one began over his brother. Benvenuto was already in a rage because his father had allowed Cecchino to borrow his best clothes.

"Benvenuto, you are right, but you've got to help me with Cecchino. He's obstinate and headstrong - not like you. He won't do anything I ask. We, you and I, have got to stop him from this madness of wanting to be a soldier. We've got to get him to study Law, as his father wishes."

"As his father wishes? Why should he follow some dreary occupation just because you want him to? Is that your revenge because your father made you do something you didn't want to? Is that why you make me keep on trying to get me to play that revolting tube of spit? Flute you call it? A portable spittoon, I call it! And you know where you can stick it - it's just the right shape!"

With this final insult, Benvenuto, with tears of rage running down his face, grabbed up all his remaining clothes, the few coins he had left, and the little bag in which he kept all his other possessions including, although he did not think of it at the time, his flute, and rushed out of the house and took the road to Pisa.

That was why Benvenuto was feeling nervous. What would his father do to him? No thunderbolt arrived from Heaven; the wrath of God or Giovanni did not descend on his head. Perhaps his father realised he had been right and had forgiven him for his outburst. Perhaps it was because he had gone to Pisa, only forty miles away.

To be on the safe side, he wrote a conciliatory letter to his father, telling him that he had found a good job with Ulivieri della Chiostra, a goldsmith, who was teaching him his trade, that he would send as much of his wages as he could, and promising that he would practice on his flute every day.

Giovanni replied with a long letter full of pious expressions.

"Not to see you every day is like losing the sight of my eyes....I shall carry on leading our family in the paths of righteousness....be a good craftsman.... Follow the upright way, in whatever house you stay."

The most embarrassing thing about the letter was that Ulivieri read it, and from then on he started to treat Benvenuto as his son, rather than as his employee and pupil.

Benvenuto spent a fruitful twelve months in Pisa, learning his craft, and, in his spare time, studying the antique sculptures in the Campo Santo.

At the end of the year, Ulivieri had to go to Florence to buy some gemstones, and naturally he took Benvenuto with him.

Ulivieri found in Giovanni a kindred spirit, and between them they persuaded Benvenuto to stay with his father. In any case, Benvenuto was unwell, suffering from the after effects of a dose of malaria he had picked up in Pisa.

The day after Ulivieri left, Benvenuto fished his flute out of his bag. It was full of dust and fluff since he had not touched it for a year. His father came into his room upon hearing him playing.

"Oh, Benvenuto! I can tell you've been practising while you were away. Just as you promised. Listen how your fingering and tonguing have improved. You've made wonderful progress. I can't tell you how proud I am of you! I'll make a musician of you yet."

"Some hopes!" Benvenuto thought.

-4-

Benvenuto was now almost twenty three years old, very hot tempered and addicted to violence.

After his return from Pisa, he stayed at home only for a short time, and then, more or less on an impulse, went on the long journey to Rome where he spent two years working hard, improving his already impressive skill in his trade, and earning quite a lot of money, most of which he sent home to his father.

He also got involved in several fights, including one with his employer whom he had threatened with a sword in a quarrel over money. The employer had paid up, despite being a far better swordsman, because he had more sense than to risk injury over a triviality, but Benvenuto was convinced that it was due to his own ferocious reputation.

Nevertheless, when news of the incident got round the small community of Roman goldsmiths, Benvenuto found it hard to get work, so he decided to return to Florence.

Now he was involved in another feud. Once again it was over money. He had done some freelance work for a family of goldsmiths named Guasconti, headed by two brothers, Salvadore and Michele. They owned three shops, and were very wealthy and influential. Benvenuto did not consider that the amount they had paid him was nearly enough.

One day, Benvenuto "just happened" to be leaning against the door of one of their shops. It was, of course, only "accidentally" that he was blocking the entrance, and he was really not talking to anyone in particular, when he made disparaging remarks about their goods to passers-by. Not surprisingly, Salvadore Guasconti was annoyed.

"Clear off, you lout, or I'll come out there and teach you some manners! If you found some work to do, you wouldn't have time to interfere with honest men. Why don't you go down to the dairy? I hear they're hiring labourers there to shovel manure!"

"Honest men?" retorted Benvenuto. "You wouldn't recognise an honest man if he stood on your foot." He raised his voice, "Still putting lead in your gold, are you then?"

While these insults were being exchanged, Salvadore's cousin, Gherardo, came along leading a mule loaded with bricks. "Somehow" the mule nudged Benvenuto in the back so that he staggered forward and tripped over, falling, face down, onto a pile of stale vegetable leaves that littered the gutter.

Benvenuto got up. "I suppose you think that's funny?"

"As a matter of fact, I do," Gherardo replied.

"Well, try laughing at this then!"

Benvenuto swung his open hand against the man's ear with such force that Gherardo's head banged against the door post and he, too, fell down, dazed, onto the same pile of filth.

Salvadore and his brother, Michele, stepped forward and Benvenuto drew his dagger.

"If one of you leaves the shop, the other one had better run for a priest. There won't be any need for a doctor."

He edged back, and, slipping between the inevitable crowd of onlookers, he ran off.

The Guasconti's lodged a formal complaint that Benvenuto had made an armed attack on their workshop - something that was unheard of in Florence, even in those turbulent times.

Benvenuto was arrested, and once more he found himself before The Eight. There were three members of the Court sitting this time. After the Magistrates had heard both versions of the incident, they ordered the three Guasconti's to step forward.

"We have no doubt that you were provoked, but one of you struck the first blow, and we are not going to have this brawling. You will each bind yourselves to be of good behaviour for a year under pain of a fine of fifty crowns if you are involved in another disturbance in that time."

"But, your Excellency, we didn't do anything," Michele protested.

"Well, so long as you continue not doing anything, nothing will happen to you, will it?" said the President of the Court. "You may leave."

Benvenuto grinned to himself. He thought he was going to get away with it too.

"And now, as for you, Benvenuto Cellini, You've been in trouble with us before. In fact you're always in trouble. You will also give the same security for your future good conduct."

"Gladly, your Excellency." Benvenuto sighed with relief.

"But because you punched Gherardo Guasconti, you will in addition, pay a fine of four bushels of flour, to be given to the Convent of the Murate."

"I haven't got any money," muttered Benvenuto, sullenly.

"Well, I suggest you borrow it, or better still, sell or pawn that dagger and sword of yours - that way you'll keep out of trouble. We are going to dinner now. You will remain in the Courtroom until we get back. If you haven't found the answer by then, we may have an unpleasant alternative in store for you. How would you like to spend two weeks cleaning pigeon droppings off the Cathedral?"

Benvenuto alternated between panic and rage. He fled from the Court and, stopping at his workroom only long enough to snatch up his stiletto, he rushed round to the Guasconti's house.

"Those bastards! First they swindle me, then they attack me, then they complain about me to the Magistrates! They get off scot free, and I'm given a job cleaning up bird shit as a punishment. Well they won't get off so lightly. I'll kill them!"

He found the three of them in the back room enjoying their midday meal and celebrating their release by the Court.

They looked up, their spoons frozen in mid-air. Benvenuto took two steps forward, and struck with his knife at Gherardo's chest. The knife went in up to the hilt, but, because of the voluminous clothes he was wearing, it simply passed through his shirt and jacket just grazing Gherardo near to the shoulder.

He fell backwards from his stool, trying to avoid the blow, and hit his already bandaged head on the floor, knocking himself unconscious. The long dagger had a thin smear of blood on it.

Benvenuto, thinking he had killed the man, turned on the others. "Now for the rest of you Guasconti's. Let me see what your guts look like!"

The women threw themselves on the ground, screaming for mercy.

By now Salvadore and Michele had got to their feet. Considering that there were only six people in the small room, two women and four men, and one of those unconscious, the noise was incredible: stools crashing over, the women wailing, Benvenuto bellowing insults and threats, and the two brothers shouting incoherently.

"Christ! He's murdered Gherardo. He's got a knife - he's gone mad!"

"For God's sake, stop him! Hit him with something!"

Salvadore picked up an iron shovel from the fireplace, and swung at Benvenuto, who ducked just in time. The heavy blade struck Michele flat in the face, smashing the bridge of his nose and opening a "V" shaped gash on his forehead. With Michele now out of the fight, Salvadore stepping over the spread-eagled Gherardo, took a heavy iron pot from the table, and hurled it at Benvenuto who was slowly advancing towards him. It missed and fell on one of the prostrate women, spilling boiling hot soup over her back.

In desperation, Salvadore snatched up the carving knife from the meat platter. Benvenuto raised his foot and kicked the table over, scattering plates, tureens, cutlery, fruit, meat and vegetables on the floor.

The corner of the heavy table landed across the crotch of the unfortunate Gherardo, while a dish of noodles slid over his chest, leaving a large stain of tomato sauce on it, heightening the impression that Benvenuto's dagger had indeed inflicted a terrible, probably fatal, wound.

In the confusion, Benvenuto turned and fled. The servants who, attracted by the noise, were about to come into the room scattered as a screaming figure rushed through the door, waving a knife at them.

Benvenuto suddenly came to his senses, and realising what he had done, ran and ran until he found himself at the Church of Santa Maria Novella. The Friar was standing near the front.

"Father! Father! Save me!" begged Benvenuto. "I've committed a terrible sin. Give me Sanctuary"

"Don't be frightened, my son, you will be safe here."

—⚒—

The Magistrate's Court reconvened immediately they heard of the fracas and issued a warrant for Benvenuto's arrest.

Giovanni went to the Magistrates. He fell on his knees and begged, "Please have mercy on my boy. He hasn't really hurt anyone badly."

"No?" said the President. "Well, it isn't for want of trying. He provokes a fight in the street; he argues with the Court, even when we try to be lenient with him; he refuses to pay his fine; he escapes from custody; he attacks a witness with a knife, and mercifully just misses killing him, then he knocks him unconscious. The owner of the house has had his face smashed in, and his wife has been hit with a cooking pot full of broth and badly scalded. Then while the first man is still lying on the floor - dead for all he knew - your son drops a table right on his private parts, so that, never mind about having children, he may never pee straight again! Then, to finish it off, he wrecks Messer Guasconti's house and threatens his servants with his dagger.

Exactly what do you think he has to do before he gets the punishment he deserves? Get up off your knees! You're a good man. You deserve better from your son. You can do your praying tomorrow, just before we have him hanged."

—⚘—

When the Friar of Santa Maria Novella was sure that nobody had actually been killed, he sent word for Giovanni to come secretly and to bring Benvenuto's horse.

"No one followed you, father, did they?" Benvenuto asked.

"No. I rode the horse, so they couldn't even if they were watching the house. But you'll have to be quick, just to be on the safe side."

Giovanni pointed to two sacks tied to the saddle.

"I've brought all your things."

Benvenuto opened the larger sack. It was full or clothes. On the top was a suit of chain mail. Benvenuto gave his father a puzzled look.

"It's Cecchino's. He brought it for you from the Military Academy."

Benvenuto put it on and buckled his sword round his waist. The Friar gave him a monk's habit as a disguise and he put that on over the armour. He pointed at the second sack.

"Your tools and your drawings are in there," Giovanni explained. He paused. "Also your flute."

Benvenuto shook his head and smiled for the first time that day.

They took him to the gate of San Pietro Gattolini which bars the road to Rome. Giovanni gave Benvenuto five gold crowns.

"It's all I have. I saved it up. It came from you anyway. I expect when you get to Rome you will soon get work - a fine craftsman like you."

He kissed Benvenuto on both cheeks and turned away as Benvenuto rode off.

Benvenuto never saw his father alive again.

Part II: The Craftsman

-5-

When Benvenuto reached Rome, he found his route into the centre of the city blocked by a procession. He reined up his horse next to another rider at the back of the watching crowd.

"What's going on?" he asked.

"Do you mean you haven't heard?"

"No, I have only just arrived from....from Sienna."

"The Pope has died."

"Adrian VI ? Dead? You don't mean it!"

"This is his funeral."

Benvenuto sniffed disdainfully. "It looks like a pretty poor funeral for a Pope to me. Where are all the bands and choirs and soldiers? Where are the monks giving alms to the poor?"

"The old skinflint left instructions that not more than twenty five ducats were to be spent on his funeral."

"Only twenty five ducats? My Grandmother's funeral must have cost more than that!"

"Well he spent his whole fifteen months reign complaining that the Cardinals were all too extravagant and living in too much luxury. That was when he wasn't worrying that someone was trying to poison him."

"Poisoned? Do you mean he was poisoned? The Pope?"

"Well he wouldn't be the first one to go that way, and there were plenty who didn't like him because he was in favour of all this Reformation stuff, but I heard that he couldn't...that he stopped passing water and he just swelled up and died."

Benvenuto crossed himself. "I wonder who the new Pope will be."

"Well we won't know for a couple of months, until all the Cardinals arrive in Rome. Most of them haven't even heard the news yet, of course. I only hope the new one is better for business than this fellow."

Adrian's cortege was just passing by.

"What business are you in, then?" Benvenuto asked.

"Me? I'm a landlord, but with all this austerity being preached by Adrian, some of my tenants have been having a hard time: robe-makers, glass workers, cabinet makers and so on. The ones who were worst hit were the goldsmiths because no one was ordering ornaments to give to the Church."

"Goldsmiths? Do you have some goldsmiths as your tenants? "

"Just one."

"I'm a goldsmith, too."

"My tenant's name is Lucagnolo. A nice chap. A bit rough: he comes from somewhere in the country, Jesi, I think. He used to work for the painter, Raphael, but he started up on his own after he died. He makes beautiful bowls and vases."

"Well, I came here looking for work. Can you tell me how to find this, what's his name? Lucagnolo."

"Better than that, I'll take you to him. Come on, there's nothing more to be seen here."

—⚂—

Benvenuto agreed to go to work for Lucagnolo and a sort of friendly rivalry soon grew up between them as to who could earn more for the business.

This rivalry suited Lucagnolo very well, because he won either way, due to the custom of the trade, which was that one-third of Benvenuto's earnings went to him as Master of the workshop.

—⚂—

Benvenuto and Lucagnolo did not bother to join the crowds who waited in front of the Vatican that November while the

Sacred College of Cardinals were locked in the Sistine Chapel to elect a new Pope.

"We're far too busy trying to earn a few ducats to waste time on all that nonsense," Lucagnolo growled. "Besides, I've seen it all before. It takes days and days while they haggle between themselves. It's got nothing to do with who will be the best Pope. It's all politics, or who'll promise the most to the others. You know, 'I'll make your brother a Cardinal and your cousin a Bishop.' Worse than that: poor Cardinals have suddenly become rich ones after an election. Sometimes when they really can't agree, they pick a stop-gap and hope he won't last too long - just like Adrian."

Much later that day, they heard the sound of cheering from in front of St. Peter's, and a few minutes later a passer-by shouted through the door of the shop,

"He's going to be called Clement VII."

The man made as if to rush off, but Lucagnolo called him back. "Hey! Wait a moment. Never mind what his new name is, who is he?"

"Cardinal Giulio de' Medici. From Florence."

Benvenuto let out a whoop of pleasure.

"A friend of yours?" Lucagnolo asked sarcastically.

"He certainly is," Benvenuto replied. "He was always doing things for my father. He was the one who took an interest in my career - if you can call sending me to Bologna to study music, taking an interest. Anyway," he said, clapping Lucagnolo on the back, "how's that for having a friend at Court? And what a friend! You can't go any higher."

"Well, unless you plan on just popping into his Palace and asking to see him, or hope to bump into him in the street, you had better write and remind him of your existence. If you are lucky, maybe your letter will eventually get past all his clerks and reach him."

Benvenuto did just that, and shortly afterwards received his first major commission from the Spanish Bishop of Salamanca, who ordered a pair of gold candlesticks. Because he realised that this was a chance to begin to build his reputation amongst rich patrons, and more important, perhaps get some work from the Pope himself, Benvenuto was determined that these would be the finest pieces he had ever made.

They were large and tall, to take the fat yellowy-white candles which the Bishop used on the altar of his private chapel. Being gold, they were, of course hollow but with a wide top and base, but the bottoms were extra heavy so that that even when carrying long candles, they would not topple over.

Remembering old Marcone's advice when he had first gone to work, Benvenuto made sure that the bases were richly and elaborately ornamented with designs of fruit and leaves and flowers that twined their way up the stem in a complicated pattern until they reached the candle cups at the top; these he decorated with motifs referring to the various events in the Bishop's career, each separated by either his family coat of arms, the arms of the City of Salamanca, or a Bishop's Mitre.

—⁂—

"Did he like them?" Lucagnolo asked when Benvenuto returned to the workshop after delivering the Bishop's altar pieces.

"Like? He didn't just like them. He loved them He was delighted with them. He was enraptured with them. He......"

"Yes, yes, I get the idea," Lucagnolo interrupted, "but while the tears of gratitude were still wet on his face, how much did you charge him?"

"Naturally we didn't discuss anything as vulgar as money. After all I am an artist and he is a nobleman."

"You try telling our butcher that!" Lucagnolo snorted.

"He did supply me with the gold I was to use." Lucagnolo started to go red in the face.

Benvenuto pulled a purse from the pouch at his waist. "Now calm down. Here's your share." He counted out some coins and dropped them into Lucgnolo's hand.

"That's a third of what he paid you?"

"Give or take a few scudi."

"You were right; he must have been pleased."

"More than that. He's ordered something else. A silver water jug. Do you realise what that means?" Benvenuto could not contain his excitement any longer. "It means that I have got myself my first patron!"

Lucagnolo clapped Benvenuto on the back." Well, that's a good excuse for us to go to the tavern, and as you've got more money in your pocket than I have, I'll let you pay for the wine.

-6-

They were half way through their second flagon of wine and Lucagnolo was sitting with his stool tilted slightly, his back leaning against the wall, with his legs stretched out in front of him. His speech was slightly slurred.

"So, my young rival, if you are going up in the world, there's another lot of studying you've got to do."

"What's that?"

"Sculpture and painting."

"I've seen every statue of Michelangelo's in Florence."

"Seen is not the same as 'studied'. Well, there are plenty more of them here in Rome, and by lots of other sculptors, too. And if you're so keen on Michelangelo, spend some time in the Sistine Chapel and look at the ceiling he painted. It's a dozen, no thirteen or fourteen years since he finished it, and I still keep finding new things in it."

"Why must I study painting? I like them well enough, and I do draw - quite well if I do say so myself, but what good's painting - proper painting - to a goldsmith?"

"You do working drawings for your own use. If you want to sell an idea to a customer, a beautiful painting is better than anything that even a great talker like you can say."

Lucagnolo took another mouthful of wine. "Would you like to look around the Farnesina Palace?"

"In the Via della Lungara? What's there? Who does it belong to?"

"Gismondo Chigi. Don't you know the story of the Chigi's?"

Benvenuto shook his head, and Lucagnolo settled himself more comfortably.

"Gismondo's older brother was Augustino Chigi. He was a banker, probably the most important one in Europe. And rich, you've got no idea! His income was nearly ninety thousand ducats a year. You know that's about thirty times what the Pope gets!"

"He knew how to spend it, too. He once gave a dinner for Pope Leo X in his loggia next to the River Tiber. Just to impress everyone, he said that the same silver was not to be used twice, so after each course, the servants threw all the plates and dishes over the balcony into the water."

Benvenuto gave a gasp. "He must have been stark raving mad!"

"No, of course he wasn't that stupid. He had had nets spread out in the river, and next morning they just fished everything up again.

Anyway, I asked you, would you like to see inside Chigi's Palace? You can study the paintings there in privacy."

"How can you arrange that?"

"I worked for Raphael, remember? Some of my pieces are in the Palace, and I did some of the embellishments, too. Gold leaf work, chapel furnishings and that sort of stuff."

Benvenuto was genuinely grateful "Yes, I'd like to go. Thanks."

"I'll speak to Madonna Porzia, that's Gismondo's wife. She's a lot younger than he is. A real beauty. She likes to encourage artists. Especially young ones," he added with a leer.

Lucagnolo signalled the innkeeper for more wine. "You're still paying," he said.

The Loggia of Psyche in the Farnesina Palace had been designed for Augustino Chigi by the architect Baldessare Peruzzi. It had arches opening onto the Palace gardens, and had been decorated by the artist, Raphael, with tapestries and garlands of fruits and flowers so that it gave the impression that the real flower pergolas in the gardens reached right into the house.

Benvenuto was working on a sketch of Raphael's figure of Jupiter which he later intended to make in a reduced size, first in wax, and then in silver or bronze.

Madonna Porzia had noticed him about her house on several occasions. On this particular day, she had been walking in the garden with her friend, Lucia Bramante. When the two women saw Benvenuto at work, they stopped. Benvenuto rose to his feet.

"Please carry on," said Porzia. "If it will not disturb you, I would like to watch you for a while."

She turned to Lucia and said, in a whispered aside that Benvenuto could not fail to hear, "Don't you think he's handsome?"

"Tell me, young man, what is your name?"

"Benvenuto Cellini."

"Ah yes, you're the goldsmith Lucagnolo sent here. How very interesting. You know, Lucia, I've never had a goldsmith before."

She turned back to Benvenuto, who was beginning to feel uncomfortably warm. "Studying in the house I mean. Tell me, Master Cellini, being a goldsmith, do you know anything about jewels?"

"Of course. In fact, I am considered to be an expert." Benvenuto could never miss an opportunity to boast.

"Really? Well I certainly intend to find out how good you are." She unfastened the brooch she was wearing. It was a lily made of magnificent diamonds, set in gold. "How much would you say that was worth, master goldsmith?"

Benvenuto examined it carefully. "I would reckon it at about eight hundred Crowns."

"Why, that's exactly right!" Porzia exclaimed.

"But," Benvenuto continued, "it could be made to be worth much more. The setting is old and could be greatly improved. Like this." He quickly drew a design, putting Lucagnolo's advice into practice.

"Very nice," Porzia handed him back the lily. "Here, take it and re-set it, just as you've sketched, and here's twenty crowns to buy materials. You have two weeks from today, and you will give me back the gold from the old setting."

"But Porzia," Lucia interjected," you don't even know who this young man is. He might be tempted to run away with all that."

"Oh pooh! Lucagnolo sent him and that's good enough for me. Besides, I can recognise honesty when I see it, just as I can recognise talent. But in any case, I think Benvenuto will find that I will reward him very well, very well indeed if he does the sort of things I like."

She smiled again and Benvenuto actually blushed.

"Come," she said to Lucia, "let's go up to my chamber. I've just thought of something I want to show you."

The two women left, hand in hand, giggling.

Benvenuto found his own hands were trembling.

—∞—

Before Benvenuto started to work on the new setting, he very carefully studied the old one.

Then he prepared a series of design drawings, similar to the sketch he had prepared for Madonna Porzia, but now each one was finely outlined in ink and painted in water-colours. He laid the sketches on his bench, rejecting them one after another, until he was left with the one he preferred.

Finally, he made an impression of the old setting in soft wax before he broke it up. He took all the diamonds and "boiled" them in a solution of soda and lye, carefully skimming off the scum which constantly floated to the top of the pot, until the stones were all free of grease and dirt, and shone brilliantly against the dark piece of cloth on which he laid them to dry.

Lucagnolo did not conceal his amusement at these elaborate preparations.

"What a waste of time this is, Benvenuto. You can earn much more money if you help me with some silver bowls. You know we can sell them over the counter of the shop as fast as we make them. And talking about silver, you would be doing yourself more good if you made a start on the Bishop of Salamanca's jug."

"I'm still thinking about it. I have something special in mind, but I haven't finished working it out yet."

Lucagnolo laughed. "Look, I started on this wine cooler the same time as you began fiddling around with that gee-gaw. You know who it's for? The Pope, himself! If he's pleased, then we'll have Cardinals and Bishops standing in line for our work! I'll tell you what, I'll finish my piece and you finish yours, and we'll see who gets paid the most. What'll you wager? Five crowns?"

Benvenuto did not actually know what he was likely to be paid, but his pride would not let him hesitate even for a moment.

"You're on. Now clear off, I've got a masterpiece to make."

—⚬—

Benvenuto reset the diamonds in the shape of a lily, as before, but this time he made the flower appear to be in a slender vase. The vase itself was also gold, but decorated with little masks and animals, each individually and exquisitely and painstakingly enamelled with a fine brush. The handles of the vase were miniature cherubs, also enamelled.

The job took Benvenuto twelve days.

—⚬—

Benvenuto sent a note, carefully written in his finest script:

> *"Benvenuto Cellini presents his compliments to the Madonna Chigi, and begs to inform her that the work which she graciously condescended to commission from him is completed.*
>
> *He respectfully enquires when he may have the honour of submitting it to her for her approval."*

The terse answer was written at the bottom of his own letter:

"Master Cellini should attend upon Madonna Chigi on Thursday at the hour of nine in the evening."

The reply was unsigned.

—⚜—

The door to the Chigi pallazzo was opened by an elderly maid-servant.

"I am Benvenuto Cellini. The Madonna is expecting me."

"Yes sir, she is. Will you please go up the stairs? The second door to the right."

The woman led Benvenuto to the foot of the staircase, curtsied, and left him to find his own way.

The second door led into Porzia's private sitting room, adjoining her bedroom.

A red silk floral carpet covered the centre of the white marble floor. Two long divans were either side of a low table upon which was a bowl of fruit, a silver wine jug and some silver goblets. Next to the open door of the bedroom there stood a sideboard with a silver bowl of flowers on it. A heavy wooden table and a carved chair under the window completed the furnishings.

Although there were five-foot high multi-branched candelabra in each corner of the room, and smaller candle holders on the table and sideboard, the only illumination in the room came from a log fire burning in the chimney, and from four large candles, two on either side of the grate.

More light came into the room from the unshuttered windows, through which the almost full moon shone out of the clear sky.

Madonna Porzia Chigi was tall, with thick black hair which she wore parted down the middle, and gathered with a jewelled comb at the nape of her slender neck. She had brown, almost almond-shaped eyes with thin, finely arched brows. Her dark complexioned face was a perfect oval, and there were dimples at either side of her mouth.

She came from her bedroom, walking with an undulating movement of her slim figure that showed she knew she was being noticed and admired.

She was wearing a sleeveless, white silk toga decorated with the "Greek Key" pattern in gold thread. The robe was fitted at the waist, but the folds of material at the bust could not conceal the movement underneath.

As she stopped to greet Benvenuto, he could see her figure silhouetted against the firelight through material that was so fine that it clung to her legs and whispered as she moved.

Benvenuto reached into his pouch. "I have brought the Madonna's jewel."

"Not so fast, Benvenuto Cellini. We have plenty of time, I promise you. I am sure you have got exactly what I want. First, let me offer you some wine. Sit down," she commanded, "Next to me."

Benvenuto was pleased to do so. He was sure that this disturbing woman could see how his knees were trembling. She filled his goblet and Benvenuto took a sip. It was thick and red and fruity.

"What wine is this? I've never tasted any like this before."

"It comes from Verona."

Benvenuto nodded. "Over two hundred and fifty miles," he thought to himself. With transport by horse or ox-cart only, everyone, except the very wealthy, drank his local wine and no other.

"I'm afraid I can't introduce you to my husband. He's gone to Naples to attend to his boring banking business. However, I am sure that we shall be able to arrange the matter of your reward to our mutual satisfaction."

"I shall leave myself in your Ladyship's hands," said Benvenuto politely.

Porzia looked at him. "So you shall. Now let me see the jewel."

Benvenuto held out the soft chamois in which it was wrapped. Cool slim fingers slid down his as she took the package.

She undid the leather purse. "It's really beautiful, even in this light," she exclaimed. "It's even better than you said it would be. You must tell me what you want from me in return. Ask for anything you desire."

"Madonna, the fact that it pleases you is reward enough for me!"

"Is it indeed? My dear Benvenuto, I am going to see that you are properly rewarded. If you won't say what you really want, I shall make up your mind for you." She smiled the same smile that she had that first day.

"First," she said, "since I already respect your professional opinion, I would like your views about something else. Do you know anything about ivory inlay work?"

"Yes, my father is a craftsman in that trade. I learned all about it from him."

"Are you an expert in everything then?" Without waiting for an answer, she went on, "Come with me. You've heard of my late brother-in-law's famous silver and ivory bed. I'd like to know what you think of it."

She took him by the hand and led him into the bedroom.

"It's magnificent," Benvenuto said, hoarsely.

"No, not the bed. This."

She crossed her arms and undid the clasps at her shoulders. Her dress slowly began to slip down over her breasts, her hips and her thighs and then lay curled, like a sensuous animal around her ankles. She stepped out of it, and, arms outstretched, she reached for him.

—∞—

Benvenuto was awakened from a deep sleep, feeling wrung out and empty.

"Come on, my goldsmith, it is time for you to go. It will soon be dawn and the servants will be up."

Benvenuto dressed in silence. When he was done, he opened his mouth to speak. Porzia put her fingers to his lips.

"Don't say anything. Go now. I think I shall have a lot more for you to do for me very soon, and I will send payment for the lily later in the day."

"I want no payment," Benvenuto stammered. "You have already given me more than I dared to hope for."

"Don't let's start that discussion again now. I haven't got the strength."

—⚘—

The sky was just changing from the pale yellow of the Roman dawn to bright blue when Benvenuto reached the workshop. Lucagnolo was already at his bench. Benvenuto tapped him on the shoulder.

"You're in early. Couldn't you sleep?"

Lucagnolo glanced up. "God, you look terrible. Where have you been all night? Out drinking?"

"Something like that."

"I've been waiting to show you this." He stacked some silver coins in front of him. "Twenty-five giulios. From the Pope for the wine cooler."

"Very fair," Benvenuto commented.

"Fair? It's generous - damn generous, and you know it! Have you been paid for your little flower yet?"

Benvenuto was silent.

"Ha! I thought not! And you won't be. I'm sorry, it was a nice piece."

"And I'll get a good price for it!"

"We shall see." Lucagnolo turned back to his bench, chuckling, "Twenty five giulios from His Holiness and a five crown wager with His Foolishness. Not a bad start to a working day!"

In the early afternoon, the maid who had let Benvenuto into the Palazzo brought a small leather purse and a note, placed it on the bench and backed out of the workroom without looking at him or saying a word.

Lucagnolo snatched up the note and read it aloud.

"When the poor give to the rich, the Devil has a good laugh. This purse will ensure that God is not denied."

"What does all that rubbish mean? Who's it from? It's not signed. Come on, open the pouch."

Benvenuto cut the seal and undid the thong. He slowly and dramatically tipped the contents onto the bench. There were ten gold coins and a twist of paper with the gold scrap from the old setting of the brooch.

"That's about four times what you got paid," Benvenuto gloated, "and I still have another five crowns to come for the bet."

With bad grace, Lucagnolo flung some money on the bench. "Here you are then. Anyway," he said," at least I have the satisfaction that I get a third of everything that you got out of the job!"

"Not a third of everything," Benvenuto replied, and collapsed on to his stool, laughing uncontrollably.

-7-

Charles V was King of Spain, King of Naples, and ruler of Milan and the Netherlands. He was also the Holy Roman Emperor. Spain had acquired enormous wealth as a result of its recent conquests in South America, particularly Mexico. In thanks for this bounty, Charles had begun to build a new Cathedral at Salamanca, and he nominated the Bishop of Salamanca as his Ambassador to the Pope.

The Bishop, Benvenuto's first wealthy patron, was, therefore, the most important diplomat at the Roman Court, but no sooner had Benvenuto got his second influential patron, Madonna Porzia Chigi, than he found himself embroiled in a bitter dispute with him, in which Benvenuto somehow managed both to offend and publicly humiliate this powerful man.

—⚹—

Benvenuto had opened his own workshop, taking advantage of the commissions he was getting from Madonna Porzia and her friends, as well as work that Lucagnolo was sub-contracting to him. Lucagnolo had even helped him to fit up the studio and, after a mock argument about whether Benvenuto was entitled to have his sign higher up the wall than he did, "assisted" Benvenuto and his neighbours to drink the several flagons of wine that Porzia had sent as a house-warming present.

—⚹—

Benvenuto took over three months to complete the Bishop's second commission, an "acquierra", a silver water jug that was more a ceremonial ornament than for every-day use.

The main reason for the long delay was the complexity of the design that the Bishop's artist had prepared, and which Benvenuto had characteristically made even more elaborate.

The jug was to be about twenty two inches high, egg shaped, decorated in the fashion of the day with animal masks and leaves, and with a wide pouring lip at the top.

The first thing that Benvenuto had to do was to melt the silver. He chose the type of furnace favoured by Florentine goldsmiths. He took a number of strips of clean, rust-free new iron, each about three-quarters of an inch wide and a quarter of an inch thick and wove them into a dome shape. At the base of the dome he made a grating, which stood on four iron feet.

All the ironwork was coated, inside and out, a quarter of an inch thick, with a paste made from clay and cloth parings. Then he made the brick furnace from the same clay, also strengthened with cloth parings and placed a terra cotta tile on top.

The iron crucible which was also scrupulously clean, was rubbed inside and out with olive oil and filled with pieces of silver. Then coals were lit, and, gradually creating its own strong updraft, the furnace became tremendously hot.

When the silver melted, it looked like bright water. Benvenuto threw a handful of tartar on the top and laid an oil-soaked cloth over the crucible to avoid spilling any of the silver when he took it off the fire.

He quickly poured the liquid metal into moulds which were held together with clamps and sealed with clay to stop the silver from running out. When the casting had cooled, it was taken from the mould and the rough edges were pared off; then it was heated again until it was red hot and scraped smooth.

The pressure of the moulding had left it slightly oval in shape, so now it had to be heated yet again, but not too much because it might crack or split. When it was hot enough Benvenuto inverted it over a wooden pole and gently beat it with a hammer. Then he re-heated and beat it another four times until he was satisfied that the shape was perfect and that as much of the metal as possible was either in the base or in the widest part of the bulge. For this shaping process, Benvenuto relied mostly on his practiced craftsman's eye, but nevertheless frequently checked his work with callipers.

At this stage, the jug was about two inches wider than its finished form, so, using special hammers, Benvenuto began gently beating it in a spiral motion until it gradually reduced to the desired dimensions, assisted all the time by carved wooden poles - just like cobblers' lasts or hatters' blocks which also helped him to form the shape of the neck. He had to take great care to keep the metal an even thickness - no weak points and no unwanted "fat" ones, and he removed all surface imperfections as he went along.

Now he was ready to decorate the jug. He filled it with melted pitch which was allowed to harden. Then he divided the body into sections and, using a bright, fine, metal stylus, scored the outside with drawings of birds and animals and flowers that he had been instructed to do. He filled up the score marks with ink to make the drawings show up, and, using a four ounce hammer, he went round the edges of the drawings with punches of differing sizes but all shaped like a letter "C".

The pitch was gently melted out over a slow fire and the inside of the jug was cleaned with a tartar and salt solution. Next an iron rod with a blunt horn-like end (called a caccianfuori) was fastened in a clamp, and the jug was positioned over it with the end of the horn inside, touching one of the figures. Benvenuto struck a gentle blow at end of the rod; the force passed through the rod and transmitted itself to the silver which welled up or bossed out in the shape that had been punched from the outside.

Each of the designs was treated in the same way, and then Benvenuto repeated the process of filling the jug with pitch, punching from the outside and tapping from the inside until he was satisfied that every figure was perfect.

The jug would, of course, be lifted by its handle, and it was here that Benvenuto introduced his own invention: he made the handle spring-loaded. When the jug was lifted, its own weight caused it to drop down the handle and a lid covering the lip opened so that the jug could be filled or its contents poured out. When the jug was standing and the handle released, it snapped back into place and the lid closed.

The Bishop was so furious at having been kept waiting for his ornament, that when Benvenuto called to deliver it, he refused to see him.

"His Grace is very busy at the moment and says that you should leave the - the object with me," was the message that Benvenuto got from the Bishop's butler.

"I'll wait."

"You won't."

"I'll come back another time, then."

"You won't. Not unless you are sent for. You heard what his Grace commanded. Give it to me."

The butler held out his hand and Benvenuto reluctantly handed over the velvet-lined box. "Um...Er..It's customary for payment to be made on delivery," he said somewhat diffidently.

"Well, you will just have to wait until the Bishop has seen it. I will let you know when. Good day to you."

The butler opened the door in a gesture that could not be mistaken, and Benvenuto found himself standing disconsolately in the street, with the door slammed shut behind him.

"So he's sorry about the delay," the Bishop grumbled. "Said it was a very difficult piece of work, did he? Well what about all the time he wasted doing work for that Chigi woman and her friends? She's actually going round boasting that she has discovered a marvellous new artist. She did? Who gave him his first job? Me!"

The Bishop examined the jug lovingly. "It's very beautiful, no doubt about that. He wants payment on delivery, does he?

Ha! I swear to God," he thundered, "that I will take as long to pay him as he took to make it!"

—⚞—

Six weeks later, the Bishop's Butler was foolishly playing with the lid when he broke it. None of the other members of the Guild of Goldsmiths would touch it and the Butler realised that the only thing for him to do was to get Benvenuto to repair it before the Bishop found out.

The Butler was a short, fat, balding man whose wispy beard could not hide his flabby rows of chins. The Bishop obviously did not pay or outfit his servants too generously either. The man was dressed in a coarse, dingy, black woollen robe, the hem of which was not only stained with the mud and indescribable filth that covered the streets of Rome, but also it was badly frayed, too.

By the time the Butler had climbed the steep flight of stairs leading to Benvenuto's workroom, he was out of breath and sweating. He leaned against the door-post, clutching his side. Benvenuto looked up from his bench. He was not going to speak first. "I wonder if he's brought my money," he thought. "No, he's got the jug in its box. The Bishop can't be sending it back - it was his own silver I used. I wonder what's wrong."

"Ahem. Messer Cellini."

"Yes?" Benvenuto growled.

"The jug is broken."

"Broken? How?"

"I was - er - I was cleaning it, yes, cleaning it, when it broke. It was an accident, but his Grace will be furious when - if - he finds out."

"I shouldn't wonder. I hear it is very hard to get reliable domestic help these days."

The Butler ignored the insult. "Can you repair it?"

"If I made it, I can repair it. Show me."

He gave the jug an almost perfunctory glance. The hinge was made of a slender silver rod. The metal was too soft for the

lid mechanism it operated. Benvenuto decided to replace it with an iron one, capped at the exposed ends with silver studs. "Every day you learn something new," he thought to himself.
"How long will it take?" the Butler asked impatiently.

"Two hours, fourteen minutes and twenty-eight seconds," Benvenuto grunted as he turned back to the piece of jewellery on his bench.

The Butler stood at the door for a few moments, but when Benvenuto continued to ignore him, he turned and walked cautiously down the rickety stairway.

The Butler returned three hours later. Benvenuto heard him climbing slowly up the stairs and met him at the doorway. The man tried to pretend he was not panting.

"Is the jug ready?"

"Yes."

"Good! The Bishop wants to show it to someone tonight. Quickly! Let me have it."

"Have what?" Benvenuto asked, innocently.

"The Bishop's jug, you fool! What else?"

"It's not the Bishop's jug. It's mine."

"What? What on earth are you talking about?"

"It's quite simple," Benvenuto explained. "The law says that until I'm paid, then I can keep it. Just like the Bishop's pawnbroker does."

The Butler realised that Benvenuto had tricked him. He reached for his sword with one pudgy hand and tried to push the door of the workroom further open with the other.

Benvenuto stopped him, and at the same time drew his own dagger.

"You're not going to have it. You can tell the Bishop from me that until I get paid, it won't leave this studio again. Now clear off!"

"Clear off? Who do you think you are speaking to, you - you tradesman?" He made the word sound like an insult.

"Do you realise that I am the major-domo to his Grace the Bishop of Salamanca, the representative of the Holy Roman Emperor?"

"For all I care you can be the keeper of the Pope's personal chamber pot!" replied Benvenuto. "Anyway, what's a 'major-domo'? A glorified footman, that's all."

"I'll have you know that I - I - I," the Butler spluttered.

He was so angry, he could not think what to say. "I'm very important!" The words came out as a sort of squeak.

"Important? You? Ha!" Benvenuto gave a snort of derision.

"You're just about as important as a fart in a thunder storm! You just don't realise the extent of your own insignificance! Now are you going to leave on your own, or would you like me to kick you down the stairs?"

The Butler realised that bluster would not work. He fell to his knees. "Please, Master Goldsmith, please let me have the jug. I promise that I'll see the Bishop pays you, but I must take it now or I don't know what he'll do to me."

"Money on the table," replied Benvenuto. "That's my rule for dealing with you Spanish thieves. No Roman artist can be insulted by having to wait for his fee. Bring money. Lots of it. It's a very valuable jug. I hope the Bishop only needs it to keep medicine in. But, no money, no jug; no money, no jug; no money, no jug." He repeated the phrase like a childish chant, as he slammed the door in the Butler's face.

"I'll be back directly," the Butler shouted, "and with enough people to cut you to pieces!"

Benvenuto did not need to be warned twice. For the protection of his new workroom, he had bought an arquebus. This was a gun of a type that had only been recently developed. The ingenious Italian gunsmiths had reduced the weight to a mere thirty pounds, so it could actually be carried and fired from the hand instead of from a tripod! The addition of the newly invented matchlock, instead of the old lighted fuse which had

had to be pushed down the touch-hole, meant it could be fired without losing the aim. The three-foot long barrel made it a little unsuitable for the use that Benvenuto had in mind, but he felt it would give him an advantage in the first instance.

He carefully loaded it with a handful of pellets.

The Butler soon returned with several of the Bishop's servants, all carrying swords. They stood at the foot of the stairs, looking up.

"There he is. Some of you give the insolent peasant the thrashing he deserves, and the rest of you get the jug. You needn't be too gentle how you search for it either."

"Really?" As they started up the stairs, Benvenuto revealed the gun he had hidden behind the door. "I think I hear a crowd of Spanish burglars plotting to loot a Roman shop, so I'll have to protect myself, won't I? I don't know, Master Butler, how much the Bishop pays you, but I hope it's a lot. I hope it's enough to make it worth your while to die for him, because if you and your gang of thieves are still here by the time I count to one, you'll have an extra navel - about the size of an orange. Now let me see. How do you fire one of these things?"

He pretended to fiddle with the firing mechanism. "First I think you pull this thing back like this...."

He looked up. The Spaniards were gone.

—⚜—

There was no way that the story of how Benvenuto had seized the jug back could be kept a secret - not with half a dozen of the Bishop's servants involved, and with Benvenuto himself boasting about it to anyone who would listen.

The problem was now how to resolve the dispute without further loss of dignity by the Bishop.

Porzia Chigi persuaded her husband, Gismondo, to act as an intermediary. Since the Bishop refused to offer a price for Benvenuto's labour, the banker arranged for Lucagnolo to give a valuation. Although he was a friend of Benvenuto, this was a task he was often called on to perform by goldsmiths and their customers, and he had a reputation for scrupulous fairness and accuracy.

Next, the Bishop gave Chigi his personal assurance that he would pay the sum he owed immediately on delivery and that Benvenuto would not be harmed in any way.

Despite the promise of a safe conduct, Benvenuto took the precaution of putting on his brother's suit of chain mail under his clothes, and of arming himself with a dagger before he went to the Bishop's palace at the agreed time.

There were about twenty clerics and members of the Bishop's staff drawn up in two intimidating lines when Benvenuto was admitted to the reception room. He had nervously to "walk the gauntlet" until he reached the Bishop who was standing at the end of the two rows.

Benvenuto stopped a few feet from the Bishop. He neither bowed nor gave any other sign of respect. He said nothing.

The Bishop began shouting at Benvenuto in Spanish. Benvenuto hardly understood a word, although the Bishop's tone was clear enough. He stared fixedly at a point just above the Bishop's nose and still said nothing. The Bishop became even more enraged. He called to his secretary,

"Bring this - this - this person pen and paper and ink."

He glared at Benvenuto and said in Italian, "You will write a receipt in your own hand; you will acknowledge that you have had your money and that you are satisfied."

Benvenuto spoke for the first time. "Indeed, I shall be pleased to do so, your Grace, just as soon as my money is in my hand."

The Bishop's face went red with rage. Before he could say anything more, Benvenuto continued, "No money, no jug. No money, no receipt. Are we agreed, my Lord Bishop, or do I have your gracious permission to leave?"

"Give him his money," the Bishop said to his Secretary, "and get a receipt."

As the Bishop walked away, he flung out a threat, "I only hope you live long enough to spend it!"

Benvenuto had the last word. "Amen," he said.

- 8 -

When Lucagnolo came visiting one evening, he found Benvenuto sitting at his kitchen table, fiddling with a silver see-saw. It was about seven inches long and four inches high with a little man at each end.

Benvenuto slid a tankard in Lucagnolo's direction and silently pointed to the wine flagon and bowl of fruit.

"Thanks," Lucagnolo said as he sat down. "Who did you make that toy for?"

"Me. I made it for myself. That's me at this end."

"Who's the other fellow?" Lucagnolo touched the figure of a thin man with a bent back, dressed in a monk's robe with a cowl covering his head. Benvenuto had made the eyes out of two dark red garnets.

"I don't know, really. I just see him sometimes when I have a nightmare. Here, look at this."

He took his hands away and the figures balanced by themselves. Then he inserted a short silver rod into a hole under one of the seats, and that end sank down.

"Why are you down and him up?"

"It goes either way, but that's how things are with me at the moment. That's how it always is. Sometimes up; sometimes down. More down than up, but only two weeks ago I was more up than I have ever been in all my life and now look where I am."

He pointed miserably at the see-saw.

"Why? What's wrong?"

"Wrong? Well I've lost the Bishop of Salamanca as a customer for a start, and I wouldn't be surprised if that fat pig isn't trying to tell all the other diplomats that I tried to rob him."

"No, on the contrary, the Pope is letting everyone know how pleased he is that you took a Spaniard down a peg or two.

You know there's going to be trouble with the King of Spain before long. A war maybe."

"Don't talk to me about the Pope. So far he's done nothing for me, except, you know what? He's making me play my damned flute at his August festival at the Belvedere Palace! 'For the sake of your respected father, my son!' Peh!"

"He sent the Bishop to you, and also the Standard Bearer of Rome."

"Governor Ceserino? Another marvellous customer! Just as bad as the other one."

"Why? I gave a very high valuation on that hat badge you made for him."

"Yes? Now let me show you something." Benvenuto crossed to a cupboard, unlocked it, and took out a velvet wrapped package.

"Here it is. The Standard Bearer's hat badge. The story of Leda and the Swan turned into a breathtaking example of the jewellers art, even if I do say so myself! Zeus, the king of the gods comes down to Earth in the form of a Swan and impregnates Leda, the Queen of Sparta. She lays two eggs and hatches Helen of Troy and Castor and Pollox, the Heavenly Twins."

"I don't suppose the King of Sparta believed her," said Lucagnolo.

Benvenuto ignored the interruption. "See, here's the story all painted in enamel on gold. A back view of an almost undraped Leda looking at the Swan to her right. Look at the detail in the tapestry, and her necklace is made of real jewels. And there's Cupid and his bow. I even picked out the city gate, brick by brick. Do you know how long it took to make that filigree surround? Lilies set with four square rubies and four diamonds!"

"I agree it's very beautiful and very complicated to make," Lucagnolo said, "that's why I set the price that I did."

"Yes, but Ceserino says he can't afford it! I'm not going to let him have it for less or they'll all be doing the same thing."

Lucagnolo nodded in agreement. "So what will you do, break it up?"

"Never! My work is not for melting, I've told you that before. No, I'm stuck with it until I find another customer. The trouble is that seeing that I was dealing with the Governor, I paid for the materials. Nearly all my money is tied up in that thing!"

Benvenuto locked it back in the cupboard.

"Never mind," Lucagnolo said, "there's still Madonna Chigi and her rich friends."

"Yes, Madonna Porzia Chigi and her lady friends!" Another voice came from the adjoining room.

Benvenuto looked up. Standing in the doorway was a statuesque, busty, farm girl and a complete contrast to Madonna Porzia, of whom he was secretly overawed.

"Pantisilea darling!" he said, "How about some wine?"

"Don't you 'darling' me when you're talking about that woman! I don't think you have to sleep with her each time you deliver her something. And how many designs do you have to show her for each piece? "

"It's good for business, and if it's good for business, then it's good for you, too."

"Good for me?" said Pantisilea. "How?"

"Well, you're eating aren't you?" replied Benvenuto.

—⋘—

Pantisilea stared morosely at her breakfast, then pushed it away with a gesture of irritation which Benvenuto pretended not to notice.

"By the way, we're going to the Artists' Circle Dinner tomorrow night. Guilio Romano is going to be Master of Ceremonies," he said.

"We are going, are we? Who are you going with, then?"

"You, of course."

"Oh no! You've known the date for weeks, but this is the first time you've mentioned it. Yes, I'm going, but not with you. Luigi Pulci has already asked me."

"Pulci the poet! No! Say you don't mean it!" Benvenuto leaned back in his chair, his hands on either side of his head. A broad grin spread over his face.

"Do you know how mixed up he is? His father was beheaded for incest. I knew your Luigi in Florence, when he was living with the Bishop of Lucca. The Bishop threw him out when he caught the French Pox from one of his other boyfriends. That's why he came to Rome. He must like the Church, though," Benvenuto sneered, "I hear he's living with another Bishop now."

"So you won't have anything to be jealous about then, will you? And maybe another time you won't take me for granted."

" I'm certainly not going alone. You know the rule. If anyone turns up without a woman, he has to pay for the whole dinner. I'm not going to do that!"

"Ask who you like Why not one of those whores from the town. I'll tell you what. That's just given me an idea. Why don't you ask Madonna Porzia?" she suggested brightly, with which she flounced out of the kitchen.

—⚬—

By the morning of the dinner, Benvenuto had a problem. He had been unable to find another woman guest.

Pantisilea was wrong: he certainly was not going to demean himself by taking a prostitute from off the streets, but equally, he did not want to suffer the ridicule of his friends if he went alone, nor the indignity of having to pay the bill.

Then he had an idea. Living nearby was a Physician who had a fourteen year old son, Silvio. The boy was slim, with smooth delicate features, long slender hands, and a voice that had not yet broken.

Because he was intent on studying Latin, he rarely went out, and none of Benvenuto's friends were likely to know him even though Benvenuto had done drawings of him several times.

"Look," he said to Silvio, "I just want to play a trick on all those artists. They're so pompous, they believe they know everything there is about the human body. Well, let's show them they can't even tell the difference between a girl and a boy!"

"Yes, but wearing girl's clothes - I don't know."

"Come on, it's just for a lark, and I'll tell you what, how much do I pay you for being a model? Three scudi? I'll give you five, and you'll get a marvellous dinner, too."

Silvio allowed himself to be persuaded. "Five scudi? Make it six - double the usual."

Benvenuto clapped him on the back. "Done! And when we break the news to them, you'll be the hero of the evening!"

"Heroine, you mean!" Silvio muttered.

They borrowed one of Silvio's mother's dresses. It was far too thick around the waist, so they padded it out a little.

"If anyone says anything tell them you are pregnant. Now, here are some earrings..."

"You're not going to make holes in my ears," Silvio protested.

"No, of course not. These clip on - no one will tell the difference. Three bracelets, a couple of rings and this necklace. I'll tell you what. You'll be wearing better jewellery than any other woman - I mean any real woman there."

"What about my hair? I'm not going to wear a wig."

"I can't see why not, but don't worry," Benvenuto added before Silvio could say anything, "there's no need. Your hair is pretty long and you can wear this hat, so just the ends will show."

Benvenuto paused "Hrrumm." He cleared his throat nervously, "Now, last of all just a touch of rouge...."

"Oh, no!"

"..... and a little kohl around the eyes..."

"I said no!"

Benvenuto jingled the six coins in his hand.

"Go on. Get on with it then," Silvio said, "but don't let me see myself in a mirror!"

Guilio Romano, the Master of Ceremonies, had seated all the women on one side of the long table and all the men on the other, and none of the women was seated near the person who had brought her. To his disgust, Benvenuto found himself sitting next to Pantisilea's companion, Luigi Pulci, while on the further side of the poet was her former lover, Bachaccia.

"Quite a family gathering," he thought, and decided to ignore them both.

The meal began with **brodetto**, chicken broth into which eggs and lemon juice had been beaten so that it almost resembled a cream soup. This was followed by a delicious baby lamb-and-vegetable stew flavoured with tarragon and basil. The stew was eaten with warm round crusty loaves, ideal for mopping up the rich sauce. Next came a white soft cheese, and finally bowls of peaches, grapes and cherries, the whole being washed down with the dry white wine of the Rome Region, served from glazed pottery flagons which were kept cool by being immersed in wooden buckets of cold water.

As the fruit course was served, and after several goblets of wine, Benvenuto decided that it was time for him to have a word with Luigi. He nudged him roughly in the ribs.

"When you first got here from Florence, and I helped you to find a doctor to cure you of the pox, you said you would always be in my debt. Remember?"

"Well so I am, my dear fellow. What can I do for you?"

"You can damn well stay away from Pantisilea. She's mine, and she's only using you to get at me."

"Come on! You know I'm not interested in women - well not much anyway. And as for upsetting you, may I fall and break my neck if I do!" A prophetic oath.

—✵—

As soon as the meal was cleared away, each of the guests was called on to entertain the others. Luigi recited one of his poems, someone else sang, and inevitably Benvenuto had to play his flute. Lucagnolo was giving a reading from Dante's "Divine Comedy", when there was a sudden disturbance.

The two women sitting on either side of Silvio had incessantly chattered throughout the meal and had tried unsuccessfully to draw Silvio into their conversation about trivialities that he did not understand. When they kept asking this beautiful young stranger personal questions about "herself" that Silvio could not answer, he had pretended that his pregnancy was making him feel unwell.

They did not stop talking, even when the entertainment began. Silvio was bored and irritable, as well as being hot and uncomfortable in the unaccustomed heavy clothes and additional padding. He began wriggling about on the bench.

"What's the matter, dear? Is something wrong?" one of the two asked him, "Is the baby moving about or kicking you? Mine did, unmercifully!"

"Yes, that's what it is. It's the baby, kicking and punching."

"Really? Do let me feel!"

"Ooh, yes, me too," said the other.

Without more ado they both thrust a hand under Silvio's skirt, and simultaneously discovered that "she" was a male. They stared at each other in horror and hurriedly withdrew their hands. One of them let out a shriek,

"You beast! How dare you bring your perverted habits here?"

She swung her open hand round, and with a tremendous slap across his face, she knocked Silvio backwards from the bench, his legs waving in the air and his skirts flying.

This only seemed to incense the other one even more.

"If you want to be a woman, you can find out what it's like to be raped!" she screamed and began ripping Silvio dress to shreds, assisted by her companion.

Silvio was stripped right down to his drawers, before the men, convulsed with laughter could rescue him. They wrapped him in the remains of the dress, and sent him home, furtively flitting from doorway to doorway, shadow to shadow.

The two women were about to turn their attention to Benvenuto when the Master of Ceremonies stopped them.

"No, ladies," Romano said, "we shall have a Trial. I shall be the President of the Court and there will be two Assessors. Lucagnolo, who is his friend, and Bachaccia, who most certainly is not. Gentlemen! A conference!"

The three "judges" went into a huddle, while the other guests laughed and joked, and Pantisilea, with a fierce look at Benvenuto, drew her forefinger across her throat.

"Ladies and gentlemen," Lucagnolo announced, "Benvenuto Cellini, resident of Rome and goldsmith of sorts, has perpetrated a superb and memorable hoax on this company. As with everything he does, it was a masterpiece!"

All the women began to boo, but Romani held up his hand. "Bachaccia will announce the verdict."

"Messer Cellini has been found guilty of attending this function without being accompanied by a female. He is ordered to pay for the meal. He will also pay for the broken crockery."

"Innkeeper," Romani said, "you may present the bill to this gentleman. He will be delighted to pay it!"

As Benvenuto forced a sickly grin, the Master of Ceremonies said, "the performances will continue, but I doubt if anything will be as entertaining as what we have just seen!"

—⚜—

Although the Master of Ceremonies had proposed that the entertainment should continue, the excitement caused by the discovery of Benvenuto's hoax and 'trial' meant that no-one was really in the mood for it, despite the efforts of some of the guests to perform their party pieces.

Instead, people stood or sat around, telling each other over and over what they had seen, while Benvenuto moved from group to group, smilingly accepting their congratulations.

When he reached an open window overlooking the courtyard he stopped for a moment for a breath of air, and, glancing out, saw Pantisilea and Pulci sitting on a stone bench, with their backs to him, kissing and giggling.

"Don't worry, Luigi," Pantisilea said, "Benvenuto's too busy letting his friends tell him how clever he is, to notice we're out here."

Luigi did not stop fondling Pantisilea, but he was not convinced.

"If he could see us, we'd be for it, for sure," he said nervously.

Benvenuto snatched up a fruit knife and leaped through the window.

"You're bloody right, you miserable queer. I'm going to make your arsehole two inches longer!"

"Leave him alone, you bullying bastard," Pantisilea screamed as Benvenuto slashed the air with the knife, while Luigi cowered away, calling for someone - anyone - to help him.

The noise and the sight of Benvenuto jumping through the window, brought the guests pouring out into the courtyard, just as Benvenuto managed to grab Luigi's cloak. Luigi slipped out of it and fled while Lucagnolo and Guilio Romano held Benvenuto back.

Pantisilea stood at the gateway and shouted, "I've finished with you. You disgrace me by coming here with a boy dressed as a girl, and you have the nerve to call Luigi names. What's more I'm fed up with your telling me what I can do or who I can see while you carry on with anyone who'll let you into her bed. What about Porzia Chigi, then? Porzia Whore! Porzia Whore!"

"By God, you'll get a thrashing when I catch you," Benvenuto shouted back.

"You'll never see me again. I'm going home to my father and if you come near me, my two brothers will kill you!"

She turned and ran after Luigi, and when Benvenuto tried to follow, Lucagnolo held him back.

"That's enough. Let her go. You don't need that sort of trouble. Either she comes home or she doesn't, and if she doesn't there's plenty more just like her. Calm down. Let her go," he repeated.

—※—

It was simply not in Benvenuto's nature either to calm down or to let things drop, but he allowed himself to be persuaded to stay for a few minutes and to drink another tankard of wine before returning home.

There he picked up his sword, and saddling his horse, galloped towards Prati where Pantisilea's father lived. He was sure that, on horseback, he would get there ahead of her; he hid himself opposite the house, in the garden of an Inn which was surrounded by a large thorn hedge.

Sure enough, a short time later Bachaccia came along the road. He had obviously been sent as a scout.

"Benvenuto! Are you there? Stop all this nonsense! Luigi didn't mean it. Come out! I know you're there. The girl's not worth it. She was only trying to make you angry."

Benvenuto stepped out from the darkness behind Bachaccia and held his sword across the man's throat, pushing his head forward against the blade with his left hand.

"Well she bloody well succeeded, didn't she?" he hissed through his teeth, "and one sound from you, and I may remember what you have been up to with her too."

"Oh my God!" Bachaccia sobbed, "Don't hurt me, I won't tell them you're here."

"Don't hurt you? The least I'll do is to whack you on the head if you don't keep quiet. Now get out of it - in the other direction, and quickly, before I change my mind and do it just the same!"

"Please, Benvenuto, I've got to stay for a minute. You gave me such a fright, I've wet myself, and if I don't take a crap right away, I'll do that in my pants too!"

He hurriedly disappeared behind the hedge, bent over nearly double and with a sort of crab-like movement.

—※—

Less than a minute later Benvenuto heard the sound of several horses approaching at a walking pace.

"The bitch must have stopped to pick up a body-guard." Benvenuto thought to himself. "But she'll need more than that to save her from a beating - Luigi, too, if he's with her!"

Coming round the bend in the road, he saw three lanterns, and in their light, he could see Pantisilea, Luigi, Lucagnolo and Guilio Romano.

Benvenuto pressed himself back into the shadow of the hedge, and dozens of sharp thorns stuck into his back. There was nothing he could do but bite his lip.

The little group stopped at the gate of Pantisilea's father's house and Luigi got down from his horse. He went to lift the girl from the saddle.

As he put his hands out for her she said, "Just one more kiss, to spite that bastard."

This was too much for Benvenuto. Goaded like a bull by the thorns, and infuriated by the treachery of his mistress, he jumped out of the darkness of the hedge.

"You're both as good as dead!" he yelled.

He slashed at Luigi with his sword, hitting him on the shoulder. Luckily for him, the blade of the sword was not sharp, and the blow only broke his collar-bone, but he turned and ran straight into the thorn hedge crying,

"He's killed me! He's killed me! I'm done for!"

The horse Pantisilea was riding reared up and threw her to the ground and one of the flying hooves caught her in the face, breaking her nose and knocking out her front teeth.

At the same time, Lucagnolo and Gulio Romano's horses, frightened by the noise and the wild screaming figure that had come rushing at them from the side, were whinnying and wheeling and trying to bolt.

Bachaccio, when had heard the approaching horses while still pulling his breeches up from round his knees, had sneaked into the house to warn Pantisilea's brothers, and they now both came dashing out, swords in hand.

Benvenuto was momentarily hidden by the shadows, so all they saw was Luigi tangled up in the thorn hedge, screaming that he was dying and begging for help, and Lucagnolo and Romano on horseback apparently trying to trample their sister into the ground.

They assumed the two horsemen were part of Benvenuto's gang and attacked them with their swords. Lucagnolo and Romano, in turn, assumed the two brothers were with Benvenuto, and fought back, slashing away with their own weapons in the darkness, because the lanterns had now fallen to the ground and gone out.

Fortunately, neither the artists or the two farmers were any good at sword play, and although there was a great deal of clashing of steel on steel, no-one was hurt except that, when his horse ran sideways, Lucagnolo's leg was caught between the frightened animal and the gate post.

Bachaccio was still trying to pull the semi-conscious Pantisilea out of the way of the horses hooves with one hand, and holding up his other one shouting, "For God's sake stop it! You're all on the same side, you idiots!"

It took Bachaccio some time to make himself heard over all the shouting and crying, and by then, Benvenuto, taking advantage of the confusion, had gone to the side of the Inn, unhitched his horse and run away back to the city.

―𝓂―

Lucagnolo did not come to see Benvenuto for nearly a week after that. Then, one morning he limped into Benvenuto's kitchen just at lunch time. There was a fifteen year old boy sitting at the table, peeling an apple.

"Hello," said Benvenuto, "What happened to your leg?"

"You know damn well what happened!" Lucagnolo snarled.

He looked at the boy, pointed at him with his thumb and raised an eyebrow at Benvenuto.

"It's my new apprentice. His name's Silvio."

"Your face is very familiar. Where have I seen you before? I know! My God! You're the fellow who dressed up like a girl at the party!"

"Don't remind me about it," the boy said with some spirit.

"Well, son, you've got a marvellous craftsman for a master, but don't get on the wrong side of him, whatever you do, or he'll stick a knife in you!"

Silvio blushed and went on carefully peeling his apple.

"Silvio who?"

"Silvio Arezzo, sir."

"The physician's son?"

The boy nodded.

"What are you doing here then? Why aren't you studying?"

"Oh, for Christ's sake, don't you start!" Benvenuto said with considerable exasperation. "He's here because he wants to be a goldsmith, not a doctor like his father. I'm here because I wanted to be a goldsmith, not a bloody musician like my father, and he's a musician because he didn't want to be an architect like his father. What's the matter with you people?"

"Ducks don't give birth to chickens," retorted Lucagnolo.

He looked around the unusually untidy kitchen and at the remains of a sparse midday meal.

"Pantisilea isn't here, then?"

"No. You don't think I'd have her back after that disgusting behaviour of hers at the party, do you? Besides, I can't bear ugliness, and who wants a girl with a flattened nose and no front teeth?"

"She's right! You are a cruel bastard," Lucagnolo said, laughing. "Do you hear that, boy? Your master's a bastard!"

"In any case," said Benvenuto, "I hear she's taken up with Luigi permanently."

"Not anymore."

"What, do you mean that she's thrown him out already? I'm not surprised. He isn't all that enthusiastic about women anyway. I don't think he even knows what to do with one - the rotten little fairy!"

"It's not that. He's dead. That's what I came to tell you."

"Dead? How? When?"

"This morning. He was on that big black horse of his. You know his prize possession that he was saying the Bishop of Lucca bought for him for fifty crowns, no less."

"Who cares about the stupid horse! Tell me what happened," Benvenuto was almost shouting with impatience.

"He was riding towards Pantisilea's father's house, and when he got to the place where the fight happened the other night..."

"Fight? What fight?" Benvenuto asked, innocently.

"Oh do shut up and listen! He got to the place where . to the place.... you bloody well know where I mean! Anyway right on the very spot, the horse shied for absolutely no reason and rolled over on top of him. When they got him out, his neck was broken."

"Dead, you say?"

"Yes. Not just ordinary dead, but very dead!"

Benvenuto scratched his chin. "You know, at the party the very last thing he said to me was, 'May I fall and break my neck if I ever upset you'."

"How strange," Lucagnolo said.

"Yes, well you remember I told you how Piero Malcesine upset my father, and a few days later he fell through the floor, broke both his legs and died of gangrene?"

"What's that got to do with Luigi?"

"So, I was just wondering if I've got the same power as my father to put the Evil Eye on people."

Silvio dropped his knife with a clatter and Lucagnolo crossed himself with two long very slow movements of his hand.

-9-

The Plague. Bubonic Plague. The Black Death.

Time after time the scourge swept through the Far East, Central Asia and Europe in one wave after another. In the great epidemic in the middle of the 14th. Century, thirty-seven million people died in the Far East, while in Europe twenty-five million, (about a quarter of the population), perished. In Britain, one and a half million souls, nearly half the inhabitants, died. Such was the terror of the disease that mothers deserted their infected children and the sick were often left to die and rot where they fell.

—⁂—

In 1523 there was an outbreak in Rome. It went on for many months, and several of Benvenuto's friends caught it - and died, along with thousands of others who succumbed every week.

At first Benvenuto seemed to be immune, but then, one evening, he began to feel very tired. Not sleepy, but physically exhausted, but he could not sleep. He could not eat either as he kept vomiting. He put this down to the constipation from which he was suffering.

The next day his temperature was up, and yet he was shivering. His back, his head, his arms and his legs hurt, and he found a carbuncle on his left wrist and some swellings in his left armpit - the dreaded **buboes**. The symptoms were unmistakable, even to Benvenuto's two house maids, who at once fled, without waiting to pick up their few possessions.

Only his apprentice, Silvio, remained behind.

Benvenuto was sure that he would soon be dead because the disease was nearly always fatal.

—⚎—

Silvio's father was the personal physician to Cardinal Iacoacci. The boy went to bring him.

He said, very casually, very unconcernedly, "Father, will you come round to see Messer Cellini. He is a little indisposed, and I have told him to go to bed until you have looked at him."

The doctor only needed to take Benvenuto's pulse, and to brush his damp hair away and put his hand on his forehead to feel his temperature, and to take one look at the buboes, already beginning to ooze pus and the watering eyes which could not even bear the dim light of the shuttered room, and he too, knew.

He turned to his son. "You're not just an idiot! You're worse! You've ruined me, you treacherous boy! This man's dying of the Plague. Look at the black spots. Even if I don't catch it myself, how can I go back to the Cardinal?"

"Father, Messer Cellini is worth all the Cardinals in Rome."

"From what I've heard about him, he would be the first and only one to agree with that! Anyway, I'm here now, and I can't leave, so I may as well try to save your precious master, but I'll tell you this, boy, you've killed us all!"

Benvenuto's breathing became harsh. Sweat poured off him and he had a raging, unquenchable thirst. In a matter of hours, the flesh seemed to fall away from him and his skin, despite the fever, became pale - almost translucent.

The constipation changed to diarrhoea; the buboes suppurated, and Silvio gagged and retched and his stomach heaved as he attempted to keep the naked Benvenuto, and the straw pallet upon which his father had laid him, clean.

Benvenuto's temperature began to rise rapidly despite the cool water with which they bathed him and the dampened sheet with which they covered him and despite the primitive herbal potions they poured between his clenched, grinding teeth.

Benvenuto opened his eyes suddenly and saw the huge python. Its skin was dry and covered with scales. It made a harsh, rustling sound as it slithered towards him, and it must have been this that had awakened him. It was at least fifteen feet long and its body was so thick that he could not get his two hands round it.

Benvenuto was absolutely paralysed with fear. He could not move a muscle. The snake wound itself around him, and as the coils tightened, the beast's tail lashed at his bare ankles, whilst its loathsome head and flickering tongue nuzzled around his face.

Tighter still, and tighter. Benvenuto could hardly breathe. At last he was galvanized into action. He began to struggle, but it was no good. His arms were pinned to his side. He could do nothing as the snake crushed him even harder.

His ribs began to creak. At any moment now they would snap. He was suffocating. He became dizzy and toppled to the floor from his bed. The force of the fall made the python slightly relax its hold for just a moment. Benvenuto was able to free his right hand and wrist before the coils tightened again.

He groped about and found his dagger. He could not move his hand to strike a proper blow, so he feebly slashed at the snake as best he could. All he was able to do was to make a few shallow cuts, from which a vile green liquid oozed.

He got a better grip on his knife and, as he sawed away, he managed to cut right through the bottom of the snake's body, where it was wrapped around his knees.

This got his right arm free to the elbow but it made no difference. Everywhere else he was held just as tightly as before. In a frenzy, he stabbed with the knife time and again. Still to no effect.

Benvenuto, in desperation contorted his body left and right, and bent over double in the hope that he could hit a vital part. He was covered with the slimy green blood.

The knife sank in for the last time and the thin blade broke off in his hand.

The python gave a heave and loosened its grip. It began to convulse and thrash about. Benvenuto jerked its head away as its sharp teeth tried to bite his face.

Both of his hands were free at last. Benvenuto grabbed the snake's head and smashed it on the ground over and over until it was a pulpy ruin in his hands.

Everything went black.

—⚏—

Benvenuto felt his haggard, stubble-covered face being wiped with a cool, damp cloth. From a distance he heard Silvio saying,

"He's lying still now, Papa. Does that mean that he's going to get better?"

"Either that or he's just about to die. It's hard to tell when they get delirious like that. We'll know soon enough. Meanwhile, clean him up and get him off that filthy straw and onto his own bed. And try to get him to drink something."

The tangled sheets were black with sweat and encrusted with excrement and pus. Silvio threw them on the fire. He washed Benvenuto down, and poured some diluted lemon juice into his mouth. Then he swept the straw into the yard and set fire to that, too.

Benvenuto recovered slowly. The open sores on his back healed and his strength gradually returned.

As soon as he was able to, he got on his horse and rode out of the City and went north forty miles or so to Cerveteri, near Civitaveccia, to the home of the Count of Anguillara, a friend of Gismondo and Porzia Chigi.

He stayed there for about a month, enjoying the good wine and the best of food and spent his days walking along the sea shore, breathing in the fresh, clean air.

―⁂―

When he returned to Rome, Benvenuto was still not strong enough to resume work, so he spent his time wandering around the studios of other craftsmen. The workshop where he spent the most time was that shared by Caradosso, originally from Milan, and Lautizo from Perugia.

Caradosso specialised in medals which he chiselled out of metal plates, half reliefs made from bronze and gold, and the ornate, fashionable hat badges.

Lautizo made seals and coins. In those days, every nobleman and every cardinal had his own seal. A cardinal's seal would be about three inches in diameter with decorative figures as well as the coat of arms of the cardinal engraved on it.

Benvenuto decided that as soon as he was better, he would break into this market in competition with his two unsuspecting teachers.

Apart from being very profitable - a good Cardinal's Seal would fetch a hundred crowns or more - cardinals and noblemen were the ones with money to spend, and Benvenuto believed he had at last found a way to break into the influential spheres of the Roman Court.

On the day he resumed work, he tilted his end of his see-saw up again.

Part III: The Killer

-10-

Benvenuto wrote in his diary, "The whole world is now at war."

An exaggeration, but a pardonable one in the circumstances.

There were no newspapers. Information was passed from mouth to mouth, gaining nothing by way of accuracy in the process. Very few people had any real idea what was going on - or why - except for those in office or in the highest positions of power.

The King of Spain was at war with the King of France. The battlefield was mainly Italy. Apart from not wanting to devastate their home countries, there was the added advantage that the armies could pay themselves by looting and pillaging the unfortunate Italians.

As well as Spaniards, Frenchmen and Italians, the armies included a collection of Germans, Swiss, Austrians, Dutchmen, Belgians, and Bohemians, all involved, either because they were the subject of one or other of the warring States, or because they were mercenaries, fighting for pay and plunder.

Charles V, the King of Spain and of the Spanish Colonies in America, had also inherited, through his mother, the Kingdom of Naples, which covered the whole of Southern Italy, Sicily, and Sardinia.

On his father's side, he inherited the thrones of Burgundy, Holland, Belgium and Luxembourg.

Also from his father's father, Maximilian I, he had a claim to be the Holy Roman Emperor, and in 1519, when he was only nineteen years old, he was confirmed in that title too, with the aid of a great deal of intrigue and bribery.

Thus, this young boy, in addition to his considerable American possessions, was the ruler of Spain, Holland, Belgium, and large parts of France, Germany, Italy, Switzerland, the Tyrol, Austria, and Bohemia - in other words, of most of the western part of Continental Europe.

In 1520, after Charles' Coronation, Pope Leo X tried to persuade the new Holy Roman Emperor to bring Martin Luther to trial for his life. Leo had already excommunicated the priest as a heretic. Charles demanded a quid pro quo from the Pope.

The French, under King Francis I, had captured the Duchy of Milan, one of Charles' hereditary possessions in 1515. Charles demanded that the Pope should support him in ejecting the French and getting this dominion of his back.

War between France and Spain broke out almost at once. Milan was not the only bone of contention. Francis I of France, for his part, was demanding that Charles should acknowledge that he only ruled Burgundy and Belgium as the French King's subject. The dispute was also a struggle for the control of the western Mediterranean and, on the French side, to prevent their country being completely surrounded by Charles' Empire.

At first the war went Charles' way. He won an important victory and regained Milan without fighting a single pitched battle. It was at the celebration of the retreat of Francis back over the Alps that Leo contracted the fatal chill from which he died. He was succeeded, first by Adrian VI, then, a little over a year later, by Guilio de' Medici - Clement VII.

Fighting for the Spanish Emperor, Charles, and against Francis, was the French King's own most important subject, Charles Bourbon, who was descended from two powerful branches of the great Bourbon family.

He had fought for his French king at the Battle of Marignano back in 1515, when the army of Francis I crossed the Alps and brilliantly defeated the Swiss army, killing thirteen thousand of them and capturing Milan and Lombardy in the first place.

Bourbon's bravery was so great, and his leadership was so decisive in the battle, that Francis rewarded him with the honorary title of "Constable of France". The jealousy that this caused in France, and the machinations of his political enemies, undermined his relationship with King Francis and his titles, dignities and possessions were threatened. Indeed, Francis I himself had designs on Bourbon's rich estates, so in retaliation, Bourbon changed allegiance and sided with Charles V and Spain against Francis.

Charles V's recapture of Milan did not put an end to the war. It went on, first one way and then the other.

By 1524, the Spanish King had completely driven the French out of Italy and invaded southern France, where an army of German mercenaries, led by the renegade Frenchman, Bourbon, laid siege to Marseilles. They were unsuccessful and had to withdraw.

Then in the Autumn of the same year, Francis counter-attacked. He crossed the Alps yet again, this time with a large and magnificently equipped army, and once more cleared the Lombardy Plain. He forced the out-numbered Holy Roman Imperial army to retreat, except for four thousand men who were left to guard the key town of Pavia.

However to protect his rear, the victorious Francis, in turn, had to lay siege to this city, but the garrison defended it so stubbornly that Francis' advance was held up and Charles had time to regroup. He brought up his German troops under the command of George von Frundsberg, a Tyrolean nobleman who had survived twenty major battles, and fresh Spanish troops under the command of Constable Bourbon.

The French king was caught in a pincer between von Frundsberg and the garrison of Pavia, and on 24th February 1525 his army was annihilated. Francis' horse was killed under him, but he fought on foot until he was captured and taken off to a Spanish prison.

—⚋—

Francis remained a prisoner for a year until he surrendered all his claims to Milan, Belgium and Burgundy, and entered into a number of other humiliating commitments, including restoring Bourbon's estates.

He also had to give his two eldest sons as hostages, but despite this, no sooner was he back in France than he was plotting to renew the war.

This time he sought the support of the rulers of the various independent Italian States, including the new Pope, Clement. The Italians had discovered that, in ridding themselves of one tyrant, Francis I of France, they had got themselves into the power of what seemed to be a worse one - Charles V of Spain.

For this reason, and with the devious complexities of Renaissance politics, the Italians were now preparing to ally themselves with their former oppressor, against their new one!

—⚋—

Fortunately for the Spaniards, and unfortunately for the Pope, his French ally was totally unprepared to resume fighting, and Clement was too naive to realise that it would take time for the French King to assemble an army to support him.

The Pope had recruited armies from the States of Florence, Venice and Rome, the so-called "Italian League", and even though the French troops had not arrived, minor skirmishes broke out between the League and the Spaniards. These lasted about a year, with the Pope and his anti-Imperialist allies scoring some initial successes.

Charles had other troubles. Despite the wealth crossing the Atlantic from his American colonies, Spain had been virtually bankrupted by the war. He had been forced to disband the greater part of his armies but he could not, of course, allow the Pope's provocations to go unpunished. In defence of his position as Holy Roman Emperor, he was bound to react as strongly as possible.

"I shall go into Italy and revenge myself on that poltroon Pope," he swore.

But how? The opportunity presented itself when, Clement was forced to withdraw his own Papal troops to meet a threatened diversionary attack from bitter enemies of his at home: the warlike and powerful Colonna Clan.

Their headquarters were in the Alban Hills, in the Roman countryside. Apart from being traditional supporters of the Spanish Kings, who were the hereditary rulers of Naples, the head of the family, Pompeo Colonna, had the ambition of being Pope himself.

If he could defeat the few remaining soldiers around Rome, the capture and murder of Clement would mean that no one, especially the hated Medici family, would stand in his way.

Colonna failed to capture the Pope, but nevertheless the damage was done and Clement had to withdraw from the Italian League and retreat from Lombardy to protect Rome.

—⚜—

Charles did not really trust Constable Bourbon, especially now that Francis had been forced to give him back his estates.

"If he can stab one King in the back, he can just as easily do the same to another one," he confided to his advisers.

Nevertheless, after the Battle of Pavia he had felt compelled, because of his own political and financial position, to give Bourbon the command of the Spanish armies in the strategically important North of Italy. Now the Imperial Army, numbering about twenty-four thousand men, with Bourbon as its general, began its slow march south.

It included twelve thousand tough, brutal Landsknechts - lance knights - provided by George von Frundsberg who had mortgaged his estates and castle and even pawned his own personal possessions to pay his Germans.

This money did not last long especially when divided amongst twelve thousand men. For Charles' Spanish troops, there was nothing, and in those days, soldiers had to be paid every thirty days - or else it was the worse for the local populace, their own officers and anyone else unfortunate to cross their path.

For one month the Spaniards were fobbed off with one ducat each in cash and a pair of shoes, fortuitously recently expropriated in Milan.

But soon the Spanish troops were on the verge of mutiny and incited the crack, disciplined, Landsknechts to follow suit. One officer was taken hostage; another was murdered. Constable Bourbon was forced to take refuge in von Frundsberg's stables, while the Germans rioted outside shouting, "Pay! Pay! Pay! Pay!" and threatening their officers with their pikes.

Von Frundsberg arrived at the scene at a gallop, and flung himself off his horse.

"What the hell is going on here?" he bellowed.

He was a tall, burly man, massively broad. He was dressed in a short-sleeved coat of mail with a sheepskin cloak around his shoulders, and carried a ferocious looking long double bladed sword unsheathed in his hand. With his hair and beard bristling, and the firelight making his eyes glow red, he seemed like the reincarnation of an ancient Viking.

"You miserable scum! I've sold every damn thing I own to pay you. I don't eat unless you do; I don't drink unless you do. Christ! When some of you cissies are too tired to march, I even carry your bloody swords for you! Pay? What do you need pay for right now? What are you going to spend it on in this God forsaken place? You've already stolen everything worth having, and you've worn out all the women for twenty miles around, anyway."

He pointed his sword at a little group of pikemen.

"Don't let me see you raise a sword to one of our own side again! Save your energy for the Pope and for carting home all the gold we're going to find in Rome."

The mercenaries shuffled their feet, but none of them made as if to move away.

"I haven't nursed you all this far to have you act like a bunch of mooing peasants. Discipline is what brought you here, and discipline is what will keep you alive!"

His face had become mottled with rage, and his voice hoarse with shouting. The sinews and veins in his thick neck stood out like chords.

"Go on! Get back to your quarters before I.... before I...."

He staggered, dropped his sword, and clutched at his throat. He fell backwards in an apoplectic fit, crashing through a large ceremonial drum. It made a hollow, booming sound before the skin tore and the wooden frame splintered under him.

As his aides rushed forward to put his rigid, convulsing figure onto a rough plank to carry him back to his tent, the mob of soldiers slowly dispersed into the darkness.

—⚍—

The Imperial army slowly made its way down the spine of Italy. Piacenza, Modena, Ferrara, Bologna, Castiglione, and many other cities, towns and villages were swept through as though by locusts.

Food for the huge number of men was a perpetual daily problem: foragers scoured the countryside. Sometimes they were lucky, sometimes not. Near Florence they found wine but no victuals. That, as can be imagined, did no good for the local population.

Elsewhere, starving soldiers were even forced to kill and eat their own donkeys.

If a town agreed to pay a satisfactory tribute it was left untouched - usually. Sometimes, even then it was not. If it resisted or refused, the soldiers took what they wanted by pillaging and looting.

Charles himself was having political difficulties with some of his supporters who did not want him, as Holy Roman Emperor, to go to the final extreme of attacking the Pope. Bourbon, therefore, encouraged his soldiers, their ranks swelled by Italian deserters, to persist in their demands for pay - or loot - as a justification for continuing their violent advance.

In desperation, the Pope rejoined the Italian League. But it was too late.

-11-

On 18th April 1527, Holy Thursday, Pope Clement was about to pronounce the pontifical blessing to the crowd in St. Peter's Square. Practically the entire population of Rome was there.

Standing next to Benevento was a strange looking creature, half-naked, with long red hair hanging down to his shoulders, clutching a crucifix in one hand and a human skull in the other. No sooner had the Pope appeared than the man elbowed his way through the crowd, and climbed on to the statue of St. Paul.

"For Christ's sake, who's that?" Benvenuto asked Lucagnolo.

"He calls himself Brando of Sienna. He says he is a Prophet." Lucagnolo gave a sniff. "Mad fanatic, I call him. You know, Hell and Damnation for everyone. End of the world at any minute if we don't all repent. Second Coming any day now. Shush! He's going to say something."

Brando braced his back on the statue and shook both the crucifix and the skull at the startled Pope.

"Thou bastard of Sodom! For thy sins, Rome shall be destroyed. Repent! Rome! Romans! Do penance! They shall do with thee as God did with Sodom and Gomorrah!"

Before he could say anything more, some of the Pope's Swiss Guard had reached him, and dragged him away ranting incoherently, while the people near him averted their heads so that he could not look directly at them. Obviously this creature possessed the Evil Eye!

Only a little over two weeks later, the madman's prophesy began to come true.

—⚜—

On 5th May Bourbon's army reached the highest hills to the north of Rome. The scene was now set for the greatest act of wanton destruction and pillage that the centre of Christendom had suffered since the time of the Goths, a thousand years previously.

The army and the civilian militia manned the city walls. They had been built by the Emperor Aurelius over fourteen hundred years before. Their upkeep, vital to the defence of Rome, had been a constant drain on the Papal revenues ever since. The thick stone battlements had been weakened by too many buildings being allowed close by or even against the walls, and by being pierced by too many gates and bridges. They were also too long to be defended against artillery, and had not been modernised to allow the defendants own cannon and musketry to give overlapping fields of fire.

In the first, probing skirmishes, no sooner had some of the enemy's scouts approached the walls than some of the already-demoralised defenders fled from their posts. This was immediately discouraged by their officers by the simple expedient of instantly and summarily executing all deserters.

—⚜—

Not that Sant' Angelo was itself fully prepared. On the day before the attack, it was suddenly realised that it was not provisioned for a siege, and the Castilian had to send out men, hurriedly to requisition such supplies that could be found in the neighbourhood.

A few rich Cardinals, bankers and merchants had taken the precaution of recruiting their own private guards to protect their Palazzos, shops and warehouses. These might be of some use against, at best, lightly armed civilian looters, but would not deter the enemy troops if they ever broke through the City walls.

Benvenuto himself had headed a troop of fifty men on behalf of one such merchant, Piero de Bene, during the raid by Colonna's men a few months before. Once it was clear that a battle for the City was about to begin, Benvenuto went to re-assemble his band of irregulars. He found that most of them had already gathered outside de Bene's house. Benvenuto did a rapid count. Thirty-nine.

"Where are the others?"

"Don't know," said one of the men, "but we'll manage without them."

"You think so?" Benvenuto replied, sarcastically. "If you will take a look, Captain, or is it General, you'll see thousands of the bastards out there. Personally, I'd be a lot happier with a few of them on my side than some of you lot. Now, you, you and you," pointing at three of the men, "go and look for the others or anyone else who wants to help and looks if he can carry a sword without falling over it, and bring them back here."

He turned to another of his troop. "You know where Lucagnolo's shop is?"

The man nodded.

"See if you can find him and tell him to come. Then get along to my studio; see if my apprentice is there and fetch him, too. He saved my life so I suppose I might as well try to save his."

Benvenuto clapped his hands twice. "Go on! Go! And back in five minutes, not a second more."

"What if it takes longer? You'll still be here, won't you?" the last man asked.

"No we bloody well won't," replied Benvenuto. "We're not going to stop around to guard this pile of worthless junk. We're going into the castle."

"To defend the Pope?"

"No you fool, to put as thick a wall as possible between us and those Spaniards. Now move!" Benvenuto ordered. "It's not just bandits like the Colonnas this time. These are real soldiers, and they could kill us all before breakfast, just for practice! If you're not back by the time I said, you'll be on your own. One of our military geniuses will remember to close the Castle gate any minute."

—⚌—

When the first shots were fired the population panicked. Thousands of them rushed up four of the roads that led into St. Peter's Square, and then set off down the fifth towards the Castel Sant' Angelo.

Rioting broke out and mobs of angry and frightened Romans attacked the Spanish and German quarters of the City. There were over seven thousand Spanish workers and a large number of Germans, mostly merchants, who lived in Rome. They, and the Pope's own elite, and entirely loyal Swiss Guard, were unjustifiably regarded as potential traitors.

Some rioters seized a heaven-sent opportunity, and forced their way into foreigners' houses and shops under the pretext of "looking for spies" and then helped themselves to the contents, killing or beating the owners if they protested.

—⚌—

Piero de Bene's warehouse was on the edge of the jewellers' section, and like the Vatican itself was close to the Castel Sant' Angelo.

The man Benvenuto had sent to his studio was the first to return. Neither Lucagnolo nor Silvio was with him.

"Couldn't find them," he said in reply to Benvenuto's unspoken question.

"Oh well, they can't say I didn't try." Benvenuto dismissed them from his mind with a shrug of his shoulders.

Benvenuto and his troop, now swollen to forty-six strong, began to force their way through the crowds trying to get to the castle.

"Make way there! Clear the way all of you! Come on, do you want the Spaniards to get to the walls before we do?"

Benvenuto punctuated his commands with slaps from the scabbard of his sword, which he carried in one hand or prods from his arquebus which he carried in the other.

Terrified though they were, the people like sheep, pressed themselves against the walls of the houses to let Benvenuto and his men pass. They marched to the drawbridge of the castle which was guarded by pikemen who had been forcibly keeping the civilians out while the last of the provisions and ammunition came in.

As Benvenuto's little company reached the row of levelled pikes, he turned to the crowd behind him in the street.

"Go home you people, or go to your posts at once! These brave men can't just stand here guarding this bridge. They've got some hard fighting to do." Then, to the guard commander, "Alright, corporal, let us through, and carry on with your duty, and good luck!"

The bluff worked. The row of pikes opened up, and Benvenuto started to cross. Just at that moment, a bell was rung inside the castle, and at this signal, the pikemen too turned and ran across the drawbridge which began to rise.

Benvenuto and his men and the pikemen scrambled under the rapidly descending portcullis and peered through the grille. He nudged the volunteer nearest to him.

"See, we got here just in time. I told you we couldn't spend more than five minutes looking for the others. God's Blood! What's going on now?"

The crowds in the street were rushing down the narrow causeway leading to the drawbridge. A few managed to leap on as it slowly went up, but they were all defeated by the steepness of the angle and were either crushed between the heavy planking and the gate, or dropped off into the moat.

The terrified crowd, surging forward, pushed dozens of their number over the now open edge of the bridge and into the water. Some sank under the weight of their belongings; some sank under those who fell on top of them. The lucky ones were fished out, covered with stinking slime. The others drowned.

One of the cardinals, who arrived too late to get across the drawbridge, had to suffer the indignity of being hauled up to the top of the battlements and to safety in a wicker basket, with his feet dangling over the side, while the frustrated citizens shouted abuse and mentally hoped for the rope to snap or for him to over-balance and fall out.

With the raising of the drawbridge and the closing of the gate, the siege of Castel Sant' Angelo had begun.

Castel Sant' Angelo, a large imposing stone and brick tower, shaped like a half star, with its back protected by the River Tiber, was originally intended as a tomb. All of the Roman Emperors, from Hadrian, who built it, to Septimus Severus, were buried there. It was Aurelius who incorporated it within the City walls when he built them, and it had only been as recently as the last thirty years that Pope Alexander VI had re-fortified the Castle with parapets, turrets, a new wall and the moat.

It was connected directly to the Vatican by a covered footbridge, especially intended to provide an escape route for the Pope. Clement had put it to good use on this occasion because when the main assault itself began, the Pope was at his morning prayers and only managed to get to the fortress at the very last moment.

The main tower commanded the Ponte Sant' Angelo, the nearby bridge over the Tiber.

The castle was impregnable against everything except starvation and siege guns, but Bourbon had no heavy artillery. He could not persuade his men, who were hungry for loot, to hold back, and the speed of his advance had outstripped his clumsy ox-train, which dragged the huge weapons and great cannon balls along unsurfaced roads, through fields, and across muddy fords.

For the defence of Rome, the only trained men consisted of four thousand regular infantry, two thousand Swiss Guards and two thousand "Black Band" irregulars.

By the ancient laws of the city, the sounding of the alarm drum should have been the signal for the assembly of all able-bodied men, but only six companies turned up, and because the best and fittest men had already been recruited, as Benvenuto and his group had, as private guards, those who did respond were the dregs of the population.

It was these inadequate, disorganised defenders who had to face Bourbon's large army of hardened, seasoned soldiers, very well experienced in attacking cities and street fighting - as the trail of destruction that they had left on the way to Rome, testified.

But the Romans were behind the walls of the city. Safely protected, so they thought.

—ɷ—

On the 5th May, Bourbon's scouts had suffered heavy losses in their first probing tests of the defences, but they brought back valuable information from which Bourbon was able to plan his assault. At midnight he gave his troops the customary harangue to inspire and motivate them. In this case it was not really necessary. The men were desperate, half-starved and clothed in rags. They knew there was food, wine women and unlimited booty on the other side of the wall. That was all the encouragement they needed.

They began lopping down trees and lashing poles together and uprooting garden fences to construct makeshift scaling ladders.

At 4 a.m. on 6th May, the battle began.

Bourbon launched two feint attacks at the Belvedere Palace and Porta Pertosa behind the Vatican. The main attack was made near to the Porta San Spirito, to the South. The walls here were lower than elsewhere, and the ground outside was slightly higher, giving an advantage to the Imperial troops.

The battlements were also weaker at this point because part of the wall was a house which had not been properly buttressed, and it also had a large window which served as a gun port.

The first attack was repelled with heavy losses, mostly from the crossfire from the Pope's artillery in Castel Sant' Angelo and on Monte San Spirito.

Then nature took a hand to help the attackers. A heavy dawn mist rose up from the marshes. The gunners on San Spirito were unsighted. Bourbon took advantage of this by moving the focus of the attack nearer to Sant' Angelo so that its big guns could not be depressed enough to be effective. With both defending batteries temporarily useless, the attackers were able to deploy their light field guns against the Castle's heavy artillery.

The defenders had to resort to throwing rocks over the walls on the Imperialists. The attack was gaining ground and momentum.

"Gunners to the battlements!" was the cry inside the castle, and Benvenuto and the others rushed to the walls. The Pope and his commanders were already there. They peered over the top. The enemy were just bringing up their scaling ladders for yet another assault.

They were being directed by a magnificent figure dressed in silver and white. It was Constable Bourbon himself!

"Quick, you men!" the Pope shouted. "Fifty gold crowns to the one who shoots that fellow down."

There was a rattle of hastily and badly aimed shots, and a few men around Bourbon fell, writhing and screaming, but Bourbon himself was untouched and did nothing to move himself under cover.

"Come on, Messer Cellini," said Clement, "you've used that gun of yours to good effect on a Spaniard before, so I hear."

Benvenuto looked puzzled.

"The Bishop of Salamanca's butler," the Pope reminded him. You're a huntsman, and you claim to be a pretty good shot. Let me see what you can really do."

Benvenuto carefully measured some powder into his arquebus, added a linen wad and selected from his pouch a perfectly round bullet that he had moulded himself, and rammed it home. Instead of just firing from the shoulder, as his modern gun permitted, he rested it on one of the old-fashioned tripods and took careful aim. He slowly squeezed the trigger; the trigger ignited a match and the match made contact with the fine powder in the firing pan which in turn set off the main charge.....

An ounce and a quarter of lead struck Bourbon just above his sword belt. The soft, superheated bullet flattened and spread on impact with his hard leather jerkin and tore a gaping wound in Bourbon's stomach. Then it broke up. Pieces of it ripped their separate ways in all directions through his insides.

The force of the blow flung Bourbon to the ground, sprawling on his back. He struggled to a sitting position, his legs spread apart, his right arm extended behind him as a prop, while his left hand involuntarily clutched at the fearful hole through which his entrails were trying to force their way out.

He looked down at the bright arterial blood pumping from between his fingers, and forming a fast spreading puddle between his legs.

"Oh shit!" he said. And died.

The news of Bourbon's death rapidly spread among attackers and defenders alike. The Romans, shouting, "Victory! Victory! We've won, we've won!" began abandoning their posts. The attackers were at first demoralised, but were rallied by Ferrante Gonzaga, a renegade Italian, who called on them to avenge their leader.

The Imperial troops tore into the walls with renewed ferocity. Wave after wave attacked. As each one fell back under a hail of bullets, a new one took its place, and every time a few more defenders were killed or wounded, and the old walls were damaged a little more as the attackers pulled down parts of the fortifications with poles, grappling hooks, ropes, or even their bare hands.

The Imperial troops were too numerous. When the fog lifted, it could be seen that the walls had been breached in three places by sheer manpower, and the Spaniards and Germans began pouring through.

They might have still been held back until the Roman cannon could be brought to bear, but many of the irregular troops and the civilians had fled from the walls, some to barricade their own houses, others to try to escape. Those who took to the river were drowned when their overloaded boats were sunk and their heavy armour dragged them to the bottom.

By seven o'clock in the morning, only three short hours after the start of the battle, all organised resistance, except for the besieged Castel Sant' Angelo, had ceased. The invaders bypassed the fort. They had other things on their minds.

According to the customs of warfare, if a city was taken by storm, no quarter was given, and the victors did as they wished. Brutal, perhaps, but it did at least discourage futile resistance.

Rome was no exception. Wounded defenders were clubbed or stabbed where they lay. Houses were burst into, and the men killed, the women raped and valuables stolen. Buildings were indiscriminately set on fire.

One of the Imperialist officers was slashed in the face as he fought with a Swiss pikeman. In revenge he led his men in a rampage in which they cut down every person, young or old, man, woman or child, armed or unarmed, soldier or civilian who crossed their paths.

The inmates of the San Spirito Hospital were all killed, mostly by being thrown out of the windows into the river. All the orphaned children of the Pieta were slaughtered.

Even with the free reign given to the victors after a battle of this sort, the Church and its ministers, and those whom they gave sanctuary were normally safe. Not so in this case. The

German Landsknechts were Lutherans. They hated the Pope. It was the Pope himself and his Church that they were fighting. Hadn't their own leader, Von Frundsberg, told them so himself.

"The Pope is our Emperor's worst enemy. For the honour of God, he must be hanged, even if I have to do it with my own hands."

"Hang the Pope! Hang the Pope!" became a sort of battle cry as the Germans desecrated and robbed the Churches, cutting priests to pieces as they did so.

One old monk was found by a gang of drunken soldiers in the street, trying to escape on a donkey. When he refused to give the beast Holy Communion, they left him to die, slowly, and struggling feebly, impaled on a door, with a spear through his belly.

Nuns were dragged out of their convents. Those who were judged to be too old or too ugly had their throats cut. The younger ones were raped by one man after another and then "sold" by one band of soldiers to another until they tired of them, and then they were hanged or shot or dispatched with a sword thrust between their legs.

At the High Altar of St. Peter's itself, five hundred armed men were brutally murdered and Holy Relics burned, while the greatest Cathedral in Christendom was turned into a stable for the Imperial Cavalry.

—☙—

The indiscriminate butchery only stopped when the looters realised that they were depriving themselves of a valuable source of revenue. Ransom.

Some unfortunates had to be ransomed several times over, first from one group and then another. If a wealthy Roman, whether Cardinal or Bishop, landowner or merchant, refused to pay, he or his family were tortured until he did.

Torture was also used to "persuade" other people to say where they had hidden their valuables, but because the owners of some of these treasures had been murdered before they could reveal where they had been buried, hoards were still being dug up hundreds of years later. In 1705 a chest with 60,000 gold pieces was found.

Not even the homes of opponents of the Pope, or supporters of the Colonna's or the Holy Roman Emperor were safe from the violence of the Germans who were now completely out of control, unless they paid their Spanish allies huge amounts for "protection". In gold.

-12-

There was nothing that the besieged garrison of Castel Sant' Angelo could do to interfere with the killing, raping, looting, torturing and burning that was going on in the city below them.

There was no question of their making any sorties out of the fortress: no one would have got more than a few hundred yards from the gate; no one would have returned alive. The largest patrol that could have sallied out would have been outnumbered, hundreds to one. The Romans shut up inside the Castle therefore had to content themselves with sniping at any of the enemy who came within range, and harassing them with artillery fire.

Benvenuto became an artilleryman by accident.

There were several cannon sited on the castle tower which commanded a wide field of fire over the whole of the city.

Benvenuto made his way to the roof to take his turn as a sniper. He saw a short, bow-legged bombardier named Giuliano lying along the length of one of the guns, his arms around it, as if embracing it. An officer was standing over him, sword upraised.

"I can't do it," sobbed Giuliano. "That's my street down there. If we fire, we'll hit my house; we'll kill my family."

The officer ground his teeth. "Open fire at once! At once, do you hear? Or I'll ram my sword right up your backside!"

Before Guiliano could refuse again, Benvenuto stepped forward. "Alright, Captain, I'll do it."

The officer looked at him. "You? What do you know about guns?"

"Enough," Benvenuto replied, "it was me who gutted Bourbon himself at four hundred paces. Anyway, the Bombardier will help me, won't you?" he added with uncharacteristic gentleness. "If we don't do something, they'll be in your house and up your wife's skirt while you watch. Are the guns loaded?"

The soldier nodded his dirty, tear-streaked face. Benvenuto picked up the lighted fuse and got the crews of three of the guns to line them up.

"You'll need more elevation," said one of the men.

"Well, do it then."

Benvenuto put the slow match to the touch-hole of the first gun, and, as the explosion roared out, he remembered to jump aside just in time to prevent the trolley from recoiling across his feet.

The heavy ball fell short and crashed through the roof of a nearby house in a spout of tiles and the roof dust of centuries. They raised the sights and fired again. Too long, but only just. The ball hit the house right at the end of the road, smashing a hole through the wall.

They made another fine adjustment and waited until a Spanish patrol turned into the street. Then, on Benvenuto's signal, all three guns of the half-battery fired, one after the other.

The left hand ball struck the parapet of one of the houses and then bounced along the roofs for the length of the road, showering masonry and jagged broken tiles on the men below. The second shot went down the centre of the road. At the first bounce it disembowelled a horse and took off its rider's left leg, bounced again, sending up a lethal spray of stone splinters from the cobbles, and smashed another man into a bleeding pulp before crashing into the wall of the end house.

The last ball was a little too high. It hit the same house, whose walls could not stand the strain of three massive impacts like this. The building collapsed into the street, pinning several Spaniards under the rubble. Benvenuto could not help gloating.

"God! That was fun. By the way, I hope that wasn't your house."

"No it wasn't," replied Guiliano, "and look, the rest of the bastards are running away."

"Yes, we stopped them just in time for your wife, I'd say. Let's find some more. Christ knows there are enough of them." Benvenuto was carried away with excitement.

He and the bombardier ran round the platform looking for targets. Down near the castle was an inn with the sign of a red sun. There seemed to be some sort of disturbance going on and the shutters were closed.

"Look at all those horses tethered there. There must be a crowd of them inside."

The bombardier nodded in agreement. Together they got the crews to line up three more guns.

"Wait!" commanded Benvenuto. "Let's get the range to the side of the inn first. We may as well catch as many inside as we can."

"You've only fired four shots, and you're already an expert," the bombardier grumbled, "but you're right." He extended his arm, held up his thumb and squinted along it with one eye.

"Five hundred paces, I guess," he said.

The cannon boomed out.

"Just short. We'll call it five-fifty. We can't risk another shot, or it may warn them."

Three fuses were touched to the holes simultaneously. Three explosions and three balls sped on their way, side by side.

One crashed through a window and ploughed along the floor boards, sending razor-sharp lumps of wood flying in all directions, liked barbed arrows through the main room.

The other two smashed through the walls, simultaneously, cutting joists and beams. The fragile building collapsed inwards, trapping and crushing the soldiers who were inside celebrating their victory too soon.

The Prince of Orange, who had assumed command of the Imperial army after Bourbon's death, could not permit the constant threat from the castle to go unchallenged. He gathered together a full company of Spanish and renegade Italian soldiers, diverting them from their looting and carousing and other pleasures, and forced them into building a gun position.

A barrel was filled with pitch-impregnated rags and was pushed on a cart to a spot to windward of the partly built trench and set alight. Under the cover of the dense, oily smoke, the soldiers began feverishly deepening and widening the ditch, while others brought up baskets and barrels filled with earth and stones to use as makeshift ramparts. Despite the odd random shot from the castle, the Spaniards managed to complete the gun site and dragged a field gun into position. It was too small to be really effective - the attackers were still hampered by the lack of their heavy artillery - but it was the best they could do.

As soon as the gun was in position, it opened fire. That served to keep the defenders' heads down while a second gun was brought up. The two then began firing in salvoes. The defenders could not depress their big guns enough to hit back, and the light falconets, loaded with grapefruit-sized balls, and fired by Benvenuto and his new friend, Bombardier Guiliano, could make no impression on the earthworks.

Guliano installed a demi-culverin in place of one of the falconets. It was longer barrelled, so it could be mounted higher; it also took a larger charge of powder which enabled it to shoot a sixteen pound lump of iron at the enemy's fortifications.

Small though the cannon balls were that the Spaniards were in turn firing, the constant pounding on one small area eventually broke through the top of the castle wall. Two shots from the field guns hit the ramparts simultaneously.

One struck the dismounted falconet. The huge sliver of metal it peeled off, pierced Guiliano's head just behind his right ear, killing him instantly. The second ball brought another section of the wall crashing down on the gunners, and Benvenuto was buried with them under a pile of rubble.

When he was dragged out, there was a thin trickle of blood coming from his nose, his face was covered by a film of white dust, and his mouth was half open, his lips drawn back from his teeth. He was unconscious but his breathing was so very shallow that, in fact, at first they thought he was dead, but when he began to groan and stir, they forced a mixture of spiced wine laced with wormwood down his throat to revive him.

He could still only move with difficulty, so, despite all his shouts of protest, they dragged off his chain mail, jerkin and shirt and treated the enormous bruises they found on his chest with hot poultices, to the accompaniment of even louder cries of pain.

By now the Pope had come up to the battlements to inspect the damage. When Benvenuto saw him, he struggled to get up.

The Pope motioned with his hand. "Stay where you are, Messer Cellini. You're not too badly hurt, I hope?"

"Oh no. Just some bruises and perhaps a cracked rib or two. Nothing serious."

Benvenuto glanced past the Pope to Guiliano's body, still lying on the ground. The realisation of the situation suddenly struck him.

"I was spared by God's grace. If I had been standing just the other side of that gun where that poor fellow was, those would be my brains spilling out of my head."

He flung himself to his knees before Clement.

"I'm not afraid to die, Your Holiness, but how can I meet my God with the blood of so many men on my hands? How many men have I killed in the past few days? Ten? Easily! Twenty? At least! It must be fifty or even a hundred. And worse still, I've enjoyed doing it. I've gloated and boasted about it."

The Pope looked at him sympathetically. "Your conscience is clear. You've only been doing your duty to defend the Holy Church from the heretics."

"Grant me absolution, so if I do die, God will forgive me. Your Holiness, please," Benvenuto begged. He seized the Pope's hand and kissed his ring.

Clement drew a long loud breath between his teeth and made the sign of the Cross over Benvenuto's bowed head. The other men also dropped to their knees.

"*Ego te absolvo*," the Pope intoned. "I absolve each of you from all blame for the deaths you have caused in this battle." He paused. "I also absolve you from responsibility for the lives you may take in the future in defence of God's Law."

He raised both of his arms above his head and spoke to all the men on the tower. "God save you all," he said.

He walked to the stairway. At the narrow doorway leading down into the castle he paused, turned, and beckoned to Benvenuto.

"Come with me, I have some work for you."

—⚜—

He led Benvenuto down to a tiny underground room and unlocked the door with a large key which was hanging from his belt.

There was no furniture except for a heavy wooden table in the corner away from the door, a stout chair and, surprisingly three ten-branch candelabra, all lit. The once-whitewashed walls and ceiling were grimed by the soot from the thousands of candles that had been used over the years to light the room, while the flagstoned floor was spotted everywhere with candle grease.

The Pope snapped his fingers at one of the two aides who were with him, and, without a word, the man dragged a heavy sack from under the table. The other priest helped him lift it up, grunting loudly as he did so.

The neck of the sack was opened and the contents poured out. Benvenuto had never seen anything like it in his whole life. The table was covered in jewel-encrusted gold tiaras, crucifixes, chalices, communion cups, plate, rings, and all the other rich ornaments of the Apostolic Camera.

The gold reflected spots of light on to the walls while the candlelight winked back from rubies, emeralds, sapphires and diamonds.

"What...." Benvenuto began.

The Pope interrupted him. "Master Goldsmith, break these pieces up and give me the jewels. If the worst happens, Charles isn't going to have them."

"And if the worst doesn't happen, Your Holiness?"

"Then you and your colleagues will be kept busy for years making new ones. Now hurry. There may be less time than we think, and in any case I'm sure you want to get back to the walls now you have a personal debt to repay the Spaniards."

He gave Benvenuto a friendly slap on his bruised shoulder. Benvenuto winced and opened his pouch and took out the small tools that he had been able to bring with him into the fort.

Clement and the two priests stood and watched closely for the two hours that it took to finish the work. As Benvenuto threw the last piece of gold onto the pile, the Pope nodded in approval.

"That was quickly done, Messer Cellini."

Benvenuto shrugged. "I didn't have to take care with the mountings. I just dug the jewels out. I tell you, sir, I take no pride in it, destroying all that craftsmanship."

"You've destroyed enough of God's craftsmanship these past few days," one of the priests interjected.

"Be silent," said the Pope. "I have given him absolution, and it was in the same good cause."

They sorted the jewels into four piles. The two priests wrapped them in thick parchment which they sewed into the hem of Clement's robe. The table was littered with a great mound of gold. Benvenuto guessed there was nearly a hundred pounds of it.

The Pope waved his hand. "Can you melt it down?"

"Of course, if I can find something to make a furnace with. Will Your Holiness have it weighed first?"

"Weighed? What for? Oh, I see. No, goldsmith. I don't think anyone would fight for the Church like you have, and then rob it. Just do the job as quickly as you can, and don't let anyone see. Here's the key."

Benvenuto went into the kitchens and collected some charcoal and earthenware dishes. He looked speculatively at the large ovens, and then at all the cooks. "He told me not to let anyone see," he thought regretfully, and snatching up a large pair of bellows hurried out before anyone could argue. He deposited his booty in the locked room and then went up to the battlements from where he got a sackful of loose bricks, of which were there in plenty. Once back in the basement dungeon, he constructed a small furnace, placed an earthenware crucible on it, broke the gold up into pieces and began to melt them down.

While the metal was melting, he locked the door, went to the armoury and got some of the moulds used for making lead shot. He poured in the molten metal, and while it was cooling, began to melt some more.

By the time the job was finished, another four hours had passed. The cell was almost as hot as the furnace itself, and Benvenuto was soaked with perspiration utterly exhausted and all the stooping, lifting, bending and operating the bellows had made his injured chest burn in agony.

He put the hundreds of little balls of gold into the sack.

"The most valuable bullets ever made, I should think."

The sack was too heavy to lift, so he pushed it under the table and went out and locked the door. The Pope was standing at one of the gun slits, staring morosely at the buildings burning in the twilight. Benvenuto held out his hand, the key in his palm.

"Finished?"

Benvenuto nodded.

"I don't know how to show my appreciation, my son."

"If you would simply excuse me, and let me get some rest, there is nothing more I could ask. I'm ready to drop."

The Pope pointed up the stairs. "They've made a dormitory up there somewhere."

"Thank you, Your Holiness."

"You're welcome, Benvenuto," the Pope said, and smiled for the first time in days.

Benvenuto forced a sickly grin, and turning on his heel, he limped up the stairs to find himself a bed.

-13-

Benvenuto awoke the next morning, the third day of the siege, to the sound of sporadic gunfire and feeling ravenous. He ran up the steps of the tower to the roof, briefly pausing at the officers' mess to grab a hunk of cold, stringy mutton and a corner of bread which he gnawed from alternate hands while he walked round the parapet, surveying the scene below.

There was a sooty haze all over the city. Thin clouds of smoke were blowing everywhere from hundreds of fires, making it difficult to see clearly and the acrid smell of burning wood made his eyes water.

A group of gunners on the west side of the tower were pointing in the direction of the Santo Spirito gate.

"There they go again, exactly on time as usual."

"There who goes?" demanded Benvenuto, "and what do you mean, 'the same time as usual'?"

"It's those bloody Spaniards. They change the guard outside the gate every three hours, on the dot. Look! You can just see their lances now."

Benvenuto was incredulous. "Do you mean to tell me you've watched them going by every three hours and you haven't done a damn thing about it? The least thing you can do is to wave them bye-bye! What the hell do you think you're up here for? They're just taking a little morning stroll after fucking your wives all night, and you stand and watch them! What are you, a crowd of pimps?"

The men looked down at their feet. One of them said, apologetically, "We've only just realised they were so regular. The gate's only just in range - if that. And," he finished lamely, "we were waiting for an officer."

"Waiting for an officer? Ha! I never heard anything so bloody stupid. When one of those Spaniards tries to shove his pike in your guts, what'll you do? Tell him you can't shoot him 'til your captain comes? Come on, it is too late this time, but get one ball off like it's a stray, just for range, and be quick about it!"

The cannon roared out at maximum elevation. They watched the flight of the ball and saw it fall somewhere a little beyond the street leading to the gate.

"Good," said Benvenuto, "not, 'just in range', but 'well in range'. Down about forty paces, and we'll have it."

"Thirty," suggested the gunner.

"Thirty then," Benvenuto agreed.

The second shot fell into the street, although they could not see exactly where because of the houses. Benvenuto drew a line on the gun carriage with a piece of charred wood to show the exact elevation and then he measured the same mark onto the other four guns that could be brought to bear.

"Alright," Benvenuto said, tapping his chest with two fingers. "Guiliano's dead. I'm your officer now. I'll be back in a couple of hours and I want all the guns loaded and trained. Best powder and roundest balls, mark you, and we'll be waiting for them."

He went towards the stairway and then stopped. "Oh by the way," he added sarcastically, "if in the meantime you do happen to see any soldiers down there within range, you'll know for sure they're the enemy. You have my full permission to kill them."

—⚏—

The ambush was set. Benvenuto and his gunners waited. They saw the soldiers coming through the gate, their lances glinting in the hazy sunlight, then they disappeared between the houses of the Borgo Santo Spirito which ran parallel with the River Tiber and at an oblique angle to the Castle.

"Wait for it, ragazzi," said Benvenuto, "we don't want to go too soon. Wait 'till we see their lances between the houses. Wait - wait - wait. Good, they're well into the street now. Ready? Fire!"

The five cannon shot as one.

"Come on! Reload! Let's try for another salvo."

They quickly swabbed the remains of the burning powder out of the barrels, rammed in a new charge, then a cloth wad, and finally, the great iron ball. The first shot in a salvo is always the most important: the guns have been carefully loaded and aimed and the whole battery fires together.

This time the gun crews fired a ragged volley. In their excitement one of the crews had spilled half their gunpowder and their shot only carried part of the way and crashed into the San Spirito Church. However the remaining four balls followed the first five and landed in the narrow street or on the parapets of the houses on either side.

There had been about fifty pikemen, with their officers and NCO's on horseback, passing through in double file. Two salvoes of twenty-five pound cannon balls careering down the roadway, bouncing from one side to another, from wall to wall, or bringing great lumps of masonry down on their heads, left the via Santo Spirito littered with sobbing, cursing, moaning men, and some who just lay silently in the mud, their eyes wide open, as if with surprise, and their mouths also open, as if frozen by their last breaths.

—◊—

Still the killing did not stop, but the first relief came to the citizens of Rome from a totally unexpected quarter: the Colonna's, the Pope's personal deadly enemies.

Pompeo Colonna had cunningly delayed committing his own private army until the outcome of the battle was assured. He had also held back while Rome was systematically ravaged by the Imperial Army. That way he was not tainted by the destruction of the city, even though, when his troops did arrive on the fourth day, they naturally joined in the looting for a while, and even though Colonna also arranged for the Pope's own private estates outside of the city to be burned out.

However, with all discipline gone from the Imperial Army, Colonna's men were the only ones who could restore order. They enforced a separation of the different nationalities, Spaniards, Germans, renegade Italians and all the others, and saw to it that they attended to their military duties, including attempting to wipe out the last defended enclave in the castle and killing or capturing the Pope. Colonna still wanted him dead.

An earthwork trench encircling Sant' Angelo was completed and the attackers then began to burrow three tunnels towards the castle walls. Two of them collapsed and the third was blown up by a countermine dug by the defenders.

"To hell with it, and the Pope," the Prince of Orange decided. "Our men haven't got the stomach for an assault anyway. We'll starve those idolaters out. It shouldn't take too long. There must be nearly a thousand of them in there. How much food can they have?"

Just to make sure, the Imperialists summarily executed any Roman carrying food anywhere near the castle although there was no chance of anyone smuggling anything in. Even one simple minded old woman who was caught with a few lettuce leaves as a gift for the Pope was strangled in full view of the horrified watchers on the battlements.

Although the defenders were eventually brought to the edge of starvation, Charles' generals found that they could not afford the time to await the outcome because the German and Spanish troops were getting completely out of hand again. It was axiomatic that an army which was allowed to sack a city invariably disintegrated. The old problem of arrears of pay was again rearing its head, and the soldiers were on the verge of mutiny. Some even attacked their officers and the different nationalities began fighting each other, too.

Food was another serious problem and civilians and invaders alike, as well as those in the castle were going hungry and faced certain starvation in the not-too-distant future.

The Prince of Orange learned of a new threat. A relief column was advancing on Rome from Clement's home city of Florence.

There was also another, more immediate problem. Drains and sewers were open and damaged and the entire water supply was contaminated. Typhus, the inevitable aftermath of war struck indiscriminately at both sides.

There were decomposing bodies lying in great heaps in the streets: those who had died in the battle, those who had been murdered by the rampaging troops and those who had died of disease. Even graves and tombs had been opened by the looters in their insatiable search for treasure. The smell was unbelievable.

There was no alternative. They would have to negotiate. The Prince of Orange decided that Colonna should be the one. Despite his feud with the Pope, they had one thing in common, their distress - their disgust - at what had happened to their city. At the moment that they met in the castle under a flag of truce, they fell on each other's shoulders and wept.

―⁂―

On Clement's side, he had been utterly defeated militarily, and he was a prisoner in his own castle, with the time fast approaching when he would inevitably be killed or captured.

As if that was not enough for one man to contend with, government had completely broken down in the Papal States, and political enemies in Florence had taken advantage of the Pope's situation and the dispatch of reinforcements to Rome, to stage a revolt against the Medici rule.

With no cards at all to play, the Pope was forced to negotiate. The terms were agreed. A large ransom for the Pope. A huge payment of tribute from the Papal States, restoration of Colonna's titles and privileges, and the appointment of a number of his supporters as Cardinals. They would increase Colonna's influence while Clement lived, and would probably secure the succession for him when Clement died.

There was one problem: the Pope could not raise the money. The gold that Benvenuto had salvaged from the regalia and the jewels that Clement had hidden were handed over. They were nowhere nearly enough. Bankers were persuaded to give money, bonds and promissory notes against the security of future tax revenue. Still it was not enough.

Hostages were offered and six fortresses, including Sant' Angelo were to be handed over to the Landsknechts as further security.

Time was also running out against the Imperial Army. Afflicted by hunger and pestilence, hundreds of the soldiers were dying in the streets daily. Spanish troops left the city on a foraging raid, searching the already denuded countryside for food. They returned empty handed.

Gold and silver coins were hurriedly minted from the plate and bullion extracted from the Pope, but this was not enough to pay the whole army from which there were wholesale desertions, some making their way home, while others took to banditry and highway robbery. For fifty miles around the city, the country was a wilderness.

The Landsknechts threatened to execute their nine hostages and the slogan, "hang the Pope" was again heard on the streets. Even Colonna went in fear of these uncontrollable Germans. The men were temporarily bought off with a few ducats each.

In an attempt to get out of the impasse, the Imperialists offered to accept a smaller ransom, but the Pope still could not raise enough money.

A face saving formula had to be found. So from the totally surrounded, besieged, and closely guarded Castel Sant' Angelo in the middle of the camp of a strong hostile army, the Pope mysteriously "escaped" to his still intact fortress city of Orvieto, nearly half-way back to Florence.

From his original position of great power and immense personal wealth, he had become an impoverished nonentity who had lost everything except his title.

The Pope's escape was taken as the excuse by the occupying army for further excesses on the already crushed and cowed Romans.

Finally Colonna succeeded in buying off the angry Landsknechts in return for three months' arrears of pay to everyone, plus a bonus of thirteen ducats to every officer if they packed up and left.

It has never been accurately calculated what the sack of Rome cost in terms of lives and property. Practically everything that could be carried away had been stolen or destroyed - gold, silver, jewellery, furniture and works of art. In terms of money, it was estimated that between seven and twelve million ducats - a phenomenal sum in those days - had been taken. Nearly every building had been destroyed. Even those left standing had been stripped of their very floorboards to feed the camp fires.

The number of the dead, both those killed in the fighting, slaughtered by the rampaging troops in the early days, tortured to death in the frenzied search for treasure or who died of hunger and unspeakable disease could not be counted. Over ten thousand rotting bodies were shovelled into common graves on the north bank of the Tiber alone.

As the occupying army was leaving Rome on 13th February 1528, just nine months and seven days after the start of the battle, the first babies conceived in the orgy of rape were being born.....

-14-

The siege of Castel Sant' Angelo was finally lifted and the garrison was allowed to leave.

Benvenuto made his way back towards his shop, staring round at the burned and damaged buildings, wrecked carts and all the other debris of war, and smelling for the first time, close up, the stench of death and fire.

He threaded his way across the heaps of rubble in the via dei Corridori, and stopped when he reached Giulio Romano's studio. A dishevelled figure was sitting in the burned-out doorway, his elbows on his knees and his head sunk in his hands.

"Hello, old friend," Benvenuto said softly. "I'm sorry I missed the last few Artists' dinners. I've been a bit busy."

"Why Benvenuto! You're …."

"Don't say it," Benvenuto warned him with a laugh.

"I was only going to say, you're still alive."

"Where's everyone else?" Benvenuto asked.

"Which everyone else? Most of the Artists' Circle are dead. Killed in the fighting, murdered by the bloody Germans, starved, or shitted to death with dysentery or typhoid. A few clever ones ran off before the fighting started. If anybody had come by here five minutes ago and asked me about you, I'd have told them you were dead too!"

"Lucagnolo?"

"I've no idea. I haven't seen him since the battle began. His place is burned to the ground. He wouldn't have just stood around letting that happen. They'd have had to kill him first."

"I don't see him leaving Rome either," Benvenuto agreed, at least not without telling me. "And what about my apprentice, Silvio?"

"Oh yes, the physician's boy. I heard that his family all went off with the Cardinal the father worked for. To Naples, I guess. That's where most of them went."

Benvenuto bent down and took Romano's hand between both of his. "Goodbye, Giulio. Maybe we'll meet again someday."

"Why? Where are you going?"

"The answer to 'why' is that there's nothing for me here in Rome. Nor you. Nor any other artist. All my customers must be dead or gone away or bankrupt. There'll be no work for a goldsmith for a very long time. Or a painter for that matter. We'd be better off if we were carpenters!"

"And where?"

"Florence. I'm going home."

"My home is here in Rome," Giulio said sadly.

—⚬—

Benvenuto's shop was still standing - just. The walls were intact, but the interior was completely stripped and wrecked. The kitchen grate was full of ash and the soldiers had obviously used his workroom as a toilet.

Benvenuto's eyes filled with tears and he was about to turn away when a thought struck him. He gingerly picked his way across the floor. In the corner was a square flagstone. With the palms of his hands he slid it towards him a fraction of an inch and pivoted it on a hidden hinge. The bottom of the stone went down into a recess revealing a metal box concreted into the foundations. He took a key from his belt and unlocked it.

There was a solitary gold coin. Benvenuto held it between thumb and forefinger and examined it glumly.

"That's the fruit of two years of my life," he said to the wall as he put it in his purse.

Next he fished a cloth bag out of the safe. In it was his seesaw. He adjusted the weight and put the toy on the floor. The model "Benvenuto" sank down. "You don't know how right you are," he thought.

The last thing in the safe was his flute. He blew a cracked note and tapped it in the palm of his hand a couple of times.

"Even the looters didn't want it" he said. With a shrug he dropped it into his pouch, too.

—⚘—

He made his way back to Florence carefully keeping out of the way of marauding bands of deserters. The first part of the journey had to be made on foot because it was a long time before he could find anyone who had a horse left, let alone someone who would sell it to him.

When he eventually reached his home town after over three weeks on the road, he was filthy. His clothes were in rags and, because of the months of starvation, his skin was drawn tight over his face. His cheeks were hollow, and his eyes, red rimmed and bloodshot from dust and fatigue were so sunken into their sockets that if it had not been for his unkempt beard, he would have looked like a walking skull.

His father's house was faced with stucco which had painted with red tempera. The sun had faded the colour in places so that there were three or four shades, from umber to pale pink. Near to the ground patches of plaster had fallen off through rising damp leaving the bare bricks exposed.

Beams angling from the roof to the wall supported a broad overhang which supplied a little shade to the upper windows, and pieces of broken tile on the ground gave the same impression of neglect and dilapidation as did the peeling paint on the loose shutters and wood-work.

The dingy door was opened by a scraggy, hunched-backed old woman who was even dirtier than Benvenuto. Her long grey hair hung in a tangled mess around her wrinkled face, falling down to her bent shoulders, and her ragged skirt was encrusted with grease.

Benvenuto and the old woman looked at each other with mutual horror and disgust. She was the first to speak. She made the sign against the Evil Eye.

"Get out of it!" she shrieked. "We don't need any beggars here. We've little enough for ourselves. Go away! You make me sick to look at you." She started to shut the door.

Benvenuto pushed it open with the flat of his hand. "I make you sick to look at? What about you, you twisted old cripple? Who else is at home, you ugly witch?"

"No one else, damn you." She leaned on the door, trying to close it.

"Well, I'll just have to throw you out myself then. I'm not having a thing like you in my house."

The shouting brought out one of the neighbours.

"It's Benvenuto Cellini isn't it? What happened to you? No, don't tell me. I'd rather not hear. It takes me all my time to worry about my own troubles."

She took him by the arm and leading him into her house, and set some bread and milk in front of him.

"I'm sorry, it's all we have," she said apologetically. "Look, there's no easy way to say this. It's not your house any more. Your sister Cosa is in a convent. Convento della Oblate, I think. She knows where your brother is."

"Where are my mother and father?" Benvenuto asked, although he already guessed the answer.

"Dead. The Plague."

—⚜—

After a tearful reunion with Cosa under the watchful eye of the Abbess, the Sisters gave him some clean clothes and let him take a bath. He refused their offer of a bed for the night and rode straight over to the barracks where Cecchino was stationed.

Cecchino held his older brother at arm's length. "Well, look at you. After all these years! What did you do in Rome during the fighting?"

"I was a soldier. Artilleryman. What were you doing? I can tell you we could have done with some of you. There were thousands of them fighting us."

"It's mad isn't it? I spend all these years learning to be a soldier, and when there's a war, I don't even get to fire a shot, and a civilian like you has all the fun! Tell me all about it."

"It wasn't fun, and I don't want to talk about it, not just yet anyway, but we'll have plenty of time. I'm staying in Florence for a while - maybe for good."

"I don't recommend it," said Cecchino.

"Why not? Don't you want me here?"

"It's nothing like that. You remember the Chief Magistrate swore he'd have you hanged for escaping and trying to kill the Guasconti's."

"Yes, but that was years ago. The whole world has come to an end since then. Do you know how many have been killed this last year? Really killed I mean, not just frightened by an angry boy?"

"You may not think it's important, but right until father died, he went to see his bloody Excellency time after time, begging him to pardon you, but he wouldn't. He said if he caught you, you'd be for it, however long it took."

"I'd better go then."

"You can stay here in the barracks for a few days. No one will tell him you're here, and we wouldn't let him take you even if they did. It will give me a chance to get you some money."

"No, I don't want …"

"It's yours anyway. I know you kept sending father money. You might as well have what's left. Er…I didn't know you were still alive, and Cosa doesn't need any so, I've spent most of it."

Benvenuto shook his head and smiled. "You haven't changed, have you? By the way, have you still got that cloak of mine?"

"I'll buy you a new one when you come back again - after the old swine dies. He can't live forever. Maybe he'll catch the Plague."

"The Plague? It's not still around is it?" Benvenuto asked nervously.

"It is, but it seems to have missed us up here in the hills, and Cosa's convent. They wouldn't have let you in if you lived in the city. It's not nice."

"I know. I've had it."

"Have you? You should be alright then. They say you can't get it twice."

"No, once is usually enough to finish you off! Anyway, thanks for telling me, but I'd rather not take a chance. What a home-coming! A choice between the gallows or the Black Death! You're right. I'll go as soon as I've rested up a bit."

Three days later, Cecchino came into the barracks dormitory, jingling some gold coins in his hand and his pack on his shoulder.

"It looks like we are both off then."

"Both?"

"Yes, my company's going on the road to Rome to meet the Pope. He's on the way here with some troops to clear the rebels out of the Medici territory. We're going to help him. Some real fighting at last!"

By the way, there's a message for you from His Holiness, no less. He said he heard you were coming to Florence, and he wants you to join the relief column. He says he needs you in his artillery."

"That's not funny, Cecchino."

"It's true. Go and see my captain. He told me to tell you. Isn't that marvellous? We'll be together."

"We won't. I'm going to do what any sensible person would."

"What's that?"

"I'm going to pretend I never got the message."

"Where will you go this time?"

"Mantua, I think. Its a hundred miles and a whole world away. Then I'll go back to Rome once the situation clears up, unless you tell me it's safe to come here instead."

"Keep in touch through Cosa then. She's not going anywhere. Good luck to you."

The two brothers embraced.

"You too," said Benvenuto, "and try not to get killed if you can help it!"

The three warring rulers, for their separate reasons, each wanted an end to the war.

The Pope, of course, because he had been totally beaten, and peace with Charles was the only way to restore his own personal position.

The Holy Roman Emperor, in his turn, was still fighting the French under King Francis. There a danger that the Papal States, where Clement was still immensely popular, might come to his aid. Also the Turks, taking advantage of his preoccupation with his other two enemies, were knocking on his Austrian back door.

Francis, too, was on the verge of a major calamity. The French army had been defeated before Naples and was in retreat, while he and his Venetian allies were still fighting in Lombardy. His only wish was to get out of this costly war which was bleeding his country to death, and which he had no hope of winning now that the Pope had been effectively removed from the scene.

Charles and the French King began discussions which Francis insisted should be kept secret from the Venetians - so secret in fact, that the actual negotiations were conducted by Francis' mother and the Emperor's aunt.

As a result, the Treaty of Cambrai, signed in August 1529, became known as "the Ladies' Peace." Under it, Charles gave up his claims to Burgundy and Francis gave up his in Italy and Belgium. To cement the bargain, Charles married his sister, Eleanor, to Francis.

So, after eight years of war, there was at last a fragile peace in Europe.

-15-

As soon as Benvenuto heard the good news that there was peace, he returned to Rome. He found his Landlord, Raffaello del Moro, a fellow goldsmith who had survived the war, and moved back into his old shop. His next task was to get an audience with the Pope on the strength of his services during the siege of Castel Sant' Angelo.

Benvenuto approached Clement and humbly kissed his feet. The Pope motioned him to rise.

"Ah, Messer Cellini! So you've come back to Rome. Benvenuto! You are welcome."

The Pope looked at the courtiers gathered around him and they all dutifully laughed, while Benvenuto bobbed his head and forced a grin through clenched teeth.

"Well, my son, what have you come to see me about? Not the matter of the gold that was missing from Castel Sant' Angelo, I suppose." The Pope was just guessing.

Benvenuto blushed. "Your Holiness," he stammered, "all there was, were the melted drops mixed up in the ash of the furnace. They were impure anyway. Your Holiness told Monsignor Cavalierino to give me some small reward for my trouble, although I was willing to serve your Holiness for nothing."

Benvenuto was positively babbling by now. "Anyway, I only got a few ducats for it, and I intended to pay you back - I mean I intend to pay you back. I only took enough to see me home and to give a little help to my poor old father, may he rest in peace."

Benvenuto's voice trailed off. He looked anxiously at the Pope who smiled flicked his hand at him and said, "Oh, never mind about it now. I owed you fifty crowns for shooting Bourbon and it is better you should have had it than the Germans. Tell your confessor what you've told me and say that I have forgiven you. So your dear father's dead is he? He was a talented and honest and upright man. An example to us all."

He stared hard and meaningfully at Benvenuto. "Well, if you aren't here to give me back my gold, what can I do for you?"

"What can you do for me? I came to find out how I can serve your Holiness."

The Pope was overtaken by a fit of coughing.

"Messer Cellini, you know what with the war, the looting and the ransom, I - all of Rome - have been ruined. It will be a long time before there will be much work for goldsmiths. I've only been able to order the most essential regalia, and I've given the work to those who returned to the service of the Holy See the soonest." An oblique reference to Benvenuto's absence from the expedition against the rebels in Florence.

Benvenuto looked crestfallen. The Pope said, "I'll tell you what. I've asked several artists to compete in designing a button for my Cope. In gold of course. About six inches in diameter. The design is to be God the Father in half relief. In the centre you'll set a diamond as big as this." He made a circle with his finger and thumb indicating a stone about three-quarters of an inch across.

"There are also four oblong emeralds, so big." He showed Benvenuto the top joint of his little finger. "And two rubies and two sapphires."

"Your Holiness does me too much honour. How can I thank you?"

"Thank me? What for? You haven't won the competition yet."

"Oh, I'll win that for sure, don't you worry!"

The Pope laughed. "I'm not worried. You're the one to worry."

He offered Benvenuto his ring to kiss. Benvenuto was dismissed.

The few survivors of the Guild of Goldsmiths, had agreed between themselves to share what little work that was available.

They certainly did not want a late entry for the competition for this important commission, so they sent their oldest, most senior, member to see Benvenuto.

"You see Benvenuto, they have all been working on their designs for weeks, so it wouldn't really be fair for you to try to join in now."

"It wouldn't be fair for me to starve to death either."

"We are sharing out all the work that becomes available. When anything new comes in from today onwards, and you want to join in, you'll be welcome."

Benvenuto gave a little growl.

"I'm sorry," said the old man, "I wasn't trying to be funny. It just slipped out."

"And just who is going to have the honour of making the Cope button?"

"Pompeo."

"Never heard of him."

"He comes from Milan."

Benvenuto shrugged.

"Anyway, we have agreed that he is going to get the job."

"So he shall," Benvenuto said, amiably. He closed his fist and tapped his chest with his thumb. "So he shall, if his design is the best!" His voice rose to a shout. "But it won't be! No one, do you hear me, no one is going to make that button except me!"

Without another word, he opened the door and still with his thumb, he pointed down the stairs. He slammed the door, hard, as the old man left.

—⚜—

The messenger reported back to the Guild.

"He won't agree," he said simply.

"Damn him to hell," the President of the Guild shouted. "We had to put up with his bragging and arrogance for years, and now he's back again. How is it that with so many good men killed in the war, God spared this upstart?"

"What are we going to do then?" Pompeo asked.

"We'll honour our agreement of course. Every member of the Guild will prepare a design. No matter which one is chosen, you'll make it. Surely between the lot of us we should be able to produce a better design than just one man."

"Perhaps a small honorarium to the one whose idea is used?" suggested the old man.

"Done!" Pompeo said with alacrity.

"And I," said the President, "will speak to the Pope's new Chamberlain about it. What's his name?"

"Tommaso da Prato," someone replied.

"Oh yes. Well I'll put a word in his ear."

"You're all mad!" Rafaello del Moro was the only one to speak up for Benvenuto.

"Worried that your tenant won't be able to pay your rent?" the President sneered.

"No, you're mad because the Pope won't take any notice of you. He'll choose the design he prefers whatever you say. You'll just make fools of yourselves. "

—᜵—

On the day that the competition was to be judged, Benvenuto and Pompeo presented themselves at the Belvedere Palace at the appointed time. In the ante room while they waited they did not even look at each other. The Chamberlain, Tommaso da Prato, came and showed them into the Pope's presence.

Clement voiced his disappointment. "Only two of you? Why are there only two entries? Don't the goldsmiths need any work?"

"Pompeo here represents the entire talent, such as it is, of the Guild of Goldsmiths, while I," said Benvenuto, "represent no one but myself."

"Is that so? Do you hear that gentlemen?" He turned to his courtiers. "The successor to St. Peter offers the membership of a Guild the chance to make the first important piece of jewellery since the war, and they can't even be bothered either to enter the competition, or to do me the courtesy of turning up. Well, if they think that this way I will have to accept whatever bit of rubbish they offer me, they are mistaken."

He moved behind the long wide polished table on which it had been intended to set out all the entries the Pope had expected. "Let's see how much of this so-called talent you have between the lot of you."

Pompeo handed over a folio of drawings. There were thirty of them.

"My, you have been busy, haven't you?" the Pope said.

He looked at the first dozen. The Bishops, priests and wealthy Romans that the Pope had invited to help him judge the entries craned their necks to look over his shoulder, straining to avoid jostling the Pope in their anxiety to see. One by one Clement passed the drawings around, shaking his head as he did so and echoing him, the spectators did likewise.

In every case, the artist had placed the large diamond in the Centre of God's breast. The designs were all very similar and only the decorations and supporting figures were different.

The Pope wrinkled his nose and sniffed. "Are they all like this?"

"Why yes," replied Pompeo, "more or less."

Clement tossed the rest of the drawings on the table without looking at them. "Now Messer Cellini, let me see your sketches."

"May it please your Holiness," said Benvenuto, "I have not brought any. I have only one design and I have made a full-size model of it."

He opened the flat, round box that he was carrying. The wax model lay firmly in place in the recesses that Benvenuto had constructed for it.

Benvenuto had not fallen into the trap of incongruously setting the great diamond in the middle of God's body. Instead, three kneeling cherubs, one in high relief facing front and the other two, back to back in half relief, supported the huge stone on their shoulders.

God, traditionally represented with flowing robes, full beard and bare feet was seated sideways on the diamond, gracefully turning His body full-face forward.

His right arm was bent, with his elbow supported by an angel, while His hand and fingers were raised in the Sign of Benediction. His left hand held a golden orb surmounted by a Cross.

The four large emeralds were set diagonally around the button, alternately with the two rubies and the two sapphires and each of the stones was supported and surrounded by other cherubs.

Around the outside of the central main design was a rim about a quarter of an inch wide, ornately decorated with leaves and even the rounded edge of the jewel was similarly, exquisitely adorned.

The Pope sucked in his breath and his eyes lit up.

"I wouldn't have had it any other way if I had designed it myself!"

"Your Holiness, however long I live, this will be my greatest masterpiece in jewellery. It will be the finest piece the world has ever seen!"

"Let us hope so," replied the Pope. He turned to Pompeo. "As for you and your colleagues, I don't think you could have found a better way to show yourselves as a bunch of amateurs, than by producing these tasteless scribbles!"

He brushed the drawings to the floor and dismissed Pompeo with a contemptuous flick of his hand. The members of the court crowded round to look at the model, so they did not see Pompeo shake his fist at Benvenuto as he left, but Benvenuto did, as he was meant to.

He had made another enemy.

"One thing, Benvenuto," the Pope said, "the only snag I can see is that it's easy to work in wax, but how will you get on in gold?"

Benvenuto flung out his arms sideways. Holy Father, if you're not satisfied that the finished piece isn't ten times better than the model, then don't pay me for it!"

The noblemen standing round murmured in protest at this impertinent piece of boastfulness, but the Pope silenced them by holding up his hand.

"Well Messer Cellini," Clement signalled his own disapproval by reverting to his surname again, "if you are sure you can do it, then I am satisfied too."

He turned to his Chamberlain. "You see, Tommaso, Cellini's design was far superior to the others. I told you that you shouldn't have listened to that jealous gossip you were repeating. Incompetent and inartistic, indeed!"

Benvenuto realised that the Pope was giving him a warning about da Prato, who flushed and scowled at this public reprimand.

"That's all the time I can spare on this business today," the Pope continued. "Tommaso, fetch the jewels and five hundred gold ducats."

When da Prato returned, Clement himself handed the heavy leather bag of gold and the little purse of stones to Benvenuto.

"I hope you will finish the piece while I'm still alive to enjoy it," he said. "I'm not the Bishop of Salamanca, you know!"

-16-

Benvenuto wasted as little time as he could on buying the bare essentials for re-furnishing his house and re-equipping his workroom, using some of the money given to him by the Pope.

Raffaello del Moro had helped by running errands, begging and pestering carpenters, blacksmiths and potters to make or sell whatever Benvenuto needed and then hauling them back to the shop on his handcart. It took two frustrating days.

When it was done, Benvenuto sat in his old familiar kitchen drinking wine with del Moro.

"Thanks for all your help," Benvenuto said, "I can't think why you bothered."

"Well, if you don't earn a decent living, you won't be able to pay my rent, will you? Besides, I want to bask in your reflected glory when you finish the button - as well as teaching those crooks at the Guild a lesson," he added as an afterthought. "By the way, have you met my daughter, Gina?"

He jerked his head in the direction of the seventeen year old girl who had been sweeping and cleaning round the house.

"You mean the same Gina you've introduced me to four times since yesterday?"

Benvenuto smiled at the girl. Quite pretty with long lashed brown eyes and a dark complexioned face, framed by thick black hair.

"A bit too short," he thought to himself, "and judging by those pudgy arms she might run to fat when she's older."

"She's a virgin, you know," del Moro said.

"Oh father! Really!" Gina protested and, covering her face with her pinafore, ran into the scullery.

"Virgins are rather thin on the ground in Rome since the Germans were here," Benvenuto replied.

"I hid her in a secret cupboard in my cellar 'til Colonna got the Germans under control, and even then after that never let her out unless she was disguised as a boy."

"And he won't let me out of the house without one of my Aunts," a voice came through the scullery door.

"You know, Benvenuto, there will be quite a generous dowry if she marries the right man."

"Very nice too, but don't look at me. No one ever accused me of being the right man yet. Besides, I like sharing myself out too much to get married, yet"

"Did you say, 'yet'? So we'll talk about it again another time, then."

"Anyway," said Benvenuto, "dowries are also a bit hard to come by these days. How did you manage to hang on to your money?"

"Sheer cunning," said del Moro tapping the side of his nose with his finger. "My house was raided a few times, and each time I left something hidden, but not too well, and just enough to convince them that they'd got the lot."

"Yes," came Gina's voice again from the next room "and then you set yourself up to help the Spaniards by melting into bars all the gold and silver that they'd stolen from everyone so they could take it away easily."

Seeing Benvenuto looking at him quizzically, del Moro spread his hands wide. "At least they left me alone after that. And you too, miss," he called out. "Also, since those ignorant animals never knew or cared what they had, I managed to lose a few drops here and there in the moulds or on the floor or in the crucibles - just getting my own stuff back really."

"None of my business," Benvenuto said gruffly and changed the subject. "I'll be able to start work tomorrow. Can you find me an assistant to do some of the labouring - looking after the furnace and so on?"

"Yes, I know a good lad. I'll send him round. Anything else?"

"A girl to take care of the house and do the cooking. Not an ugly one."

"Gina's a very good cook," said del Moro hopefully.

"Oh do shut up! Virgins need not apply. That's the last thing I'm looking for!"

From the scullery came the sound of dishes being rattled loudly.

At last Benvenuto was ready to work on the Cope button. He began by selecting from the coins given to him by the Pope the twenty that were in the worst condition and melting them down, making sure that he had more than enough metal for his purposes.

He beat out a disk about an inch wider than he intended the finished button to be, and having marked out the main figure in the same way as he had with the Bishop's jug, he gradually bossed it out from behind so that it stood out in high relief.

When he had spent a careful, painstaking week on the work, he had a visit from the Pope's secretary, Traiano.

"His Holiness wants you to come to see him right away. Bring your work so he can see how you're getting on."

Traiano saw Benvenuto begin to bristle with rage and held up his hand.

"Now, now, Messer Cellini, His Holiness wants to offer you another important task. It's my suggestion that you bring what you're doing with you. If you forget your professional pride just this once, I think it will help you to get the new order."

Benvenuto slowly relaxed and smiled. "Why, Messer Traiano, I'm sure you should have been a diplomat. I shall be delighted to accompany you."

He wrapped the piece of gold in a soft cloth and set off for the Vatican.

Clement was surrounded by the usual crowd of courtiers. Benvenuto recognised amongst them the sculptor, Baccio Bandinelli.

"He and I were boys together in Florence," Benvenuto whispered to Traiano. "I worked for his father for a short while, but we never got on. His father kept telling him I was better than he was. Still, it's nice to see a face from home."

He smiled and waved at Bandinelli who sniffed loudly and turned his back.

"Alright, if that's the way you want it, then up yours," Benvenuto muttered under his breath.

The Pope interrupted this unseen little byplay.

"Ah, Benvenuto, you're here at last. What's that you've got with you?"

He unwrapped the cloth and peered at the barely started button for a moment.

"Yes, very nice. I'm sure it will work out very well. So sure, that I'm going to give you something else to do that's even more important - if you think you're up to it, that is."

"Holy Father, if its work with metal or jewels, then whatever it is, I can do it, and better than anyone in the whole of Italy."

"Yes, yes of course," Clement said testily. "Now what I want are some dies for the Mint. We need some new money to replace what those thieving heretics stole. Have you ever made dies?"

"I made the Seal for the Cardinal of Mantua. It showed the Ascension of Our Lady and the Twelve Apostles. It was so beautiful that his Eminence paid me two hundred ducats for it."

The Pope waved his hand impatiently. "I'm sure it must have been very good for him to have been so extraordinarily generous. I could never afford to pay anything like that, especially in these hard times. Can you make dies for coins or not? Yes or No?"

"Yes."

"Good. That's all I wanted to know. What I want is the designs for two gold doubloons. Now what I have in mind is this. The first coin will have my bust on the front and Christ, naked, with His hands tied on the reverse."

"The inscription?" Benvenuto asked.

"My name and titles on the front. On the back put '**Ecce Homo.**' 'Behold the man'."

Benvenuto wrote it down. "And the other coin, your Holiness?"

"A Pope and a King supporting a falling Cross. The inscription will be '**Unus spiritus et una fides erant in eis.**' That means 'They were of one heart and of one accord,' you know?"

"Yes, I studied Latin in Your Holiness' own school. Will the front be the same as the first one?"

"No, I want Saint Peter and Saint Paul. Now is all that clear?"

"Perfectly," replied Benvenuto.

"Excuse me your Holiness!" The interjection came from Bandinelli. "May I suggest that the goldsmith should be given proper designs from a trained artist for important work such as this?"

Before the Pope could answer, Benvenuto turned on Bandinelli. "I've no need of your designs for my work, thank you very much! There's nothing you can do for me. You never could draw very well, as I remember, and according to Michelangelo, you're not much of a sculptor either!"

The Pope's Chamberlain, Tommaso da Prato, joined in the argument. He pointed a long, bony finger at Benvenuto.

"Be silent, fellow! The Pope himself personally commanded Messer Bandinelli to come to Rome to help in the reconstruction of the city. How dare you interrupt him when he is speaking to His Holiness? The Holy Father doesn't need a tradesman to answer for him."

Benvenuto had enough sense not to reply even when da Prato turned to the Pope and continued, "Holy Father, you are showering this young man with too many favours. He's so anxious to make a name for himself that he'll promise you anything. You've already given him one important job. Now you're giving him one that even he admits he's never done before."

Clement had been sitting listening, with his interlaced hands in his lap, impatiently tapping his thumbs together in time with his right foot.

"Have you finished, Messer da Prato?"

The Chamberlain ignored the danger signals. "If his designs are no good, he will just have wasted valuable time, and he'll have an excuse to delay the Cope button too."

Clement stared around the room. "Has anyone else got anything he wants to add to this? Any more helpful advice?"

There was a discreet silence.

"Fine! Now, Messer da Prato, you were good enough to scold Cellini for speaking on my behalf. Well the same goes for you too!"

The Chamberlain's thin face flushed, and his deep set eyes glittered with rage, but the Pope was not finished with him yet.

"I expect you have got one of your favourites in mind. Maybe that Pompeo. I've told you already that unless the Guild apologises for the trick of trying to foist their choice on me to make the Button, hair will sprout from here," he pointed to the palm of his hand, "before one of that gang gets another job from me!"

"And you, sir," he glared at Bandinelli. "I invited you to Rome to advise me on sculpture and architecture, and that's what you'll do. No diversions, do you hear?"

Bandinelli mumbled something which might have been taken for "yes", and Clement then rounded on Benvenuto.

"I've known you since you were a boy and you've no reason to look so smug."

Benvenuto hastily assumed what he thought was a solemn expression.

"Don't remind me about my school." Clement said. "I sent you to Bologna to study music and you disobeyed me. It's only a few months since I ordered you to help my army in Florence and you defied me. And stop quarrelling with everybody. I only hope the war has satisfied your taste for fighting or you'll be on your way back to Florence where I hear there's still someone waiting for you with a rope!"

The Pope hoped that by impartially reprimanding all three of them, no one would be aggrieved. In fact, Benvenuto left the room with two more implacable enemies than when he had come in.

So now Benvenuto was engaged on two major commissions at once, but as the Pope had clearly told him that the new one was more important, that was the one on which he concentrated his energies.

There was one distraction. Gina del Moro came in each day to help tidy up and to make Benvenuto's midday meal. Her father had deliberately not found him a housekeeper and since, naturally, a well brought-up girl could not be left alone in the house with a man who was not her husband, del Moro came with as her chaperone and spent his time watching Benvenuto at work.

"You know," said Benvenuto, "I learned to make coins from Lautizo and Caradosso when I was getting over the Plague. They didn't realise they were teaching me. They thought I was 'just watching'. Is that what you're doing? Learning to be my rival?"

"No fear!" del Moro replied with some feeling, "It's much too hard work. Besides, there's no secret. You'll be doing it the same way as they have since Julius Caesar's time - or longer."

"The tools are better, so is the metal for the dies."

Benvenuto produced two carefully smoothed and polished pieces of half-inch thick steel. Holding them by their edges between the fingers and thumbs of both hands, he said "You see? They are just a fraction smaller than the coins are supposed to be and I've already cut and punched the designs for each side."

"Why not engrave them? Surely that would be easier and more delicate."

"Delicate is just what we don't want when you think what a beating they're going to take. The punch compressed and hardened the steel, and even then I had to reheat and temper it."

Gina had come into the workroom with some cool juice. She peered at the dies.

"What's that funny writing, Benvenuto? It doesn't look right to me."

"That's because it's **intaglio**."

"Oh don't confuse the girl!" del Moro said. "It's back-to-front, just like in a mirror. Anyway, you couldn't read it even if it was the right way round."

"Well, what does it say round the head of that man?"

"It says who he is. '**Clemens VII - Pont Max.**' 'Clement VII, Supreme Pontiff'," Benvenuto explained. He walked over to his bench and picked up two thick iron rods.

"Look. Here are two more of the same dies fixed on to the ends of these bars. I'm going to clamp the first one with the Pope's head, into this block of lead. Can you see, this rod is square and tapered so it fits exactly into this hole so it can't twist."

Del Moro gingerly touched the block.

"Don't worry," said Benvenuto, "it weighs about a hundred pounds. It won't move." He turned to Gina. "We call this die the 'pile.' This other tool is called the 'punch' and we use it to make the reverse side of the coin."

"How? And why is one end all bent over and split?"

"We call that a 'beard' and its flattened like that because it's the end that I hit with this great iron mallet. Let me show you."

He selected a coin blank cut from a thin metal strip and carefully placed it between the two dies, making sure that it was not off centre.

"Do you see these little marks on the front of each die?"

Gina and her father both nodded.

"They are to make sure that the 'heads' and 'tails' are exactly the right way up. Now, I hold the die steady - very steady - with my left hand and I strike it as hard as I can with the hammer. So!"

Benvenuto grunted with the effort. "The first blow has to be hard enough to set the impression in the disc so the dies won't move, because if they do, the images will be blurred when I hit it again, and yet once more like this. And that should be it," he said as he examined his work.

Del Moro took the coin. "You certainly made it look easy."

"Don't you believe it! I've spent hours practicing. I've only got to get a few perfect ones to show the Pope and the Master of the Mint. The coiners at the Mint are really skilled. They take ages to train."

"Wouldn't it be simpler if the blanks were heated first?"

"No, the dies would also get hot and wear out more quickly. Not that I would mind. If - when - the Pope accepts my designs I'm going to have a regular income making replacement dies. The more they need, the better I'll like it!"

"That's not gold though," said Gina, pointing to the blank.

"No, it's copper. That way I could practice as much as I needed to without having to stop and melt them down again each time. The Pope will get real gold ones of course."

"Have you got some?" del Moro asked. "You haven't earned anything since you came back. I'll lend you some if you need it."

"No, thank you just the same. The Pope gave me more than I needed for his Cope Button. I'll just quickly make a few blanks out of that."

Benvenuto did not realise that he was about to make a very costly mistake.

A few days later Benvenuto was working on the tools for the second coin when Gina came running into the house, screaming,

"Please help me! Hide me! Don't let them hurt me! Please Benvenuto ....." She stood there with her knuckles crammed into her mouth as if to hold down her sobs.

Benvenuto snatched up his sword and dagger which were always to hand when he had valuables in the shop.

"Who? Who wants to hurt you? Where are they?"

At that moment her father came through the door, followed by two strangers.

"There you are, you foolish girl. Come on, come home at once. We're waiting for you."

Gina clung on to Benvenuto. "Don't let him take me. I don't want to go!"

"What's going on, Raffaello? She says someone wants to hurt her. Who? You?"

"No of course not. She's frightened of the surgeon."

"Surgeon? What surgeon? What's wrong?"

"It's her hand. Haven't you ever noticed how she tries to hide it?"

Del Moro took hold of her right hand and showed it to Benvenuto. The third and little fingers were bent downwards.

"It's tuberculosis in the bones. If we don't operate, it will spread and she could lose her whole hand, or even her arm. They have to lay the fingers open and scrape away the bad parts."

Benvenuto felt his teeth go on edge and he gave an involuntary shudder, while Gina clung tightly to him.

"Come on. I'll stay with you. I won't let them hurt you." Benvenuto put his arm round her shoulder and led her, still resisting slightly, back down the road to her father's house.

As soon as she got into the kitchen and saw the surgeon, she began struggling.

Benvenuto, please don't let him touch me! I don't care what happens, don't let him cut me. Just don't let him cut me!"

Benvenuto looked at the instruments in the surgeon's hands. One was a clumsy thick iron knife, the blade of which was pitted and stained and as jagged as a saw; the other was a sort of chisel with a curved iron blade which was also very badly worn and blunt-looking.

"Holy Mother of God, Doctor! You're not going to use those things on this girl, are you? No wonder she's frightened! All that knife's good for is chopping wood. Just wait a few minutes and I'll bring you something much better. Don't worry Gina, he won't hurt you, I promise!"

He rushed back to his workroom and scattered the contents of cupboards and drawers until he found one of the Turkish-style daggers that he had made. He tested the long narrow blade against his thumb and then quickly honed the steel until it was as sharp as a razor.

Next he fished out from amongst his tools two of the crescent-shaped gouges that he used for working gold. Benvenuto always made his own, and these too were of the finest steel, brand new, and with their cutting edges unblemished.

Back in the del Moro kitchen he handed them to the surgeon without a word, and then turning to the terrified girl said, "You'll never feel a thing with those. I don't know how many times I've accidently taken lumps out of myself with them and never even noticed it."

Before she could protest, Benvenuto put one arm around her waist, stooped and put his other arm behind her knees, and swept her up and laid her on the bare kitchen table.

She started to shout and struggle, but in a moment the doctor and his two well-trained assistants flung themselves on her and using thick leather straps they tied her down, one belt tightly across her breast and left arm, one around her middle and another across her thighs.

She was still screaming, "No, no, no! Please stop it! Papa, please don't let them!" when one of the assistants pushed her shoulders down on the table and held them there while the other thrust a well-chewed piece of leather between her teeth to prevent her from biting her tongue.

Benvenuto gently took her head between his hands and forced her to look away.

"Shush, shush, Gina. I promise it won't hurt, but don't move or the Doctor will get the wrong fingers."

He kissed her forehead. "Now stay quiet and as soon as it's done, if you are a brave girl and don't make a fuss, I'll make you a gold ring. Maybe a twisted plait or perhaps one like a snake."

"What about a plain gold wedding band?" said del Moro, hopefully.

Two big sobs made the girl's body shudder, then she screwed her eyes up tight and clamped her teeth hard on the strap.

The second assistant roughly pulled her right hand behind her head and spread out her fingers.

Benvenuto was right. She did not feel the knife cut into her soft flesh, but when the doctor began chipping away the diseased bone, she screamed and fainted.

-17-

Benvenuto had been sitting in the ante-room waiting to be admitted to the Pope's audience chamber for nearly half an hour before the Secretary came out to fetch him.

"What sort of mood is he in today, Messer Traiano?"

"Oh, excellent for him. He hasn't ordered more than two people to be burnt at the stake in the past hour."

"Very funny! Go on, lead the way. I've wasted enough time here today already."

Clement barely glanced at the great gold button before impatiently waving it away.

"It looks the same as last time to me. Bring it back when you've made some more progress."

"Your Holiness instructed me to concentrate on the doubloons, which I am happy to say are finished. With your permission ....."

Benvenuto pulled a length of black velvet from his pouch and laid it on a table. Then he took four perfectly struck samples of the gold pieces from four separate strips of cloth and laid them out, "heads" and "tails", "heads" and "tails". He made a grand sweeping gesture with his hand.

Clement picked up each coin in turn and looked at them closely. "Very nice. Very nice indeed. A very good likeness of me - flattering perhaps - and all the other figures are absolutely clear."

He turned to his Chamberlain. "Well, Tommaso, don't you agree, he's done them very well, hasn't he? Despite all your doubts."

Da Prato sniffed. They seem to be alright, your Holiness."

The Pope gently tossed the coins up and down in the palms of his hands. "Come on, you can do better than that. You didn't think they would be as fine as this, did you? They are good enough aren't they?"

"Yes, I suppose so," came the grudging reply.

"Then," said Clement, "how shall we reward him?"

This was the moment that Benvenuto had been waiting for. He produced a Petition from the pocket of his doublet. In it he asked to be appointed to the vacant position of "Superintendant of the Apostolic Dies." The Post carried a salary of six gold crowns a month, and in addition, the Master of the Mint paid a fee for every die and seal that had to be cut. At the rate at which they were worn out, a great number were needed and Benvenuto and the skilled workmen he would employ could earn him a substantial regular income.

The Pope glanced at the document, relieved that Benvenuto had not asked for an immediate fee. He was going to have to appoint a new Superintendant anyway, so it was like getting the dies for the coins for nothing. Benvenuto had relied on this when he planned how this interview would go.

"That seems a reasonable suggestion to me." He gave the document to da Prato. "Don't you agree, Tommaso?"

The Chamberlain looked grim. "Holy Father, you should take time to deliberate. These matters should not be decided in a hurry. Besides, it takes time to draw up the proper papers."

The Pope snatched the document back and clapped his hands together. "Pen," he commanded.

A servant ran forward from the other side of the room with a quill. The Pope looked at it. "Well, either cut your throat so I can dip the pen in your blood, or get me some ink as well."

The man scuttled back to the desk and returned with an ink pot which he offered to the Pope who scrawled the word "Granted" at the bottom of the petition, added his signature with a flourish and waved it backwards and forwards once or twice to dry the ink.

He thrust it back into back into da Prato's hand. "There, seal it. You can send it to the Monastery and have the monks make fifty illuminated copies if you like, but it's done. From this minute!"

—⚹—

As it happened the Pope would have been better advised to have listened to his Chamberlain and to Bandinelli and not given the commission to make the new gold coins to an inexperienced craftsman, however skilful in other fields and Benvenuto would have been better off to have got some expert assistance in designing them.

The reason was that the new coins turned out to be a disaster. The two coins were "doubloons", worth two ducats each. However, because of the richness of the design and the size of the dies, the pieces used slightly more than two ducats of gold. In other words the coins contained more gold than their face value.

Da Prato arranged for Bandinelli and his own favoured goldsmith, Pompeo, to have a private audience with the Pope, and Clement looked surprised when they entered his study, accompanied by the Master of the Mint.

"You stay, Tommaso. So gentlemen, to what do I owe a visit from such a distinguished delegation?"

Without replying, the Master of the Mint produced a box containing a set of jewellers' scales. He laid them on the Pope's desk and steadied them with his hand, then he took a brass disk from his pocket.

Bandinelli handed him one each of the new coins while the Pope looked on, perplexed.

"Will someone please tell me what is happening?"

"If your Holiness will just watch," said da Prato.

The Master of the Mint placed the brass disk in one pan of the scales. "That is the official weight of two ducats of fine gold. And here is one of your doubloons."

He put it on the other scales pan which immediately dropped to the table top. At that moment Benvenuto's side of his see-saw should have sunk in sympathy!

"What does that mean?"

"It means, your Holiness," said the Master of the Mint, "that the coins weigh too much."

"It means that that fool Cellini has used too much gold," Bandinelli added with sneer.

"You, goldsmith, what's your name? Oh yes, Messer Pompeo. How could this happen?"

"He made the coin too wide and the design too thick, your Holiness."

"That's obvious, but I asked you how it could happen."

"Ignorance, carelessness, stupidity, who knows?" Bandinelli said. "You will remember that Messer da Prato and I warned you against giving this commission to an inexperienced boaster, at least without adequate supervision."

The Pope rounded on the Master of the Mint.

"That's not what I meant. You, sir! How was it allowed to pass? Don't you check these things before you start to make them?"

"Yes your Holiness, well no. Actually...."

"Come on. Stop dithering, man which is it? Yes or no?"

"Both. I mean, er, you see, normally yes we check every new gold or silver coin, and we test a few coins each day on these same scales."

"Normally?" asked the Pope. "So what was abnormal this time?"

"Your Holiness demanded - ordered - that the coins should be produced as quickly as possible. We - I - assumed from what I heard when you gave Cellini the job in my presence, and despite Bandinelli's advice about having someone else do the designs that he knew what he was doing," he added defiantly.

"But it's your job to weigh them, isn't it?"

"Yes, but the coins were taken straight from the mint by your Treasurer to pay your Holiness' urgent bills as fast as we made them."

"And," da Prato interjected, "as fast as they were put into circulation, the goldsmiths were melting them down again for the excess gold."

"How much excess?" Clement asked anxiously.

"Not much." Pompeo said. "A few grains each. Just enough to make it worthwhile to spend the time and trouble to melt them, especially in these hard times."

"I asked you, 'how much' - in total, not just per coin? By all the Saints! Must I drag the story out of you one piece at a time?"

"Ten ounces, maybe twelve. Fifteen or sixteen at the outside. We haven't finished the audit yet," the Master of the Mint replied.

"What audit?"

"After we completed the first batch of coins we found there was a shortage of gold, but the Treasurer took them away before we could find out why. We thought it was an accounting error or larger than usual losses on the melt."

"So you did nothing? Just pretended everything was alright." Clement said, with mounting anger.

"Before we could be sure, you were asking for more coins, and the Treasurer was actually standing in the mint snatching them out of the coin-makers' hands as soon as they were done."

Clement interrupted him again. "So you still did nothing?"

"Yes we did. When we found a shortage on the second lot as well, we assumed that we had a thief somewhere, but by then stories were coming back from the jewellery quarter, and goldsmiths were asking for unusual quantities of coins and were offering to pay for them in gold ingots."

"And that is when you realised what had gone wrong?"

"Yes, your Holiness. And we came to see you immediately. After all, the coins have only been issued for three days."

"Very well. Ten, twelve, maybe sixteen ounces lost," the Pope said. "Let's say sixteen. I'll get that back from Cellini, one way or another. Now, Tommaso, about that office of Superintendent of the Dies that we gave him......"

"We gave him, your Holiness?" da Prato could not resist asking.

-18-

Allesandro, Duke of Penna, had recruited a corps of soldiers for his private army from the Medici training school in Florence. Amongst them was Benvenuto's younger brother, Cecchino, so the two Cellini's found themselves reunited in Rome.

These young soldiers were always getting into trouble for fighting with civilians, intimidating shopkeepers, insulting women in the streets and for senseless acts of vandalism, hooliganism and wilful damage.

Early one afternoon a group of them were taking their siesta at an inn they used to frequent. The fact was that they had eaten too much for their midday meal and drunk to much rough red wine, and some of them were sleeping it off.

A police patrol marched along the street with one of their number, Cisti, under arrest for some offence or another. As he passed by the courtyard of the inn he called out, "Hey, you fellows! I'm being taken to prison. Tell the Captain I'll be away for months and months, I shouldn't wonder. And tell my section I won't be able to pay them the money I owe them."

The four men in Cisti's section of course understood this not-too-subtle message, and chased after the police, getting ahead of them and circling back to prepare an ambush.

Despite the disdain that the brash young Florentines had for these lowly Romans, they were no match for the patrol, which not only out-numbered them, but also was heavily armed with pikes and arquebuses as well as swords.

"Come on, you can let him go now," they shouted to the sergeant leading the police. "We'll take him back to our own Captain. He'll punish him for you if he's been a naughty boy!"

"Just stand aside, or it'll be too bad for you. He's going to see the Magistrate. Now get out of the way or we'll march right over you."

The four soldiers drew their swords. The police levelled their own weapons.

"March!" ordered the sergeant.

The clash was over in moments. When it was, one of the four was lying on the cobbles, fatally wounded. Another with a slash on the arm had dropped his sword and run away, quickly followed by the other two.

They got back to the barracks found their Captain and told him what had happened. He hurried to see for himself and arrived on the scene just as the wounded man was being driven away on a cart with blood dripping off its tail to the ground.

The Captain in turn was hurrying back to gather his men together when he bumped into Cecchino.

"What's up, Captain?" he asked.

"Those damned policemen have murdered your friend Bertini Aldobrandi, that's what's up! The street at the Banchi is smothered with his blood, that's what's up! Lucca's arm is cut to the bone and they're going to lock Cisti up in a stinking cell. I'm going to get some men and teach those bastards a lesson!"

"What do you mean, they've killed Bertini? Which one of them did it?" Cecchino shouted.

"A corporal. A big fellow with a blue feather in his hat. He's carrying a double handed sword. But wait until I get the others. We need reinforcements. Wait I say!"

It was too late. Cecchino was already half way down the street, sword in hand. He ran towards the jail and quickly caught up with the patrol. The man with the feather in his cap was on the outside file, and as soon as Cecchino saw him he let out a tremendous yell and charged at him full tilt, his sword held stiffly out in front.

The corporal turned but did not have a chance to defend himself. Cecchino was going so fast that his sword ran the man right through, almost to the hilt and he fell to the ground, dying.

Cecchino put his foot on the policeman's chest to help himself withdraw his sword. At that moment the sergeant recovered from his surprise, and, raising his arquebus, aimed and fired.

The heavy, soft ball of lead struck Cecchino in the side of his knee. It pulverised his knee-cap, smashed the knee-joint and shattered the bottom of his thigh-bone. The flattened lump of metal and jagged pieces of bone tore through flesh and muscle and Cecchino's leg was left hanging by a few threads of sinew.

In less than ten seconds one healthy young man had had his life snuffed out and another had been turned into a helpless cripple.

Just then the police spotted a crowd of Florentine soldiers running towards them. They hastily picked up the corporal's body and threw it on the back of the cart with the dead Bertino and hustled their prisoner, Cisti who had started it all towards Sant' Angelo, now restored to its role of a prison.

Cecchino was left lying where he had fallen, screaming in agony. His friends lifted him up and carried him to a nearby doctor's house. Someone sent for Benvenuto.

—⁂—

Cecchino was in deep shock and barely conscious. His breathing was laboured as he said, "Don't be upset. It's just bad luck. An occupational hazard you might say. Oh God! It hurts! It hurts!"

He gave an involuntary groan of pain and bit his lower lip. "Benvenuto. I've only got a little time left. Promise me you won't do anything stupid, "

"You're the stupid one," said Benvenuto, "for thinking you're dying. All that's happened is that your leg's messed up a bit. The doctor will fix you up in time for you to go to the funeral of the fellow who shot you, if there's anything left of him to bury after I'm through with him."

"No, don't. Please, promise me!"

Benvenuto just grunted and looked up at the doctor who slowly shook his head and then, with his eyes, signalled Benvenuto to follow him from the room.

Outside the door the doctor said, "I'm sorry my friend, there's nothing you can do for your brother. His leg is ruined and I ought to cut it off, but there's no point. He's already lost a lot of blood, and if that doesn't kill him, gangrene will set in and do it instead. Also you know, when anyone gets hurt as badly as your brother, they seem to die, no matter what you do."

Soon Cecchino's temperature began to rise. Blood poisoning was setting in. The muck from the ground onto which he had fallen when he was shot, and the dirty bits of cloth from his uniform forced into the wound by the musket ball and the doctor's own unwashed hands had all contributed their quota of deadly germs into Cecchino's weakened system.

He began to thrash about on his cot. His wound started to bleed again, and it was only after they had tied the raving man down that they could staunch the flow.

Cecchino opened his eyes to find a priest standing at his side.

"My son, if you will make your Confession, I will give you Communion."

"Oh no!" whispered Cecchino. He seized the priest's hand. "Father, I don't want to die, tell me I'm not going to."

"Perhaps not," replied the priest. "It's in God's hands, but you've got the blood of a man on your conscience so we'll pray for your deliverance just the same. Now, your Confession."

The priest waved Benvenuto, the doctor and the others out of earshot of the bedside. Tears filled Cecchino's eyes and the priest had to bend over him to catch the murmured words as he began to recite, "I confess to Almighty God, to the Blessed Mary, ever a virgin, to the Blessed Michael the Arch-Angel, to Saint John the Baptist, to the Holy Apostles Peter and Paul and all the Saints and to you, Father, that I have sinned in thought, word and deed...."

—⚘—

At dawn the priest was standing near the foot of the bed, quietly praying, when Cecchino suddenly cried out as if he was a child again,

"Mama! Papa! Cosa!" Then he seemed to realise that his parents and his sister were not there and he moaned, "Benvenuto! Help me! Good-bye, good-bye."

Before Benvenuto could cross to his side he was gone.

—⚘—

Benvenuto had him buried before nightfall, and arranged for a large slab of marble to be set over the grave which he carved himself.

As he blew the last of the marble dust from the monument and brushed it clean with his fingers, he said, "There Cecchino! It's finished. A memorial to you and a reminder to me that your death has to be avenged. You said I shouldn't do it. I never promised you I wouldn't though, did I? But you thought I did. I deceived my own dying brother! Oh God! What shall I do?" he cried aloud.

For two weeks after Cecchino's death Benvenuto's mental turmoil continued. He could not work properly and he made hardly any progress on the Cope Button. His dreams were haunted by a strange hooded man with a body twisted like a capital "S" who somehow reminded of something, but what? Perhaps the serpent he had fought in his delirium when he had the Plague? No, someone real. But who? Benvenuto could not think, but he shuddered and crossed himself.

—⚘—

Finally he made up his mind. Whether or not he had deceived his brother, he owed it to his own peace of mind to avenge him. His killer would not live when Cecchino was in his grave.

Benvenuto knew who the policeman was. It would have been virtually impossible to keep his identity a secret anyway, but the man went round boasting of what he had done.

"What a shot it was! And if I hadn't got him, he'd have spitted a few more of my men."

Benvenuto found out where the sergeant lived and spent hours hanging around, watching him, but always taking care not to be seen himself.

One evening, just as darkness fell, Benvenuto decided his chance had come. His victim was standing in the doorway of his lodgings, taking the air. Benvenuto, seeing the street was empty, nonchalantly began to stroll along with his drawn dagger concealed at his side.

As Benvenuto drew level with the policeman, he aimed a savage sweeping blow at him, but the man was a trained soldier, and instinctively he swayed backwards, so that the knife just glanced off his shoulder, only wounding him superficially.

The man was unarmed, and as Benvenuto came at him a second time, he ran away up the street and round the corner, dodging into an alley where he hoped he could hide. Benvenuto saw and followed him. The sergeant began to run further up the narrow passageway.

The street was covered in mud, muck and garbage. Sanitary arrangements were primitive and the occupiers of the houses had the habit of emptying the contents of chamber pots out of the window, straight onto the street below.

The man glanced over his shoulder, then he lost his footing on the slippery surface and sprawled full length on the ground.

Benvenuto was on him instantly, his knee in the small of the sergeant's back, left hand entwined in his hair, viciously pulling his head backwards with the sharp blade of his knife pressed against the man's throat so hard that an ever so thin line of blood seeped from a tiny nick in the skin.

"Who are you? What do you want with me, for God's sake?" The frightened man's voice started to rise.

"If you make just one more loud noise, it'll be your last," Benvenuto hissed, and to emphasise the point he gave another tug on the man's hair.

"Is it my purse you're after? Well take it. It's only got a few scudi in it anyway."

"Your purse? I don't want your money you scum! Who am I? I am Benvenuto Cellini, the brother of Giovanfransesco Cellini, the boy you murdered."

"Oh sweet Jesus! No! No!" the policeman's voice began to rise, but quietened down again when the dagger was pressed harder against his throat.

"It was an accident. I didn't mean to kill him. I only fired to warn him off. Please let me go. Please," the sobbing man begged, "I didn't even aim at him."

"You can make your excuses to the Devil. Tell him Benvenuto Cellini has sent him another customer."

Benvenuto suddenly changed the position of his knife, and placing its point against his enemy's arched back, just below the left shoulder blade, he leaned hard on the hilt with all his weight.

The blade slipped through skin and muscle and burst the man's heart. Muscle and flesh sucked on the steel in a sort of obscene kiss of death, and Benvenuto had to twist the knife round before he could get it out.

The whole incident had only taken a little more than a minute, but despite Benvenuto's attempts to keep his victim quiet, heads were appearing at windows overhanging the alley, attracted by the noise of the pursuit and of the sound of the two voices, one frightened and the other angry.

Benvenuto rose, aimed a last senseless kick at the dead man's head and ran through the darkness to the shelter of his own house. He leaned against his door, holding it shut with his back, trembling. He did not know whether it was with terror or elation, but he felt purged and cleansed and his mind was clear for the first time in weeks.

—⚜—

The investigation of the murder was only perfunctory. Suspects there were in plenty. Apart from Benvenuto, there was the whole of Cecchino's company, and every person whom the sergeant had ever arrested - or the families of the many who had gone to the gallows because of him.

The police gave up. After all what was one more dead man in a city where every day new skeletons and mummified corpses were being dug up from the ruins of buildings being repaired after the war.

—⚜—

Suspecting was one thing; proving was another. But **knowing** was something entirely different. There was one person who was certain that Benvenuto had done it. That person was the Pope.

He sent for Benvenuto on the pretext of wanting to see the progress he had made with the Cope Button. To Benvenuto's surprise, when he was shown into the Pope's presence, Clement was not surrounded by the usual crowd of officials and noblemen: he was alone except for his Chamberlain.

Benvenuto stood at the door waiting for the Pope's signal to advance. Clement stared at him grimly for what seemed to be an age. Actually it was only for ten seconds or so. Then he held out his hand for Benvenuto to kiss the Pontifical ring.

Benvenuto rose from his knees. "Messer Cellini," the Pope said. Benvenuto noted with some dismay the dropping of his first name. "Messer Cellini, I hear you've been very troubled since your brother died. Very troubled indeed. I hope you're better now."

"Yes thank you, your Holiness." Benvenuto's reply was just mumbled. "I'm sure I will be alright from now on."

"And I'm sure we all hope you'll be spared any further sorrow, but I want you to remember this: when you are troubled, you go to your Confessor for help. No one else, and you don't try to cure yourself. Do you understand my meaning?"

Benvenuto nodded. He saw da Prato gazing at him steadily, and he quickly averted his eyes.

"I want to be sure. Answer me. Have I really made myself perfectly clear?"

"Yes, your Holiness." Benvenuto's reply was barely audible. "Perfectly clear."

"Good. Well then, how's my work coming on …… Benvenuto?"

-19-

The rich, those who had survived the Sack of Rome, bounced back to their former positions.

Then there were the new rich, including those who had managed to acquire the estates and property of others who had perished in the war. In many cases they were trusted ex-employees who had helped their dead masters to hide their valuables from the looters.

Orders flowed into the shop of the well-known Benvenuto Cellini. Never mind his unfortunate error about the doubloons. After all, his only fault had been giving too much gold for the money, and that couldn't be bad, could it?

Benvenuto prospered. In a short time he had five assistants and apprentices working for him, and as was customary, since none of them was married or had a family, they slept in a room behind the workshop.

To cook and clean for his establishment, and to Gina del Moro's disgust, Benvenuto engaged a young, and as always a very pretty and very busty housemaid. She slept with Benvenuto in an outhouse away from the shop, and Gina pretended not to know - or even to notice the girl on the fewer and fewer occasions that she found a pretext to visit.

Apart from Benvenuto, the girl and the five workmen, there was an eighth resident: a wolf-hound called Cassius, who doubled as Benvenuto's hunting dog and guard dog.

One night after Benvenuto and his assistants had celebrated a particularly profitable sale with too much heavy food and too much wine, the workers were fast asleep in their tiny, non-too-pleasant smelling room. Benvenuto and the girl were asleep in their large bed.

Soon after midnight, a thief broke into the shop. He picked up and pocketed a few gold and silver rings and charms, and was just forcing open the drawers where the more valuable jewels and the supplies of gold were kept, when the dog sprang at him, snapping and barking furiously.

The robber drew his sword and slashed at the animal. Its thick fur protected it from injury, and the dog ran off and tried to rouse the drunken workmen by barking loudly, tugging at their bedclothes, and even nipping at their arms and hands dangling over the edge of their beds.

It was no use. The men were too stupefied by drink to wake up properly. In the end, one of them did get up, and giving the dog a kick, forced it out of the room and slammed the door shut, muttering about a "noisy brute" as he did so.

Cassius ran back into the workroom, still barking, and this time he bit the man's arm so hard that he let go of his sword, and, fearing that the noise would wake up the household, he fled, with the dog snapping at his cloak.

The next morning when the workmen somewhat shakily came into the shop rubbing their bloodshot eyes, they found the place in disorder. One of them went to wake Benvenuto up.

"God help us, Master! We've been robbed; the shop's been ransacked!"

Benvenuto was in an instant panic. "God help **us**? God help **me** you mean. If the Pope's jewels have been stolen, he'll have me crucified."

The Pope's jewels. Three months after Cecchino's death Benvenuto had still not completed the Cope Button. For once it was not his fault.

The gold-beating had long since been finished and all that remained to be done was to set the nine stones, but the Pope, short of money as ever, had had to pawn the great central diamond with a Genoese banker. So Benvenuto was simply holding the button and the remaining jewels until the Pope could get the diamond back.

Benvenuto threw on a robe and rushed into the workroom.

Ignoring the other opened drawers, he made straight for the iron chest which stood in one corner. Hardly daring to look, he stood in front of it.

There were some scratch marks round the three locks where someone had tried to jemmy it open, but the locks were still fastened. Despite the fact that it was still the cool early morning, Benvenuto's hair was prickly with sweat, while perspiration ran down his forehead as he undid the locks, fumbling with the keys as he did so.

He lifted the lid a little, and with his head cocked to one side, he peeped in. The Cope Button box was still there! He snatched it from the chest and opened it.

He was so agitated that he held the box upside down, and the contents spilled out. He scrabbled on the floor and counted as he picked them up: "Gold Button, one sapphire, two sapphires; one ruby, two rubies; one, two, three, four emeralds. They're all there! They're all there."

Benvenuto guessed that his rivals would lose no time in suggesting that the robbery was just a cover up for him having misappropriated the jewels himself.

He was right. The Chamberlain, Tommaso da Prato said to Clement, "I hope your Holiness will remember that both I and Bandinelli warned you against trusting this young man. He seems to have prospered too quickly, and Pompeo thinks that we'll soon have him round here with some hard luck story."

Early that afternoon, Benvenuto went to the Vatican and asked the Pope's secretary, Traiano, for an immediate audience on a matter of urgent business. His suspicions about mischief making by his competitors was confirmed when the normally friendly secretary neither expressed any surprise, nor asked him what it was about.

He was left waiting in an ante room for nearly an hour, then he was summoned into the Pope's chamber. Again Clement had only one attendant, Tommaso da Prato.

Benvenuto knelt and kissed the Pope's ring and rose to his feet.

"What is this urgent business that you want to see me about, Messer Cellini?" Again the use of his surname.

"Holy Father, you may have heard that last night I had the misfortune to be robbed in my sleep by a thief who broke into my shop. The man has escaped and we don't know who he may be."

The Pope and da Prato exchanged glances. "Yes Messer Cellini, I had heard something about it. How does it concern me, though?"

"May it please your Holiness," Benvenuto spoke extra deferentially and paused for effect, "may it please your Holiness, this unfortunate affair doesn't concern you at all."

"What?"

"Holy Father, I came to tell you that your property is perfectly safe. Naturally I had it hidden in a very secure place, even though that meant that there was not enough room for my own goods which consequently got stolen. Not that I am complaining, because I have always considered it an honour as well as my duty to place your Holiness' interests above my own."

Benvenuto pulled the jewel box from his pouch and held it out to the Pope. Clement peered inside and Benvenuto could see his lips moving as he counted.

"My dear Benvenuto, with all the trouble you have had today, there was really no need for you to take the time to come to see me."

"I only wanted to reassure your Holiness. I know there are trouble-makers and gossips who would like nothing better than to suggest that I have been careless with your property."

He hit his forehead with the palm of his hand as if the thought had just struck him. "Why, I'll wager that there might even be malicious libellers who would even suggest I had stolen your jewels myself."

The Pope looked at da Prato from the corner of his eyes. "Oh come now, Benvenuto. Why would anyone be so wicked?"

"Because, your Holiness, some people know I am your most loyal subject." Benvenuto stared at da Prato. "Some people would like to get their own untalented favourites into your service. Some people might not even be averse to accepting a ducat or two for a good word in your ear."

Clement started to put his hand in front of his mouth, but instead stroked his beard.

"No, Benvenuto, you're too hard. I think some people sometimes jump to the wrong conclusions. I think that some people don't always show Christian charity. What do you think Messer da Prato?"

"I'm sure your Holiness is right."

"Of course I'm right. That's why I'm the Pope! I think the best thing those people should do when they discover their mistake is to ask their Confessor to fix a penance for them."

Da Prato did not reply. What was there for him to say?

The next morning Benvenuto heard shouting in the street outside his shop, and when he joined the crowd of onlookers, he saw that in the centre was Raffaello del Moro, a policeman and a young man dressed in a ragged and torn cloak.

The policeman was saying, "Look here sir, I've already told you I can't arrest a man just because he acts suspiciously. I searched him for you and you agreed he hadn't got anything of yours on him. I'm sorry, I've got to let him go."

At that moment, Cassius, Benvenuto's wolf-hound, caught sight of the young man and, barking furiously leaped straight at him through a gap in the crowd.

As the man instinctively threw his arm up to protect his throat, the weight of the large animal caught him off balance and knocked him to the ground, with the dog still snarling and growling and trying to bite him.

The onlookers drew back, prepared to flee from what they thought was a mad dog, but Benvenuto ran forward and pulled Cassius off, quietening him with several cuffs to the head.

"If you don't keep that beast of yours under control, I'll run it through," the policeman said, reaching for his sword.

"Yes, I'm sorry Corporal," replied Benvenuto. "It's not like him to do something like this." He turned to the young man. "Here, let me look at your arm."

Benvenuto caught a glimpse of the ring on the man's little finger. "Hey! Show me that!" He wrenched the ring off. "That's one of mine. That's why the dog went for you. He recognised you. You're the one who robbed my shop last night!"

He turned to the corporal. "Well, if you can't arrest him for robbing del Moro, you'd better arrest him for robbing me."

The policeman tied the man's hands and led him away, accompanied by Benvenuto who had to sign the complaint.

As the trio trooped off, someone in the crowd shouted out, "Corporal, don't you think you'd better take the dog with you? You'll need him as a witness!"

—⚜—

The false alarm over the Pope's jewels was soon followed by another incident where Benvenuto's integrity was called into question.

Counterfeit copies of his gold doubloons began to appear. In those days counterfeiting of gold and silver coins was not uncommon. It was usually done by making castings of a real coin out of gold or silver mixed with cheap base metals.

Detection was not easy when the real coins themselves were not too well made, and the forgeries could be passed off among ignorant people who did not see silver, or more especially gold, all that often anyway.

However, the new doubloons were a different matter. Because of the mistake in the weight of the gold content, the coins were being snapped up and melted down as fast as the goldsmiths could get their hands on them, and it was soon noticed that some of them were counterfeit and contained lead.

Naturally, there was an outcry which soon reached the ears of the Pope.

Benvenuto received an urgent command to go to the Vatican immediately. With the Pope in his study were four men. The first three were Tommaso da Prato, Jacopo Balducci, the Master of the Mint and Bandinelli the Sculptor. The last person was Benvenuto's hated rival, Pompeo who stood there, grinning at him with a mixture of triumph and glee.

"Messer Cellini….." the Pope said.

"Oh Lord!" thought Benvenuto. "What is it this time?"

"Messer Cellini, what do you make of these?"

He tossed three coins on to the long table. Two of them skidded on the polished wood; the third went rolling and spinning like a top until it clattered and fell flat alongside its two fellows.

Benvenuto picked the coins up and, one at a time, tossed them in the palm of his right hand to feel their weight. Then he carefully examined them front and back, held them up between forefinger and thumb and squinted at them edgeways on, and finally rubbed them against the soft skin inside his wrists.

Frowning, he squatted on his haunches, and dropped the three coins on the marble floor, one by one, checking the sound they made against the sound of a doubloon that he taken from his pouch.

"So what do you say about them?" Pompeo asked scornfully.

Benvenuto ignored him and took out a sharp pointed instrument and showed it to the Pope.

"Do I have your Holiness' permission?"

Clement nodded. Benvenuto scraped a thin scratch on the surface of the three doubloons, and taking them to the window, he peered at them closely in the strong light.

He turned to face the Pope. "They're false."

"Are you sure?"

"No question about it."

"How would you class them?" asked the Pope.

"They're good. Very good indeed. Excellent in fact."

"Obviously you are a connoisseur of craftsmanship," da Prato said, sarcastically.

"At least as much as your friend over there." Benvenuto jerked his head towards Pompeo.

"Never mind all that, can you tell whether they are castings or if they've been stamped?"

"Oh, they've obviously been struck from a die."

Da Prato turned to the Pope. "That, your Holiness, tallies with what Pompeo and the Master of the Mint have already told you."

"I also agree." Bandinelli spoke for the first time.

The Pope was ready to spring his trap.

"Messer Cellini, you've said often enough that no one but you was expert enough to make dies for the doubloons. How do you account for the fact that these absolutely perfect counterfeits have been struck from a die as good as yours? Some people think you've gone in for making false coins."

He flicked his eyes at da Prato.

"Your Holiness!" Benvenuto was livid with indignation. "Some people will never stop spreading vile slanders about me, especially if they're jealous of the confidence your Holiness reposes in me."

"But can you prove you had nothing to do with it, Cellini?" Bandinelli asked.

Benvenuto flung his arms sideways, and with a resigned expression on his face, he counted off the points one by one on his fingers.

"First, if I had wanted to, I could have stolen his Holiness' jewels by pretending the man who robbed my shop took them. The robber who I myself, personally, detected and handed over to the police.

Secondly, I've got so many customers, I don't know where to turn. I can earn more money in my shop by honest work, than I could by wasting my time trying to make a few miserable scudi mixing lead with gold.

Lastly, Bandinelli, admit it, is there more than one single person in Rome - in Italy even, who has ever complained about my honesty?" He glared ferociously at da Prato.

Bandinelli shook his head. "No, for all your faults, nobody can say you're not honest," he said reluctantly.

The Pope held up his hand.

"Benvenuto, enough! You've convinced me. Now, do you have any suggestion as to who might have done this?"

He thought for a moment. "Only one, Holy Father. A coin maker in the Mint."

The Pope looked at the Master of the Mint. Balducci shrugged his shoulders, and then sadly and very slowly, nodded his head. So did Bandinelli.

"Right. See you find him then, Messer Balducci. And Benvenuto, you may go."

"Thank you, your Holiness. Before I do, I have a suggestion for Messer da Prato also."

The Pope raised his eyebrows and Benvenuto continued, "I think as a priest of the Holy Church, he ought to tell some people to learn from the book of Proverbs where it says, 'Accuse not a servant unto his Master lest he curse thee...' Don't you think that's a valid point, Messer da Prato?"

"Damn your impertinence, goldsmith," snarled da Prato. "I won't teach you your business, and don't you try to teach me mine!"

Benvenuto made an exaggerated, mocking bow towards him and left.

—ɷ—

The investigation at the Mint did not take long. It was not difficult to catch the counterfeiter. It was a coin maker called Ceseri Salvestro. His accomplice was a metal founder who had made the blanks of gold mixed with lead.

—ɷ—

One morning later that week, a huge crowd gathered on the banks of the Tiber, near to the Ponte Sant' Angelo. There was almost a carnival atmosphere. Hawkers were carrying trays with slices of melon, warm almond cakes and peaches, while others were selling cups of wine and fizzy fruit juice from leather skins and earthenware jugs.

Whole families were there, with fathers carrying their children on their shoulders to give them a better view.

Half a company of soldiers confined the crowd to one side of the square and the roadway leading into it by leaning against the linked shafts of their pikes which they held lengthways as a makeshift barrier.

The road on the opposite side of the square faced the exit from Castel Sant' Angelo which had now reverted to its normal use as a prison.

When the gates opened and a wide, wooden wheeled cart trundled out, drawn by two horses, the crowd gave a loud cheer.

The flat bed of the truck was about five feet from the ground, and the sides consisted of widely spaced horizontal poles with upright supports through which the passengers could be seen.

There were four despondent wretched-looking men seated on a bench crossways on the truck. Their arms were tied behind their backs at both their wrists and elbows, and their ankles were also bound with thin cord. Standing in front of each man was a soldier pointing a gun.

Behind the four was a priest reading from a prayer book held in one hand while, with the other, he clung to the latticed side of the cart to help him keep his balance as it rattled over the cobblestones.

The last passenger was seated on a stool near the back of the cart. His head was bowed and he seemed to be wearing the cowl to his cloak over his ears and head.

Running alongside the cart were six more soldiers, armed with pikes, three on each side.

When the cart reached the centre of the square, it swung round in a wide arc facing back the way it had come, jolting to a halt under a long thick beam supported on the perpendicular sawn-off trunks of two Lombardy poplar trees. Suspended from the beam were four nooses.

As soon as the truck stopped, the last man who had sat alone stood up and lowered the tail-gate. The crowd saw he was not just wearing a cowl, but a black hood and mask covering his face. A low murmur rang through the people, and many of them, Benvenuto included, crossed themselves.

The soldiers on the truck drew their daggers and prodded the prisoners, forcing them to rise and hop forward until they stood under the ropes, looking around them fearfully.

One was the young man who had robbed Benvenuto; another was Ceseri Salvestro, the counterfeiter. The others were two convicted murderers.

The six soldiers who had escorted the cart formed a semi-circle at the tail-gate with their pikes levelled at the crowd and were joined by the guards from the truck, one at a time as the executioner adjusted the noose around each of the victims' necks.

So far, less than a minute and a half had elapsed since the truck had emerged from the prison gate, and less than twenty seconds since it had come to a complete halt.

The masked man climbed back on the cart, leaned over the rail and took both the whip and the reins from the driver.

He cracked the whip over the horses and shouted "A-van-ti." He said the word in three syllables. Then he shouted, "Basta." Between the two words, the cart lurched forward about five yards, leaving the four men hanging by their necks from the gallows.

The crowd went "Aaaah" as they spontaneously let out their own breath as if in sympathy with the choking men.

One of the murderers was in a sense luckier than his companions. A fortuitous combination of the length of the rope, the height of the drop and his own weight meant that his neck snapped in the fall and he died instantly.

The other three jerked and kicked their tied feet while their clothes darkened with urine as their bladders involuntarily emptied themselves. Their bitten tongues hung out of their mouths and the whites of their eyes went dark red, almost black, as the tiny blood vessels burst.

The hangman stood at the back of the cart with arms folded staring intently until they stopped slowly twisting round and round, back and forth on their ropes and until the only movement was their gentle swaying as the cool breeze blowing off the river caught them.

Then he nodded, almost imperceptibly, to the sergeant who shouted the one word command, "Andiamo!" "Let's go."

At this the four guards turned and leaped on the cart which drove off as fast as the horses could gallop towards the prison, followed on foot by the soldiers who had been holding back the crowd, leaving only the six pikemen to guard the hanged men.

It was nearly two hours later, when the noon gun sounded from the castle battlements that the victims were cut down, their heads lolling grotesquely on necks that had already stretched several inches from the weight of the dead bodies.

Only the corpse of Ceseri Salvestro was claimed by his widow. The other three friendless men were loaded onto a hand cart by the pikemen for burial later that afternoon somewhere in the hills outside the city.

Most of the morbid crowd had stayed until this very moment, Benvenuto and Raffaello del Moro amongst them.

"Well," said Benvenuto, that will teach those two not to cross my path with their villainy."

"What about the foundryman who gave Salvestro the lead blanks?" asked del Moro.

"Oh him," said Benvenuto. "His confession helped to convict Salvestro, so they only sentenced him to hard labour for life down the sulphur mines. He got off quite lightly, really!"

-20-

Benvenuto had at last finished the Cope Button, and dressed in his best clothes, and accompanied by two of his apprentices and two of his workmen, he presented himself to the Pope.

Before entering the Audience Chamber, Benvenuto carefully arranged what he intended to be a dramatic unveiling.

First there was a large black velvet cushion hung with gold braid and tassels. The Button was carefully placed in the centre and covered with a white brocade cloth heavily embroidered, also in gold thread.

Benvenuto led his little procession into the room, followed by the boy carrying the cushion. Behind him were his two workmen, and then the last apprentice. The formation resembled a crucifix.

When Benvenuto reached the Pope, they all knelt together in a well-rehearsed movement. The Pope offered his ring to be kissed and Benvenuto and his little company rose to their feet.

"May it please your Holiness, I humbly present the Cope Button that has been made to your most gracious command."

Benvenuto took the cushion and presented it to the Pope with a low bow, and swept off the cloth cover.

Clement gingerly picked the great button up. Ever so slowly he nodded his head up and down several times.

"Beautiful. Yes it's really very beautiful. It does you great honour."

He showed it round to the courtiers standing about him, who, in response to the Pope's enthusiasm broke into polite applause.

"You know," Clement said to nobody in particular, "when someone creates a marvellous - a unique - work of art like this, it's absolutely impossible to find a suitable reward for him. The terrible war. The extortionate reparations I have had to pay, and now the floods. I must be the poorest Prince in Christendom!"

He gave a big sigh and assumed a doleful expression.

"If only I were rich, I'd load you with gold. Less of course what you owe me for what I lost on the overweight doubloons."

His face brightened as if a thought had just struck him. "Don't worry Benvenuto, I'll see you always have bread to eat."

Benvenuto's bushy eyebrows nearly shot to the top of his forehead. Money - a lot of it - and right away, was what he had in mind, but he realised somewhat gloomily that he would have to find a solution very quickly.

"To serve your Holiness is its own reward." Benvenuto gave a deep bow. The Pope looked relieved as well as mildly surprised, but his expression soon changed as Benvenuto continued, "It is a matter of deep personal regret to me that to provide the necessities - the barest of necessities - of life for myself and these craftsmen who are dependent upon me for their very food, means that matters as repugnant as money have to arise between us."

Benvenuto gestured towards his four workers who grinned sheepishly.

"Your Holiness does not concern himself with such mundane matters, so you are probably unaware that my contract as Die Maker to the mint has not been renewed. Doubtless it was due to the evil, jealous influence of some people."

He looked hard at Tommaso da Prato, who snapped back, "Doubtless it was due to the mess you made over the doubloons."

Benvenuto pretended he had not heard.

"Now it so happens, Holy Father, that I was going to petition you to allow me to serve you as one of your Holiness' Mace Bearers."

In mediaeval times the Mace was a weapon of war, and the Mace-bearer was part of a sovereign's personal bodyguard. However, by now the duties were largely ceremonial, but they did involve the collection of a few taxes on behalf of the Pope, of which the office holder was allowed to keep two hundred ducats.

Although there was currently a vacancy, the Pope was keeping it in hand in case he needed it as a political favour.

"Appoint you to the office of Mace Bearer?" Clement said, "Oh yes, what an excellent suggestion."

He did not manage to convey much enthusiasm. Instead, he said to da Prato,

"Tommaso, be kind enough to see that this, ... this request, is dealt with through the usual channels. All the usual channels. All of them."

"Before you go...." the Pope said.

Benvenuto jerked himself upright. He had not realised that he was going to be dismissed.

"..... before you go, Messer da Prato will give you a sketch for a new Chalice I would like you to make. He will also give you five hundred ducats for the gold and expenses for which you will give him a full accounting. I expect that I shall see you again soon. Good day to you."

He held out his ring for Benvenuto to kiss again, and to his bewilderment, instead of being feted with a little celebratory **colazione** as he had expected, he found himself out in the street, blinking in the harsh sunlight, the bag of gold - not even his gold - clutched in one hand and a crumpled drawing in the other.

Angrily he kicked one of his apprentices. "Get out from under my feet, you oaf! Isn't the whole of St. Peter's Square wide enough for you?"

—ɷ—

The Chalice was to have three figures in full relief depicting "Faith", "Hope" and "Charity". At the base of the Chalice there were three circles and on these Benvenuto showed scenes of the Nativity, the Resurrection and the Crucifixion of St. Peter.

When the wood and wax model was ready he took it to the Pope for his approval, and as soon as Clement signified that he was satisfied, Benvenuto said deferentially, "Your Holiness, about my appointment as one of your Mace Bearers....?"

The Pope frowned. "Oh yes, well I suppose the papers are working their way through the Clerks' Office. You know how slow they are."

"Indeed I do, Holy Father. That is why I have an alternative suggestion."

Benvenuto handed him yet another roll of parchment. He did not notice the Pope's eyes rolling upwards, as if appealing to Heaven.

"What is it this time?"

"The Master of your Holiness' Foundry has just died. His post is vacant."

"So it is," replied the Pope, "and the annual fee is six hundred ducats. That's three times a Mace Bearer's! If I gave you that job, you'd grow fat and lazy and stop making beautiful things like that." He pointed at the model of the Chalice.

"I've no chance of growing fat if my clients don't pay me, and if your Holiness won't even pay me a small annual retainer. The Holy Father is right as always," Benvenuto added bitterly. "I would only sit scratching my belly if you were to give me the job. Your Holiness should undoubtedly give it to an artist who is more talented, more industrious, and who has served you more faithfully than I!"

Little globules of spit shot out of his mouth as he spoke.

Benvenuto snatched up his model and flung himself out of the room without waiting for the Pope's permission, pausing at the door only to say, "No doubt your loyal Chamberlain, Messer da Prato will have some advice for you on the subject!"

—⚬—

Tommaso da Prato, escorted by two soldiers, ostensibly to protect him from footpads, called on Benvenuto with a message from the Pope.

His Holiness was most displeased with Messer Cellini's display of temperament. His Holiness never made appointments to important positions without careful consideration. On a recent occasion he had had reason to regret the hasty appointment of an inexperienced die-maker to the Mint. Messer Cellini, would when it was convenient to His Holiness, receive such reward as His Holiness deemed proper for his few past services, so long as he observed a respectful attitude to the Holy See and its officers. Every one of them. Did Messer Cellini clearly understand?

"Is that all?" he asked.

"No, there's another thing. His Holiness has commanded me to enquire when he may expect some further progress on his Chalice."

"Really? Well I have this terrible, this disgusting habit that I can't seem to break, of needing to eat every day. It means that I have to give preference to my paying clients. I haven't got too much time for charity work for those who tell me they are paupers!"

"That tongue of yours is long enough to hang you by, Master Goldsmith," warned da Prato. "I'll give him your message with pleasure."

Benvenuto backed down. "Tell him I'm doing it as fast as I can," he growled. "Now perhaps there's something I can show you? A silver back-stabber, perhaps?"

Da Prato turned to leave. "His Holiness is going to Bologna, and he's left you in my charge. He asked me to keep you up to the mark. Hard up to it. I'll be seeing you again quite soon I expect, shopkeeper!"

—⚒—

A week later da Prato sent for Benvenuto, and ordered him to bring the Chalice with him. Benvenuto arrived late and without the cup.

"Where's that hash you're supposed to be working on?"

"Oh dear, your most Reverence, it isn't quite finished.

I can't make a hash, as you call it, without vegetables. You know my terms of business. No money, no goods!"

"What I know," said da Prato, "is that I think I'll send you to the Galleys. Just for a little lesson in manners. Say about ten years' worth."

"When I do something to deserve the Galleys, you can send me there, but I'll tell you this now. I am not going to do anything to the Chalice until I get some money. Shall I spell it for you? M-O-N-E-Y. And don't you ask me to come here again. I'll see your master, what's-his-name when he gets back, but if you want me, tell the guards to bring me by force."

—⚉—

Da Prato, of course, lost no time in reporting what had happened when the Pope returned from Bologna. In a terrible rage, Clement sent for Benvenuto who happened to be suffering from conjunctivitis - inflammation of the eyes.

Benvenuto was feeling very sorry for himself and was in an unusually docile and chastened mood. He was even ready to apologise. He was sure he was going to lose his sight and he might need every friend soon.

The Pope, however, was not prepared to be friendly.

"Messer Cellini," he said without ceremony, "the Chalice, if you please." He held out his hand. "Is it finished?"

He looked in the box. "You've hardly done anything. How dare you? What's your explanation for this disobedience?"

"Not even a Pope can make a blind man work on something like this, can he?" Benvenuto retorted.

"What do you mean blind? Who's blind?"

"I am, Holy Father. See for yourself." Benvenuto raised his head and showed his red rimmed bloodshot eyes.

"How on earth did you get in that state?"

"He did it!" Benvenuto pointed straight at da Prato with an accuracy that was remarkable for a supposedly sightless man.

"First he came and bullied me, then he threatened me with the Galleys. I think the shock has made me start to go blind. Or perhaps he put a curse on me."

It's more likely that God is punishing you for your disrespect to his Vicar on Earth," said the Pope. "Get out of here now. If your doctors don't cure you quickly, we'll try one of my remedies. It starts with a ride to the river bank on the back of a cart."

During the next week, Benvenuto's rival Pompeo, with the help of da Prato, introduced a new goldsmith to the Pope. He was called Tobbia. Pompeo had concealed the fact that Tobbia had just fled from Milan to escape from a charge of making counterfeit coins, and Clement was persuaded to commission him to make a candlestick for King Francis.

Benvenuto's jealousy knew no bounds, and although he had been working on the Chalice since his last meeting with the Pope, when the Pope's secretary, Traiano, came to get a progress report, Benvenuto obstinately refused to show it to him.

"Can a baker make bread without flour? Well, Sir, I'm a goldsmith, and I can't make Chalices out of thin air. I have to give priority to customers who pay me."

"Look, I'm not da Prato. I'm the only ally you've got at Court, although Heaven only knows why I bother with you. Just let me see what you've been doing so I can tell his Holiness you've been making progress."

Benvenuto turned his back on his friend. "Tell the Pope what you like, but I'm too busy trying to earn this week's wages to get the damn pot out of the safe."

An hour later, four soldiers and a sergeant arrived at Benvenuto's workroom and kicked the door open.

"Benvenuto Cellini," said the Sergeant, waving a paper, "this is a warrant for your arrest, and in case you are thinking of trying any tricks, we've got permission to shoot you if you resist."

Benvenuto looked at the soldiers fingering the triggers of their guns.

"What's the charge? What have I done?"

"Done? You don't have to have done anything for us to get one of these things." The Sergeant waved the warrant again. "We just do what we're told: bring them in, beat them up, string them up or whatever. I don't get paid for asking questions. Nor for answering them either. Now, are you ready? Oh, by the way, it says here you're to bring some Chalice with you. Do you know what that means?"

Benvenuto's eyes gleamed. "Yes, I know." He picked up the goblet that he had started to work on again as soon as Traiano had left, and wrapped it in a cloth.

As the little group turned to leave the shop, one of the soldiers gave a little cough and jerked his head in the direction of the counter on which were lying a few gold coins that Benvenuto had left there to pay some commission due to one of his master craftsmen. The Sergeant picked them up and dropped them into his doublet.

"Hey, what's the idea?" said Benvenuto. "Why are you taking those?"

"Evidence," said the Sergeant laconically.

"Evidence? Evidence of what?"

"They may be stolen."

Benvenuto was furious. "They're mine. They haven't been stolen."

"Well they have now," replied the Sergeant, "and where you're going you won't need them anyway!" He laughed raucously at his own joke. Somehow, however, Benvenuto did not find it so funny.

—⚜—

Benvenuto was taken to the courtroom. He was surprised to see that the Magistrate was none other than his old client Gabriello Ceserino for whom he had made the "Leda and the Swan" hat pin for which he had never been paid.

"Clement certainly picked himself a sympathetic judge," he thought to himself. Out loud he said, "You're back too, then?"

"So many judges were murdered in the war, that the Pope insisted I came to Rome to help him out," Ceserino explained.

"Messer Cellini, I'm very grieved to find you here, but it's your own fault really. The Holy Father has kindly told me that if you hand over his Chalice, I may release you."

"**His** Chalice? It's not his Chalice; it's mine, and he shan't have it. Not now, not ever."

"You realise I can have it taken from you by force?"

"Certainly. If the Pope wants to rob me, I can't stop him, but I'm not just going to quietly hand over my goods to the first highwayman who kidnaps me."

"Why do you keep saying the Chalice is yours? The Pope had it designed, he ordered it and he gave you five hundred ducats for the gold."

"He can have the five hundred ducats back at any time, minus the money those thieves you sent stole from me on the way here."

Ceserino glared at the Sergeant as Benvenuto continued, "The Chalice is mine until I'm paid for it. Some people's eyes are bigger than their pockets. I remember a Florentine nobleman once ordered a hat pin from me that he couldn't afford. He didn't get it either."

Ceserino ignored the insult. "Very well, I'll tell the Pope what you say. Meanwhile, Sergeant, lock him up."

—w—

Ceserino returned from the Vatican after a long discussion with the Pope. He ordered Benvenuto to be brought up from the cells and sent the guards out of the room.

When the two men were alone he cleared his throat several times. "Benvenuto, my old friend, you realise that the Pope is entirely above the law. However, as God's representative, he will always hear a plea for justice, even if it is misconceived and comes from an ungrateful subject who only imagines he has a grievance."

He had to raise his hand to silence Benvenuto.

"Therefore, although the Pope will condescend to review your claim, there is one matter that he cannot possibly overlook - your public insolence and disobedience to him. So this is what he has commanded. Do you understand? Commanded."

Benvenuto nodded.

"You will place the Chalice in a box in my presence and seal it. I will take the box to His Holiness. He will return it to you with the seals unbroken. That way the honour of both of you will be satisfied. Then, and only then, will he instruct Tommaso da Prato to discuss payment for the Cope Button with you."

He waited, but Benvenuto stayed glumly silent.

"You have no choice. Did I say that this was what His Holiness has commanded.?"

Benvenuto hesitated for a moment or two and then he said, "May I trouble your Worship for some sealing wax?"

Ceserino lit a candle on his writing table and dropped a few pellets of sealing wax into a long spoon-shaped brass crucible. As soon as the wax melted, they poured a few blobs on to lid of the box, and Benvenuto quickly pressed them down with his signet ring.

Ceserino again set off for the Vatican, his fat face streaming with perspiration in the heat of the early afternoon.

—⋙—

Clement took the box from Ceserino and turned it over in his hands a few times, and then the sight of the carefully applied seals seemed to infuriate him.

"Tell Messer Cellini," he shouted at the Magistrate, "that Popes have power to undo much greater things than this."

"But your Holiness promised....." Ceserino protested.

"Silence!" ordered the Pope. He ripped open the box and took out the partly finished Chalice. He looked it over, and despite himself, nodded with approval.

Without another word he handed the cup to Pompeo who in turn passed it to the Pope's new goldsmith, Tobbia.

"Well," Clement asked, "can you match this work?"

"Easily," Tobbia replied. "In fact I'd be ashamed if I couldn't do it ten times better."

"Madonna!" Clement silently swore to himself. "I'm cursed with yet another boaster."

Aloud he said to Ceserino, "You, will return this - this thing to Messer Cellini. The order is cancelled. Messer Pompeo will collect my five hundred ducats back from him and if he doesn't pay at once, I'll have him rotting in Sant' Angelo until he's ninety.

And as for you Messer Tobbia, I'll be satisfied if you can do half as well as Cellini, but I'm not going to stand any nonsense from you. You'll finish the Candlestick for King Francis and my Chalice in six weeks or I'll send you back to Milan.

Tell me," he added sweetly, showing that his information was as good as ever, "do they hang counterfeiters there, or do they behead them?"

When Ceserino returned to his office, he prudently took two soldiers with him into the room where Benvenuto had been kept waiting.

Silently, he handed the box to Benvenuto, who only needed one glance at the seals to see what had happened.

"Thank you, my dear and Honourable Magistrate. Thank you, and thank God, for showing me what the solemn word of a Pope is worth. May I go now?"

"Benvenuto, believe me, I'm sorry. No, I'm ashamed. Certainly you can go, but I want to warn you. Pompeo is coming to collect the five hundred ducats from you, and if you don't pay, the Pope's only looking for an excuse to lock you up. Have you got the money?"

"Of course I've got the money. I am Benvenuto Cellini, master craftsman, not some jumped-up priest rattling a begging bowl on the balcony of St. Peter's!"

After Pompeo had collected the gold, Benvenuto went out and got drunk. Very drunk.

On his way back from the Inn just before dawn, he got into a row with a crowd of equally drunk men coming from another part of the town. There was an exchange of mindless insults, mostly about the morals, or lack of them, of their respective mothers, but as the others passed by the jeering rang in his head.

"Why me?" he thought. "Why is it always me? No sooner do things start going right, then something happens. Da Prato. Not getting paid. That prick, Pompeo."

"Oh shut up, you arseholes!" he yelled and picking up a clod of earth, he threw it wildly into the crowd, but staggering from the drink he fell to the ground. At the same moment, one of the other men dropped. A stone in the lump of mud had knocked him cold, with blood streaming from a scalp wound.

Someone shouted, "He's dead! Look at the blood! You've killed him!"

Benvenuto got up on his knees, and then hauled himself upright and ran.

As luck would have it, Pompeo was just riding by on his way home from celebrating his victory over the famous Cellini.

When he saw Benvenuto running away and heard the crowd still screaming "He's killed him", he jumped to the conclusion that it was Tobbia lying there. After all, what other enemies had Benvenuto made that day? Actually the stranger was only stunned, but without waiting to check, Pompeo raced off to the Vatican where Clement, da Prato, and the Secretary, Traiano, were finishing their early morning prayers.

Pompeo burst into the chapel. "Holy Father, Benvenuto Cellini has just murdered Tobbia. I saw it myself!"

It was too much for the Pope. In a blind rage he sent for the Magistrate Ceserino.

"You'll have Cellini found. When you've got him, take him straight to the place where he killed Tobbia, and hang him. Don't bother with a trial, and don't come back until you've done it!"

Unseen by the Pope and da Prato, Traiano slipped away and sent a messenger hurrying to Benvenuto's shop, while Ceserino, with extra slow deliberation gathered an escort.

There was nothing for it, Benvenuto hastily gathered together his stock of gold and jewels, got on his horse and rode off towards Naples.

Before he had gone very far, Tobbia was of course found unharmed and working in his studio, and in fact no-one was reported as having been killed anywhere near the scene of the incident.

Traiano sent the same messenger galloping along the road to tell Benvenuto that it was safe to return.

"Thanks for the news," Benvenuto said to the man as they rode back to Rome. "I suppose I ought to be pleased, but I might as well have gone on to Naples just the same. I haven't been paid for the Cope Button, and now it looks as if I never will. And, I suppose you heard I lost my job at the Mint, well, to cap it all, now they've taken away the commission for the Chalice."

"But you've got lots of other customers apart from the Pope haven't you?"

"For the moment, but no doubt some of them will go to that Pompeo as soon as they discover that he's in favour and I'm not. God! I'd like to watch that bastard dying in agony at my feet!"

"Don't talk like that. You nearly got yourself lynched over Tobbia."

"It's very kind of you to remind me," Benvenuto said bitterly. "That's another reason for me to go to Naples. Just let any of that gang so much as cut his finger and they'll be after me with a rope again!"

He fished in his saddle bag and pulled out his flute. "Now shut up. I think we'll have some music instead of all this jabbering."

—⚬—

Who was to blame? Not himself, Benvenuto thought, No, it was all the fault of Tommaso da Prato, Bandinello and above all Pompeo. There was nothing he could do about as important an official as da Prato or a celebrity like Bandinello, but Pompeo. "One day…"

The situation was aggravated by Pompeo going around boasting that he had been personally responsible for the downfall of the high and mighty Benvenuto Cellini and even taunted him publicly about it.

Benvenuto lay in wait for Pompeo as he returned home one night. As Pompeo passed the doorway where he was hiding, Benvenuto, his face masked, leaped on him and slashed out with his short, but very sharp dagger.

It had only been his intention to mark his enemy's face, but Pompeo instinctively jerked his head back exposing his throat to the blade which cut through the great carotid artery. Pompeo died in moments in a great gout of blood.

Benvenuto was again deep in trouble, and this time seemingly with no hope of escaping the gallows.

But for once, the Gods favoured Benvenuto through the misfortune of another.

That same night Pope Clement died.

The politicking and jostling for position began at once, and nobody had the time or inclination to worry about one murder - at least not for the moment.

Perhaps later.

Part IV: The Prisoner

-21-

It was October 13th 1534. Benvenuto Cellini was nearly thirty-four years old and still struggling to make his fortune.

Allessandro Farnese was sixty-six when he was elected as Pope by the Sacred College of Cardinals in succession to Clement VII.

For once, the different parties were more or less in agreement in their choice, and the Convocation of Cardinals was amongst the shortest on record. Farnese was the oldest, and a very influential member of the College. He had been made a Cardinal as long ago as 1493. His age and poor health suggested that he would be a "stop-gap" Pope, reigning for only a few years until recovery from the war was complete. He could initiate essential changes that the Reformation was calling for, without involving any of the political interests in any backlash.

Those aspirants for the Throne of St. Peter who were hoping for a short reign were to be disappointed. He remained Pope until 1549 - fifteen years later.

Pope Paul III, for that was the title he had taken, owed his very early appointment as Cardinal when he was only twenty-five to the fact that his sister, Guilia, was the mistress of the Borgia Pope, Alexander IV.

The rule of celibacy of the priesthood was then as often broken as observed, especially among the Bishops and Cardinals, and, just as Paul received favoured treatment as a result of Alexander's liaison with his sister, so did Paul, soon after his Coronation, begin to shower honours and favours on his own illegitimate offspring.

First, he appointed his three grandsons, one aged fifteen, and one aged sixteen to be Cardinals. Later he engineered the marriage of his grandson, Ottavio, to Margaret, the widowed daughter of Charles V. Years later, and contrary to the Emperor's wishes, he appointed his illegitimate son, Pier Luigi as Duke of Parma and Piacenza.

These machinations did him no good in the end, for when Paul died in November 1549, confessing on his death bed to the sin of Corruption, he was actually at war with his own grandson, Ottavio.

For a politician like Paul III, all potential friends, all possible allies, and all men of influence, were important.

So it was that when Benvenuto, through the good offices of three very powerful patrons, Cardinal de' Medici, Cardinal Cornaro, and the Bishop of Pavia, sought an amnesty from the "suspicion" of being Pompeo's murderer, his request was not rejected out of hand. Pope Paul took time to consider.

He needed time anyway, because Benvenuto was just one of many Petitioners besieging the new Pope for dispensations, indulgences, offices and favours of all kinds. The election of a new Pope was a great opportunity for wiping the slate clean of all sorts of past problems - if only for administrative reasons. It was also the time for paying back political debts and for collecting new obligations that the new Pope could call in at a later date.

—⚜—

Paul was discovering for himself that despite his great, and theoretically unlimited powers as secular ruler of the Papal States as well as spiritual head of the Church, he was hemmed in on all sides by a vast bureaucracy, by a huge political and diplomatic staff, by strange customs and rituals, by noblemen and others having rights and privileges that they had inherited or purchased, and by the monumental, crushing burden of the minute administrative details of the great office to which he had just been elected.

In all the pressing decisions that the new and inexperienced Pope had to make, advice, often conflicting, was tendered to him, not only by long-established officials, but also by interested parties, and by greedy and ambitious men jockeying for position and promotion in the new hierarchy.

Consequentially and despite his influential sponsors, Benvenuto's plea for an amnesty did not proceed either smoothly or quickly. In fact, one of those attempting to influence the new Pope against it was none other than Paul's own illegitimate son, Pier Luigi Farnese.

Pier Luigi had actually fought against Clement at the Sack of Rome, and had been excommunicated as a result, but had later been given Absolution as a result of the intercession of his father.

Apart from being egged on by Tommaso da Prato, Pier Luigi's interest in Benvenuto's affairs was only coincidental. One of his friends had just married the dead Pompeo's daughter who had received a substantial inheritance from her late father. Typically, when Pier Luigi began making trouble for him, Benvenuto, instead of keeping quiet, spread the slander that Pier Luigi was doing so in return for a share of the dowry!

Benvenuto's heart was pounding as he entered the Audience Chamber for his first meeting with Pope Paul, but not because he was overawed. What he was feeling was fear.

As he approached the Pope who was flanked by his two enemies, Tommaso da Prato, now even more powerful than before because of his long service as an administrator, and by Pier Luigi Farnese, Benvenuto wondered if he was safe. Would he be arrested? Had he taken his last walk as a free man before jail and the gallows?

He really had no reason to worry. His invitation from the Pope had been arranged by Cardinal de' Medici who was himself escorting Benvenuto and making the formal presentation.

"So you're Benvenuto Cellini," the Pope said.

Benvenuto cringed as he awaited the joke about being welcome. It did not come. Instead the Pope continued, "We have your petition for a free pardon under consideration."

"I beg that your Holiness will be pleased to grant it, so that I may have the opportunity of devoting myself to your service." Benvenuto bowed his head in genuine humility.

"We shall consult with our advisers...."

Da Prato seized what he thought was his cue. "May I respectfully suggest that it is too early in your Holiness' reign to be granting petitions of this sort?"

Without even glancing at him, the Pope silenced da Prato with one upraised finger.

"As we were saying, we shall consult with our advisers - in due course, because it is too soon for us to be considering petitions of this sort. Now perhaps you will say what reason there is why we should pardon you for this terrible crime."

"Your Holiness, there is no reason."

The Pope's mouth fell open,

"None, that is, except that I am innocent." Benvenuto lied. "It is only that some people decided to blame me for the act of a street robber. And there is no reason to pardon me except for my years of loyal and devoted service to your Holiness' illustrious predecessor."

Da Prato leaned over and whispered something in Paul's ear.

"A good answer Messer Cellini," the Pope said, "but isn't it a fact that you had behaved in a disgustingly impertinent way with the late Pope, and when he died you were in disgrace?"

"To my sorrow and shame, your Holiness, that's true. I believe I must have been mad. Maybe it was all the cares and worries that I had, and the fear that some people," he shot a malevolent glance at da Prato, "were poisoning the Holy Father's mind against me."

"Mad?" said the Pope. "But you're fully recovered now, of course."

"By God's Grace."

"Has your Confessor given you absolution?"

Benvenuto was not sure which crime the Pope was talking about: Pompeo's murder, or offending Clement.

"No, he says that only God can forgive me, and only your Holiness can pardon me, and that I must repent every day of my life."

"My, my!" the Pope was impressed. "Certainly the Roman air does something for the power of eloquence. Well, you shall have our answer on Lady Day."

"On the Feast of Our Lady?" Benvenuto was aghast. That was still nearly four months away. "But I could be arrested, tried and hanged long before that! Will your Holiness at least grant me a safe conduct until then?"

Before the Pope could say another word, Benvenuto had opened his ever-ready pouch and pulled out a folded parchment.

The Pope clutched his long white beard with both hands. "Messer Cellini! We had already heard about your powers of anticipation. No doubt it is to do with those necromancers you mix with. Come on, we shall sign it before you bewitch us! Messer da Prato, the Seal, if you please."

Benvenuto decided to press his luck.

"May it please your Holiness, I do have something else to show you."

Even Cardinal de' Medici looked surprised.

Benvenuto held out a small black oblong box. Embedded in it were the designs for a new gold crown piece, a little more than an inch across. On one side was the Farnese family coat of arms and on the other the figure of St. Paul with the inscription, "S. Paulinus vas electionis."

Very nice, master goldsmith," said the Pope, "but if we commission the design, it might be thought that you had already been pardoned, which you haven't. Perhaps later.... Now you have our permission to withdraw, and see you stay out of trouble until we send for you again."

Da Prato and Pier Luigi were not going to let matters rest there. Whatever Benvenuto said or the Pope chose to believe, Pompeo's friends knew who the murderer was. Pier Luigi had promised the dead man's daughter that Benvenuto would be punished, and yet there he was walking about a free man with the Pope's safe conduct in his pocket, a pardon as good as granted, and a fair prospect of the commission to design the new coinage as well.

What happened to Benvenuto was of no actual importance to Pier Luigi personally, but if he, the Pope's son, was to be regarded as a man of power and influence in the new regime he had to deal with this nonentity. Since Benvenuto had a safe conduct, there was only one quick solution. Murder!

The assassin who was hired was a Corsican soldier - and not a very good one at that.

Benvenuto was suspicious when he received an invitation to call on Pier Luigi to discuss an order for a pair of silver vases at a time which would take him through one of the less frequented streets at dusk. Why that particular time? Why would Pier Luigi pick him, of all people, to make them?

Benvenuto decided to take no chances. He wore both his sword and a dagger, a coat of chain mail and long studded heavy leather gauntlets. He walked down the centre of the road, keeping a careful watch in all directions, whirling round on his heels every fifty yards or so to see if he was being followed, and sprinting past each alleyway.

He left the Piazza Madama, and passed by the French Church, Santa Luigi dei Francesi. Now he was crossing the Largo Toniolo going towards the Via del Pozzo delle Cornaccia. "Street of the Well of the Crows. Where did they get a ridiculous name like that?" he thought. It came from the Coat of Arms of Cardinal Wolsey who had built himself a Palace there - and never used it.

Just as he reached the corner, he saw what he had been half expecting. A furtive movement in a doorway; a head peeping out and hurriedly withdrawn.

He quietly unsheathed his sword and hid it under his cloak. Moving closer to the wall, he ran on tiptoe till he was nearly level with the doorway. Then, with a loud yell, he leapt into the entrance and pinned a very surprised Corsican to the door, his sword pressed hard against the man's throat.

"Drop your dagger my friend, and quickly."

The weapon fell to the ground and Benvenuto kicked it clattering away over the cobblestones.

"And now perhaps you will tell me what you were up to."

The point of Benvenuto's sword scratched painfully at the man's skin and his Adam's Apple nervously bobbed up and down.

"Up to? Nothing sir. I don't know what you mean. I was just...."

"Listen carefully. I'm going to give you some very good advice. This is no time for lying. Not unless you want to find yourself dead."

Benvenuto moved his sword slightly so that its point dug under the soldier's chin, forcing him to stand on his toes. Benvenuto pressed harder and the man jerked his head back, banging it with a loud crack against the door behind him.

"Sir, please take the sword away. I can't breathe."

"Will it help you if I give you another air hole in your throat? Now what were you up to?"

"Robbery. That's it. I thought you were an old drunk I could steal a few scudi off."

Benvenuto drew his dagger and stuck it under the terrified man's eyeball. "Last chance," he hissed.

"They paid me. They told me to look out for you and to stab you."

"Who did, damn it?"

"I don't know." The two points pressed harder against the quivering skin. "In God's name! I swear I don't know! Digi the pickpocket told me to do it. He said I'd be paid."

"How much?"

"Five Crowns."

Benvenuto was genuinely insulted. Later, whenever he told the story, he increased the figure to a hundred, although a hundred crowns could have bought the murder of a bishop.

"Five crowns. Madonna! If that's all they could pay, no wonder they got a donkey like you. You're not worth blunting my blade on. Anyway, you're lucky I promised the Pope I'd stay out of trouble and not kill anyone else - at least for a few months."

His dagger flashed in his left hand and cut through the thin leather thong which held the man's drawers up around his waist.

Contemptuously he turned his back on the Corsican, leaving him trying to pull his fallen hose up from around his knees.

—m—

Pier Luigi, when confronted by Benvenuto of course denied all knowledge of the "invitation" which had led him into the ambush. It was left to Pompeo's daughter to continue to try to avenge her father's death.

Digi the pickpocket was instructed to turn informer. He went to the police and told them that he had heard Benvenuto boast of killing Pompeo and that he was hiding in his own shop.

The police, really part of the army, were ignorant soldiers, and knew nothing about proper methods of investigation. They would arrest a suspect, and in the absence of concrete evidence, would simply beat and torture him until he confessed.

The policeman to whom Digi went with his story was the same one who had arrested Benvenuto when he had defied Pope Clement.

The first Benvenuto knew about it was when his door burst open.

"What the hell do you want?" he shouted. "I know you were born in a cave, but haven't you found out how to open a door yet?"

"You are Benvenuto Cellini?" the Sergeant asked.

"You know damn well I am. I asked you what you wanted. I haven't got anything for you to steal this time."

"You're under arrest."

"Arrest? What for?"

"Listen my friend, I'm taking you for murdering Pompeo the Milanese, and while I'm at it, for blasphemy, heresy, larceny, resisting arrest, and anything else I can think of between here and Castel Sant' Angelo. After I've finished charging you, they'll not only hang you, but they'll have to keep your corpse in jail for another fifty years."

Benvenuto laughed. "You're arresting me for murdering Pompeo? Who put you up to this lunacy? Don't you know I've got a safe conduct from the Pope himself? Here, see!"

He took out the document and threw it on the table. The Sergeant picked it up, unfolded it and screwed up his eyes as he looked at it.

"You've got it upside down," Benvenuto jeered. "What's the matter, Emperor Ignoramus the First, can't you read?" He turned on the grinning soldiers. "What about you lot? I suppose none of you can read either, or else they'd make you a Captain."

Benvenuto took command. "You," he said, pointing to the man nearest to him. "Three doors down the road is the house of Marco the Scribe. Bring him here, and quickly. I've no more time to waste on you idiots."

The Sergeant had the grace to look crestfallen when Marco confirmed the contents of the safe conduct to him, but Benvenuto saw he was in half a mind to tear it up.

"My safe conduct, if you don't mind, Sergeant. I can easily get another copy from my friend the Pope!"

The Sergeant threw it on the floor and signalled his men to leave.

"I say, Sergeant, before you go, do you happen to have a silver scudi on you?"

The startled Sergeant took a coin out of his doublet. Benvenuto pocketed it.

"Thank you. That'll pay for the broken lock. Now you only owe me the five crowns you stole last time." He pointed at the door with his thumb. "Give my regards to Digi the Pickpocket," he shouted after the retreating soldiers as they clattered down the stairs.

"Your Eminence," Benvenuto said to Cardinal de' Medici, "my luck can't hold. First they tried to have me murdered and then arrested. The Feast of Our Lady isn't till the end of March. There's plenty of time for Pier Luigi to think up some more unpleasantness for me."

"The Pope's son is far too busy with his own affairs now to bother about you any more, with all due respect," said the Cardinal.

"Well, Pompeo's daughter then, or any of his friends. And da Prato never seems to be too short of time to try to think of ways to get me into trouble."

"Look," the Cardinal said with some exasperation, "I've told you, I can't possibly ask the Pope to give you an earlier decision, and he wouldn't if I did. The best I can do for you is to tell him I've given you permission to leave the city until Lady Day."

"I suppose another exile is better than the cemetery."

"You're learning, at last. Now mark this, you had better make sure that I know exactly where you are, and if I do tell you to come back, I don't want any of your arrogant nonsense that you'll come when you're ready. You'll get the fastest horse you can find and ride it till it drops, and when you get to wherever you're told to report, you'll be there two hours ahead of time. Understood?"

"Yes, your Eminence," Benvenuto said meekly.

"And if I don't send for you sooner, I'll see you at 8 o'clock in the morning on Lady Day. What time are you to be here?"

"Eight o'clock, Lady Day."

"No, you fool! Don't you ever listen? You'll be here at six. Two hours ahead of time."

Benvenuto's newest exile was not a happy one. First he went to Ferrara and then to Venice, all the time watching while his small supply of money dwindled away.

He did manage to eke it out with an odd commission here and there, but nothing really profitable. Even when he managed to earn a fee, he had to share it with whichever Master Goldsmith had sub-contracted it to him or who had given him workshop facilities.

It was therefore with some relief when it was at last time for him to make his way back to Rome to keep his appointment with the Cardinal and the Pope.

Perhaps he would not have been so relieved if he had known what was still in store for him when he got back....

-22-

On Cardinal de' Medici's instructions, Benvenuto presented himself immediately after Matins on Lady Day to the Chief Magistrate, Gabriello Ceserino.

In the room with Ceserino was the hated Police Sergeant, and, standing against the wall, four other soldiers. Ceserino pretended to study a document on the table. The Magistrate signed the parchment with a great flourish, shook some sand onto the wet ink, threw the pen down, and leaning back in his chair stared at Benvenuto, and then nodded at the Sergeant, who took Benvenuto's sword and dagger.

"So you're here at last," Ceserino said. "Benvenuto Cellini, you are here to answer a charge of murder. You will wait until you are sent for. Show him where, Sergeant."

"Hup!" The Sergeant gave a sort of bark and the four soldiers fell in behind and in front of Benvenuto.

"Hup!" Again the bark, and the soldiers stepped off, the rear two barging into Benvenuto when he did not move with them, making him stumble.

They climbed several flights of winding stairs and along the corridor to the farthest room on the top floor. It had a thick door which opened outwards. In place of a lock there was a long bar which fitted into slots on either side. On the inside there was not even a handle.

The Sergeant held the door open, and with his hand held across his stomach, bowed low and said, "Illustrissimo, pray condescend to enter your suite."

As Benvenuto took a pace forward, the Sergeant gave him a push in the small of his back which sent him staggering. The door slammed shut behind him, and Benvenuto heard the bar swinging into place.

He looked around the room. It had a wooden floor, bare stone walls and a small barred window set near the ceiling. The only furniture was a table and a wooden chair.

Benvenuto sat down, but after a few moments stood up again. He went to the door and pushed at it futilely. Then he ran to the window. It was too high to see out of, so he dragged the table beneath it and set the chair on top and climbed up. The chair wobbled dangerously and he had to clutch on to the bars to stop himself from falling.

From far below he could hear the clatter of carts on the cobblestones, the noise of the crowds in the nearby market and even the sound of a band in one of the Lady Day Processions, but he could not see the ground. All that was visible was the roof and upper floors of the building opposite, and even that had its shutters closed against the morning sunlight.

He jumped down and began pacing backwards and forwards across the narrow room, his mind racing with his fears.

"Oh God! Why did I come back? Why did I trust de' Medici? Why didn't I stay safely in Venice? Oh Christ! This time tomorrow I could be dead! Hanging from that terrible gibbet with my feet kicking and my tongue half bitten off."

—⁂—

Time passed. Benvenuto had no idea how long, but the sun grew brighter and the room hotter. Suddenly the door opened and a soldier came in and put a wooden bowl filled with lentils, a pewter mug of water and a spoon on the table. He left without a word, and the door slammed shut again.

Benvenuto looked at the black stew with distaste. Ceserino had paid out for Benvenuto to have a proper meal, but the Sergeant had kept the money and sent up the food being served to the other prisoners.

Benvenuto had no appetite, but for want of something better to do, he swallowed down the peppery mess, and then drank the water in a couple of great gulps. He thought he was going to be sick. Worse still, he felt his bladder was going to burst. What was he going to do about that? He speculatively eyed the empty food bowl, but as if he had read his thoughts, the jailer came back into the room.

"Piss?" he asked. Without waiting for an answer, he turned and walked out of the room and Benvenuto gratefully followed him up a ladder to the flat roof.

The man pointed to the chimney stack. When Benvenuto had finished the man gave a jerk of his head and Benvenuto obediently went back to his cell, absolutely humiliated and degraded, just as it had been intended that he should be.

Before the door of his cell closed, he turned to the jailer. "Can I have some more water?"

"Maybe you'd prefer some white wine?"

"Oh yes please!"

"Well you can't have that either! Do you think this is an inn?" The man cackled with laughter and slammed the door shut.

—m—

More time passed. Benvenuto had measured his cell lengthways and widthways with his feet, toe-to-heel, toe-to-heel. He had counted the floorboards and the tiny panes of glass in the window. He was frantic with worry and boredom.

He emptied out his pouch. Four doubloons, twelve gold crowns, six silver scudi and six copper coins, a tiny pair of pliers, a couple of gouges and his safe conduct.

"Fat lot of good that was," he thought.

He started to play a childish game with the coins. He divided them into two equal piles and began tossing them. Heads went to the right, tails to the left. There were too many coins and it was taking too long for one side to win. Impatiently he put the money back in his purse.

The door of the cell opened again. It was not the jailer this time, but the Sergeant, and behind him the same four soldiers.

"Face the wall, your Excellency."

Benvenuto turned.

"Hands behind your back."

Benvenuto felt his himself being tightly tied at wrists and elbows.

"Downstairs!"

In the street was a covered wagon.

"Inside."

Benvenuto climbed into the back of the wagon, assisted by a sharp push on the rump from the haft of one of the soldier's pikes. The wagon lumbered off.

"Surely they're not going to hang me now? No, they'd let me see a priest first. Anyway, I haven't even had a trial and it's the wrong time of day. But where are we going then, for God's sake?" He could not see out of the canvass screen.

—⚜—

The cart stopped.

"Out." Benvenuto blinked in the bright afternoon sunlight. He was at the Vatican. Passers-by stared curiously as the bound man stumbled up the steps, assisted none too gently by the four soldiers. Benvenuto hung his head, hoping that there was no one about who could recognise him.

They reached the door of the Pope's Audience Chamber.

"Wait." The Sergeant pulled out his dagger and cut the cords. Benvenuto massaged his wrists.

The prisoner and escort entered the room. The Pope was seated on a throne-like chair. At his side, sitting at a small desk, was Tommaso da Prato, smiling wolfishly.

Benvenuto was wheeled round to the right, where he noticed for the first time that Ceserino was also seated at a long table, flanked by four other men whom he took to be magistrates too.

"Benvenuto Cellini," the Chief Magistrate said, "You are accused of the murder of the Milanese, Pompeo Sforza. How do you plead?"

"Sforza," thought Benvenuto. "So that's what his family name was. I never knew. That's what all the fuss is about. They're big noises in Turin. Pompeo came from Milan. He must be a distant relative."

Ceserino broke into his thoughts. "Answer me Messer Cellini. What do you say? You've as good as publicly confessed it already."

"Yes, I killed him," Benvenuto whispered.

"Killed him? That's not what I asked you. You won't quibble if you know what's good for you. Did you have a fight? Was it a duel? Were you defending yourself?"

Benvenuto's mumbled reply was inaudible. Ceserino answered for him.

"So it was murder then. You know the penalty?"

Before Benvenuto could reply, Ceserino went on, "It's hanging, that is unless clemency is granted."

The Magistrate rose and said to the Pope. "Your Holiness, Benvenuto Cellini has freely confessed to the murder of Pompeo Sforza. He has petitioned for mercy. Unless your Holiness is willing to grant him a pardon, it will be our duty to sentence him to death. Your Holiness is aware that a pardon cannot be granted until the criminal has been tried and convicted, which he now has been."

The Pope cleared his throat. "Messer Cellini."

"Face the Holy Father when he is talking to you," da Prato interjected. Benvenuto turned round.

"Messer Cellini, you have committed a murder. It is in your favour that you confessed. We didn't actually hear you, but the Magistrate says you did. It has been said on your behalf that you were temporarily insane. That is no real excuse, but we are going to grant your plea for mercy because so many good people have spoken to us favourably on your behalf, and in view of your past valuable services to the late Pope Clement and to the Holy See in the late war."

Benvenuto let out a long silent breath from between his pursed lips. He felt his knees begin to buckle and he leaned against the Magistrates' table for support.

"However," the Pope continued, "Pier Luigi Farnese advises us that her father's untimely death has left Messer Sforza's daughter with an inadequate dowry. You will therefore pay one thousand crowns compensation."

"One thousand crowns, Your Holiness? Gladly, but I only have about twenty crowns in the world. With this hanging over me..." Benvenuto inwardly shuddered at the word, "...I've not been able to work for months, and before that, due to my regrettable - my unpardonable - difference with Pope Clement, my income had already been substantially reduced."

"We had already anticipated this problem. When Messer da Prato hands you our sealed pardon, he will also give you the order for making the dies for the coins you designed, under the supervision of the Master of the Mint. The fee will go towards the damages, but as that will not be sufficient we shall give you two other important commissions.

The Holy Roman Emperor will be paying a State visit in six weeks' time, on his way back from Tunis. You will design two gifts. A Crucifix for the Empress' Chapel, and a solid gold and jewelled cover for a Book of Offices of Our Lady for King Charles."

"That is a lot of work," da Prato said.

"Yes, thank you Tommaso, for pointing that out," the Pope continued, "however we will tolerate no delay. The dies, the Crucifix and the cover will all be ready in good time. We will accept no excuses. Messer da Prato will make all the necessary arrangements with you."

"I thank Your Holiness for your great mercy and generosity." Benvenuto flung himself at the Pope's feet.

"Alright! Alright!" Paul said. "Now go."

Benvenuto rose and turned to leave.

"Just a moment, Cellini. Not so fast," da Prato said.

Benvenuto's heart sank. "Here, you've forgotten your Pardon!"

Benvenuto's hand trembled as he took the scroll.

—⚏—

When Benvenuto reached the street, the thought struck him: all that horror, all the mental torture he had gone through had just been a pantomime. What had Ceserino said? "A pardon cannot be granted until the criminal has been tried and convicted."

The Pardon had already been prepared and sealed! They'd known all along they were going to let him go, and no one had even given him a hint! The bastards!

His stomach heaved. He leaned against one of the great pillars of St. Peter's and vomited until he was empty. He continued to retch until his ribs and throat were sore and his eyes and nose ran.

-23-

At least Benvenuto was back at work; at least he was able to do something with some prestige to it instead of the petty, tawdry jobs he had been forced to do to eke out the barest of livings during the months of his latest exile. At least he had the chance to rebuild his reputation.

"At least?" he thought. "It's also the most. I'm not going to get paid. I've got months of work to do in just a few weeks. How will I even live in the meantime?"

He rechecked the coins in his purse. "I've got less than twenty crowns to my name."

His tools, those he had not taken with him, and his small stock of finished goods were safe. Raffaello del Moro had taken care of them, but without customers, the goods were worth no more than the value of the gold.

Then there was his shop. Despite having been shuttered for months, it had been vandalised. The furniture had been stolen and the work-benches, the cupboards, the fittings and the very floor boards had been broken up and used as firewood by a gang of tramps who had forced their way in and lived there through the long cold winter.

They had been chased out by an almost berserk Benvenuto at the point of his sword, leaving a horrible mess of rags, bones, and bits of useless rubbish scavenged from the heaps of refuse found in every street in the city.

Benvenuto's gagged at the stench and sight of the piles of filth in the corners of his shop and home.

A few silver coins bought him the labour of a couple of the City's beggars whose hunger did not permit them to be too fastidious, and they cleaned out the worst of the dirt until it was in a fit state for the finishing touches to be put by Gino del Moro and the girl whom Benvenuto quickly hired as a maid.

Then, helped by Raffaello del Moro, he rushed around to get new work-benches, stools, tables, a bed, and cooking utensils. This took the better part of two precious days and a good part of Benvenuto's remaining cash.

"I've got to get some money from somewhere," he told del Moro. "I need some assistants, and I can't pay and feed them on nothing. And I've got to try to look prosperous or I won't be able to get any of my old customers back."

"My dear fellow, if you need some money, why don't you just ask me?" said del Moro.

"I thought that was what I was doing."

"You know, Benvenuto, my Gino's still not married, and neither are you....."

"For God's sake! I want a loan, not a dowry. Besides, you don't really want a son-in-law who seems to be just one jump ahead of the hangman, do you?"

Del Moro looked at Benvenuto thoughtfully and nodded. He pulled out his purse. "How much would you like to borrow?" he said.

—⁂—

Finally, with the help of a new assistant, a plump thirteen year old boy, the son of a local tradesman he took on as an apprentice, he was able to set about repairing his tools, making some new ones, and starting on his three big, important and utterly profitless jobs.

Benvenuto realised that the most important thing for him to do was to produce some results, and quickly. Something he could show the Pope at once.

The dies for the coins! They were the easiest. A few dies, perhaps a dozen, would last the Mint for at least a week, and in the meantime he could get on with the Crucifix.

Making coin dies was no problem. After his last short career working for the Mint, he could do them almost mechanically.

The Crucifix was also easy: he had made dozens of them before. He would design something simple and, above all, quick to make, and yet sufficiently decorative to satisfy the Pope and not affront the dignity of the Emperor who was to receive it. That meant nothing unique, elaborate or original. Just a mixture of the better parts of works he had done before.

—⚏—

Benvenuto worked at a frantic, almost feverish pace on his sketches and the clay model of the Crucifix.

It was to be half a cubit - about eleven inches - high. Its base was circular, about five inches in diameter, rounded like a melon, and Benvenuto intended that it should be enamelled green to represent the Hill of Golgotha, which in his ignorance he thought was grassed over, instead of merely being a rocky prominence.

The Cross would be hollow, and about three-quarters of an inch square, and starkly plain except for some very fine engraving to give just a hint of the grain in the wood.

The thickness of the Cross was actually governed by three little figures that Benvenuto had already made and which he had got with the remains of his stock. He had prepared them for the Chalice that he had started to make for Clement before that job was taken away from him at the beginning of his troubles. Then, the figures were to have been "Faith", "Hope" and "Charity", but now, with the addition of a halo for each, Benvenuto decided they would just as easily symbolise the Three Marys witnessing the Crucifixion.

Christ was not to be shown slumped and dead or dying as was traditional, but with His head thrown back and straining in His agony, at the height of the Passion, at the moment when He cried out to God.

Benvenuto also decided to cast Christ as a solid figure, both to give weight to the piece, and because it would be quicker and less complicated to make than a hollow one. Time, how to save time, was his problem, and after all he was not paying for the gold!

The written description that Benvenuto prepared to accompany the model specified that Christ's halo was to be set with twenty-five tiny diamonds, and those of the three female figures with ten each. These would catch and reflect rays of light from the Altar. Three small rubies at Christ's feet and hands, and five more round his forehead were to indicate the blood from the wounds.

Despite having been cobbled together with ideas from half a dozen or so similar works with a minimum of designing, Benvenuto's natural talent had produced what would be a simple, but powerful, and very acceptable piece.

Accompanied by his apprentice carrying the tall box containing the wax model of the Crucifix, Benvenuto presented himself at the Vatican and asked the Pope's Secretary, Traiano, for an immediate Audience.

"Come this way, Messer Cellini. I'll find out if His Holiness can see you. He's very busy."

He led Benvenuto into the same small, narrow ante-room in which he had been kept waiting on previous occasions. There was just a long wooden bench along one wall under the window and no other furniture at all. A candelabra holding eight candle stumps stood against the opposite wall, at one end of which hung a wooden Crucifix.

At the other end was a painting of Pope Julius II by some unknown, and not very proficient artist. Julius had died in 1513 so the picture was at least twenty-one years old. "More than that," Benvenuto said to himself.

He had seen the gloomy portrait many times, but for want of something to do, he examined it again. Julius was seated on his throne, hands folded on his lap, a large ruby glinting from the Papal ring in the light of some hidden lamp. The Pope's robes, probably once bright and richly embroidered, now seemed dirty with soot, and the paint was flaking in places all over the canvas from neglect and damp.

The room was stifling in the Spring sunshine. Benvenuto crossed to the window. It was nailed shut. He shook it angrily and his apprentice flinched as if he expected someone to rush into the room and punish Benvenuto for this disrespect for the Pope's Palace.

Benvenuto impatiently paced around the room, cracking his knuckles and muttering to himself. He stood for a while at the window with its thick uneven glass which distorted the view so that the crowds and carts seemed to be swimming along the street below. Then he began drawing little vertical lines with his finger on the dust that coated the ledge, but after a few moments he rubbed them out with his palm. He looked with disgust at the dirt on his hand and glanced round for something to clean it on. No curtain; no tapestry-backed chair; nothing.

He wiped his hand on the shoulder of the boy's jerkin and crossed to the candelabra and began digging at the dirty, slippery spots of candle grease on the floor with his heel. They came up at first in curly flakes, then large lumps began to separate from the edges of the pools of wax as their grip on the flagstones broke under Benvenuto's shoe.

Tiring of this useless exercise, and finding his ankle and the calf of his leg were beginning to ache, he had just started to straighten the Crucifix which was hanging lopsidedly on the wall, when the door behind him opened.

Benvenuto swung round. Instead of Traiano, it was Tommaso da Prato. He stared at his enemy as if he had never properly seen him before.

Da Prato was aged about sixty. The upper part of his painfully thin body seemed curiously twisted, with his left shoulder thrown forward of, and higher than the right; his back was bent and stooped from the many hours he had spent hunched over his interminable documents.

The first two long fingers of his right hand were permanently stained black with ink up to the second joint. Another mark of his trade.

Da Prato's wispy iron-grey beard clung to his hatchet face like clumps of grass to a sand dune, and the tufts of hair that sprouted out of the wide cavernous black nostrils beneath his beak-like nose and from his ears were matched by the thick eyebrows framing his sunken, watery, pale blue eyes.

In his threadbare black robe, dusty and almost rusty with age, he suddenly seemed to Benvenuto to resemble the Angel of Death, and it was all that he could do to stop crossing himself.

"What do you want?" both men spoke simultaneously. Then there was silence as they each glared at the other, waiting for a reply. Benvenuto was the first to break.

"I've come to see the Pope."

"What about?"

"Are you the Pope now?" Benvenuto's voice was heavy with sarcasm.

"You know perfectly well who I am."

"Well, if you're not the Pope, what the Hell's it got to do with you what I want to see him about?" Benvenuto's apprentice winced, and wished he could hide somewhere.

"What's it got to do with me? Let me remind you, my murdering friend, that when His Holiness was merciful, if misguided enough to spare your worthless life the other day, he put you in my hands. Do you remember? He's not going to have you crawling up his backside all the time like you did with Clement. So, if you've got business with His Holiness, you can tell me about it or you can clear off. This Pope doesn't deal with tinkers!"

"And I don't deal with underlings" snapped Benvenuto. "I've got the model and drawings of the Emperor's Crucifix here for the Pope to look at. The Pope, not some damned pen-pusher."

"Give them to me."

"Piss off!"

"Very well," da Prato spoke very quietly and menacingly.

"I'll tell His Holiness exactly what you've said. That you refuse to obey his instructions to deal with me. I once told you that your tongue will be long enough to get you hanged in the end. Just make sure you don't trip over it as you leave."

As da Prato turned to go, Benvenuto realised that he was beaten. He had no option but to climb down.

"No wait," he said, and da Prato came back into the room showing his crooked and blackened teeth in what, for him, passed as a smile. It soon changed into a snarl as Benvenuto continued, If His Holiness really wants me to use you as a messenger boy, who am I to argue? He knows what you are best suited for. Here take them. Try not to drop the model, and don't get the drawings dirty with those filthy paws of yours."

He turned to the boy. "You know, his threats don't frighten me. No one frightens me. No one. I'm no coward."

—⁂—

Da Prato returned after a surprisingly short time with the models and the drawings.

"His Holiness says that if this is the best you can manage, he supposes it will have to do."

"He is too kind. What else did he say?"

"He asked how long the cover for the book was going to take, and why you haven't made any progress so far."

"In only one week?" Benvenuto retorted. "Because my work requires planning and designing. I don't spend my time reciting out of books or scribbling rubbish on parchment. And what's more, I don't believe that the Pope said any such thing - but if he wants to help he can pray for me to get some Divine inspiration. Even a genius like me needs it. Now, I'll ask you again, what else did the Pope say?"

"What would you have liked him to have said?"

"Well, for example, how about, 'Give that great artist, Messer Cellini, the two hundred crown's worth of gold, and the fifty-five small diamonds and eight small rubies that he needs to make the piece'?"

"Oh, that's what you wanted him to say?"

"Yes, that," said Benvenuto. "The Pope may be generous enough to give expensive presents to Emperors, but I can't afford to pay for them for him."

"Here." Da Prato took a small twist of cloth and a heavy leather bag from the folds of his robes. "These are the stones, and here is the gold. I'd like a receipt, please. You know all about receipts, don't you?"

"Well in that case you won't mind if I count the money first," Benvenuto replied, unceremoniously brushing his apprentice off the bench as he spoke.

He emptied the money from the sack and began arranging it in piles. "I can't be too careful, especially with your friend Pompeo not being here to bribe you anymore, you must be a bit short of cash these days."

"How dare you!" da Prato shouted. "How dare you! I'll..."

"Oh do be quiet, there's a good fellow," said Benvenuto.

"You've made me lose count. Now I'll have to start all over again."

Da Prato waited impatiently while Benvenuto first played with the little heaps of coins and then signed the receipt with a crayon he took from his pouch, because the Pope's Chamberlain had forgotten to bring an ink horn and pen with him.

Da Prato snatched the paper angrily. "Don't forget what I told you - shopkeeper!"

He placed the thumb and forefinger of his hand round his throat and threw his head over his shoulder in a pantomime of a hanging.

Benvenuto's response was an age old, timeless obscene gesture with the upraised middle finger of his right hand, but it was lost on da Prato's retreating, unseeing back.

As Benvenuto left the Vatican, he paused at the pillar he had vomited through fear and relief at his reprieve just eight days before. The buzzing flies had long since gone, but the dark stains and the dried remains of the lentils were still there. It would take a good few rain storms to remove this reminder of his greatest humiliation.

He looked up at his apprentice.

"Well, what's so funny then?" he said to the bewildered boy and aimed a kick at his fat rump that sent him staggering and tripping down the stairs, desperately trying to avoid falling and dropping the model, or even worse falling on it and crushing it flat.

If he could not afford trained assistants, he could at least pay for components to be made by other craftsmen and hope that the Pope's book-keepers would either not notice, or at least let it pass. But who would help him?

Benvenuto looked up and stopped in his tracks. He was outside the shop of his friend, Raffaello del Moro. He whistled to the boy to come back and went in.

Del Moro agreed to have one of his men make Benvenuto an iron-work furnace and brushed aside any question of payment. What was it? A few bars of iron, and one or two hours work from a labourer. It was the least he could do to help a neighbour. Was there anything else?

Actually there was. Benvenuto also needed three very thin sheets of gold with which to make the cover of the book. Two would have to be about five inches by three, and the other one would have to be five inches by one; they all would have to be a perfect sixty-fourth of an inch thick. These plates were larger and thicker than were required for the finished cover, but the extra gold would be taken up by the raised figures and rich decorations that Benvenuto was already planning.

This time, it was not just a question of repaying del Moro for the gold. The beating out of these smooth plates was a long and skilled job. Del Moro, or one of his craftsmen would have to do it, and despite their friendship Benvenuto would have to pay for the labour involved. He could only hope that del Moro would be generous so he could get the cost past the scrutiny of the Vatican auditors.

―∿―

Benvenuto spent the afternoon instructing del Moro about the gold sheets and negotiating the price. Then del Moro insisted on his staying to seal the deal with some wine and sweet cakes, "just made by Gina."

It was almost dark when Benvenuto at last got back to his own workshop. Late or not, he was determined to begin work right away. He would get a supply of dies ready for the Mint. With that tedious job out of the way, he could make a clear start at moulding the Crucifix first thing in the morning.

Moulding the Crucifix! Benvenuto hastily scrabbled through cupboards and drawers. He had no casting boxes in which to make the moulds. Of course not!

Those damned tramps must have burned them! He quickly sketched out the dimensions of the few simple wooden trays that he needed, and sent the boy to the nearby carpenter's shop.

"Tell the man they must be ready by sunrise. And you hurry back" he yelled after the boy as he scampered up the road. "We've work to do before bed time."

Now he could get on with the dies. He laid out his tools on the bench, lit the charcoal furnace and set two of the steel blanks on it to soften.

Benvenuto had specially made the tools for these coins; every part of the design had its own shaped cutter. He did not believe in making the dies freehand with chisels or graves because he wanted every die to be identical. Not only did that make forgery harder, but it was also the secret of his speed in die making.

When he had last worked for the Mint he used to make nine sets of dies every morning. Now he would make at least a dozen before bed! And he'd cheat a bit too! He would make two upper dies to each lower one since the bottom ones took less wear and lasted longer. Thank goodness it was dies for gold coins and not silver or worse still copper. They would strike far fewer coins and use the dies even longer, especially as the new Pope couldn't afford much new gold coinage anyway. With luck, twelve dies would last a week or even ten days.

The door of the workroom opened and the maid poked her head in.

"Well, what the hell do you want?" he shouted. "Can't you see I'm busy?"

"It's your supper, Master. I just wondered when you want it."

Benvenuto snorted. "Supper, ha! I've got no time to eat supper. The Pope's eating supper. Da Prato's eating supper, may he choke on it! I'm just a slave. Slaves don't eat supper. Just bring me candles. Lots and lots of candles. I've got to work half the night. I must see what I'm doing."

He took the first softened piece of steel and bent over his work.

—⚒—

After three-quarters of an hour he paused to stretch his arms, straighten his back and rub his eyes. Now that the tapping of his little hammer had stopped, he could hear the sounds from the kitchen. The rattle of pewter plates, and giggling and laughing from the maid and the boy.

"Damn sauce! I'm here working by myself, and they're guzzling and enjoying themselves. What the hell am I paying them for?"

"Mario! Claudio! Whatever your stupid name is...." Benvenuto always had trouble in remembering the names of his never ending procession of apprentices and assistants, and he would call them by anything that came into his head. As he rarely used the same name twice, when he had a full staff no one could be sure who he was talking to, and he would then fly into a rage when the right one did not answer.

"Frederico! Can't you hear me damn it? Come in here! At once!" The boy whose name was really Busbacca sheepishly shuffled into the workshop.

"Ah, there you are at last." Benvenuto's voice was deceptively mild "I trust you had an enjoyable supper."

"Oh yes, Messer Cellini, it was very nice, there was chicken and..."

"Well now you can bloody well help me with my work. That's what you're here for!"

Benvenuto pointed towards the coin blanks. "Get some more charcoal. Keep the furnace going. Put two more blanks on the gridiron. Heat them. Don't let them get too hot."

Busbacca nodded his head like a demented puppet at each order, and as he turned to obey them, Benvenuto added, "Oh, and sharpen up those punches and matrices. They're blunter than... blunter than...." Benvenuto could not think of a simile and his voice lapsed into a mumble as he went back to tapping on the next die.

The maid crept back into the room and put a plate and a mug down on the bench next to Benvenuto. Two chicken drumsticks, a hunk of bread and an apple. The mug was filled with milk.

Benvenuto looked at the girl and said, with unusual gentleness, "Thanks. Thanks a lot. Now get off to bed. Go to sleep. I'll be here quite a while yet."

—⁓—

Two more hours. Now there were four top dies and two bottom dies lying in their little wooden boxes. Half the job was done.

The boy's shoes were slapping the floor as he went backwards and forward, flatfooted with exhaustion, and he was nearly crying, he was so tired.

"You don't know what work is," Benvenuto said cheerfully. "When I was an apprentice, I never set foot in bed for nearly three years! Come on, Alfonso, let me have another blank."

He leaned over to pick up the piece of metal that Busbacca had scooped up with a trowel from the tray over the furnace. He dropped it on the bench with a curse.

"Christ Almighty, boy! I told you to warm it up, not bloody well melt it. Give me another one. And for God's sake stop that snivelling! I'm just as tired as you are. Just make up your mind to it, we won't be finished for another two hours - three if you don't get a move on. Here, sharpen up these punches, and put some more charcoal on the furnace."

—⚬—

While Benvenuto worked on the last die, Busbacca sat on the floor, legs spread out and his back against the wall. His eyes gradually closed and he dozed through the tapping of Benvenuto's little hammer.

And then it was done.

Benvenuto put the final metal disk into its box, stood up, stretched and yawned emitting a loud mooing sound, and gulped down the last of the milk.

He walked over to the boy and gently nudged him in the ribs with the toe of his shoe.

"Come on, sonny. It's finished. Douse the furnace, we don't want to suffocate while we're asleep, do we? Blow out the candles and then you can go to bed. You can have a lie-in in the morning..... 'til sunrise!"

Laughing at his own joke, he walked shakily to his room holding his hand on the wall to steady himself as he went.

-24-

Benvenuto woke well before daybreak. He was still tired and did not know what had disturbed him. Then he heard it again: from the kitchen was coming the ferocious clatter and rattle of pots and the sound of someone energetically cleaning out the stove.

He struggled out of bed, crossed to the night stand, and with the tips of his fingers, he splashed a few drops of tepid, dusty water on his face. Not to wash - that was not a daily ritual in those days - but to get rid of the cobwebs. His head still ached and his mouth was gummy with mucus. He opened the window, hawked, and spat out into the street, wiping his mouth with the back of his hand.

He put on his shirt, leaving the tails flapping loose outside his doublet, stuck his feet into his shoes without bothering to pull them over his heels and shuffled into the kitchen.

The maid, black under the eyes, and hair dishevelled set a pewter plate and mug of watered wine in front of him as he sat down. She said nothing but dropped a round loaf of bread on the table and a plate with some white cheese, sweaty and crusted with yellow at the edges from yesterday's heat. Benvenuto broke off a piece of the bread. It was stale.

"Oh well, it's too early to expect any fresh food," he said, dunking his bread in the wine to soften it. "Go and wake the boy."

—☞—

Busbacca stood in the kitchen doorway, rubbing the sleep from his eyes.

"Ah, Good morning young man! I hope you are refreshed and invigorated after a sound night's sleep! Are you ready for another day's work?"

"No Messer Cellini, not really. I'm still very tired."

"Too tired to eat right now, I suppose?"

"Yes, Master."

"Good, well in that case you can skip your breakfast. It's not fit to eat anyway." Benvenuto glanced at the girl. "Now here's what you have to do. First you'll go to the carpenter and get the moulding boxes. Come straight back here with them, I need them right away. Then you'll go to the Mint with one set of dies."

"Why only one set, Master?"

"We won't tell them there's any more ready; maybe they'll be a bit more careful with them and make them last longer.

Make them give you a receipt. I'll get it ready for you. Now shut up and don't interrupt me again, I'm not finished yet. Where was I?"

He tapped his lips with his finger. "Oh yes, on your way back from the Mint, call in at the blacksmith. I want a pair of shears for cutting up coins. He knows what I mean. Also ask him for a sack of charcoal. Tell him I'll pay him later. The carpenter too. Lastly, call in at del Moro's and collect the furnace. Is that all clear? Off you go then."

The boy scampered towards the door but pulled up short when Benvenuto called to him again, "By the way, when you get back, I want to see you sweating and out of breath! Understand? Now, RUN!"

The girl had been standing, hands on hips, smiling as she watched Busbacca's mouth open wider and wider as if he was trying to catch Benvenuto's stream of orders in it.

Benvenuto turned towards her. "And as for you, see there's something decent to eat at noon. The next time you serve me rubbish like this, you'll find yourself back on the farm, milking the pigs or whatever it was you did there!"

He swept the dishes and food from the table with his arm as he stamped off into the workroom, slamming the door shut behind him.

—⚬—

By the time the boy returned to the workshop for the first time, Benvenuto had scribbled out the receipt for the Master of the Mint to sign and had carefully wrapped one lower and two upper coin dies in separate pieces of cloth and packed them into a box.

He had separated the base of the model of the Crucifix, which was slightly larger than the finished piece was intended to be to allow for the fact that the metal would contract on cooling.

He was just carefully splitting the Cross itself into two vertical halves with the aid of a hot wire when the boy came in.

"I've got the casting boxes, Master."

After a few moments when he had finished cutting through the wax, Benvenuto put the two pieces on the bench very carefully and looked up.

"Maybe you'd like me to give you a pat on the back?"

"No, sir."

"What about a kick up the arse then?"

"No."

"Well get off to the Mint then, for God's sake!" Benvenuto roared. As the boy turned to the door, Benvenuto could not resist calling him back again.

"And don't forget! Hurry back, sweating and out of breath."

—⚬—

Benvenuto prepared a mixture of sand and Fuller's Earth. He rammed it tightly around the bottoms of the vertically split patterns of the parts of the Crucifix as they lay in the casting boxes and sprinkled some fine, very dry sand over the surface to enable the casts to be easily divided in two.

Then he placed the upper halves on top and surrounded them with the same mixture, reinforcing it this time with thin metal bars laid across the width of each box.

Now he had to open the moulds again, remove the wax patterns gently, so as not to disturb the impression of the Crucifix in the sand, and add funnels into which the molten metal would run, and vent holes through which the hot gases could escape.

Finally, before he clamped the moulds shut and weighted them down, Benvenuto inserted and pinned in place the "core", a piece of hardened clay, the same shape as the pattern but marginally thinner than the outside. It was in the cavity between the core and the outer sand impression that the hollow shell of metal would be formed.

Very carefully he placed the casting boxes over the top of the cooking stove to help the sand to harden and dry.

"Don't touch them," he warned the girl. "Don't even look in their direction. If they get damaged, kill yourself at once. Don't just run away, because I'll find you wherever you are...."

Her fingers tightened around her broom handle, but as she looked up, eyes flashing, she saw Benvenuto was grinning again. She turned her head away so as not to let him see her smiling back.

"Master, I'm here!" It was Busbacca, clutching in his fat arms a large sack of charcoal, with the new furnace perched on top, held in place by his chin. There was a red weal where the iron had dug into his pudgy skin, and a large pair of shears was tucked into his belt, the points of which had scratched his legs as he hurried home.

Benvenuto pretended to inspect the boy.

"Sweating?"

"Yes Master!"

"Out of breath?"

"Oh yes Master! I ran all the way and it was so heavy!"

"Good for you. Now we'll get some real work done. You've been having it too easy so far.....!"

The new furnace had been lit and while Busbacca fanned the charcoal to red heat, Benvenuto snipped the gold coins into shavings so they would melt more quickly in the crucible and poured the liquid metal into the sand moulds. When the parts cooled, Benvenuto would fit them together and smooth out the joins.

The small figure of Christ was to be solid in three quarters relief. He had already made a little cast of the wax model out of plaster of Paris - Benvenuto called it "gesso" - mixed with two parts of brick dust. Then, having reinforced the moulding with fine wire and coated it with more plaster, he melted out the wax and poured in the gold in its place.

Now it was only a question of time while the gold hardened, then the figures of Christ and the ready-made three Marys could be soldered to the Crucifix, the jewels set, the base enamelled and the piece would be finished.

But time was what could not be spared, so while the boy quenched the furnace, Benvenuto began to sketch the designs for the book cover he had been planning in his mind while his hands had been busy on mechanical jobs in the past few days; then he added the description in his pointed handwriting.

While the pen was still in his hand, he also wrote a letter to the Pope.

"Benvenuto Cellini, Master Goldsmith presents his humble duty to the Holy Father and begs to inform him that the Crucifix that His Holiness graciously commissioned for Her Majesty, Queen Isobella of Portugal, the Holy Roman Empress, is completed.

In accordance with the recognised custom, he respectfully requests the honour of an Audience so that he may witness the acceptance of the work and its consecration into the service of the Church.

Benvenuto Cellini will also seek the opportunity to submit the designs he proposes for the Breviary Cover that His Holiness has commanded him to execute for His Majesty, King Charles V, in the hope that His Holiness may find it convenient to signify his approval thereof in person, rather than through an intermediary.

As His Holiness' most dutiful and obedient subject, a favourable reply is most earnestly solicited."

The barb was in the tail, and the Pope smiled in his beard as he read it. "Rather than through an intermediary." It's a wonder that he didn't say, "through some people."

He scrawled across the bottom of the letter, *"Tomorrow at 11 O'clock."*

Benvenuto arrived at the Vatican in good time, dressed in his best black velvet doublet, new black hose, a fine white linen shirt and with his cloak held in place by a large pair of enamelled gold clasps linked by a heavy gold chain.

He had skirted the Castel Sant' Angelo by the Piazza Pia, turning left into the Borgo Sant' Angelo where he had wreaked such havoc amongst the Spaniards with the cannon during the Sack, and stood for a moment staring at the Via dei Corridori bordering the fortified passage through which Clement had escaped from the Vatican to the Castle.

"Was it as long as eight years ago," he thought. "God, how the time is rushing by and I'm still getting nowhere."

He turned right into the Via de Porta Angelica, passing by the works on the new Basilica of St. Peter's.

"Look at it," he said to Busbacca. "They've been working on it for twenty eight years already, and it's no nearer to being finished than when they started."

Now they turned into the Via Leone, sharp left into the Viale Vaticano, and a few minutes before the hour he slipped through the Palace door, averting his eyes from the column where he had disgraced himself a few weeks before. He surreptitiously made the sign against the Evil Eye and mentally vowed never to look in that direction again.

They were ushered into the familiar dingy ante room and settled down for the usual long wait. But not this time. Promptly at 11 o'clock, the secretary, Traiano, came in and led them into the Pope's presence.

To Benvenuto's disappointment, once again the usual crowd of courtiers was absent. Just Cardinal de' Medici and an old customer, Cardinal d'Este of Ferrara. And of course the hated da Prato.

"Thank God for a couple of friendly faces," he muttered to Traiano as he waited for the signal to approach the Pope.

"Well Messer Cellini, have you finished your tasks?"

"Not all of them, Your Holiness. I have supplied your Mint with dies for the new coinage…"

"Yes, we have heard how you keep them waiting from hand to mouth for each new set."

Benvenuto pretended that he had not heard.

"….. and whilst making the dies, I have finished the Crucifix. Will Your Holiness deign to inspect it?"

Without waiting for a reply, he flicked his hand at Busbacca who came forward with the casket. Normally this would have been made in Benvenuto's own workshop, but with no assistants he had bought it. He winced at the crimson velvet interior which clashed with the wine-coloured heavily-gilded exterior. No matter, it was the contents which counted.

Paul took the Crucifix by the tip of one forefinger at the top of the Cross and the tip of the other under the enamelled base. He held it out at arm's length and stared at it for almost a minute, then he set it down on the table and slowly turned it round and round as he carefully inspected it from every angle.

Finally, he crossed himself and knelt before the figure and bowed his head for a moment in prayer. Rising, he turned and faced Benvenuto.

"Yes, Messer Cellini, it is quite satisfactory." Faint praise indeed. "And now perhaps you will tell us your plans for the Breviary."

Again Benvenuto signalled to Busbacca who handed him a tube of parchment tied with ribbon.

"With Your Holiness' permission." Benvenuto unrolled the skin and laid his sheets of drawings and notes on the table.

The front cover would have allegorical figures, one in each corner, and a fountain with five bathers. They would be shown in a garden depicted by rich foliage and flowers, all worked in heavy bas-relief.

On the corners of the back cover, he had put four more allegorical figures connected by heavy garlands of leaves and flowers. For the centre panel he had chosen the theme, "Birth of Eve in the Garden of Eden", which he surrounded with a wreath on top of which he mischievously he put a Florentine Lily.

The spine of the book, with five horizontal rings would be decorated with daisies matching those on the covers.

On the top edge of the covers he would provide ornamented gold loops through which ribbons would pass to tie the prayer book to its owner's belt while he was in procession, and the book would be held closed by a pair of heavily decorated gold clasps.

Lastly, to bring out the beauty of the strongly embossed figures, Benvenuto proposed to use a combination of coloured enamels.

The Pope studied the half-dozen sheets of sketches and notes in silence for about ten minutes, then he started to hum to himself as he re-read the specification from the beginning. When he finally straightened up and looked at Benvenuto, he was actually smiling.

"Congratulations, Master Goldsmith. This is very beautiful, very rich, but tell me where are the jewels?"

"The jewels are in your Holiness' Treasury. I can add as many as it may please you to give me. Small stones, diamonds to go in the centre of the flowers and the Lily; emeralds and sapphires for the clasps and rubies for the rings."

"This is a very elaborate piece of work. It will of course be ready in three weeks, in time for the Emperor's visit." It was really a question, not a statement.

"Unhappily, no, Your Holiness."

"What! Everything was to have been done in good time. Have you forgotten what we commanded you?"

"No, Holy Father, believe me, I haven't forgotten, far from it. But ….."

"No buts!" the Pope barked. "Haven't you learned your lesson yet.?"

"No Your Holiness, I mean yes," Benvenuto stammered. "Your Holiness set me an impossible task. It isn't just that the work is delicate and complicated. It's also the amount of time that's been wasted."

"Wasted? How?"

"I'm not complaining about the four hours Messer da Prato kept me waiting before he approved the design of the Crucifix and gave me the materials."

The Pope gave da Prato a puzzled look.

"Doubtless he was engaged on important matters of State," Benvenuto said magnanimously. "Besides my apprentice and I made up for it by working through the night." He laid his hand on his breast as a gesture of humble submission to Fate.

"The real waste of time is because if you won't pay me, I can't afford an assistant." He counted on his fingers. "I had to spend three hours making the sand moulds and the casting of the Christ; another three melting the gold; two hours joining the parts and fettling the seams. I even took an hour fitting out the casket. That's a whole day's work on its own that an assistant could have done. Shall I go on?"

"No, we understand. Are you saying that if we allow you something for an assistant, you can still be ready in three weeks?"

"No, Your Holiness, I fear not. Too much time has been lost already, which I can never get back. All I can promise is that with money to pay a skilled assistant instead of an untrained apprentice…" he glared at Busbacca as if it was his fault, "…I could be much more advanced by the time the Emperor comes."

"What would you have ready?"

"The front cover would be done; the design of the back would be etched; the clasps would be finished and the spine and the loops at least started."

"Ten ducats."

"I beg the Holy Father's pardon?"

"You can have ten gold ducats for general expenses over the cost of materials. And you'll keep the Mint supplied with dies too. We are very disappointed at the way you've let us down after the chance we gave you. Messer da Prato see to the money at once. At once."

The Pope turned on his heel and abruptly left the room.

Benvenuto was able to make more rapid progress on the Breviary now that he had secured the services of a new assistant, a tall thin youth of nineteen called Ascanio who did have the advantage, so far as Benvenuto was concerned, of having finished his apprenticeship and of having a few customers of his own, so that he could not only help with the work, but also was bringing in a little income into the workshop.

The book cover was still far from complete when the Emperor Charles V and all his vast entourage of servants and courtiers, not to mention his large personal bodyguard, arrived in Rome to be entertained by the Pope.

The Emperor had come as part of the complicated politics of the sixteenth century, with its kaleidoscope of constantly changing alliances and enmities. It was a world where diplomatic pressure was discreetly applied by anything from a lavish gift, to a carefully contrived marriage and where a new power position could be established by the promotion of the supporter of a Head of State by the Ruler of another, or conversely by the demotion or even the imprisonment of the same supporter, or as in this case, by a State visit.

Charles V was returning from Tunis which his army had recently captured from the Moslems, so that despite his implication in the Sack of Rome, he was still regarded as the Champion of Christianity.

When he came to Rome, Charles was once more at war with the King of France, Francis I, who by now was married to Charles' sister, Eleanor.

The machinations of Francis I had even involved him in sheltering the Turkish pirate, the infamous Barbarossa, in Toulon Harbour after forays against Charles' merchant fleet.

Worse still, Francis had reneged on the Treaty of Cambrai which had ended the last war, and by which Francis had specifically given up his claims to Italy. However, the marriage of Francis' eldest son, Henry, to Catherine de' Medici was a subtle signal that Francis was reviving his Italian aspirations.

When Fransesco Sforza, the Duke of Milan and the Emperor's puppet ruler died, Francis demanded his "rights", but Charles rebuffed him by refusing to let either a Medici or a member of Francis' family, the Valois, to inherit the vacant Throne.

So while the Emperor and his armies were engaged in Africa, Francis I seized the opportunity to join in a local war between the Swiss and the pro-French Duke of Savoy whose territory included Milan and the Northern Italian State of Piedmont. In March 1536, without even bothering to look for a pretext to take sides, the French troops invaded and occupied both Savoy and Piedmont.

Charles was so incensed at this treachery that he offered to meet Francis in personal combat, a proposal made in all seriousness, but which was treated with derision by the astonished rulers and ministers of Europe.

So now Charles V was in Rome, attempting to involve the Pope. He remained there for three months, and the exaggerated courtesies of diplomacy, and the elaborate rituals of the Court masked the bitterness of the private negotiations in which the Pope remained obdurate and unmoved.

Part of this charade was the exchange of ostentatious and costly gifts as tokens of what was really non-existent regard and esteem. That was why the Pope was anxious that both the Crucifix and the Breviary should be ready, and why he was so put out that the book cover was only partly finished by the time the ceremonials began. It was as if the Pope seriously hoped that he could placate the Emperor with a few baubles in place of an army.

When Benvenuto received an invitation to a banquet at the Vatican, he really believed that his luck had changed at last and that he was once more in favour with the Pope; that he could expect a flow of prestigious commissions from influential members of the Court and the rich merchants and bankers who invariably followed them. He was even optimistic enough to move his see-saw so that the model of himself was again up.

He looked through his meagre wardrobe with distaste. Everything was threadbare.

"Nearly thirty-seven years old and not a damn thing to my name. When am I going to get some real money? Get it and keep it?"

He went back into the workshop.

"Ascanio, I can't possibly dine with the Pope and the Holy Roman Emperor in the rags I've got. Show me what you have."

Before Benvenuto employed him, Ascanio had been apprenticed to another goldsmith who was something of a dandy and who had given him a parting gift of a trunk of splendid, hardly-worn clothes.

Ascanio was as thin as the boy Busbacca was fat. His height and build was almost identical to Benvenuto's.

Benvenuto picked a pair of white pantaloons, puffed and tied with silk ribbons at the knees above white stockings, and a boat-necked over-shirt of voile with white and crimson four-inch stripes to the waist with its skirt and hem falling to the knee in white pleats embroidered with thin gold thread. The leg-of-mutton sleeves, also with crimson and white stripes slashed with gold ribbon knots were caught at the wrist with lace frills.

To complete the outfit, Benvenuto selected a black velvet cape, richly decorated with gold scrolls and whorls and a matching flat hat with its high brim also trimmed with the same lace as the shirt. It was an elegant, almost dazzling costume.

Unfortunately, Benvenuto's feet were too big to cram into Ascanio's shoes, so he would have to make do with his own old black pair. He decided that he would have to do something about the scuff marks. He quickly sketched a large, simple buckle.

"Come on Ascanio, we'll make a pair of these in silver.

You do one and I'll do the other, but let's get moving, we've only got a couple of hours."

Benvenuto set out for the Vatican in the early afternoon, with his hair combed, beard trimmed and even freshly bathed and perfumed, and carrying a little velvet bag which held the Emperor's partly finished Breviary which he had been instructed to bring with him.

—⚜—

The Vatican Palace was not really suited for the giving of State Banquets, and the site chosen was the largest room of the Borgia Apartments.

The Imperial party entered the Palace by the **Sala dei Paramenti,** and the Pope took them to see the ceiling of the Sistine Chapel, Michelangelo's masterpiece, which he had spent over four years painting while lying on his back, covering the ten thousand square feet with fresco while paint steadily dripped into his eyes. Michelangelo had only recently started his new great work in the Chapel – "The Last Judgment" - but this was hidden behind screens, and the fiery artist would allow no one - and that included the Pope and the Holy Roman Emperor - to look at it.

From the Sistine Chapel, the Pope conducted the Emperor and Empress back through the **Cortile di Sentinello,** the sentries being members of the Papal Swiss Guard, and into the Borgia Apartments themselves. The six rooms had been decorated by

Alexander VI, the second of the Borgia popes after his succession in 1492.

As the procession of Pope, Emperor, Empress, Princes and Cardinals proceeded through the first five rooms of the Apartments, they paused briefly at the beautiful frescoes: the "Room of the Sybils", with its little door leading to the Raphael Rooms above; the "Room of the Apostles", depicting the scrolls upon which they composed the Screed; and the "Room of Liberal Arts and Sciences" which had been Alexander's own Study.

At last Charles and Pope Paul entered the **Sala dei Pontifico,** the ceiling of which had once collapsed, nearly killing Alexander. It had been rebuilt for Leo X and decorated with stucco and fresco, and its walls covered with Flemish tapestries. It was used as the Cardinals' dining room when they were locked incommunicado at the time of electing a new Pope.

After Pope Alexander VI's death, the Borgia Apartments had gradually fallen into disuse because of the superstitions arising from their sinister connections, particularly with Alexander's notorious children, Caesare and Lucrezia Borgia, but the neglected Borgia Apartments had been dusted and cleaned up in honour of the State Visit, and the dining room was brilliantly lit with hundreds of candles and decorated with a profusion of flowers.

There was a long table to the right of the entrance, with eight shorter sprigs extending at right angles across width of the room like the teeth of a comb. Individual chairs were set behind the high table, but the other two hundred and fifty guests sat crammed shoulder to shoulder on wooden benches on either side of the sprigs. There was barely enough room between the rows of tables for servants to pass with food and wine.

In those days one's social station was indicated by how close one sat to the top table. To his dismay, Benvenuto found he was placed near the bottom of the left hand sprig, and on the inside position to boot, so that he had his back to nearly everyone in the room. He could only see the Pope and the

Emperor by peering past his neighbour, a fat cleric with a pasty face, already beaded with sweat and whose garlic-laden breath made Benvenuto flinch.

The man had a few wisps of gingery hair brushed sideways across the middle of his freckled head, dividing it into two, like a dome-shaped pair of buttocks. The pungent smell exuding from him made Benvenuto think that even in those far-from-sanitary days, the priest's last contact with water must have been at his baptism.

With a sigh of resignation, Benvenuto glanced at the priests and minor officials with whom he was seated, and then craned his neck round to see who else was there. Seated near the top was Michelangelo with his pupil George Vasari. The sculptor inclined his head in greeting as his eyes caught Benvenuto's.

Across the room, discreetly away from Michelangelo, was Antonio da Sangallo, the architect of St. Peter's. Next to him was Baccio Bandinelli, the great old man's hated rival who taken sides against Benvenuto at the beginning of the feud with da Prato and Pompeo. Benvenuto glared at Bandinelli balefully, but he never even noticed.

Amongst the dignitaries were of course Pier Luigi, the Pope's illegitimate son, other members of the Farnese and de' Medici, Colonna and Chigi families, with Cardinals and members of Charles' own Court.

The procession entered, and all the guests stood uncomfortably with the benches pressing into the backs of their half-bent knees, while the Pope pronounced a long benediction, totally inaudible to all but those nearest to him.

—⁂—

The menu had been carefully chosen. Not so lavish as to impress the visitors with the Pope's wealth - he would want to argue that apart from other considerations, he could not afford to join in the war - but yet not so mean as to be insulting to the distinguished guests. Members of the Swiss Guard would act as waiters, except on the top table which would be stewarded by the Pope's own personal servants.

The first course was **cacciucco:** a spicy fish stew, served in bowls which the common guests had to pass up the length of the tables. When this was cleared away, great platters of different roasts were placed at intervals along the tables; roasts of beef, of veal, and of pork. Benvenuto found himself faced with a dish piled high with baby chickens. He helped himself to one.

When the platter was nearly empty, it was replaced with a great lump of beef from which Benvenuto and his neighbours hacked jagged pieces with their daggers.

There were no speeches. They would never have been heard in all the vast hubbub of conversation and the clatter of metal plates. Instead, the Pope and Charles' top table guests pledged each other with shouted toasts in goblets of Trebbiano supplied from flagons that were refilled as fast as they were emptied.

Benvenuto helped himself to some chops and a few spoonfuls of **piselli** - peas.

When the meat course was finished, Benvenuto grunted in satisfaction. He had not eaten and drunk so well, or so much, for a long time. He surreptitiously wiped his greasy fingers on the skirt of the priest's cassock as the dishes were cleared away ready for the fruit and the slabs of **straccino**, the soft white cheese he loved so much.

All through the meal different groups of musicians and soloists played on harps, lutes and mandolins, more or less to no effect because of the din going on around them.

From time to time the Chamberlain, Tommaso da Prato, pushed his way up and down the aisles between the tables, squeezing past waiters and dodging performers as he approached one or other of the guests and summoned him to the three high-backed thrones on which the Pope and Charles and the Empress were seated. A brief introduction, a conversation that varied from terse to brief, depending on who it was, and then the guest was dismissed to make way for another, who, by then da Prato would have located and brought for his audience.

—∞—

Suddenly, Benvenuto felt a tap on his shoulder from da Prato's ceremonial wand. He looked up.

"Come on, you. And bring the book cover with you."

He turned on his heel and left Benvenuto to scramble to his feet and awkwardly clamber backwards over the bench, holding on the shoulders of his two neighbours for support and taking the opportunity to wipe his fingers clean again as he did so.

He hurried after da Prato as he led the way round the edge of the room and waited for the sign to approach the Pope.

Paul looked up. "Ah, Messer Cellini, there you are. If we remember rightly, you were first trained as a musician. Would you care to borrow a - a flute was it not? - and give us a performance?"

"It is many years since I last played seriously, Your Holiness."

The Pope turned to Charles. You see how it is, Sire? If you expressed a hint of the most modest wish to any of your subjects, doubtless he would jump to perform it. In Rome, ours just make excuses. And that is why, your Majesty, this man who did make the Crucifix, to give him credit, has embarrassed us by not completing the Breviary we have commissioned as a token of esteem for you."

Benvenuto's face burned with rage and humiliation at this public reprimand.

"Messer Cellini, perhaps you will at least be good enough to show His Majesty what you have managed to do so far."

Now it so happened that Charles was looking for an opportunity to offer a mild - an ever so mild - rebuff to Paul. "**Uno pequino pase - A little dig**," he thought. The Emperor was well aware of the significance of the use of the Borgia Apartments of all places for the banquet, and his intelligence services had told him that the Pope's present attitude to an active alliance against Francis I was negative.

A small hint would do. A small reminder that he, Charles V, the Holy Roman Emperor, was the greatest, the most powerful ruler in Europe. This gaunt artist, standing with his fists clenched as he tried to hide his anger at the Pope might prove to be the pretext. Even though he was of no importance, he had obviously irritated the Pope in some way, and taking the man's side would act as a small tug on the reins.

He examined the pieces of the book cover with genuine approval.

"This is your own design, Master Goldsmith?"

"Yes, your Majesty."

"And the Crucifix that His Holiness has given the Empress.?"

"Yes indeed, your Majesty."

Charles turned to the Pope. "You know, your Holiness, I believe you should try to be tolerant of the temperament of artists. It's in their nature - otherwise they wouldn't be artists.

Princes and Popes have the burden of being reliable at all times and always doing the right thing. Don't you agree?"

Actually Paul did not agree. His idea of what was right did not coincide with what Charles wanted him to do, but he was not going to get involved in a game of words, pretending that Cellini was the subject when they were really talking about something else. Before he had the chance to say anything, Charles was speaking to Benvenuto again.

"Cellini. Your name is Cellini? I know you. Aren't you the man who shot my general, Constable Bourbon back in '27? By the blood of Christ - begging your pardon your Holiness - if I'd have caught you, I'd have gladly strung you up from the Sant' Angelo Tower!"

"Another one threatening me with the rope. Is that all you bastards can think of? And if I'd got you in my sights I'd have just as gladly blown your bloody royal head off!"

Of course Benvenuto did not say this out loud, but as the thought flashed through his mind he said deferentially, "I am indeed fortunate to have been of some service to your

Majesty. - And to the Holy Father," he added after a pause. "I can only hope that I may in some way assist in cementing the friendship between both your Excellencies!"

The Pope ground his teeth and his eyes rolled heavenwards as he silently prayed for God immediately to strike this meddling talkative fool at least dumb, if not dead.

God didn't.

Paul rapped on the table with his ring. "Messer da Prato. Next!"

The Audience was over.

―∞―

Benvenuto returned to his seat, took a deep swig of wine and then bit savagely into a plum, spraying juice on both his neighbours.

The fat priest nudged Benvenuto in the ribs. Benvenuto pretended not to notice, so the priest jabbed him with his arm again.

"Well, come on. What did he say to you? What did the Pope say?"

Benvenuto glared at the man.

"Actually, he apologised for seating me next to you. He said he had asked all the other guests, but none of them had a strong enough stomach. Now for God's sake, keep your damned elbows to your sides, otherwise all the fucking fleas will escape from your stinking armpits."

-25-

Eventually Benvenuto's sentence to virtual slavery came to an end.

The Master of the Mint finally told him that "for the time being" they now had sufficient dies to complete the issue of the new coins as well as spares for replacements.

The Breviary had been finished, delivered, accepted and signed for and Benvenuto's detailed statement of account and vouchers had been receipted without da Prato bothering to do more than glance at the total and count the change. He had obviously no stomach for the abuse to which he knew he would be subjected if he so much as queried an item.

Benvenuto waited for another summons to the Vatican; waited for another commission for some important piece which he would be well paid for this time. He waited in vain.

Weeks passed, but nothing came except minor orders from old customers. Enough to keep him busy, but nothing to show the world that he was once more back at the top of his profession.

He made a minor modification to his toy see-saw. He fitted another weight so that it could now balance, with the two figures exactly level. He stood in front of it and blew gently. The see-saw rocked.

"That's how it is with me, Ascanio" he said to his new assistant. "Just one little puff of wind and I could be up again. Or down, "he added morosely.

His hopes were momentarily raised when, eventually, Traiano told him he was required at the Vatican. He did not see the Pope. Da Prato was waiting for him. Each man eyed the other warily. Da Prato spoke first.

"His Holiness has received this ring as a gift from His Majesty. He'd like your opinion of it."

He held out a large ring which Benvenuto took to the window and examined carefully. Then he delicately pressed it against the pane. There was a harsh grating sound as he made a small scratch on the glass.

"Well, what do you want me to tell you? It's a diamond. It's a nice big stone, but a bit on the thin side. I would expect a stone of this size to have a few flaws, but it's been tinted so I can't see properly. The tinting was done by Miliano Targhetto, from Venice. He's an expert."

Tinting stones, particularly diamonds, was quite fashionable in those days. It was a process of laying colour behind a jewel with a vegetable mastic resin. It was used to change or improve the shade of a jewel and to hide any imperfections.

"How can you tell whose work it is?"

"Because it's my business to know" Benvenuto snapped. "There aren't many people who can do this sort of work properly, and I recognise his style. I spent some time in his studio when I had to go …. when I was in Venice last year."

"How much is it worth?"

"Hard to say without removing the tint to see what's underneath. Targhetto wouldn't bother with a really bad stone. In its present condition I'd say about twelve thousand crowns."

"That's what we've already been told. What do you mean by, 'in its present condition'?"

"I mean that the tint is worn. If that is improved and if the stone is re-set, it would be worth more - anything up to twenty thousand."

"Who could improve it?"

"Me."

"I thought you said this fellow - what's his name? - Targhetto, was an expert."

"So am I, and I'm here and he's in Venice."

"How long would you take?"

"Three days. Some of it is slow work that I prefer only to do in daylight."

"Wait here." Da Prato left with the ring and returned after a few minutes.

"His Holiness says you may take the ring and deal with it as you think fit. He says the setting is a little too small for his finger."

"I know his ring size."

"I'm authorised to pay you two per cent of whatever the Pope's experts say you have increased its value by. Bring a certificate from both of these."

Benvenuto looked at the names on the slip of paper that da Prato gave him and nodded approvingly.

"Now, I expect that you're in a hurry to get on with your work, so I won't detain you. Be here at three o'clock on Friday. You know how to find your own way out," Da Prato, said over his shoulder as he stalked from the room.

—⁂—

Benvenuto re-tinted and re-set the diamond, collected the valuations from the two jewellers and stood in the ante-room, waiting for da Prato to return from showing his work to the Pope.

Da Prato came back with a heavy canvas bag.

"The Holy Father thanks you," he said gruffly. "The experts agree the ring is now worth twenty thousand crowns, so here's your hundred and fifty."

"A hundred and fifty? That's not two per cent of eight thousand."

"Why so it isn't! I decided that the other ten crowns would be your contribution to the Church. Allow me to thank you for your generosity."

—⁂—

More weeks passed without another summons to the Vatican, even though Benvenuto's competitors were getting valuable commissions from members of the Court. Finally, he asked for an appointment with one of his old customers, Cardinal d'Este of Ferrara.

The Cardinal's Palace was near to the Piazza Borghese on the east bank of the Tiber. It was in a part of the City which had been partly saved from the worst excesses of the Sack as a result of the efforts of Cardinal Andrea, who had paid a ransom so that his own palace, the Palazzo della Vale, and the neighbouring properties might be spared.

The Cardinal's study was on the first floor at the back of the building. It was a cool quiet room, with a wide balcony overlooking a courtyard garden with a fountain in the centre surrounded by ancient Roman statues and carvings.

Benvenuto kissed the Cardinal's ring and politely waited for permission to speak. D' Este got up from his high-backed chair and led him to the window.

"I love this room. Here a man can think, and forget the troubles of the World - or solve them." The Cardinal turned his back on the garden, walked back to his chair, and sat down.

"So, my son. Tell me what your trouble is, and how I can help you solve it."

"It's just that I don't know what to do. I'm at my wits' end. I simply can't earn my living here in Rome any more. Your Eminence may well look surprised. I'm a first class craftsman. The best in the city. Why only recently I took a diamond belonging to the Pope and increased its value by three-quarters."

"No one questions your skill, Benvenuto. Why can't you get enough work then? I would have thought you would have been the busiest goldsmith in Rome."

"So I should be, but I've hardly earned anything for three years. First I had that stupid quarrel with Pope Clement, may he dwell forever among the Saints." Benvenuto crossed himself.

"Then I committed a terrible crime and had to hide for months. Finally, with my nerves absolutely shattered with the thought that I had just escaped being hanged, I had to do six month's work in as many weeks with no help and no pay."

The Cardinal made a sympathetic clucking noise.

"Alright, so now I've done the penance His Holiness set me, and yet the customers still avoid me as if I've got the Plague or something. I can earn a living anywhere. Anywhere it seems except Rome! I don't want to have to leave, but is there any hope for me if I stay? Why is the Pope keeping my customers from coming? Why does he hate me? I haven't done a thing wrong in his reign."

Benvenuto was nearly in tears.

"My dear fellow, you are absolutely mistaken. The Pope isn't punishing you, and he doesn't hate you either. On the contrary, didn't he spare your life when you were sentenced to death? If His Holiness hadn't fixed the damages and given you work so you could pay them, Pompeo's family would have been suing you for years. They would have bled you dry."

"You mean that he's soon going to give me something worthwhile to do?"

"I doubt it. Not soon."

"But ....."

The Cardinal held up his hand.

"Listen, Benvenuto. Don't you realise what's happening here just now? The Pope's got all his work cut out to stop getting involved in this war between Charles and Francis. He's certainly got no time to think about art, artists or gold vases. What's more he may need every scudo he can raise to buy the Emperor off. Money instead of men!"

"So I had better go away then?"

"For a while, perhaps. Where to? Florence?"

Benvenuto looked up at the ceiling. "Not really. There are too many unhappy memories there - of my father and mother and brother."

The memories he was really thinking about were the notoriously long ones that some Florentines had. Maybe someone would still remember that he had a long overdue appointment with their hangman too.

D'Este snapped his fingers. "Wait a minute. I've got an idea! France!"

"France?"

"Yes, to France - to the court of King Francis I."

"You mean while it's still possible that the Pope will have to go to war with the French, you want me to go to work for their King?"

"Exactly."

"With the greatest deference and respect, your Eminence, I've already been as near to the executioner as I ever want to be."

The Cardinal shook his head in exasperation.

"No, no, my son, you don't understand. His Holiness doesn't want to fight the French, but he can't convince the Emperor that he doesn't. Now if he allows his favourite Goldsmith - that is you - to go to France, maybe Charles will get the message. Perhaps it will also reassure King Francis" he added as an afterthought.

"I'll get Cardinal de' Medici to write to Catherine de' Medici about you. She's married to Francis' second son, Prince Henry."

Benvenuto was not convinced.

"I tell you, Benvenuto, I'd be amazed if Francis didn't welcome you with open arms when he learns from Cardinal de' Medici that it was you who did him the big favour of shooting Constable Bourbon."

"How lucky I am!" Benvenuto thought. "That's two kings who owe me a favour for shooting the same man!"

He shrugged his shoulders in a typical Italian gesture of resignation.

"I expect you'll need some money for the expenses of such a long journey, so I'm going to give you three hundred and f...." D'Este corrected himself. "I'm going to *lend* you three hundred gold crowns out of my own pocket. And do you know why?"

Benvenuto had no idea. He shook his head.

"Because I'll tell the Holy Father that I thought of it - which I did - and if he agrees, it will stand me in good stead with the Holy Office, and I'll be greatly in your debt."

Benvenuto had never had anyone even half as important as a Cardinal greatly in his debt. And who was he to argue if both a Cardinal and the Pope wanted him to go to France as a ploy in some diplomatic charade? Maybe the Pope would also consider he was greatly in Benvenuto's debt!

He did not hesitate any more. He nodded, and then knelt and kissed the Cardinal's ring.

—⚒—

Raffaello del Moro bought Benvenuto's stock of finished goods, and agreed to collect the few debts that were owing by his customers, but he refused either to buy his furniture or to cancel the lease of the shop.

"You can have the shop rent free unless I decide to find a new tenant, and if I do, I'll store your furniture somewhere. You can't sell it: it's not worth a bucket of horse's sweat. Besides, you'll need a shop and your stuff when you come back. I don't want to have to go chasing round buying beds and benches for you for a third time."

"What do you mean, 'when I come back'? Why do you think I'll ever come back?"

"Well, there's my lovely Gina."

"Oh do shut up!" Benvenuto said with a smile.

"Then you'll come back because you don't really want to go, and because you're going for someone else's reasons, not your own."

And so, on a warm, early-summer afternoon Benvenuto, Ascanio and Busbacca, three horses and a pack mule set off for France by what was a rather circuitous route.

First skirting round Florence by the country lanes he knew so well. He was never going back until he was sure that the old Chief Magistrate was dead and buried.

Then on to Bologna and Venice, carefully avoiding the Lombardy Plain and the possibility of getting mixed up in the war between Francis and Charles. The whole of this part of the journey was conducted at a leisurely pace, not stretching the horses at all as they would need all their strength when they went over the Alps.

Most nights were spent at country inns in the noisy and frequently drunken company of other travellers, and where, more often than not Benvenuto was able to find a serving girl to share his bed.

He stayed a week in Venice, not bothering to look at the palaces and churches, but poking round the workshops of the many goldsmiths, amongst whom were the finest in Italy. He was as anxious as ever to learn what he could about other craftsmen's techniques and about the newest fashions, and he had at last discovered how important the goodwill of colleagues was. They could tell him about customers in other towns or could praise his work when submitted to them for an opinion - and that in itself was as good as a recommendation.

From Venice Benvenuto went to Padua and while allowing the horses to rest, he was introduced to the poet Pietro Bembo who asked him to make a small bronze portrait. When he had completed the die, he asked to be excused from making the actual casting on the grounds that he did not have a foundry.

Bembo agreed that any competent craftsman in the town could finish the job and offered to pay Benvenuto's full fee, but Benvenuto refused to accept any money, so Bembo insisted that he accept the gift of another horse, a big, rich chestnut coloured one, which Benvenuto would be able to sell later in France or Switzerland without insulting the poet.

Benvenuto's little party made its way into eastern Switzerland through the Bernina Pass, with the tiny, isolated farming village of St. Moritz a few miles away to the west. Continuing roughly northwards over the steep mountain roads through the Alpine valleys, via Arosa and Chur, it was late June when they reached Walenstadt, at the head of the Walensee - a ten mile long lake.

During his overnight stay at the local inn, he learned that he had two choices for the route of the next leg of his journey to Zurich. He could either travel the length of the lake by the twice-daily ferry, or he could follow the trail round the shore, which was a hard dangerous ride along steep cliffs, with nothing more than bridle paths to follow.

Benvenuto had never been on a boat before - it would be a new experience, and besides it would save a couple of days. It was early afternoon when the ferry tied up to take on its second load of passengers. Benvenuto had decided not to get up before dawn, even for the pleasure of his first boat trip.

The boat had a square mainsail and was steered by a large tiller. The crew of four men and a boy in addition to the captain could assist with the oars in case of need, but usually the strong winds circulating round valley meant that they had little more to do than to tend the sails.

To the rear of the mainmast was a platform surrounded by a rail and sub-divided into separate pens into which any livestock, from sheep to horses, could be put for the journey. The passengers would sit or stand in the well of the boat, forward of the mainmast unless the crew needed to get into the space to row.

As Benvenuto's four horses and his pack mule were dragged, prodded and coaxed along the gangway and on to the boat rocking at the jetty, he glanced over the other travellers. Because of the load he was putting on board, there was hardly room for anyone else other than Benvenuto's group.

The ferry captain did a little calculation and pointed to two women dressed in black with no luggage other than baskets of fruit which they were carrying to market, and also waved on board the inevitable priest whom he would not have dared to leave behind. Half-a-dozen other would-be passengers would have to wait until the next day.

A fat farmer leading a large black pig by a rope tied to a ring in its nose, began shouting at the ferryman. Benvenuto nudged his companions and watched with amusement while the sailor first reasoned with the man, then pantomimed a sinking boat with his hands, and finally shrugged his shoulders and walked up the gangway which he untied and threw with a great crash on to the planking of the jetty, making the farmer jerk his wretched pig out of the way to prevent it getting flattened.

To the accompaniment of a stream of invective from the farmer, which made Benvenuto - no mean performer himself - grin with admiration, two of the crew pushed the boat off with long poles while the sail was raised by two others, with the captain operating the tiller.

There was a fairly stiff breeze blowing and despite it being early on a summer afternoon, it was dull, almost dark. Heavy black clouds were tumbling over the mountains. The boat had only been moving for a few minutes when large drops of rain began splashing on the dry wooden planking.

The crew hurriedly rigged a tarpaulin for the passengers to huddle under to keep dry. However, the boat began to wallow in the choppy swell whipped up by the increasing wind, and one by one, the wretched passengers turned pale and made for the side.

Lightning started to flash and frightened the horses, who tugged at their halters and shied with their hobbled hooves, slamming them down on the deck like echoes of the crashes of thunder.

Now it was Benvenuto's turn to be frightened. Maybe the boat would turn over. Maybe it would fill up with the water and sink - already waves were slopping over the side and the boy was frantically bailing out with a metal cooking pot. Or maybe the horses would kick the thin planks of the boat to bits or break loose and fall over the side. Suddenly he remembered the sailor pantomiming a sinking boat to the farmer who had been lucky enough to be left behind.

He struggled to the stern, clutching on to the rails, at the same time dodging the horses, and found the captain and one of the crew pushing hard on the long wooden tiller, trying to steer the heavily loaded boat as it pitched and rolled in the mounting waves.

"Captain, I want to get off."

"You what?"

"I want to get off the boat. Right away."

The captain shrugged his shoulders. "Go on then, but don't make too much of a splash. I'm wet enough already!"

"No, you don't understand, I want you to put me ashore."

"Look, we're two miles along the lake, and it's almost a mile from either side. Why on earth do you want to get off?"

"Because this boat's going to sink, that's why - if we don't get struck by lightning first!"

"Look here, sir, your Lordship - I can tell you're a well educated gentleman. No doubt you're a rich merchant or banker or something and know everything about your business. Now me, I've been sailing up and down this lake four times a day for thirty years in all weathers. I want to get home just as much as you do, and I tell you it is perfectly safe. A bit rough, yes, but perfectly safe."

"And I tell you we're sinking, and I can't swim."

By now the captain as thoroughly irritated.

"Well if the boat is sinking, now would be a bloody good time for you to learn. Me, I can swim very well."

"With your throat cut?" Benvenuto drew his dagger. "Listen to me sailor, you get this wreck to the shore, or you'll see your head floating behind the rudder."

"But there's nowhere to land."

"Oh come on! A man who's been sailing up and down the lake for thirty years must know a spot. Now find it and be quick about it!"

He jabbed the dagger in the captain's direction for emphasis.

The captain did indeed know a spot. A little rocky promontory which formed a natural jetty. It was obviously much used, because there was a rowing boat tied to a tree branch and a wide but well-worn path leading up towards the top of the high overhanging cliff.

Benvenuto hoped there was a farm there where he and his companions could get shelter from the storm. The path was too steep to ride up, especially with the animals in such a very nervous state, so they all had to go on foot. Benvenuto led the way, holding the bridle of his horse. Ascanio was next with the mule and his horse and, in the rear, Busbacca with his own horse and the new one given by Bembo.

Before they began the climb, they paused to watch the crew trying to row the boat out of the shelter of the cliff so that the flapping, empty sails could pick up the wind.

As they reached the cliff-top, there was a blue flash and instantly an extra loud crash when a tall tree nearby was struck by lightning.

The new horse, only recently "broken", and far less trained than the others, pulled itself free from Busbacca's hand and bolted. In its panic, it attempted to rush past, first Ascanio, and then Benvenuto. The path was so narrow that there was simply not enough room. It barged into Benvenuto's horse, and then with its hooves scrabbling on a slab of wet, slippery rock, it lost its footing and pitched over the cliff. It hit a small ledge and bounced off and outwards, down to the lake, far below.

Rushing to the edge, Benvenuto and his two employees saw that as luck - as bad luck - would have it, the horse had landed right on top of the boat, which, because of the force of the waves and adverse wind had still not cleared the shore.

The effect of half a ton of horse falling from two hundred feet was like a direct hit with a bomb. The animal had struck the fore part of the boat, crashing through the canvas awning and smashing the boy and one of the women to a pulp before breaking a great hole in the flimsy wood of the hull.

The whole front of the boat broke away, throwing the four crewmen and the priest who had been pressed into helping with the rowing, and the surviving old lady, into the water.

The stern of the boat, overbalanced by the weight of the mast and the sodden sail, first tipped end up, and then rolled over and floated upside down, inches below the surface. The captain only just managed to leap clear to avoid being trapped underneath.

He struck out for the shore without stopping to see whether the others, struggling in the water, clutching on to pieces of wreckage and impeded by their heavy clothing needed any help.

Benvenuto sat on a boulder and roared with laughter until tears streamed down his face.

"What's so funny master?" asked Busbacca. "That horse and those poor people are all dead."

"Funny? Of course it's funny." Benvenuto pointed to the captain, far below, still swimming desperately for safety. "I told that idiot his lousy boat wasn't safe. Now maybe he'll believe me!"

-26-

Francis I "by God's Grace, King of France," was born at Cognac at 10 o'clock at night on the 12th September 1494 to Louise of Savoy and Charles, Count of Angouleme.

On his father's side he could trace his ancestry back two hundred years and more - to Philippe V the founder of the House of Valois, and to King Jean II and to Charles the Wise - King Charles V of France.

The Count of Angouleme had married Louise when she was twelve years old. She was still only eighteen when the future king was born. At 19 she was a widow, and the baby Francis inherited his father's title.

The King, Louis XII had two daughters but no sons, so Francis, the Senior Prince of the Blood Royal, was recognised as the Heir Presumptive. He was given the additional title of Duke of Valois and with it the magnificent Palace of Ambois.

Francis secured his place as the next King by his betrothal, when she was only seven, to Louis' older daughter, Claude. The marriage of this connoisseur of feminine beauty to the small, fat, rich princess who walked with a limp and whose dumpling face was marred by a ferocious squint, took place in 1514.

Francis became the fifty-seventh King of France at the age of nineteen, when Louis died on New Year's Day 1515.

He began his reign with a country-wide series of extravagant celebrations, banquets and tournaments as well as the gratification of the large sexual appetite he had acquired at an early age. It was said that his mother's lady-in-waiting had seduced him at the age of ten. Whether or not this was true, by the time he was sixteen he was taking his first cure for venereal disease.

—ᴡ—

Francis soon turned from the pursuit of pleasure to the pursuit of French claims to the Italian States of Milan and Naples.

His chance came when the Republic of Venice sought his aid against Spanish invaders and the Pope's armies. At the same time Genoa was being threatened by the Duke of Milan and the Genoans also begged for France's help.

By diplomatic bargaining he arranged for the neutrality of Archduke Charles of Flanders. Henry VIII of England was too weak militarily to intervene, and too politically inept to take advantage of the situation. So, in accordance with the best military tactics, the French rear was well secured when Francis launched himself against Lombardy.

Spain and the Pope were heavily committed in the war against Venice and were unable to divert troops to Northern Italy to meet Francis' advancing armies.

—ᴡ—

Francis' army consisted mostly of paid professionals - mercenaries. Twenty-five hundred heavy cavalry with full armour, swords and lances; fifteen hundred stradiots, mounted light skirmishers wearing light half-armour and carrying crossbows and lances; nine thousand crack German Lance-knights and ten thousand infantry under the Spanish renegade, Count Pedro de Navarro - an expert siege engineer.

There were seventy large cannon and three hundred smaller guns of the latest design, capable of shooting iron balls, not just rocks, and with the new trunnions which meant their elevation could be altered too, for greater accuracy.

With the addition of French noblemen's' private forces, it was a formidable army of thirty thousand men, with, as its General, the brilliant Constable Bourbon, who was then still Francis' loyal subject.

On 31st July 1515 Francis and his troops left Lyons, and twelve days later they simply disappeared into the Alps. The Swiss believed that there were only two ways the French could come: either through the Mont Cenis Pass or through the Mount Geneva Pass. Ten thousand of their best troops were strategically stationed between the two at Suza.

However, in a brilliant stroke, Pedro de Navarro found a precarious southerly route into Italy across goat tracks and tiny defiles, blasting rocks out of the way until he and a thousand labourers had made a path along which the carts and cannons and cavalry could cautiously inch. Deep chasms were bridged with wooden beams. Otherwise cannon and terrified horses were swung across on slings and ropes. In some places one slip from the narrow track meant a messy death five thousand feet or more below.

Francis did not however rely on military strategy alone. He got rid of most of the Swiss army by bribery. He stripped the French noblemen of every piece of gold coin or plate he could lay his hands on as a down payment.

Even so, he still had to fight a bloody pitched two-day battle with the Swiss at Marignano starting on the 13th September, through that moonlit night and on until the 14th when, with about fourteen thousand dead and wounded, the Swiss pikemen were finally defeated by the French army's massive fire power and the way was open for the speedy capture of Milan.

—⚔—

Over the next ten years Francis' fortunes ebbed and flowed, culminating with the defection of Constable Bourbon and Francis' defeat and capture at the battle of Pavia, his subsequent year-long imprisonment, and his signing under duress of the humiliating Treaty of Madrid in 1526.

Now here it was, another nine years on. Twenty-one into Francis' reign and the same old war for the same old reason was about to begin once more.

Charles V's army was fighting in North Africa and Francis had seized the opportunity to invade Italy again. While Charles was still in Rome vainly trying to enlist the Pope's support, Benvenuto was on his way to the Court of King Francis as a minor demonstration of the Pope's unwillingness to become involved.

The Chateau of Fontainebleau was originally built by Robert the Good in the twelfth century as a hunting lodge. It was near to Paris, and ideally sited on the route into the Loire Valley, so that the French Kings could enjoy hunting the abundant game while making the frequent tours of their Kingdom that were vital to help keep order.

Louis VI – "Louis the Gros" - decided that a dungeon tower was a vital addition.

Louis VII built the Chapel, later to be enlarged by Louis IX - Saint Louis - and the building was consecrated by Thomas a Beckett when he fled from the wrath Henry II in 1169.

In 1313 Charles V established the library encircling the Cour Ovale and which was to be the foundation of the National Library.

Of all the rulers who left an imprint on the Chateau, it was Francis who transformed it. This was his favourite Palace, his real home, indeed that is what he called it – "Chez moi."

He began work on it in 1527 with one drastic step. He demolished all the old buildings with the exception of Louis VI's prison tower and began again.

He worked on the Castle for the rest of his life, employing a succession of distinguished architects, beginning with Gilles le Breton who built the Porte Doree - the Golden Gate - a four storey mixture of the Italian and French style from which stretches the long avenue into the forest.

Externally Fontainebleau is severe in appearance, partly because the local sandstone does not lend itself to embellishment, and partly because it is a random collection of rather indifferent buildings. But the interior; that is sumptuous!

Francis, over the years summoned the greatest decorators, artists, sculptors and carvers, and the most skilful craftsmen he could find.

Giovanni de Jacopo, il Rosso, created the beautiful, allegorical frescos high on the wall of the "Francis I Gallery", between the elaborately carved wainscot with its gold letter "F"s and crown-surmounted lilies, and the gilded carved ceilings, each separate picture being flanked by a confection of stucco sculptures.

Then there were the artists: Fransesco Primaticcio, Niccolo del Abbate, Bartolommeo de Miniato, Charles Carmoy, Leonardo Thiry, Andrea del Sarto and a host of others. But towering head and shoulders above all of them was Leonardo da Vinci, who spent the last years of his life, until he died in 1519, working for the King, who purchased many of his paintings, including the Mona Lisa.

In his lifetime, Francis called together what came to be known as "the School of Fontainebleau". It was probably the greatest assembly of artists ever to work on one project. He also he made a collection of works of art that demonstrated an unparalleled eye for greatness. Apart from his Leonardos, there were Raphaels, Titians, Fra Bartolommeos, Clouets, van Cleves as well as paintings and sculptures by many other artists.

He even managed to acquire Michelangelo's "Hercules", for his long gallery, in which he intended to house Roman antiquities.

"Fontainebleau," he said, "is to become a second Rome."

-27-

Benvenuto arrived at Fontainebleau in the middle of July, tired, saddle-sore and travel-stained and presented his credentials to Catherine de' Medici.

Catherine de' Medici, daughter of the Duke of Urbino, was orphaned within three weeks of her birth and was made the ward of her cousin Giulio, who later became Pope Clement VII, and who unashamedly used her as a matrimonial pawn in his politicking.

Her importance was recognised during the Florentine revolt against the Medicis in 1529, when, still only 11 years old, she was the subject of a bizarre plot by a group of fanatics to kidnap her from the convent where she lived and to house her in a brothel, or to chain her, naked, to the city walls, or worse still, to arrange for her to be raped by the soldiers. It was only because she was so well guarded that she escaped from all of these fates, any of which would have destroyed her marriageable value.

On 28th October 1533 she was married by Pope Clement himself to Henry, Duke of Orleans, and the second son of King Francis. Bride and groom were both 14 years old.

She was certainly no beauty. A Pale complexion, fat face, heavy eyebrows over bulging eyes; a large nose with uneven lips, the top one thin and the bottom one thick. And yet, young as she was, she was already a mature woman, possessed of considerable culture, intelligence and personal charm.

She brought with her as her dowry, her late mother's estates and castles in Auvergne, a hundred thousand gold ecus, a large collection of valuable jewellery and a magnificent trousseau of clothes, silks, linens, plate, and household goods.

Despite all this, her father-in-law, King Francis, complained that "she came naked as a new-born babe." The Pope's Ambassador had to remind him that by the marriage, Clement had promised the King three additional jewels: Naples, Milan, and Genoa.

Francis did treat her with kindness and affection, unlike most of his Court who called her "the shopkeeper's daughter," and it was she who arranged for Benvenuto to have an audience with the King.

Benvenuto had to cool his heels in a nearby inn for several days after his meeting with Catherine de' Medici before the summons to the palace came. All it said was:

Messer Benvenuto Cellini is bidden to present himself to His Majesty's Chamberlain at 10 o'clock the morning on the twenty-second of July.

There was no signature; just a red wax seal.

Benvenuto arrived wearing the best clothes he could find in Ascanio's trunk.

There was a fine white linen shirt with a lace collar and cuffs. Over this there was a thigh-length coat with gold brocade vertical panels about two inches wide. The sleeves were puffed out at the shoulders where they were slashed with pieces of crimson silk, and then fell to the lace at his wrists in overlapping circular layers of brocade. His pantaloons were in the same layers and were tied off at his knees with gold silk ribbon where they met his white stockings.

On his head he wore a soft squashy beret of matching gold trimmed with white feathers. Fortunately he had time to buy a new pair of shoes from the local cobbler in a pale, very light brown shiny leather.

The ante room into which he was shown was a marked contrast to the one at the Vatican. Its windows looked out on to a large courtyard, and the room was light and bright and airy, and gleamed with fresh paint and gilded wood-panelling.

There was even a great silver bowl of yellow and white flowers in the middle of the long rectangular polished table that ran the length of an elaborately patterned carpet.

There were a number of other men waiting in the room, but Benvenuto barely had a minute to glance around before another servant came in. He was dressed in the household livery, a black velvet doublet, black stockings, silver-buckled shoes and a rather old-fashioned tabard embroidered with a shield and three fleurs de lys and the monogram letter "F" on either side.

He came directly to Benvenuto. "Monsieur Cellini? Please follow me."

Benvenuto tucked the large leather folio case he had with him under his arm. It held his collection of sketches and designs, including those for the book cover and Crucifix that he had made for the Holy Roman Emperor and Empress.

―ᴍ―

If he had expected a personal interview he was disappointed. The large audience chamber, with its high ceiling and carved walnut panelling held about fifty or sixty people, all in little groups.

There was a tapestry-covered throne on a dias at the far end, but the King stood talking to one of the groups, sometimes sending for someone to join him, and sometimes walking with his secretary to join a different group altogether.

Those not in the King's actual presence spoke only in whispers as they watched his slow progress around the room, while those nearest to him blatantly eavesdropped. This was in fact more of a levee than an audience, and nothing private was transacted.

The servant led Benvenuto directly to where Catherine de' Medici - the Duchess of Orleans was now her correct title - was standing with two of her ladies-in-waiting. Benvenuto removed his hat and bowed.

"Your Grace."

"Good morning, Messer Cellini. I see you have some drawings with you. I doubt if His Majesty will look at them today, but give me your testimonials."

Benvenuto handed over the letters from Cardinal de' Medici and Cardinal d'Este.

"Stay here."

The Duchess left him with the two ladies and stood near the King. Her status as a Royal Princess entitled her to that privilege. While she was waiting for Francis to finish his conversation, Benvenuto had his first chance to look at the King.

He was a massive man - a giant by the standards of those days. Six foot tall with a heavy broad frame and a long thin nose; delicately arched eyebrows over almond shaped, rather sly looking eyes. Except that the thick black beard he had been wearing for the past twenty years was fuller, darker and more luxuriant, he bore a remarkable resemblance to the smaller, stouter, red-haired Henry VIII of England.

This then was the paradoxical King of France. His Court had the reputation of being the most lecherous and debauched ever known, while on the other hand his reign saw the fusing of the cultures of Gothic France with the Italian Renaissance. Again, while he was the cruellest of tyrants, his Court was filled with artists, scholars, poets and writers.

His buildings were magnificent. Apart from Fontainebleau, he was responsible for the Chateau de Chambourd and a new wing at Blois, and yet his needless wars destroyed many of the beauties of Italy. He founded both the College de France and the National Library but was directly responsible for the death and of hundreds of thousands in the vain pursuit of his empire-building ambitions.

Fortunately for Benvenuto, whose French was limited, Francis, because of his Italian daughter-in-law and his dealings with many Italian artists, understood some Italian, and, as did every educated person on the sixteenth century, he spoke Latin.

Catherine de' Medici too was surprisingly well-educated for a woman of that era. Apart from her native Italian, she spoke fluent French, Latin and Greek and studied mathematics, natural history, astronomy and astrology.

Catherine handed the King the two letters. Francis gave them to his secretary who broke the seals and translated the sonorous Latin. When he had finished, the King said something to Catherine who first pointed to Benvenuto and then beckoned to him.

Benvenuto was not sure whether he had to bow or kneel. He attempted to do both and dropped his folio. With his face and ears burning with humiliation, he scrabbled on the floor, cramming loose papers in a crumpled mess back into the case while the King stood, hands on hips with a condescending smile on his face.

So you are the goldsmith, Messer Cellini of Florence. Messer Benvenuto Cellini."

"Yes, your Majesty."

"And this is your first visit to France?"

"Indeed it is, Sire."

"Well, let me say, 'Benvenuto!' You are welcome." The King roared with laughter while those around him, whether they understood or not, politely joined in.

Benvenuto ground his teeth. "Dear God!" he prayed, "take a year from my life, but have mercy and don't let me have to hear that stupid joke again!"

He forced a smile and said, "How droll! His Highness' wit is only exceeded by his generosity to a stranger."

The King grunted. "Cardinals de' Medici and d'Este recommend you highly."

"They are very kind."

"They say His Holiness holds you in high esteem."

Benvenuto nodded.

"And yet he has most generously divested himself of your services so that you may come to us. Hum! I wonder what that crafty old fox is up to."

There was nothing for Benvenuto to say.

"You are also well thought of by our Director of Stuccos and Paintings, Master di Jacopo."

He pointed to a corner of the room where the artist was standing.

"Il Rosso," said Benvenuto as he recognised him.

"We call him Maitre Roux," said the King.

"He was my friend in Rome," Benvenuto replied.

"Indeed?" the King continued, "We understand from our daughter that you shot that traitor Bourbon at the Siege of Rome."

"Yes I did, your Majesty."

"Well the way that show-off stupidly used to expose himself, someone was bound to have done it sooner or later. If it wasn't you, it would have been somebody else. Anyway, you only saved our Headsman a job."

The King patted Benvenuto on the shoulder. "Well, Master Goldsmith, we are delighted to have a craftsman of your skill and eminence in our household. While we have nothing in mind for you at the moment, we are sure we shall find you something very soon. Our Chamberlain will arrange quarters for you, and in the meantime, you can wander round the Chateau and see what suggestions you yourself have to offer."

A wave of the hand, and Benvenuto was dismissed.

Benvenuto could not have chosen a worse time to enter Francis' service.

The war sparked off by his treacherous invasion of Lombardy had begun in earnest. In that same month of July 1536, Charles had launched a two pronged attack, one in the North through Picardy and the other in the South through Provence.

Charles himself personally led an army of fifty thousand men over the Alps and easily captured the undefended town of Aix. Pausing only to have himself crowned "King of Arles," he thrust on to Marseilles - and straight into a trap.

Francis stationed most of his army at Avignon under the command of Constable Montmorency, with strict instructions not to attack unless Charles attempted to cross the Rhone.

At the other end of the line, Francis anchored his forces, well supported with artillery, in Marseilles. Between the two wings, the cities of Arles and Tarascon were also packed with troops and munitions so that Charles was faced with an impenetrable semi-circle of fortresses which brought his advance to a complete halt.

By mid-September Francis' strategy had worked. Charles' army had to live off the land, and since they were unable to advance they soon ran out of food. Francis sent in saboteurs who poisoned the wells behind the lines so that, in the heat of the summer, with the rivers low, the Imperial Army began to get short of water too. Dysentery broke out.

Charles had learnt nothing from his unsuccessful campaign of 1524. Once again he had wasted his forces against the impregnable city of Marseilles.

His columns and stragglers were harassed by local peasants seeking loot and revenge for the stripping of their farms, crops and stock. For those not killed by these guerrillas, there was death from hunger and disease.

The roads and fields were filled with twenty thousand dead and dying men - two fifths of Charles' army - and the rotting corpses of their horses.

When the Count of Nassau, the leader of Charles' army in the North, heard of the disaster in Provence he lifted the siege of Peronne, abandoned his attempt to advance on Paris, and retreated across the border.

When Benvenuto was being introduced to the King, these victories had not yet happened. Francis was still anxiously awaiting the outcome of his tactical plan. Furthermore, the King had little enough money to spare for works of art. He had a war to finance - and one that would be fought on his own land, with no chance of booty.

But worse than this, On 10th August his eighteen year old son Francois, the Dauphin, died.

There had been a strong bond of affection between the King and his heir, despite differences in their personalities: the Prince was always in black while the King always dressed like a peacock; The Prince preferred his books to soldiering, and was as quiet and reserved as his father was boisterous and extroverted.

They were frightened at first to break the news to the King, but even as the Cardinal of Lorraine started to tell him in a gentle, roundabout way, Francis guessed and broke down. Then he reacted in a typically savage senseless way.

The Dauphin had been taken ill after drinking some iced water brought to him by his Italian Secretary, and died a few days later.

The Italian was known to be interested in poisons, and that was enough for Francis. Despite the absence of a credible motive or advantage for Charles, Francis decided that the Italian must be an Imperialist agent. Under the skilled hands of the King's torturers, the wretched man eventually confessed and Francis "mercifully" ordered his sufferings to be put an end to by his being torn to pieces by horses. His severed head was given to the mob to use as a football.

—m—

Benvenuto soon realised that there would be absolutely no work for him for a long time in the French Court, because Francis was grief-stricken over the death of his son, and at the same time was preoccupied with the war.

Also, Benvenuto heard rumours round the Palace that the invading armies were expected to attack Paris from the North and South, and he had no wish to be caught in the middle of another battle.

"What is more, your Highness," he said to Catherine de' Medici, whose husband was now the new heir to the Throne, "after what happened to Count Montecuccoli, I am not so sure it is safe to be an Italian round here at the moment. Can you imagine what could happen if Prince.... if there was another tragedy?"

Catherine gave him permission to return to Rome and promised to see that the King sent for him again as soon as possible.

-28-

No one could question Benvenuto's reasons for leaving France, or suggest that he had failed to be accepted by King Francis. On the contrary, he had a perfect excuse. He reached Rome in October, ruefully reflecting that yet another half a year had passed him by without profit, but very soon things started to go well for him.

Cardinal d'Este lived up to his promise to show his appreciation, not only by commissioning a gold jug and basin for himself, but also by touting for work for Benvenuto from anyone over whom he had the slightest influence and from the many suitors seeking favours, absolutions and indulgences from him and his bishops.

Soon Benvenuto had a flourishing workshop, with as much work as he could cope with, and he had to hire more assistants to help Busbacca and Ascanio. More assistants also meant more shares of profits from their personal customers. On the shelf above his bench, his end of the see-saw was firmly up once more.

The one thing that spoiled Benvenuto's triumph was the absence of any commissions from the Pope himself. Benvenuto explained this by claiming that far from being out of favour, the Pope was simply trying to find some suitably magnificent reward for his having carried out a diplomatic mission of vital importance and extreme secrecy to the King of France.

In a city where half the Spanish colony was in the pay of the Holy Roman Emperor, and the other half would liked to have been, this sort of indiscretion was an embarrassment to the Pope and a source of annoyance to his son and chief adviser, Pier Luigi Farnese.

Pompeo's family also complained to Pier Luigi that his murderer was strutting the streets, flaunting his new-found affluence, while they had been fobbed off with a derisory pittance.

"There's nothing to be done about it," Pier Luigi told them. "The man's been pardoned, and that's that. Now if there was something else he's done...."

Digi the Pickpocket's assistance was once again sought. He soon "discovered" that Benvenuto had eighty thousand ducats hidden away, in the form of precious stones, the property of the Church, stolen from Pope Clement during the siege of Castel Sant' Angelo.

This story, incredible though it was, was sufficient for Pier Luigi. He issued a warrant for Benvenuto's arrest.

—⚜—

Benvenuto was strolling home late in the evening after a pleasant dinner with his friend Sugherello the Perfumer from whom he was negotiating to purchase a larger shop. He had had just a little more than enough to drink and was wearing a warm cloak against the cold winter air.

He was carrying his flute. He had grown to enjoy the praise of others when he was occasionally persuaded to play a few tunes as part of the usual after-dinner entertainment.

He was walking along the Strada Guilia, the grandiose approach to St. Peter's, created by Pope Julius II after whom it was named, even though he ran out of money before it could be completed. When he reached a small palace just being built by Pope Paul for his daughter, Constanza, he had to step into the roadway to avoid the scaffolding used by the plasterers moulding the stucco design of Farnese Lilies mixed with the Papal emblems.

A figure stepped out of the shadows and Benvenuto instinctively reached for his dagger. He relaxed when he saw that the man was obviously not a robber. He was wearing a uniform, and then he recognised the hated police sergeant.

Benvenuto greeted him with venom.

"Hello! Just coming home from your reading lessons? Or are you a footpad in your spare time? No, don't tell me, you've come to give me back the five crowns you stole from me." Benvenuto had a long memory.

"Are you Benvenuto Cellini, the goldsmith?"

"No, actually I'm the Sultan of Turkey making a pilgrimage incognito. What the hell do you want?"

The Sergeant took a step towards Benvenuto, who raised his flute like a club.

"Listen you. Just come one step nearer, and you'll be picking splinters of this out of your mouth. I asked you what you want."

The Sergeant pulled his pistol out of his belt, cocked it, and pointed it at Benvenuto.

"Cellini, you're under arrest. If it was up to me, I'd shoot you now for attempting to escape, but I've orders to bring you in alive. Mind you, they didn't say I couldn't put a ball through your foot."

He lowered his gun a little, and Benvenuto took an involuntary step backwards.

"What's the charge?"

"I don't know. What difference does it make? They told me to arrest you, so I've done it. Threatening a police officer and resisting arrest will do for a start. Is it is illegal to bleed all over the roadway? No? Pity, I could have arranged that too. Come on, put your hands behind your back."

Out came the usual lengths of cord, and Benvenuto's wrists and elbows were viciously tied behind him while he was relieved of his dagger and flute.

Benvenuto glanced round and realised he was standing only a few yards away from where he had killed Pompeo. At that moment the Sergeant gave him a sharp push in the small of his back and sent him staggering towards the Castel Sant' Angelo.

—⚜—

The Sergeant stopped at the gate of the Castle and identified himself to the sentry. For the first time Benvenuto discovered the man's name: Crespino.

Benvenuto was led down the stairs to a windowless basement room. It was well lit with a cartwheel of candles hanging from the ceiling, directly under which was a table with three chairs. The only other piece of furniture was a stool near the door, on which Crespino sat himself. Another soldier came in and stood next to him.

Benvenuto perched himself on the edge of the table. He looked at the Sergeant sitting with his legs stretched out, his back leaning against the wall. Crespino stuck a grimy forefinger into his mouth, and with his nail began digging in the gap between two teeth. He excavated a shred of meat left over from his supper and examined it for a moment or two as it lay on his finger tip, then he popped the fragment back in his mouth and noisily sucked his teeth.

Benvenuto turned his head away and looked at the other soldier and saw that he was staring at him curiously. Benvenuto fixed his eyes on a point just below the man's hair line and stared back. After about fifteen seconds - it seemed much longer - the soldier, blushing furiously looked down and began to fiddle with the buckle of his belt.

Benvenuto did not have time to enjoy his petty victory.

The door opened and three men came in.

The first was Gabriello Ceserino who had now been appointed Castellan - the keeper of Castel Sant' Angelo. Next was another magistrate, Benedetto da Cagli. The third man, carrying a sheaf of documents under his arm, was Tommaso da Prato.

—⚜—

Benvenuto and the Sergeant rose to their feet, and the three newcomers took their seats behind the table, da Prato pulling the writing paper and ink pot nearer to him as he picked up a pen.

Ceserino spoke first. "Benvenuto Cellini?"

"I can't hear you."

Ceserino raised his voice. "I said, 'is your name Benvenuto Cellini?' You're not deaf are you?"

"No, your Excellency, I'm not deaf. I just don't hear too well with my hands tied behind my back."

Ceserino waved his hand at the Sergeant. "Undo him at once. It's too late at night for these games."

"Now Messer Cellini, you know why you're here, don't you?"

"Yes, I'm here because that man," Benvenuto pointed at Crespino, "set upon me in the street and threatened to shoot me if I didn't come."

Ceserino shook his head. "I mean, the Sergeant has read you the Warrant hasn't he?"

"Read me the warrant? Don't you know he can't read? He's so stupid he can't find his own arse using both hands."

Again a shake of Ceserino's head. He held out his hand, beckoned with all four fingers. "Sergeant, the warrant if you please."

Crespino came to the table, and as he reached in the folds of his cloak for the document, Benvenuto's dagger and flute fell out of a pocket on to the table. The Flute started to roll to the floor, but the sergeant caught it.

"What in God's name are those?"

"Prisoner's property, Sir," the Sergeant mumbled.

"Well, I'll take charge of them. He can have them back when - if he's released."

Ceserino opened the warrant and began to read.

"This is a warrant to authorise …..Oh, what does it matter? You're here anyway, so just answer Judge da Cagli's questions. His Excellency has been appointed a Magistrate by Messer Pier Luigi Farnese," he added with heavy emphasis.

Benvenuto ignored the hint. "Would it be alright if I sat down then? I find that if my feet are tired it also affects my hearing."

Ceserino hit his head with the palm of his hand in exasperation. "Sergeant. Your stool!"

The policeman angrily kicked it across the stone floor. It Toppled over at Benvenuto's feet and he picked it up and sat down.

Judge da Cagli spoke for the first time in a dry, rasping voice.

"Now that's enough of all this nonsense. This is no joking matter, and the quicker you answer my questions, the quicker we'll be done. It will be a lot less painful too. I'm sure the Sergeant here will be pleased to give you a fitting for a pair of thumb screws if it will assist your memory."

"Your Honour, I don't mind answering questions. It's just that I don't know what this is all about. It's a fine thing when an honest man can be picked up with no reason given and....."

"Honest man?" said the Judge. "We'll see about that. Just answer the questions. Were you in the garrison of Sant' Angelo during the siege?"

Oh yes, indeed I was. I didn't get excommunicated for being a traitor to the Holy Church."

Benvenuto was referring to da Cagli's sponsor, Pier Luigi. The Judge flushed red and da Prato felt obliged to intervene.

"Don't be impertinent! His Excellency has already told you to ....."

"Oh, so you've found your voice have you? I wondered when you were going to join in. I suppose it's you who's behind all this. Once you thought you were the Pope; now you think you're a Magistrate. Stick to your scribbling, there's a good fellow. I expect you've got enough to do."

The Judge slammed his hand down on the table so hard that the ink pot jumped up and a few drops splashed out.

"Cellini! I'm warning you for the last time."

Benvenuto spread his hands submissively. "I'm sorry, Sir, but it was this man who interrupted you. What was your next question?"

"Did the late Pope give you some gold to melt down for him?"

"He did."

"What became of it?"

Benvenuto gasped in amazement. "Holy Mother of God! Not that story again! Surely not? I melted it down and gave it back to His Holiness. Messer da Prato was in the Castle. I expect he's got it written down somewhere."

Da Prato leafed through his papers and extracted a sheet. He showed it to the Judge, pointing to a line half way down.

"It seems that between ninety and a hundred ducats' worth were missing," da Cagli said.

"Fifty Crowns were my reward for shooting General Bourbon. The rest were wages."

Da Prato pointed to a lower part of the page. The Judge coughed.

"Hurrumph. So it seems."

Well, never mind about the gold. What we want to know is what did you do with the jewels? We believe that there were eighty thousand ducats' worth, and we have been informed that you kept them."

Benvenuto burst out laughing.

"Eighty thousand ducats' worth of jewels! Me?" He slapped his chest. "Do you think I would have come back to Rome after the war if I'd stolen all that? Do you suppose I'd have come back to Rome last year and risked getting myself hanged if I'd got all that?"

Da Cagli pursed his lips. "You could have spent it," he said lamely.

"And what was Pope Clement doing all this time? Do you mean he didn't notice the jewels were gone? Or perhaps he was too embarrassed to ask for them?"

The Judge realised that Benvenuto had taken charge of the situation.

"Cellini, this attitude of yours will get you nowhere."

"I'm not anywhere I want to be right now," Benvenuto muttered sullenly.

"What was that you said?"

"I said, 'I'll help you all I can right now,' sir."

Da Prato, who was seated nearest to Benvenuto, repeated the question. "Alright, so tell us what you did with the jewels."

"Would you believe me if I told you we were so short of musket balls, we shot them at the enemy?"

Again the Judge's fist crashed down on the table. "Cellini!" he shouted.

Benvenuto turned to face him.

"My apologies, your Honour, but I don't know why this person keeps on interrupting. Perhaps he thinks you don't know how to do your job." He tried to drive a wedge between his two tormentors.

"After I took the stones from their settings, I sorted them into their different kinds. Diamonds, rubies, emeralds, sapphires and so on, you know?"

Da Cagli nodded.

"Then we counted and listed them."

"We?"

"Me and two priests."

"Who were they?"

"I don't know. With those funny clothes they wear, they all look alike to me. It wasn't Messer da Prato. He was hiding in the cellar from the Spaniards, I suppose. He should be able to check who they were. He knows who was on Pope Clement's staff, and he's got records of everything that ever happens."

"What happened next?"

"One of the priests made little purses out of linen." Benvenuto tapped his forehead with his finger. "No, it wasn't linen, it was parchment or paper. Anyway, it isn't important. He sewed them into the hem of his Holiness' best robe."

"What did the Pope do with them?"

"I heard he used them to ransom himself. Can't he find out?" He pointed at da Prato.

"In time," said the Judge, "but isn't there any other proof that you have. A copy of the list, perhaps?" His tone was less accusatory now.

"After all these years, after the whole city was destroyed, and after all the travelling I've done, would it be reasonable to expect me to have it?"

Grudgingly the Judge admitted, "Perhaps not."

"Well I have got it!" Benvenuto exclaimed triumphantly.

Da Prato could not help himself. "With you?" he asked.

Benvenuto pretended to pat his pockets and his pouch, and then snapped his finger and thumb.

"There, there! Isn't that stupid of me? Fancy walking about without a whole lifetime's business records on me just in case I get unexpectedly arrested."

"Messer Cellini!" said the Judge, his voice rising higher at each syllable, although he was smiling - almost.

Benvenuto was pleased to hear himself being addressed by his title again. "I'll go and find them and bring them to you first thing in the morning," he offered.

"You're going nowhere. The warrant says you stay here until this business is cleared up. The Sergeant will go and collect it. Tell him where it is."

"With the most humble respect, sir, I don't want that man in my house. He's stolen things from me before. Five crowns it was, and I don't suppose I'll ever get it back," he added wistfully.

"And if he does get his hands on it, I don't trust him not to destroy it, just to get me into trouble. Let me send a note to a friend to fetch it. Please!"

The Judge turned to da Prato. "Give him a pen and paper," he ordered.

Benvenuto scrawled a few lines to Raffaello del Moro.

"I'm in trouble through a ridiculous and false accusation. Please open my black leather chest and bring the folio of documents labelled 'Clement VII' to Sant' Angelo. Deliver them to Messer Ceserino. No one else. Please hurry as they won't let me out."

He signed it with a flourish and held up the finger on which he wore his signet ring. Reluctantly da Prato heated a blob of wax for him.

The Judge rose and Benvenuto, Ceserino and da Prato did likewise. "Well, that's it for the moment," da Cagli said. He turned to Ceserino. "Master Castellan, have him locked up until I want him again."

When da Cagli left, Crespino signalled to his man to take hold of Benvenuto, but the fat little jailer held up his hand.

"It's alright, Sergeant, he's my prisoner now. He can't escape, and so far I've heard nothing which makes me want to treat him like a convict. He'll stay in my quarters tonight."

As the Sergeant started to protest, he added firmly, "It's my responsibility. Go about your business!"

The next day's session was very short.

Del Moro arrived early in the morning and Ceserino brought him to Benvenuto who extracted the document he wanted after a second, slow and heart-bumping search through the leather wallet. The first time, in his haste, he had missed it altogether.

The Judge read the list, and then sent it skimming along the table to da Prato, who just glanced at it and looked at da Cagli with a silent shrug of his shoulders.

"It's not signed," the Judge said. "Do you recognise the handwriting, Messer da Prato?"

"No, your Excellency."

"Have you managed to find out which secretary his Holiness had with him at the time? Or the name of the priest who is supposed to have sewed up the jewels?"

"No, your Excellency."

"Can you say for sure that this is the list of the jewels we are looking for?"

"Again, no your Excellency. This could be a list of anything. I don't even know if this is eighty thousand ducats' worth. Suppose it is: maybe the jewels that were broken up were worth much more."

The Judge turned to Benvenuto. "It's not much help, is it?"

"But at least it's something for your Excellency to start on. I will be at your disposition to give you any further assistance you want once Messer da Prato has finished his enquiries."

"You can be sure you'll be at my disposition," said the Judge, "because you're not leaving here until I'm satisfied."

"But how long will that be? I have my work - my business." Benvenuto protested. "Messer da Prato has all the records. It shouldn't take him any time at all."

Da Prato grinned, his tongue flickering like a thin pink snake between the gaps in his yellow and blackened teeth.

"Oh, I don't know. As you so rightly remarked yesterday, with all my scribbling, I've already got more than enough to do as it is. Don't worry, I won't keep you waiting longer than I think necessary."

"Messer Ceserino," said the Judge as he left, "there's just one other thing. Naturally I reported the whole of my conversation with Cellini to Messer Pier Luigi Farnese. The whole of it." He stared hard at Benvenuto.

"His Excellency asks me to remind you, Messer Ceserino, that he appointed you to this very comfortable post, and that until this Tribunal is satisfied - if it ever is - that this man is innocent, he's a prisoner, not your house guest. See he's locked up. This is a jail, not a blasted inn!"

-29-

Despite Pier Luigi's instructions, Gabriello did not lock Benvenuto in the dungeons, but in a room reserved for the more distinguished prisoners of the Pope. As his imprisonment extended from days into weeks, he was allowed to move about the building against his promise to go back to his cell whenever Pier Luigi's men were around and, above all, not to try to escape.

He was also permitted as many visitors as he wanted. Del Moro and Ascanio came often as they tried to keep Benvenuto's shop running, and Benvenuto was allowed to do some work so long as he could manage with small tools and without a furnace.

Cardinal d'Este of Ferrara discreetly came to see him while in the Castle "on other business," which included watching Benvenuto working on his jug and basin. Each time he reassured him that he was doing what he could to get him released.

At the request of Cardinal de' Medici, the French Ambassador made representations to the Pope but was rebuffed on the grounds that Benvenuto was "just a trouble-making murderer." Actually the French King's intervention did more harm than good, because the Pope deviously decided that he might be able to use Benvenuto as a minor bargaining pawn at some later time.

It soon became clear to Benvenuto that the Pope might never let him go. He lapsed into a state of depression and despair.

—⚜—

Thirty or forty days into his imprisonment - he had lost count - Benvenuto was locked into his room for the night. He looked anxiously at the single candle he was allowed. When it went out his windowless cell would be pitch black.

Even the passageway outside the room was so poorly lit that there was no light to creep under the door - the only thing that got in was a draught that made his candle flutter and burn more quickly.

When it went out there would be nothing left to do except to lie on his bed and try to sleep. Some nights he would wake up and not know whether he ought to try to go to sleep again, or whether it was nearly morning. He would frantically toss and turn in the blackness, alternately tormented by the fear of never being free, and fantasising about how he would be released, rehabilitated and showered with honours by an abjectly repentant Pope.

At other times he would be awakened by the door crashing open. The guard would order him up to perform his first degrading task of the day - to empty his chamber pot. Then, after eating the breakfast of fruit brought in the day before by Ascanio, he would have to sweep out and clean his cell.

—⚍—

But now he was sitting on the end of his bed, waiting for his candle to go out. His feet were planted flat on the stone floor, a few inches apart, his elbows on his knees, his chin in his two hands as he stared at the door, as if by doing so he could miraculously make it open. He stared so hard that his eyes became glazed and gradually crossed until the very nails in the door hinges began to dance and merge into one another.

The nails in the hinges! Benvenuto jumped up and went over to the door and peered at it as if he had never seen it before, although from the countless, long boring hours he had spent in the cell, he knew every bolt, every nail, and every knot in the woodwork as well as every name and date scratched in the brickwork by previous occupiers.

The door had no key-hole. It was secured outside by a large cast-iron latch. Inside it had three metal hinges bolted to the door by two rows of nails with big, square heads.

He picked up a pair of pincers from among his tools, got hold of one of the nails and tugged and rocked it, up and down and side to side until he gradually eased it out. He pushed it back into its hole and seized a nail from the next hinge. After a few minutes work he was looking at it clutched in the end of his pincers.

He went back to his candle and passed the nail through the hot melted wax and pushed it into its hole, the hardening wax holding it tight; then he did the same with the first one.

Excitedly, he started on a nail on the bottom hinge, but in his impatience, when he wrenched it out, it was bent.

"God! Now I'm for it! I'll be caught before I've even begun! I'll finish up changed to the dungeons chained wall."

With the nail held tight in the jaws of his pincers he started to tap it with his hammer, but he had picked the wrong moment. The guard, just passing on his half-hourly patrol, banged on the closed door.

"What the Hell is going on in there? What's that noise? What are you up to?"

Benvenuto quickly snatched the nail and hid it behind his back.

"Doing? Nothing. I'm just getting on with a bit of work on Cardinal D' Este's bowl. Why officer, is something wrong? Am I disturbing someone?"

"Oh, shut up!" the jailer shouted through the door. "Don't let me hear another sound from you, or I'll come in and quieten you myself."

Benvenuto listened to the footsteps disappearing along the corridor. That was another thing. The guards. He would have to take them into account. It would be no use just rushing into an escape. It wasn't simply a matter of getting out of his cell - the whole thing would need careful planning. Benvenuto looked heavenwards in gratitude for a timely warning.

He quietly snipped the nail in two about half way down, applied the hot wax and slipped it into its hole and dropped the other half in the one place the guards would never search: the chamber pot. He would get rid of it in the morning.

Then he threw himself on his bed and began to daydream of what he would do when he escaped. Where would he go? Venice? France? "Anywhere away from Rome!"

The candle spluttered out, and Benvenuto wrinkled his nose at the acrid smell of the burning wick.

Benvenuto began his planning the first thing the next morning. He took advantage of his freedom to wander round the fortress by making a mental note of every sentry post outside the walls and the beats patrolled by the guards on the inside, as well as how long they took to walk them. He could only hope that the night-time routine was the same as the day.

When he was locked up in his cell that night, he measured the length of the guards' patrol by the amount of candle that burned between each round. He was able to work out what was the shortest time, and on the day he broke out, that would be the time he would allow himself.

Next, refreshing his memory of the layout of the upper parts of the castle from his garrison duties in the siege, he worked out his best escape route, and decided that he must make some sort of rope.

The more privileged prisoners were allowed two coarse linen sheets each. Under the pretext of getting them changed, he managed to steal one which he hid in his mattress. A few days later he repeated the trick, and a few days later he did so yet again.

As his mattress was now noticeably too bulky, he then had to smuggle out some of the damp, insect-ridden straw with which it was usually stuffed and disposing of it, a handful at a time. Some he dropped over the battlements; some he dropped in the yard where the horses came, and some he surreptitiously threw on the fires burning in the grates in the various parts of the building.

—⚌—

Now came his first alarm. A sudden search of the cells. Benvenuto did not know whether they were suspicious of someone or whether it was just a routine spot check. Whatever the reason he had something to hide. Not his tools - the guards knew they were authorised - but his extra sheets and the loosened nails.

Benvenuto was sitting in his cell eating his unpalatable midday meal: a cold mutton chop left over from last night's dinner, a piece of dry bread saved from his breakfast which he smeared with a little of the mutton fat, and a couple of apples, somewhat soft and wrinkled from having been stored since the summer. Ascanio would bring his main meal late in the afternoon; it would be tasty, but tepid by the time it got past the sentries, unless he could heat it in one of the fireplaces.

He was preoccupied with gnawing the last of the meat off the bone when Crespino and two guards stepped into the room.

"We're going to search the cell."

"Please make yourself entirely at home, but what on earth for?"

"Weapons."

Benvenuto was incredulous. He looked round the tiny room with its low bed, single stool, table, shelf, and bare, plastered, windowless walls.

"Weapons? You did say weapons? Well, I keep my twenty-four pounder cannon under the bed, while behind those magnificent damask draperies are a lance and an arquebus. And of course my sword is with the suit of armour in the corner."

"Very funny," said the sergeant. "I wonder if you'll still be making jokes on the day I take you off to be hanged."

"You'll never see me hanged," Benvenuto retorted. "I'll be riding round in my own carriage while you're begging for bread on the steps of the whorehouse. By the way, that reminds me, how is your mother these days?"

The sergeant hit Benvenuto back-handed in the mouth and knocked him sprawling across the bed. As Benvenuto wiped a trickle of blood from his split and rapidly swelling lip, Crespino started to draw his sword and said over his shoulder to the other two soldiers,

"You saw this violent prisoner attack me. Now I'll have to kill him to protect myself."

"Help! Help! Anyone, help!" Benvenuto yelled at the top of his voice. "Three guards have come to murder me. I'm unarmed, but they're going to kill me. If anyone can hear, please help!"

Crespino paused, his sword half-way from its scabbard. He pushed it back in.

"You think you're bloody clever, don't you? I don't think you'll ever get out of here - alive that is - but if you do, come and see me. We'll see what sort of guts you've really got. I'll cut them from your belly for you."

Crespino swept Benvenuto's tools, crockery and food onto the floor.

"Come on you two," he ordered his men, and all three backed out of the door.

Benvenuto sat up and dabbed his mouth with his sheet and shrugged his shoulders. A fat lip was a small enough price to pay for distracting the searchers, and at least his escape plan was still intact.

Methodically, and with the patience that came from his painstaking craft, Benvenuto continued with his preparations. He sent for del Moro and instructed him to sell his stock, collect his debts and to finish off the Cardinal's jug and bowl which were in their final stages. He also asked him to get rid of the staff - keeping Ascanio and Busbacca in his own service, and generally to wind up his affairs for him.

"What's the idea?" his friend asked.

"Because I've had enough, that's why. They'll have to let me out soon, and when they do, I'm off, that very day."

"Are you sure they're letting you go?"

"Of course," Benvenuto lied. "How much longer can they take? I'll be on my way so fast they won't have time to change their minds. That's why I want my money ready. I'm going back to France. I'll take the two boys with me, if they want to come."

"By the way," Benvenuto said as del Moro was about to leave, "you won't tell anyone that I expect them to let me out any day. You know what they're like. They'd probably change their minds, just for spite."

"Well, what happens if anyone finds out I'm selling your stuff? You know it's impossible to keep a secret in this town."

Benvenuto thought for a moment. "Say you're selling me up because I owe you money, and you're not going to wait for it any longer. Alright?"

—⚡—

At night Benvenuto continued with his attack on the hinges, but he carefully balanced the number of nails he could extract without making it obvious that the door was weakened, against the time it would take him to pull out the rest at the very last minute.

By putting his candle out a little early, and by changing one stump for a slightly larger one each night, he managed to secrete a whole extra candle in his mattress. Every day he checked and double-checked the sentries' routine so that he would not be taken by surprise by any change.

Then he set about turning his stolen sheets into a rope. He cut each one into strips about six inches wide, folded them in half lengthways and sewed the edges with strong twine that Ascanio had brought in with him. Now, with each one overlapping by about six inches, he very carefully joined the linen tubes together with row after row of stitches first in one direction, and then to make doubly sure, crossways.

He had two walls to scale, so he made himself two ropes. He intended that the ends should be very secure before he entrusted his weight to them. On the last night he would knot the rope at intervals to give him hand and footholds, because he was realistic enough to realise that his many illnesses and his imprisonment had left him very weakened.

The next thing to be decided was the date and time. The date was easy. The first really dark night. He decided not to wait for del Moro to get his money for him. Escaping was the thing. He was not going to risk another search or his life for money. There had been many times when he had had none, and he would manage somehow - as always.

Selling Benvenuto's stock was easy. Gold is gold. Benvenuto's debtors were all good customers and paid del Moro readily. All except Cardinal D' Este who thought he was doing Benvenuto a favour.

"Messer del Moro, if Benvenuto owes you any money, he will pay you himself when he gets out of this bit of trouble. Let's hope it won't be long now."

Del Moro indignantly reported the conversation to Benvenuto.

"No matter, my friend," said Benvenuto, "it's my money he's keeping, not yours. You don't want to get so carried away with things that you start believing our own story, do you?"

It was now about nine o'clock at night, and although the prisoners were all locked up, the building was not yet quiet, so any noise he made would not be noticed. It was on the last day of the moon and Benvenuto had seen the thick heavy clouds that afternoon and he knew there was no chance of them blowing away. He guessed that it would be pitch black outside. If only it would rain and keep the sentries in their huts, so much the better!

He had pulled out several more nails as soon as his cell was closed for the night after supper, and now he was standing with his ear pressed against the thick door until he heard what he was listening for: the sound of the guard's footsteps and the jingle of his keys as he made his rounds.

Benvenuto heard the jailer stop and not move on. His stomach had been churning with apprehension all the afternoon, and now he felt as if his chest was being crushed by thick straps, while at the same time a great ball of iron climbed up his throat.

He retreated to the back of his cell, and in a cracked voice - his mouth was so dry - he began to recite the Lord's Prayer.

"That's a good chap," the guard shouted through the door. "You say your 'night-night' prayers, and God will be very pleased with you. You'll be up there with Him very soon now, I shouldn't wonder."

He walked away chuckling, and Benvenuto made a rude gesture at the locked door before putting the mark on his candle to show when he would be back. By the time he was, Benvenuto expected to be out.

As soon as the guard left, he took out all the nails he had loosened over the past few days. There were only four he had not tampered with, two in the top hinge and two in the bottom. Every other one had been carefully drawn so that it could be replaced if there was a last minute hitch. For the same reason, he now carefully pulled one more from each hinge. Only the last two, when he reached the point of no return, would be taken out the quickest way he could.

Benvenuto looked at his candle. He had twenty-five minutes, forty if he was lucky, before the guard came back, but if he was not out of the cell in fifteen, he would wait for the next round and meanwhile hold the door shut with the short length of string looped around a nail that he had hammered in for that very purpose.

"I need three minutes to get each of the last two nails out, that will leave me six minutes. For God's sake be careful!" he grunted to himself as one of the old nails bent. "If it breaks, it'll take hours."

In a hundred years or more, the hinges had become fused into the woodwork by rust and carelessly applied paint. He would have to lever them out with the ends of his pincers. He wasted two of his precious minutes, sweating with apprehension and when he could no longer pretend to himself that he was "listening for the guard," he finally did it. Then, with his "ropes" slung over his shoulder and his tools tucked into his belt and pouch, he gently applied his weight to the edge of the door.

Nothing happened.

He pressed harder, and this time the door gave a little. It was the latch at the other end that was holding it shut. With two hands pressed flat against the door, and his feet slipping on the stone floor, he pushed as hard as he could and gradually the tremendous leverage made the soft iron bend, bit by bit, until a gap appeared between the door and the jamb.

Now he had something to get a grip on, and turning sideways, he pushed his hand through and heaved again, this time with his shoulder. As the gap widened, he forced his stool into the space to stop the door springing back and looked at his candle. He had taken more than fifteen minutes and was into his safety margin, but there was still time before the sentry was due.

With a final push, and at the same time twisting the stool inside the gap, Benvenuto made enough space to squeeze through. There was a moment of panic when his belt buckle caught on the wood, and then he was out in the passageway. He slid the stool back into the cell and leaned against the door until it was nearly back into position - not that it would withstand even the most cursory inspection, so next he created a small diversion.

The only light in the corridor came from a six-branched candelabra at each end. Quite often a candle would be blown out by the draught, and Benvenuto had sometimes heard the guard grumbling and cursing to himself when he had to relight it. Benvenuto went to the candelabra along the passage past his cell and blew out not one, but four candles. That would give the jailer something to think about other than whether the cell door was still closed!

Benvenuto took hold of the handle of the door of the short stairway leading up to the battlements. The iron ball was back in his throat again. He slowly turned the handle, and even more slowly and quietly, and with a deep breath he eased the door open, wincing at the creak of its dry hinges.

There was a feint rustling as a rat scurried along the corridor, and Benvenuto, thinking the sentry was coming back, flung himself through the door, and leaned against it, bracing his feet on the edge of the bottom step, panting and mopping the sweat from his forehead with his sleeve. He stayed there for nearly a minute - it seemed longer - and then realising he was safe for the moment, he began to climb the stairs.

The stairway led to a terrace which served as a lookout platform. Benvenuto hunted round in the dark for a water spout made from a thick hollow tile projecting about three inches from the parapet which he had noticed on one of his reconnaissances, and tied the end of his shorter rope to it. He was not sure whether the pipe would really stand his weight, but once or twice in the last day or two when he had reached over the edge and leaned on it hard, it had seemed firm enough. Now there was nothing else to do but to trust it.

He turned his face up to Heaven. "Dear God, don't let the pipe break. That's all I ask, and that's a small enough thing, considering that you've done nothing for me lately."

He swung himself over the edge, hesitated for a moment, and then, with his eyes screwed shut began to lower himself to the next level. As his feet touched the ground on a roof-top poultry yard he discovered he had been holding his breath for the last part of the descent.

He tugged at the rope, trying to bring it down, but the knot was too tight. After a few fruitless attempts, he tied a large stone on to the end and tried to throw it back over the parapet, but had to cover his head with his arms as it came crashing down again. He stood back to give himself room for an even harder throw, but this time he hit the wall and the rock fell out of the knotted sheet, hitting the pavement with a loud clatter, waking the startled chickens which let out a squawking and clucking noise which quickly subsided.

"What the hell was that?" shouted a voice from the courtyard below.

"It was probably one of those damn cats. The place is swarming with them," someone replied from the guard house. "What do you think it was? A thunderbolt or maybe an Angel?"

A door slammed shut and Benvenuto looked over the edge of the terrace, but it was too dark to see anything. He decided to abandon the rope, hoping no one would spot it before he was clear.

―⚘―

Benvenuto had planned to make his way from the chicken run to the outer battlements, but instead something went wrong. The yard had a high wooden fence round it to keep the birds in, but the gate was not just shut as it usually was during the day, but was locked. There were two bolts on the outside which Benvenuto could not reach to slide open.

He could not reach the top of the fence, so he stood back and took a run and jump, but could not get a hold of the top; instead he hit the fence with his body, bruising both his knees, while the noise made the chickens restless so that they started to make gobbling noises again.

"Oh shush!" Benvenuto hissed at them. "You'll have the guards up here in a minute!" The birds quietened down as if they understood him.

Prowling round the fence looking for a gap or a weakness, he stubbed his toe on a plank left lying on the ground by workmen years before.

Benvenuto dragged it clear of the weeds and long grass that had grown round it, swearing to himself as splinters stuck into the palms of his hands, and leaned it against the fence. It did not reach the top and when he tested his weight on it, it slipped and he had to grope around in the blackness for a rock to brace it.

"For God's sake hurry up!" he muttered, as flat on his stomach he slowly pulled himself up the rough damp wood. The fence creaked and swayed, and the chickens fluttered nervously in their coop, but at last he reached the end of the plank, which by now was bending in the middle. By arching himself backwards and reaching upwards, he was just able to grasp the top of the fence with his fingers and swing himself up.

The sharp edge of the fence dug into him painfully as he lay there, head one side and feet the other. He twisted sideways and over and slowly lowered himself to the ground and stood for a few moments, and straining to get his breath back.

He worked his way to the side of the castle facing the Prati where, at that time of night, there would be hardly any passers-by.

As he circled the fortifications, he paused at the spot from which he had shot Bourbon, raised an imaginary arquebus to his shoulder and said, "Bang!"

A few steps further on he stopped again by one of the gun positions. Benvenuto touched the stone blocks which had nearly crushed him to death, and then ran his hand over the cannon which had replaced the one at which Bombardier Guiliano had been killed and he had been spared, in the random way that death is dealt out in battle. He shook his head and continued past the obstacle course of cannons, cannon balls and wooden firing steps.

As he did so, a sweet sickly stench wafted its way up to him; a gruesome reminder of what was just below the battlements. Apart from the numerous other crimes for which the penalty was death, there was an average of fourteen murders a day in Rome. Not all those sentenced to be hanged had a ceremonial execution in the river bank square in front of the prison. Most of them were simply bundled, kicking and screaming over the wall of the castle, a noose tied round their necks and left to struggle, futilely scrabbling to find a foothold on the smooth vertical stonework to relieve the dreadful choking pressure before the last blackness set in.

A few, the brave and the realistic, would jump, hoping that the rope would break their necks, putting an instant end to their suffering. In the end the result was the same; rows of blackening, putrefying corpses hanging from the walls of the castle.

Benvenuto nervously fingered his throat. "Jesus! If I get caught, that could be me at the end of one of those!"

The thought spurred him to hurry to the spot he was looking for. He quickly tied his rope to a bolt in the wall and began to climb down.

Benvenuto's feet kicked empty air. He had reached the end of the rope of sheets, but as he looked down in the shadow of the vast bulk of the castle, he still could not see the ground. He cursed his own stupidity in under-estimating the length of the rope he would need and forgetting to allow for all the knots he had made to help him down.

He was dangling at full arm's length and the strain was becoming unbearable. There was nothing else for him to do except to summon up courage and let himself drop - blindly. He rocked himself backwards and forwards to gather momentum and pushed himself away from the wall. As he swung back again he let go, intending to bounce off the stonework with his feet braced to break his fall. He did not realise that the faster he pushed away, the faster he would swing back, so he smashed hard into the wall, banging his head and his already-bruised knees.

His rope had finished about fifteen feet from the ground and he was totally unprepared when he landed on the back of both heels. A tremendous pain shot through his right ankle, and as he fell on to the pavement he struck the side of his head yet again, this time with such force that he lost consciousness.

―⚏―

Benvenuto did not know how long he had been lying there, but a light rain had been falling long enough to get his face and clothes quite wet. He put his hand to his head and felt a sort of stickiness. He guessed he had been bleeding. As he levered himself into a sitting position, he became aware of the dull ache in his ankle. He twisted himself round so that he could lean his back against the wall, sharply sucking in his breath and biting his lip as the ache turned into a throbbing stab.

He leaned forward to feel. "It's broken. I've broken my bloody ankle. Oh God! What am I going to do now? I must get away from here before they miss me."

Clutching on to the wall for support, he managed to stand on one foot, wincing as his head, knees, back and injured leg gave him sharp twinges of pain. Still holding the wall with one hand, he gingerly put his foot on the ground but instantly lifted it off with a muttered curse his eyes watering in agony.

Wasting no more time, he began to hop away from the prison on his good leg, every jolt making his head throb even more, but he could not go far on one foot because by now, not only was his bruised left knee hurting, but also every muscle in the calf and thigh of his leg was stiff and aching in sympathy.

Benvenuto sat on a broken barrel and looked round. He was four or five hundred yards across the Tiber from the prison, near to the beginning of the "via Recta" - Straight Street - in part of a flourishing residential and business district. He was not even going in the right direction!

He picked up a piece of wood and tied it to his leg with his belt. It was not very firm, and it still would not support his weight, but Benvenuto hoped it would help a little if he accidentally put his injured foot on the ground - as he had already done several agonising times.

He looked up at the sky. It had stopped raining, the clouds were clearing and the crescent moon would soon be out. He was in danger of being seen, and even though he was absolutely exhausted and his left leg was stiff and painful, he had to keep moving away from the castle, he had to find shelter and above all, he had to find a doctor.

If he went roughly parallel with the river, passing the church of San Salvatore in Lauro, and then on for about another five hundred yards, he would reach the Palace of Cardinal d'Este. He was sure he would find help there.

He wrenched one of the staves off the barrel, and using it as a walking stick, began hopping along the road.

Suddenly a pale shape hurled itself at him from out of a gateway, and Benvenuto shouted with fright as it knocked him to the ground. It was a huge mastiff. A guard dog or one of the wild dogs that roamed the city, alone and in packs. Benvenuto did not know which, but it made no difference - he was fighting for his life!

The beast's teeth sank into the forearm that he instinctively threw up to protect his throat as he lay there, trapped under its feet and its 150 pounds and more of weight.

Benvenuto smashed his fist down on the dog's nose. The animal did not let go, but ground its teeth even harder into his arm. His instincts as a street fighter came to his aid, and a jab with his thumb in the animal's eye made it shake its head and let go momentarily, but its teeth snapped down again over his elbow, and this time Benvenuto screamed in agony.

He felt something pressing between his side and the ground. It was his pliers. He pulled them out of his pocket with his free hand and stabbed the dog's ribs with the handles. This time it was the dog's turn to yelp with pain. Benvenuto smashed the pliers down on its head, once, twice, and once again and it retreated out of reach, but still making growling noises in its throat.

Benvenuto got up on all fours and roared back while the dog stood its ground with its feet spread apart, ready either to spring or run. Benvenuto took the initiative. Picking up his barrel stave, he slashed at the animal, giving it a sharp crack across the back with its edge. The dog tried to bite the stick, but it still stayed where it was until, seeing Benvenuto raise his weapon for another blow, it turned and loped off down the road.

Benvenuto collapsed to the ground, shaking uncontrollably and started to cry.

"Oh Christ! What's happening to me? Even for killing that swine Pompeo I don't deserve all this. What's going to happen to me next?"

Benvenuto realised he had no time to waste on self-pity. Pulling himself together, he tried to stand, but he felt so weak and was still trembling so much that he simply could not do it. He gritted his teeth.

"Well, if I can't walk or hop, I'll bloody well have to crawl."

He started on his way on his hands and knees, his right knee bent upwards to try to protect his foot from contact with the ground. When he reached the corner around which the dog had gone he paused, fearful in case it was lying in ambush. By now, his hands were raw and bleeding and he forced himself to stand upright and leaned against the wall of the nearest building.

He heard the sound of hoof beats and the rattle of a cart on the roadway and pressed himself back into the shadows. As the cart got nearer, he saw that it was a water carrier bringing great stone pitchers of cool clean water down from the hills for the wealthier houses, some of which were not served by their own wells or the ancient Roman aqueducts.

The ragged, scruffy old pedlar crossed himself in terror as Benvenuto staggered out into his path and stood on one leg, supporting himself with his makeshift crutch, and held up his free hand to halt him.

"Stop. Please stop. I need help. Can you give me a ride?"

Without waiting for an answer, Benvenuto dragged himself over the tailgate of the little cart. The water seller craned his head round and looked Benvenuto up and down.

"Holy Mother of God! What happened to you?"

"Please get moving, and I'll tell you. But hurry, he may still be after me."

Benvenuto told the old man where Raffaello del Moro lived and with a prod to the donkey's ribs from the driver's stick the cart lurched off.

"So who's chasing you, and why?"

"You see," said Benvenuto coyly, "I was visiting a friend when her husband came home unexpectedly and I had to jump out of the window. And if it wasn't bad enough that I broke my ankle when I jumped, the bastard set his rotten dog on me!'

"Caught in bed with someone else's wife, and had to jump out of the window, did you? I only wish I still had the strength for it myself."

There was hardly any room for Benvenuto to sit at the back of the cart, and as it bumped over the rough roadway it made his broken ankle start to throb even more, so he took his barrel stave and used it as a prop to hold his leg out straight, sticking one end of the wooden slat under his rump to hold it in position.

He twisted round slightly and, lifting the lid off one of the earthenware jars, he helped himself to a ladle of cold water which he swished round his mouth and spat out again. His throat was raw and dry.

"It must have been from barking back at that bloody dog," he thought as the cart brought him to del Moro's door.

-30-

It was just dawn when Benvenuto arrived at del Moro's house, which was also his workroom and shop. Two housemaids were helping Gina to get breakfast ready for the workmen, but it was del Moro himself, still dressed only in his nightshirt and a pair of sandals, who opened the door in answer to Benvenuto's frantic knocking.

What he saw was his friend, one leg in a clumsy splint, propping himself up on the other with a lump of wood, his clothes in tatters, stockings in shreds, hands and knees grazed, blood on his face head and arms, and covered from head to foot with mud from the street.

He clapped his hands to his face. "Holy Mother of God! What's happened to you?" he said, echoing the first words of the water carrier. "How did you get here? How did you manage to...."

Benvenuto put a finger to his lips, jerked his head behind him in the direction of the old man and pursed his lips in a silent "shush."

Del Moro took the hint. "Come on, let's get you inside and see what we can do for you." He turned to the water carrier. "Thank you very much for bringing him home. It was very kind of you."

"That's alright. I didn't mind going so far out of my way." The old man paused hopefully. "Even though it's hard for me to climb all those hills."

"Oh, er yes," said del Moro. "Wait a moment."

He went into the house, pushing Benvenuto ahead of him. He came back a few moments later with a gold crown. The old man looked at it lying in the palm of his dirty hand. It was more than he could earn in months.

"Thank you kindly, your Honour, I ...."

Del Moro waved his hand. "There's just one more thing. You won't tell anyone where he is, will you?"

"Me? I won't say a word. I was young myself once, you know." He waved at Benvenuto through the open door. "I don't suppose you'll be doing much jumping in and out of bed for a while, but I'll tell you what. Next time you do, have one for me, will you?"

He put the back of his hand to his lips and gave himself a noisy kiss, and started to lead his donkey back the way he had come.

Busbacca was sent to get the Doctor.

"Go and fetch Jacamo Arezzo," Benvenuto instructed the boy. "His son was once my apprentice." He looked at del Moro. "He won't give me away."

Del Moro shrugged his shoulders. "It's your neck. Now let's get you on the bed and clean you up a bit before he gets here. Ascanio, come on, give me a hand. And you girl," he said, pointing to one of the maids, "bring some hot water, and some towels. Gina, you can fetch Benvenuto a drink of water."

"Wine," corrected Benvenuto.

"Wine," said del Moro.

They stripped Benvenuto of all his clothes. Del Moro looked at the heap of rags lying on the floor.

"Burn them."

Gina gathered them together and held up the shoes.

"What about these."

Del Moro wrinkled his nose in disgust. "Burn them first of all."

With Ascanio's help he began gently to sponge away the dirt. He examined the blood matted in Benvenuto's hair.

"I'll leave this alone. If I wash it off, you'll only start to bleed again. Are you going to tell me what this is all about? Did you break out of prison? You must have done. Why? I thought you said they were going to let you go soon. What happened?"

"I guess they changed their minds. How do I know what they were going to do? I saw a chance, so I took it. Anyway it's done now."

"You know, Benvenuto, the Pope will have you hanged if you're caught. The least that'll happen is that you'll rot in jail forever."

"Oh come on! I didn't do anything to be sent to prison for in the first place. The Pope just forgot about me, that's all. Anyway he once escaped from Sant' Angelo himself, you know. Nothing happened to him."

That was true. Pope Alexander VI had imprisoned Alexander Farnese for forging a Papal Brief and even threatened to have him executed, but the young man, with the help of friends and a heavily bribed guard had been lowered down the wall in a basket.

Del Moro scoffed. "Your name's Cellini, not Farnese. They don't hang Farneses that easily, and no one will start a war if you swing. Why, hardly anyone would notice you've gone," he added brutally."

—⁂—

Doctor Arezzo began by examining Benvenuto's head. He gently snipped away the knot of clotted blood and hair, and probed the wound with his finger. Benvenuto jerked his head with a sharp intake of breath.

"Does that hurt?"

"Only when you poke at it!" Benvenuto retorted.

"It certainly hasn't done anything to your famous tongue of yours anyway. Now let me see the bump on your forehead. Hmm! That's nothing. I'll just put some salve on it, and also on your hands."

He carefully studied Benvenuto's bitten arm, but at first did not touch it.

"A dog?"

"I think it was a wolf. A whole pack of them."

"Look here Messer Cellini," there was a note of irritation in the doctor's voice, "It's bad enough that I've been dragged out of bed before the birds are up. I'm in no mood for your stories. Now, was the dog mad?"

"How should I know? It was dark."

"Well, if it was, you'll find out soon enough Meantime a little of the salve on your arm, some more on your knees while I'm at it and then I'll be ready for that ankle of yours. I bet that's what you've been waiting for, eh?"

Benvenuto managed a sickly grin and quickly took another swig of his wine.

With del Moro and Ascanio holding his shoulders and Busbacca leaning on his right knee and Gina on his left, Benvenuto crammed the knuckle of his forefinger into his mouth as the doctor took hold of his calf and foot and began to manipulate them. The grating of the two ends of bone was distinctly audible in the tiny bedroom - until the sound was drowned out by Benvenuto's yelling.

Arezzo straightened his back.

"Well that's done. Now we'll bind it with these splints ...." he took them from the little leather sack he had with him "....and then I'll be off."

Arezzo poked the tip of his fore-finger in his ear and scratched vigorously.

"I won't ask how you got here. I thought you were supposed to be in prison, so as I can get into trouble for helping you, I hope everyone will forget I was here." He gave a little cough. "There's the small matter of my fee. One gold crown - no, a doubloon I think in the circumstances."

He glanced at Benvenuto's naked body - obviously he had no money on him. "Anyone?" he said, looking first at Ascanio and then at del Moro.

"Yes of course." Del Moro gave him the two coins. "Will you stay for breakfast?"

"Breakfast? I don't eat breakfast this time of day. Peasants and labourers eat breakfast this early, not surgeons. I'm going back to bed. Besides," he said, picking up his medicines, "if the police come, it won't be breakfast - it'll be more like the Last Supper."

If the doctor did not want any breakfast, Benvenuto did.

"You've got no idea what the food was like in that place. If it wasn't for what you sent into me, I'd have starved, and if I tried to save anything from one meal to the next, I had to fight the rats for it."

A plate of tortellini, little thin hot pancakes stuffed with chopped spicy meat was placed in front of Benvenuto who swallowed them without seeming to stop to chew. They were followed by a platter of cold meat and chicken left over from last night's meal and cheese all washed down with earthenware mugs of beer.

At last Benvenuto leaned back in his chair and tried to belch. He gently tapped at the bottom of his breast bone with his fist.

"I've got to get away from here."

"I know," del Moro replied, "but where."

"I haven't decided yet. Maybe Venice, or better still France. Anywhere so long as it's nowhere near Farnese and that bastard son of his."

"You won't be able to ride for at least a few days until your ankle is at least a little bit better, and the longer you stay in the city, the more chance there is of your being caught."

"I'll have to hide for a few days, but not here. If they do try to find me, they're bound to come here. Find me some lodgings with someone reliable and I'll go tonight."

Ascanio and Busbacca helped Benvenuto up to the attic and Gina laid out a mattress for him to sleep on.

"Thanks for everything. You won't forget to call me when it's time for lunch, will you?"

Gina giggled and shut the door, leaving Benvenuto in darkness, but this time it seemed friendly and protective, not frightening like his cell.

—⚭—

While Benvenuto was sleeping del Moro made a foolish error that was to cost Benvenuto dearly.

The news that Benvenuto had escaped was all over the city and crowds of people were gathered at Sant' Angelo looking at the sheet ropes hanging from the battlements like two absurd pennants mocking the Pope's authority.

Del Moro went to Cardinal d'Este and told him that Benvenuto was hiding in his house. He asked him to see the Pope and to suggest that since Benvenuto had not been convicted of any crime, he should be allowed to leave Rome, never to return.

"Well, Messer Farnese," the Pope asked his son, "what do you think of Cardinal d'Este's suggestion?"

"I believe that it would be an affront to your Holiness' dignity to allow this man to profit from his escape. He is also suspected of having stolen the property of the Holy See."

"Your Holiness," d'Este protested, "this story about the jewels is just gossip, and obvious nonsense at that. Cellini has too many important friends, Cardinal De' Medici, even the King of France among them for your Holiness to risk offending - and for what purpose?"

"For what purpose, Messer Farnese?" asked the Pope.

Pier Luigi's face swelled with rage. "I believe his Eminence Cardinal d'Este is petitioning the Holy Father to appoint his protégé to the next vacant Bishopric."

"So?"

"So, your Holiness," Pier Luigi replied, "I say that Cellini is a thief and a murderer. I say he escaped from jail and must go back. I say that the only way he should leave it again is at the end of a rope. I also say that people who want favours from the Pope shouldn't interfere in his affairs!"

Paul patted the air as if soothing a frisky puppy and made a clicking noise with his tongue.

"Tsk, Tsk. It is not necessary to speak like that. His Eminence has our interests at heart and is entitled to speak his mind."

The Pope could not see any reason to offend the Cardinal.

He turned to d'Este.

"Your Eminence must know how much we value his advice. This time however we must agree with Messer Farnese. Cellini has escaped from prison, and he must go back again. As to what may happen later ….. ," he shrugged his shoulders.

As soon as Cardinal D' Este had withdrawn, abashed, the Pope rounded on Gabriello Ceserino. The unhappy, fat little prison governor had been summoned to the Vatican to explain how Benvenuto had escaped, and had tried to make himself inconspicuous throughout the whole exchange.

"You, Sir! When I escaped from Sant' Angelo, it was with the help of a bribed guard. Find out who helped Cellini and have him whipped. And as for Cellini, he's still here in Rome. Get him. Either he goes back to his cell, or you do! Go on, you may leave."

—⚜—

Benvenuto was seated with del Moro at an early evening meal when the street door burst open. Benvenuto's dog, Cassius, now a temporary member of del Moro's household, jumped up and launched himself, snapping and snarling through bared teeth, at the soldiers led by Sergeant Crespino as they crowded into the room.

Crespino already had his gun in his hand and aimed it at the dog.

"Stop!" shouted del Moro. "I'll quieten him." He threw himself on Cassius and calmed the animal down.

The Sergeant shifted his aim to Benvenuto who was just sitting unable to move.

"Well, well! Look who's here! Come on you - up!" Crespino gestured with the barrel of his gun.

Del Moro intervened. "He can't move. His ankle's broken."

Crespino looked at Benvenuto's bandaged splinted leg stretched straight out under the table.

"Oh you poor chap. What a shame!" he sneered. "I do hope it's not too painful. By the way," he added, "do you know Giusto Sidoli?"

Benvenuto looked blank.

"He was the Sergeant of the Guard when you escaped. He got demoted because of you."

Benvenuto made what he hoped was an apologetic fluttering movement with his hands.

"He sent you a message."

Benvenuto's voice was cracked and horse. "What?"

"This," Crespino said, and kicked Benvenuto viciously on his injured ankle.

Benvenuto heard himself scream once, and then he fainted.

When he recovered, he was bound to a chair, his arms lashed tightly behind its upright back, his thighs tied to the seat and his legs to the feet of the chair.

As his eyes opened fully, he saw del Moro shaking his finger at Crespino.

"He's an injured, unarmed prisoner. If you hurt him again, you'll be in trouble, do you hear?"

The Sergeant grabbed del Moro's shirt into a bunch with one hand and with the other rhythmically tapped the gun barrel against the side of del Moro's jaw to emphasise every phrase.

"I'll be in trouble? Listen my friend, you've been harbouring an escaped prisoner. You'll be lucky if I'm not back for you too soon. And in any case, if you wag that finger of yours at me again, I'll tear it off and stuff it up your nose! Understand?"

At the last word he pivoted the long gun in his hand and cracked del Moro painfully on the shin.

Benvenuto had been free for less than a day.

The Sergeant halted the escort at the door of the castle. He pointed to the sky, now almost clear of clouds.

"That's the sky," he said, "and those are the stars."

"Really, that's very observant of you." Benvenuto had got some of his bravura back.

"Yes, really. So take a good look," the Sergeant replied. "I doubt if you'll ever see them again. Ever!"

- 3 1 -

As a fortress, Castel Sant' Angelo, Hadrian's tomb, was impregnable. There were two ways of getting in. The first was by demolishing the massive walls, but it was calculated that there was probably insufficient gun powder in the whole of Europe - or enough cannon balls - to do the job.

The other way in was through the one small entrance in the base of the tower which led into a narrow assault-proof tunnel.

When the fat and aging Roderigo Borgia became Pope Alexander VI in 1492, he decided to turn the fortress into a palace. He also instructed his architect, San Gallo, to make a new access to the roof because the long staircase to the top was too steep for him to climb, and he considered it undignified to be carried up on a litter by sweating, cursing servants.

San Gallo made one other improvement. Four large triangular air shafts penetrated the building to ventilate the new winding passageway. The architect sealed off the bottom of one of these shafts to create the terrible dungeon nicknamed "San Marocco," an oubliette - a cell, the only way in and out of which was by rope through a bottle-necked hole in the top.

It was at the entrance to this fearful pit that Benvenuto and his escort stopped, and Benvenuto's chair was dumped painfully on the ground. The four soldiers straightened their backs and stretched themselves with a chorus of grunts, while one of them was sent to collect the Governor.

—⚜—

"So you're back, are you?" Ceserino said, "You should have known better than to have tried to escape. I don't even know why you did it. I treated you well, didn't I? I gave you plenty of special privileges, didn't I?"

Benvenuto hung his head in what he hoped would look like contrition.

The little Governor wrung his pudgy hands together.

"You've no idea what trouble you've caused. The whole guard has been punished; and that won't do you or any of the prisoners any good. And they even made me pay for the door and the sheets you damaged."

"Hah! Perhaps you had better take it out of the money you owe me."

"What money? What are you talking about?"

"For the Leda and Swan hat badge of course. It's been nearly twenty years you know!"

Ceserino ground his teeth and noisily breathed in through his nose, while his fat face, even in the flickering torchlight was red with anger.

"You fool! You'll never learn who your friends are, and you'll never learn to keep your mouth shut either, will you? Alright sergeant," he ordered, "put him down."

He turned on his heel and ran up the nearest stairway.

—⚜—

Crespino drew his dagger and cut the ropes. As the sergeant stooped to release his legs and feet, Benvenuto started to rub his wrists.

"Put me down where?" he asked.

Crespino pointed with his dagger. "Why, the Palazzo San Marocco, of course."

"San Marocco! It's the condemned cell! For God's sake! I don't want to go down there."

"Oh don't you? Well not to worry, I don't suppose you'll be there for long. Most people I put down there don't want to come out again."

"Why not?" Benvenuto began to ask. "Oh!" he said as he suddenly realised why, and nervously fingered his throat.

The soldiers had rigged up a tripod over the entrance hole and tied a large basket to it. The sergeant gestured with his thumb.

"Into the basket, your Excellency."

"I won't go."

"Well that's a shame, because that means I'll have to push you down there. It's quite a drop; a lot further than the next one you'll be taking. Now move!"

As two of the soldiers grabbed Benvenuto by his arms, he began to struggle.

The sergeant pushed his bristly unshaven face so close to Benvenuto's that he could smell the man's sharp acrid breath whistling between broken, yellowing teeth and he recoiled from the little droplets of spittle which sprayed out as Crespino hissed at him,

"That's enough! I've taken all the shit I'm going to stand from you, now or ever. Do you hear? Now for the last time, get into that basket or I'll pitch you down the hole head first. The only thing that's stopping me doing it anyway is that I don't want to lose the fee for hanging you."

He landed a short brutal jab with his fist to Benvenuto's solar plexus, and as Benvenuto doubled up, the wind exploding with a "whoosh" from his mouth, the sergeant hooked his good leg from under him and pushed him backwards over the edge of the basket, and the soldiers began to lower it into the darkness.

It hit the stone floor with a thump that sent a jolt of agony through Benvenuto's ankle. He was lying sprawled on his back, half in and half out of the tipped-up basket, still trying to recover his breath from the sergeant's punch when he saw him silhouetted against the dim light at the top of the shaft.

"Get out of the basket, you!"

"Please pull me up again," Benvenuto begged.

The sergeant tried to reason with him. "Look, if you don't get out of the basket, I can't send you down your mattress, blanket or lantern, can I?"

"For pity's sake, let me out of here! I won't give you any trouble, honestly."

"Corporal," Crespino roared, "get one of those latrine buckets. Let's see how he likes having it emptied over him."

Benvenuto hurriedly scrambled to one side and immediately the basket was pulled up with a jerk. Moments later, a mattress filled with straw whose dampness he could smell through the cotton ticking, thumped down beside him, followed by a blanket and then by a leather water bottle.

"Where's my lantern?"

"Forget it. After what you did with the last lot of candles, I'm not letting you within sniffing distance of one. I'll tell you what though, I'll lower my lantern a few feet so you can get your bearings, and then you're on your own."

Benvenuto just had time to glance round his cell and to locate his all-important bucket before the light was taken away and he was left in a darkness that seemed to fold itself round him like black velvet sheet. Benvenuto imagined that the walls were closing in on him, crushing him. He felt he was being buried alive and his arms flailed around and his hands clawed the air as he tried to swim his way to the surface.

"Help! Anyone, please! Let me out! At least bring me some light. Don't leave me in the dark!"

No one came. Benvenuto could only hear the sound of the feet of the sentries and the crash of closing doors - the noises of a prison settling down for the night.

Somehow he managed to get up off the floor, but in the pitch dark it was impossible for him to balance on one leg; he could not reach a wall for support and as his right foot involuntarily touched the ground, another blinding stab of pain hit him and he collapsed on the mattress.

His body heaved with dry sobs of self-pity, but gradually he calmed down, and as his heart stopped thumping and the trickles of perspiration dried on his face, his breathing became shallower and he fell asleep.

It was the pain that woke him. Not just pain in one place, but everywhere: his ankle hurt every time he moved; his head and back throbbed from when he fell from the castle wall - was it only the day before yesterday? - and there was a dull gnawing ache where the dog had bitten him. Now to add to his discomfort, he could feel the stone floor digging into his hips and elbows through the thin mattress.

Benvenuto realised he was thirsty. He groped around for the water, but jerked his hand back in horror as he felt something soft and warm that seemed to wriggle under his touch. Then he realised what it was. It was only the water skin.

He unscrewed the stopper and took a deep swig but spat it out immediately. It was warm and tasted of old leather. He was still thirsty and his throat was dry so he forced himself to drink some of the brackish water and then rinsed his mouth and spat that out into the darkness too.

He folded up his blanket and using it as a pillow he tried to get back to sleep, but his head was too full of worry.

"How did I get into this mess," Benvenuto asked the empty air. "One day I'm peacefully running my business, not hurting anyone. I go out for dinner and the next thing I know I'm in prison for months. No charge, no trial. Alright, so I escaped."

Benvenuto was arguing with himself.

"They could have let me get away with it, and the whole thing would have been over. I'd have left this stinking city forever, but no, I'm in the condemned cell. Christ! Surely they're not going to hang me. For what? For nothing!"

He stuffed his fingers in his mouth with fear. His eyes filled with hot tears.

"Stop it you fool. You haven't been down here for a day yet."

He closed his eyes, and after a while he dozed off again.

—⁂—

This time it was the sound of the grating covering the entrance hole to cell being dragged away that woke Benvenuto up, stiff, still aching, still thirsty, and now hungry too. There was some pale grey daylight showing from above, but it barely reached to where he was lying. A guard leaned in and lowered a lantern.

"Wake up," he shouted.

"I am awake."

"Then shut up and listen. I'm in charge of you now. I've heard all about you from Sergeant Crespino and Sergeant Sidoli - no, I mean Private Sidoli, thanks to you. I can make things easy for you or hard - very hard. Just as you like.

First, nothing comes down to you or goes up except through this hole, so if you don't want to starve to death or drown in your own shit, you'll behave yourself. Do you understand?"

"I won't give you any trouble."

"Damn right you won't. Your last guard got two dozen lashes for either being bribed or being careless. I guess it hurt as much either way. Now stand clear, and you'll get your breakfast down in the basket, then you can send up your chamber pot."

"I didn't use it."

"Thank Christ for that! Send your water bottle up and I'll refill it for you."

"I've hardly used any."

"More fool you then. I'll tell you one thing, although I don't know why I should. You get fed three times a day. You get water each time. Drink all you can. It may taste terrible but you'll need every drop."

The basket slid down and immediately that Benvenuto took the stone pot out of it, it was pulled up again. The guard threw a wooden spoon down and said,

"Keep that with you. Lose it, and you won't get another."

"Hey," Benvenuto called, "What's going to happen to me next?"

"Happen? Nothing. You wait 'til they decide to hang you, then we come down, tie you up and heave you over the battlements.

Or you stay there 'til you go mad, then we come down, tie you up and chuck you in the river. Of course the Pope may come by, beg your forgiveness and make you a bishop."

He stamped off, chuckling, leaving Benvenuto to his breakfast.

Benvenuto was aroused from a sort of stupor by the sound of angry voices from the entrance of the cell.

"..... I don't care what you say, Messer Ceserino. I tell you I don't see prisoners in cells, especially that pit. You have him brought up and find me a proper room to see him in, or you may join him down there!"

It was Judge da Cagli. Benvenuto could not hear the Governor's reply as the two men walked away, still arguing, but a few minutes later the large passenger basket came down with a lighted lantern inside.

"Messer Cellini. Get in. You're coming up." Ceserino's voice was friendly and gentle, and Benvenuto gratefully crawled over the edge of the basket and steadied it to prevent it crashing against the walls of the shaft.

Even though the light in the passage was dim, he had to blink a few times before his eyes adjusted. When they did, he saw to his dismay that in charge of the escort was Sergeant Crespino.

"This way," ordered the Governor.

"Your Excellency," Benvenuto said politely, "I can't walk."

"He walked far enough when he escaped," Crespino interjected.

"Well, he'll have to be carried now," the Governor snapped. "It's only a short way, and I don't want any more arguments with the Judge, or with you, or you," he added, looking first at the Sergeant and then at Benvenuto.

"Sergeant, tell two of your men to use that." Ceserino pointed to a wide inch-thick plank leaning against the wall.

Benvenuto sat straddling the plank with one soldier at each end and the Governor hurrying ahead.

"You can take that smirk off your face sonny," Crespino muttered, "otherwise you can try riding that plank edgeways on!"

Da Cagli was seated behind a small table and the Governor took his place beside him. Benvenuto was pleased to see that da Prato was not there. The Judge pointed at a stool and Benvenuto eased himself onto it, his injured leg stuck out in front of him.

"Benvenuto Cellini," the Judge's voice was low and solemn. "I have been ordered to sentence you to death."

Benvenuto's chest tightened, and his whole stomach seemed to heave.

" ..... but I refused."

"Refused?" Benvenuto managed to croak.

"Yes, refused. God knows what it'll cost me, but I'm a Judge, not a hired assassin. I don't believe you stole the jewels."

"You don't?" Ceserino asked.

"No of course not!" the Judge said testily. "They must take me for a fool. There's not a shred of evidence except from a paid informer - and a pickpocket at that. No one has answered the prisoner's defence, which at least does make sense, however disrespectfully he presented it to me." Da Cagli looked at Benvenuto for a moment before continuing, "And what's more, da Prato, whose no friend of Cellini by all accounts, hasn't come back to disprove what he said."

Da Cagli pointed a finger at Benvenuto. "So the question is, what are we going to do with you?"

"Well, if I'm not guilty....," Benvenuto began hopefully.

"You'll stay here," the Judge interrupted. "I may not be prepared to hang you, but I'm certainly not going to take your place at the end of a rope."

"Not back in the San Marocco Pit, for God's sake!"

"No, the Governor will find you a new cell. Not as comfortable as your last one, and one you won't get out of so easily this time."

"For how long?"

"Until ......" Da Cagli let the word hang in the air.

"Until when?"

"Until Pier Luigi decides to release you, or until there's a new Pope and a general amnesty, or until ..... until they find someone else to sentence you to death."

The big iron ball climbed back into Benvenuto's throat.

-32-

Crespino led Benvenuto along a corridor which ran underground beneath the roof garden. There were a number of heavy doors set into the wall. Crespino stopped in front of one of them, undid the locking bar and pulled it open.

"I believe your Highness is an expert on prison cells, considering the number you've been in, I trust this one will meet with your approval. Go on, inside."

On this cue, the soldiers who had been carrying Benvenuto tipped the plank and sent him hopping into the cell.

The smell which hit Benvenuto was unbelievable. It was a compound of hundreds of years of human waste mixed with the unwashed, unventilated sweat of hot, frightened and desperate men.

Water which had dripped through the roof lay in pools on the uneven floor which was strewn with damp rotting straw. There was not a single piece of furniture in the room, and Crespino threw in a scrap of rush matting that was to serve as Benvenuto's bed, followed by a latrine bucket.

When the door was locked, it left Benvenuto with a tiny chink of light coming through one of the archers' slits in the outer wall, and which he would soon discover would give him just a few hours of light every day. Benvenuto heard the sound of the outer passageway door being slammed shut and bolted.

For company, the dungeon abounded with insect life of the most repulsive kind: spiders, centipedes, and earwigs seeking a cool refuge from the heat of the garden above.

The hours passed, and Benvenuto sank into an ever deepening depression. No one answered his shouts and he began to believe that he had been completely forgotten and that he would be left there to starve.

He had been in the cell for nearly twenty four hours before the guard arrived with something for him to eat. Benvenuto had fallen into such an apathetic stupor that he had stopped noticing the pain in his ankle and the throbbing ache in his head from the foul air of his prison, and he did not even hear the warder's approaching footsteps.

He sat up with a start as the man put a wooden bowl and spoon and a water skin inside the door, followed by another latrine bucket.

"In future see your things are waiting at the door or you won't get fresh ones. Bring your bucket. I'm not coming inside - the stink's so thick I reckon you could grow mushrooms in the air. You must be a special friend of Crespino's for him to have put you in here."

Benvenuto crawled to the door with the bucket and poked his head out, but hurriedly drew it back when the staff of the guard's pike whistled through the air and hit the stone floor with a ringing clang.

"Put your nose out of the cell without permission, and I'll cut it off."

"I'm sorry, I didn't know. How long must I stay here? Can I at least have my books and some candles?"

"Prisoners will not speak to guards without permission. Guards will not hold unnecessary conversations with prisoners." The warder intoned his orders as if he were reciting the Catechism.

The door slammed shut and Benvenuto was left to himself and his polenta. He was so hungry that he wolfed the unpalatable mess down in less than a minute, and then cleared the last scrapings from the bowl with his dirt-encrusted finger.

Two new guards delivered his breakfast the next morning while Benvenuto discretely stayed well back in his cell. Before he hurriedly closed the door, one of them said gruffly, "The Governor will be here to see you this afternoon."

With raised hopes, Benvenuto crawled across his cell to see what was in his bowl. He grimaced but decided that overripe cheese and stale bread was a slight improvement on polenta. He remembered the breakfast over which he had complained to his maid in what now seemed the distant past. "God! It was a feast compared to the muck I've been eating lately."

Ceserino would not come into the malodorous cell, but spoke to Benvenuto through the open door.

"It's not as comfortable as the nice room I gave you, is it? I hope you realise how much trouble you've caused your friends. You've undone all their patient work. Instead of gratitude, you abused them! You spat in their faces."

"Excellency, I ....."

"Silence!" roared the normally mild little Governor, "you've been warned not to speak without permission. In any case, don't interrupt me when I'm talking. You'll know when I've finished because you'll see my mouth stop moving! Now for once in your life, be quiet and listen!"

"You're lucky not to have been hanged, but instead you're getting no privileges. None at all. Prison food and no visitors - not unless they've got enough rank to be able to insist. You wanted to know how long you'll be here, well only God, Messer Pier Luigi Farnese and His Holiness know, and none of them have told me. Maybe they'll decide you've been punished enough next week ....."

Benvenuto brightened.

"..... or maybe you'll stay here until you die. Not many men live through the winter in this cell. But to show there's nothing personal, I've brought two of your books, just as you asked. A Bible." Ceserino handed it to a guard who tossed it to Benvenuto, "... and this one, which Messer del Moro says is your favourite. **'Chronicles,'** by Giovanni Villani."

The Governor thumbed through the book and glanced at the fly leaf. "Hum, 'A History of Florence From the Time of the Bible Until 1348 with Sixteen Years Added by his Brother and Nephew.' Very interesting. It looks as if you'll have plenty of time to read it, but you'll get no candles - you did enough damage with the last lot."

"I thank your Excellency for the books," Benvenuto said humbly.

"I told you to shut up, didn't I? Who gave you permission to speak?" The enraged Ceserino kicked the door shut, and Benvenuto heard him say to the guard, "For God's sake, let me get some fresh air before I'm sick!"

As the days and weeks of living in utter squalor crawled by, boredom and fear turned to despair.

"I'm never going to get out of here. No one can help me, not even Cardinal d'Este or Cardinal de' Medici. The rotten food's making me weaker and weaker, and I don't know how I haven't caught some disease in this stinking place already." He scratched at his body. "Look at me. I'm covered in sores and bites."

He raised his voice and shouted, "For pity's sake, let me out of here you bastards! A decent meal and ten minutes of fresh air and I don't bloody well care what you do with me afterwards!"

Two guards passing on patrol stopped outside his door and Benvenuto could hear them talking.

"There you are. It won't be long before he goes mad like they all do in here."

"Maybe he'll kill himself."

"No chance. This one's not allowed a knife or anything metal. He even has a wooden bowl so he can't cut his wrists on a broken plate."

"Hang himself then?"

"What with? His clothes are rotting rags - they'd never take his weight, even if he could find somewhere to tie a noose."

The guards moved on.

"Hang myself?" Benvenuto thought. "They've threatened me with that so many times, it's the last thing I'd want to do!"

When the absurdity of what he had just said sank in, he rolled round the floor cackling uncontrollably. The times when he could actually find something to laugh about seemed to belong to the remote and forgotten past.

Nevertheless, the guards had planted the thought. He could put an end to his misery himself. Suicide.

He wiped his eyes and focused in the dim light on the only moveable thing in the cell. Lying alongside one wall was a large wooden beam, about six feet long and over a foot square. It must have been there for decades, left behind from some construction work. Benvenuto had been using it as a sort of bench to sit on.

He dragged it away from the wall and recoiled in disgust at the army of insects that fled across the floor from behind it. The beam was tremendously heavy, but somehow managed to stand it upright on its end and prop it up flat against the wall.

Carefully measuring the distance, he lay down beneath it and pushed at the bottom with his hand. He hoped that the beam would over-balance and fall and crush his head. He gave it several hard prods but the beam did not move, so he twisted round lengthways and kicked it with his left foot. Still nothing. He kicked again, this time with both feet, wincing at the pain in his tender, newly healed ankle.

Again and again he kicked, but although it seemed to rock a little, it still stayed where it was. In his weakened condition his legs had no more strength left and he rolled to one side, exhausted.

As he did so, the beam slowly toppled over and crashed to the ground alongside Benvenuto with such force that the floor under him seemed to lift and he was splattered with the filth and water that the great lump of wood had splashed up. He lay there, with one arm thrown across it and sobbed.

Benvenuto regarded his escape from his own suicide attempt as a sign that his sufferings were part of some mysterious plan of Providence. This restored his morale for a while and he began to devote himself to reading his Bible for as long as the light permitted, and spending hours every day in prayer.

He descended into a dream world populated by imaginary visitors: Bishops, Cardinals, Pope Clement, Pope Paul, his patrons, friends and mistresses, his employees and apprentices in a continual procession; people he had forgotten he had ever known. But his most frequent phantom visitor was a handsome young man whom Benvenuto took to be an Angel. The first time this Vision appeared, he rebuked Benvenuto for his attempted suicide.

"Do you know who lent you the body you tried to destroy before its appointed time?"

Benvenuto hung his head in shame. "Everything comes from God."

"Well, let Him guide you. Don't abandon hope in His power to save."

Each "meeting" with the Angel made him a little more optimistic. He decided to start trying to do something creative. He mixed some urine and sooty brick dust, and with a pen made from a splinter broken off the wooden beam he began to use the fly leaves of his Bible to write a **Capitolo** - a poetic art form which had originated in his native Florence, usually with every third line rhyming, and often with a comic or obscene content.

Benvenuto's **capitolo** was a long tedious rigmarole, full of obscure allusions to people and events, and very bad poetry into the bargain!

> *He who would know how great is God's strength,*
> *And how far a man resembles things great,*
> *In prison must stay for a length.*
> *Family and cares a pressing weight,*
> *Body and mind pained and spent,*
> *A thousand long miles from his own estate.*

And so on for nearly two hundred verses. Anyway, it helped to while away the hours and to take his mind off his worries for a time, and to that extent it served its purpose.

Benvenuto's health had never been particularly robust, and the lack of exercise and fresh air, the inadequate food and the foul condition of his cell took an increasing toll. He became weak, tired and listless; all his muscles ached and he frequently suffered slight fevers. His skin thickened and developed abscesses and bruises and blood spots. His teeth ached intolerably and his gums became soft and spongy and began to ooze puss. Without a mirror he could not know his eyes were sunk into his puffy face.

He had in fact developed scurvy, but the realisation did not dawn on him until one morning when he rubbed the inside of his mouth with his finger to relieve the pain a little.

He felt a tooth move. Too frightened to believe it, he gave it a prod. Yes, there it was again, it had definitely moved! He touched it with his tongue. Now it seemed to be leaning right over into his mouth. He grasped it between thumb and forefinger, and, as he tried to straighten it, the whole tooth came away, root and all.

Benvenuto stared at it in horror, and when he poked his tongue into the blood-filled gap, he felt the next tooth rocking and moving too. He tugged at his beard and pinched his cheek, but it was no good: he wasn't dreaming; he really was awake; his teeth were really falling out.

He ran to the door and began to shout for help - futilely, because there was no-one to hear. The warders only came by on irregular patrols and at meal time. Benvenuto sank down on his wooden beam with his head between his hands. He knew from the symptoms that he had got the disease that killed sailors and prisoners alike.

His mind was full of terrified thoughts while he waited for the guard to come. He was dying for sure, and no-one would do anything for him. Eventually it was time for the midday meal, and he heard the sound of bolts being unlocked and feet marching along the corridor.

The door of his cell opened and his heart sank. It was Crespino. It was just his bad luck that he was on duty today. He'd certainly get no sympathy from him! For a moment his old spirit and obstinacy made him think of keeping quiet. He would not beg for help from the sergeant of all people, but then common sense and his instincts of self-preservation took over.

"Get me a doctor. I'm ill."

"Dear dear! I can't tell you how sorry I am," Crespino replied sarcastically. "No one gave you permission to speak did they? But alright, what's wrong with you? You certainly haven't caught the French Pox in here, have you?"

"My teeth are all dropping out," Benvenuto mumbled.

"Really? Do you want to know how to stop losing your teeth? Bend over and shove your head up your arse!"

Crespino walked away laughing coarsely, and Benvenuto was left shouting at the door of the cell,

"You send me a doctor or tell the Governor, do you hear, or it'll be the worse for you. BRING ME A DOCTOR!" he bellowed as the outer doors closed, one after the other.

—⚋—

Sergeant Crespino was too well disciplined to disobey his standing orders, which were to report at once to the Governor all signs of illness amongst the prisoners. Just one contracting a contagious disease could cause thousands of deaths in the city.

This time, however, the Governor did not need to send for the doctor. He too could recognise the symptoms of scurvy. Although the cause - the simple lack of vitamin C - was not understood, the cure, even then, was well known. A diet of fruit juice, citrus fruits or fresh green uncooked vegetables or even fresh milk and the results were immediate and dramatic.

That evening with his supper there were two oranges. Benvenuto winced as the acid juice bit into his sore gums but nevertheless he greedily sucked at the fruit - a rare treat, after months of polenta alternating with pasta.

The next day and the next, there were two oranges with every meal and a mug of lemon juice in the evening, provided by the Governor from his own table.

At mid-day on the fourth day Benvenuto was surprised to see that the wooden bowl was larger than usual and was covered in a cloth - an unheard of refinement. He peeped underneath. It was a beef and vegetable stew in thick gravy. Stone cold, but beef nevertheless. He looked at the guard. He did not dare to risk losing his prize by breaking the rule of silence. Instead, he simply raised his eyebrows.

"The Governor has given permission for your friends to send in your dinner three times a week."

The soldier stuck his finger in the bowl and extracted a chunk of meat, popped it in his mouth.

"Very nice," he said, sucking his teeth. "Ah well, buon appetito."

He closed the door and Benvenuto was left to enjoy his meal. He lifted his bowl in a toast to his Angel.

—⁂—

Prison Governor Ceserino's act of mercy in allowing him to have some of his food sent in from outside nearly cost Benvenuto his life.

Nothing could be kept secret in Rome for very long, and in no time Sergeant Crespino was grumbling to one of his informers, Digi the Pickpocket that he didn't know what prison was coming to when people like Cellini could live in the lap of luxury, with all sorts of tasty tit-bits being sent into him.

Digi did not only work for Crespino. He had a more important master: Pier Luigi Farnese whom he knew had a particular interest in Cellini. He lost no time in passing on this piece of gossip, and a couple of silver coins changed hands.

Pier Luigi saw an opportunity to get rid of this nuisance, once and for all. The importuning of influential people on

Benvenuto's behalf was never ending. It seemed to Pier Luigi that every time he was engaged in a piece of political negotiation, especially with the Medici supporters, someone would ask for Cellini's release or for favourable treatment for him as part of the deal.

If Cellini were dead, and if he did not die in a way that resulted in any suspicion of foul play, then he, Pier Luigi, would no longer be pestered about this nobody, whose continued existence was in any case an affront to his own prestige.

So long as Benvenuto was eating the same slops as the other prisoners, he was more or less safe from what was still the favourite Italian assassination weapon - poison. But once outsiders were involved, there was a chance to tamper with it, either by stealth or by bribery.

Benvenuto's food was supplied by a nearby inn. A few more silver coins changed hands, and the kitchen boy agreed to make a little diversion each time he delivered Benvenuto's meal.

The choice of poison was crucial. If anything violent and speedy were used, someone would be sure to guess what had been done, apart from which there was always the risk that one of the jailers would steal all or some of the dish, with fatal results to the wrong person.

No, a very slow poison was called for; one whose effect was gradual and cumulative, and one whose symptoms would not be easily recognisable amongst the various diseases endemic in the prison. Powdered glass.

A tiny quantity of the material, so fine that, mixed with food, it is completely unnoticeable and totally indigestible becomes embedded in the lining of the stomach, intestines and bowels, gradually ripping them up as it passes through the body, causing internal haemorrhages. Each successive dose adds to the damage caused by the last. An agonising death was the result and in the absence of post mortems it would be undetectable.

Benvenuto owed his survival to luck.

On the very first doctored delivery, the glass was not powdered to the finest dust. It was a feast day and the poisoner was in a hurry and became careless. Benvenuto's midday meal was soup, a stew and a salad. A small helping of glass had been added to each. Benvenuto thought the salad was a little gritty, but took no notice, he was so hungry, but when he finished a sunbeam caught on a few shards of splintered glass lying on his empty plate.

He touched them with his finger tip. There was no doubt what was there. How long had this been going on? Were his insides being slowly ripped to shreds? What could he do? He could starve, die of scurvy, or end up screaming in agony in a puddle of his own blood. Who could he trust? Who could he tell?

He told the one jailer who had occasionally shown him a little sympathy.

"For God's sake, get a message to Rafaello del Moro. Tell him they're trying to kill me. They're poisoning the food he orders for me."

The guard sucked in his lips, and half closed his eyes.

"Are they now? Well that's very naughty of them. We'll have to put a stop to it, won't we? Alright! Alright!" he added as Benvenuto started to protest, "I'll go and see him as soon as I'm off duty."

The man walked away down the corridor shaking his head. "It's strange," he thought, "how many of them go funny in the end."

"What do you think?" del Moro asked Gina when the soldier had left, jingling some silver coins in his hand. "The poor fellow's sufferings must have begun to turn his mind. Who would want to poison him, and why?"

"Yes father, but who would want to keep Benvenuto in jail, and why?"

"You're right, but what can I do about it?"

"Go and see Cardinal d'Este."

"Right again. The Cardinal is supposed to be Benvenuto's friend. He's the Prince, not me, so let him worry about it! If he wants me to do his bloody job, he'd better let me have his bloody income." Del Moro could not understand why he was suddenly angry. "You know," he said to Gina, "that Benvenuto's a fool. If he'd married a brainy girl like you, he'd never always be in trouble."

The Medici party, through their own network of spies and informers had already got wind of the fact that there was a plot afoot against someone in the prison.

The kitchen lad with the unusual wealth of a few silver scudi rattling about in his purse got himself very drunk and began bragging that a very important prisoner in Sant' Angelo was going to die soon.

"I can't tell you who, but when he does, I shall be going up in the world, you'll see."

As soon as Cardinal de' Medici got the report of the boy's indiscrete boasting, he had two of his men waylay him and "persuade" him to tell them what he knew.

It took only three minutes for the two thugs men to convince themselves that the blubbering boy had given them the whole story, including the name of the intended victim. The only thing he did not know was who was responsible, but as soon as de' Medici heard that Digi was paying the boy, only one guess was needed.

The immediate problem of keeping Benvenuto alive - of preventing him from being poisoned - was very simply solved.

The prison Governor was summoned to see Cardinal d'Este and given certain explicit instructions and warned what would happen if he did not carry them out.

"Messer Cellini, I've heard what they tried to do. Believe me, I'm sorry. I assure you that it was all done outside the Castle. It won't happen again. I promise you I'll see you're safe."

"How? Are you going to get Crespino to taste my food? Or da Prato? Or perhaps you will? That would be very nice of you. The only way I'll be safe is if they let me go. What the hell am I doing here anyway? I still don't know."

"It's not up to me how long you stay here," the Governor replied," and nobody's going to taste your food for you."

"Then how will you stop them poisoning me?"

"I've got the Bishop of Padua in jail here too."

"Well isn't that just lovely," Benvenuto sneered. "If only my poor old mother could have lived to see this day. She would have been truly proud to know that I was locked up in the same prison as a real Bishop!"

"Shut up, will you!" the Governor snapped. "The Bishop's here because of some disturbances or something in Padua, but the Pope daren't let anything happen to him. Anyway the Bishop's brother sends in all his food and you'll get some of it. Every day, not just three times a week," he added triumphantly.

"I'm very grateful I'm sure, but do tell His Grace not to order anything too hard. My teeth are still a bit loose you know!"

Ceserino's only reply was to kick the cell door shut and walk away muttering.

The Pope saw his son in private.

"What is this mad obsession of yours with this Cellini person? I simply don't understand it. Haven't you got anything else to worry about?"

"The jewels he stole," Pier Luigi replied.

"Oh piffle! There aren't any jewels. Everyone knows what Clement did with them. What's more you don't believe it either, otherwise a short session on the rack, and you'd have had him begging to be allowed to tell you where they are."

"But ….."

"But nothing! Now you listen to me. The man is nothing but a nuisance. The Medici's just use him as a pawn: every time they ask me to let him go and I refuse, I have to give them something else instead. What's worse, I've just had a letter from the King Francis saying he has some work for him, and asking me if I can release him from my service. Did you hear that? 'Release him from my service.' He knows where he is."

"That's only because that daughter-in-law, Catherine de' Medici put him up to it."

"What difference does it make what his reason is? He's asked, and how can I refuse? Do you seriously expect me to offend the King of France over this nobody?"

Pier Luigi said nothing, but rubbed his mouth with the palm of his hand as the Pope continued stalking up and down the room, waving his arms like windmills.

"There's no profit in him, and anything there's no profit in is always trouble. From what I've heard, you've tried to have him killed a couple of times, and even bungled that. Well it's the end. Do you understand? The end. So what you're going to do is this ....."

Paul came to a halt in front of his son.

"You're going to let him go. What are you going to do?"

"I'm going to let him go, your Holiness."

"That's right. The last thing I want to see of him is his backside disappearing out of the City gate. I'll give you one week so you can squeeze the Medici's for whatever you can get in return, but in the meantime, nothing had better happen to him, do you understand? If he died of old age right now, they'd only blame me."

The Pope stopped shouting. "Now," he said in a more kindly tone, "I think we had better discuss more important affairs. First of all, this business in Padua ...."

―⋙―

The following Saturday morning Benvenuto was squatting in his cell, struggling to catch enough light to read by when he heard the sound of the tramp of soldiers' feet along the passage.

He stood up nervously as he heard the door of his cell being unlocked. It was Crespino.

"Outside, you."

"Outside?" said Benvenuto. "Outside where?"

"Out here, of course."

"Why?"

"Maybe they want to re-decorate your cell and put in some carpet, or perhaps they're going to let me hang you at last, although it's a bit late in the day for that," Crespino said regretfully "Anyway, I've told you before, I just pick people up from one place and take them to another. I don't ask any questions, and neither will you if you know what's good for you. Now, I'll say it for the last time - out! And bring your things with you."

"What things? I've only got two books and a wooden spoon."

"So bring them then, and MOVE!"

When Benvenuto stepped out of his cell, he paused for a moment. It was the first time he had been through the door in nearly two years. Crespino put an end to his day-dreaming by whacking him hard across the back of his legs with the flat of his sword.

"Move, I said."

Benvenuto had to adjust himself simultaneously to the new sensations of actually walking more than half a dozen paces in one direction, of normal daylight, and strangest of all, fresh crisp, cold air.

—⚜—

Benvenuto was led to one of the lower rooms of the castle. Crespino roughly pushed him in and took up his usual position on a stool inside the door, leaving his prisoner standing aimlessly in the middle of the floor. The Sergeant scrambled to his feet again when the door swung open and Tommaso da Prato stepped in.

"Oh Lord," thought Benvenuto, "that's all I needed. What are they going to do to me now?"

Da Prato stared at Benvenuto, whom he had not seen since the day of his arrest. Instead of the tall, young, immaculate figure he knew only too well, what he saw was a scarecrow, with matted hair hanging down past his shoulders and a tangled beard halfway down his chest. Red rimmed, bloodshot eyes stared out of a pale white face as thin, blue-veined hands clutched his miserable rags around him.

Benvenuto was absolutely filthy. And the smell! Da Prato pressed a perfumed handkerchief to his nose before he spoke.

"I've got something interesting to tell you."

"The only interesting thing you can tell me is the date of your funeral." Benvenuto had lost none of his old fire.

"Consider yourself lucky that I'm not here to tell you the date of yours! Now listen to me. I hate you. I've always hated you. I don't remember why. Maybe I hated you because you hated me, or maybe you hated me because I hated you. After all this time, what does it matter? It's all over now. You're free to go."

"Free? Did you say I can go?" Benvenuto felt a rush of tears to his eyes.

"Not just 'can' go. You **have** to go. You must leave Rome. It's Saturday today. If you're still here at noon on Monday, or if you ever come back, the least you can expect is prison or hanging,"

Da Prato flicked his hand at Crespino.

"Alright Sergeant, you can throw him out."

He turned to leave and paused at the door. "Oh, and goodbye, Messer Cellini."

"Go to hell!" Benvenuto retorted.

"After you," said da Prato.

For once, at the very end, it was da Prato who had the last word.

―∞―

Ascanio and Busbacca had agreed to go with Benvenuto to Fontainebleau, and as they and the pack horse reached the crest of the hill on the route north out of Rome, they were riding a little ahead, chattering excitedly.

An old peasant walked slowly along the narrow road with a wooden frame tied to his back, held in place by a leather strap round his forehead. The frame was piled high with wicker baskets loaded with vegetables that the man was taking to market, and he was so bowed down with the weight that he was carrying that he could not even look up at Benvenuto as he trudged by.

Benvenuto stopped his horse to let him pass and followed him round with his eyes. As he did so, he caught a glimpse of the weak winter sunlight on the roofs of Rome far below.

He turned in his saddle to get a better view. There was the Vatican with St. Peter's still under construction. The hated Castel Sant' Angelo; the River Tiber and its bridges; the Artists' quarter - his home.

Twenty years of his life had been spent there.

He spat on the ground, and viciously tugging on the reins of his horse, he wheeled it round and sent it galloping after his two young men.

He did not glance back again.

Part V: The Frenchman

-33-

Benvenuto made his way north-east to the Cardinal's Estate at Ferrara, where he was instructed to wait until the Cardinal himself arrived en route for France to take up his new post as the Pope's Ambassador to the French Court.

The letter of introduction to the Cardinal's major domo said that Benvenuto was to be given suitable quarters so that he could rest and convalesce from his long ordeal in prison, that he was to enjoy the usual hospitality given by the estate to distinguished artists and, if he wanted them, he could have facilities to carry on his trade.

The accommodation, although sparse, was luxurious compared with his cell at Sant' Angelo and a good deal more comfortable than many places that he had lodged in during the "downs" in his career.

But to Benvenuto there was something essential missing. Status. He was - and there was no hiding it - just a pensioner, a receiver of alms, although he did have a fair sum in gold of his own as a result of del Moro realising his assets while he was in prison. He also had his tools and drawings that del Moro had saved for him, as well as three personal items: his flute, an ornate box containing his see-saw and his arquebus.

The food that he was served in the communal dining room was plain but good. Real meat and no polenta, even though there was a fair proportion of leftovers from the tables of the more exalted guests who dined in private when the Cardinal and his entourage were not in residence.

Benvenuto decided that his diet was lacking an important ingredient. Peacock soup.

The Cardinal's gardens were partly formal and partly wild and a number of peacocks strutted about there, more as decoration than as pets. They were certainly not there to be eaten, even though since the time of Ancient Rome peacocks had been regarded as a delicacy.

Benvenuto believed that they had aphrodisiacal qualities too, and this was just the stimulant that he felt he urgently needed.

At his farewell party on the Sunday night before he left Rome, encouraged by his friends he had with some reluctance paid a disastrous visit to a brothel.

Two years in jail, far from stimulating his formidable sexual appetite had completely destroyed it. To his acute humiliation, the girl, attractive and skilled that she was could not arouse him at all.

"Never mind, dear," she consoled him, "I expect you've just had a bit too much to drink. We'll try again another time, shall we? I'd like that," she added coyly as she went in search of a more virile customer, leaving Benvenuto blushing with embarrassment to pull on his clothes and join his companions in another part of the Inn.

Del Moro leered at him. "Well, how was it?"

"Oh, great. Simply great. You know, it's just like swimming."

Del Moro stopped smiling and looked puzzled.

"Yes," Benvenuto explained, "no matter how long it is between times, you never forget how to do it!"

—⁊⁊⁊—

So, armed with his arquebus, he sneaked out of his quarters one night soon after his arrival, and peacock soup it was.

When the Cardinal got to hear of it, he sighed with resignation and sent another note to the major domo. It arrived just in time. Benvenuto still felt that his performance with the Cardinal's all-too-willing servant girls was below standard.

The major domo found him in the garden, gun in hand, speculatively eying the peacocks. Benvenuto shaded his eyes with his hand and pretended to be searching the tree tops for crows and squirrels.

"Good morning, Messer Cellini. I have received a letter from his Eminence.

"Oh yes? And how is the dear, kind man?"

"In good health, I have no doubt, thanks be to God, but he does not write to me on such matters. He only instructs me on household affairs, and he desires me to give you certain instructions."

"Instructions?"

"Well, some commissions then."

A vision of the Bishop of Salamanca's butler flashed through Benvenuto's mind.

"I'm not accustomed to receiving instructions, or commissions either, from butlers."

"And I'm not accustomed ….." the major domo began. He was going to say something about "not being spoken to in that way by the Cardinal's workmen," but the look in Benvenuto's eye as well as his ferocious reputation made the man pause.

"And I'm not accustomed to dealing with artists and craftsmen." His tone was conciliatory and he smiled as he spoke. "All I am doing is to pass on my honoured Master's wishes."

Benvenuto was mollified. "What are they, may I ask?"

The butler began to unfold the Cardinal's letter, and Benvenuto held out his hand to take it, but the butler clutched it protectively to his chest.

"Excuse me, but it isn't for you. It has other confidential household matters in it." He puffed himself up importantly. "But I'll read what he says about you."

He began to skim through the letter, mumbling to himself.

"Blah, blah, blah, dum, dum, dum." A pause. "Dum, dum, dum." He prudently did not read out everything that the Cardinal had actually written.

> *"If Cellini continues to make a nuisance of himself, you will inform me at once, and I will deal with him. Meanwhile, I will set him to work to keep him out of mischief."*

"Ah, here we are." He began to paraphrase the letter in short sentences. "Messer Cellini is to have one of the out houses to use as a workshop. A new seal for his Eminence. About three inches in diameter. Obverse showing St. John preaching in the desert. Reverse to show St. Ambrose on horseback driving the Arians out of Italy with a whip." The butler looked up. "St Ambrose? Arians? Whip? Do you know what he is talking about?"

"Of course," Benvenuto said. A detailed knowledge of the stories of the Saints and of mythology was part of his stock-in-trade. "It's about the twelve hundredth anniversary of his birth. I suppose that's why the Cardinal's suddenly remembered him. He drove the Arians - they were heretics - out of Italy, supposedly with a whip. Mind you, they've been back a few times since," he mused.

"He wrote the old church music too, and he had a swarm of bees settle on his mouth when he was in his cradle. That's supposed to be a good omen. I wouldn't fancy it myself though. Anyway, that's why the beehive is one of his symbols, you know."

The butler nodded as if he did.

Benvenuto thought about it. A new seal would earn a fee of only about a hundred crowns. "Is that all he wants?" he asked.

"No-o." The butler hesitated. "The bowl that you were making when you were in - when you were in that place. The one Messer del Moro finished for you. His Eminence wants you to look over to see if you're satisfied with the workmanship."

Benvenuto preened himself. "Naturally he would want me to do that."

"And while you're doing that, there are a couple of dents that need repairing."

Benvenuto grimaced. There would be no fee for that.

The butler glanced at the paper again. "The jug that you made to go with the bowl. He wants another one to match it."

Benvenuto sucked his upper lip under his lower and nodded. Three hundred crowns at least, maybe five hundred.

"Is there anything else?

"Not for his Eminence just now. I would have thought that you'll have more than enough to do until his Eminence gets here, but he has written to his Grace the Duke of Ferrara on your behalf, so maybe he will be sending for you too."

"You don't understand. What I mean is 'pay.' What does he say about pay?"

"He doesn't say anything about pay, and no wonder. I believe that his Eminence spent a great deal on your behalf while you were …. in that place." The butler still could not bring himself to admit that one of his Master's guests could ever have been in prison. "And," he continued, "there's the expense of keeping you and your two employees here, and of getting you all to France when his Eminence goes. No, I don't suppose there'll be any question of payment. You wouldn't really expect any, would you?"

"Of course not," Benvenuto snapped. "I'm quite used to not being paid. Six months hiding from the hangman; another six working as a slave for Pope Paul, and just when I start to get myself straightened out, two years in jail for no reason. In fact, if I actually got my hands on some money of my own, I wouldn't even remember what to do with it! Alright," he conceded in a tired voice, "just give me fifty gold crowns and I'll get to work."

"Fifty crowns? I told you weren't being paid. What do you want fifty crowns for?"

"Oh Christ," Benvenuto snarled through clenched teeth, "you people are all the same. I want fifty gold crowns because gold vases are made out of gold, that's why! It's your Master who's in the miracle business not me. I can't conjure loaves and fishes out of the air, much less gold, so fifty crowns, if you please!"

"Come and see me later, when you've finished whatever it is you're doing here, and I'll have it for you."

"I once had a conversation like this with the Bishop of Salamanca's butler. The very same subject. Do you know what I told him?"

"What?"

"No money, no jug! No money, no jug!"

The butler turned on his heel and marched back towards the house. After a few yards he stopped.

"Oh yes, by the way, I almost forgot, His Eminence did also send you another message."

"What?"

"He says, 'P.S. Leave my bloody peacocks alone'!"

—⚭—

The Duke of Ferrara found a small commission for Benvenuto. A gold medal with the Duke's portrait on one side, and a graceful, lightly-draped female figure holding a torch as the symbol of "Peace" on the other.

Benvenuto handed the finished piece to Busbacca for him to place in its box.

"It's beautiful, Master. You haven't lost any of your skill."

"Of course not! A great Artist never loses his skill, even when some damn fool locks him up in prison for years."

"What I don't understand," said Ascanio, "is why you've got 'Peace' trampling that chained figure - 'Fury' you said it was - under her feet. It's a bit incongruous, isn't it?"

"That's the whole point, you fool! 'Peace' is about the most uncharacteristic symbol that anyone could imagine that the Duke would have picked for himself!"

"Master," said Busbacca," The Duke's Butler is coming up the path."

"Is he indeed? Well, I hope he's come with a bag of money. I'm sick of being a one-man charity to the rich."

"He's got a box with him."

The Butler, Fiaschino, was a timorous, bow-legged little man who had been reduced to such a state of constant nervousness by the bullying by his employer, that he was a figure of fun amongst the Duke's domestic staff that he was supposed to control.

He took the box with the medal without more than a quick glance inside.

"His Grace has instructed me to hand you this remembrance of him," he twittered. "He says, 'may this diamond adorn the unique hand of the artist who has done such great work.' Here." He handed Benvenuto a gold-tooled, velvet-lined box in which sat a diamond ring.

Benvenuto examined the stone and then put the ring back in the box, snapped the lid shut with a snort of disgust and grabbed Fiaschino by the buckle of his belt. He dragged the man towards him until they were standing chest to chest. Benvenuto's face was contorted by rage.

"You thief!" he hissed.

"Thief? Sir, what do you mean?"

"What I mean is this." Benvenuto waved the box under the terrified man's nose. "The Duke was entitled to pay me at least two hundred crowns for the medal - and he knew it. This piece of junk is worth about ten - from a blind lunatic, if I could get him drunk enough to buy it. You've stolen my ring and substituted this one."

"No, sir! I assure you. Look at the box. It's got his Grace's own Coat of Arms on it."

"Box? I'm not interested in boxes. What did you do with my ring?" Benvenuto shouted.

"If you please Sir, look at the setting. His Grace's initials are engraved on the inside."

"Then you can take it back to the Duke of Ferrara and tell him to keep it. I don't want it." He thrust the ring and box down the front of Fiaschino's shirt.

"Oh Messer Cellini, I couldn't do that. It would make him very angry."

"Angry! Don't talk to me about being angry! I give lessons in being angry," he yelled, with little flecks of spittle flying out of the corners of his mouth. He pushed Fiaschino staggering backwards towards the door. "Now, if you know what's good for you, you'll clear off before I really lose my temper."

An hour later, Benvenuto, still seething, was busy in his workshop. Ascanio was carefully polishing out a small dent in the damaged bowl, Busbacca was beating a gold rod round a wooden pattern the shape of the handle of the Cardinal's new vase, and Benvenuto was working on the pattern on the base, when four soldiers of the Duke of Ferrara's personal bodyguard came for him.

The Cardinal's butler was there too, leading Benvenuto's horse which was already saddled. He stood a back from the four men, out of their line of sight and gave a tiny shrug of his shoulders, palms outspread as if apologising for having brought them.

"Oh Jesus!" thought Benvenuto, "Here we go again."

He ignored the soldiers and continued to tap the piece of gold on his bench. Maybe they had only come to watch; maybe they would go away. It was no good; they did not.

One of the soldiers, obviously the leader, was carrying a long wooden club dangling from his wrist by a leather strap. He was a burly, squat man with broken teeth, a flattened nose and thick hairy arms that were too long for his chain mail jerkin. Beneath his helmet Benvenuto could see his close-cropped hair and a ragged flap of skin and a hole where his left ear should have been.

"Messer Tecchini?"

"Cellini," Benvenuto corrected, and without looking up went on with his work.

"The Duke wants to see you."

With an elaborate sigh, Benvenuto put his hammer down.

"Does he? Well that is very kind of him indeed. I'm honoured. Please convey my respects to his Grace, and tell him that I'll be along as soon as possible."

"Now," growled the soldier.

"But I'm all dirty, and in my working clothes. I can't possibly go like this."

The soldier took a grip on the handle of his club, and began to tap it in the palm of his other hand.

"Now," he insisted.

Benvenuto stood up and gave the piece of gold to Ascanio.

"What does he want to see me about? Benvenuto asked in a conversational tone.

"I don't know. I don't ask questions. When he tells me to go and bring people in, I just go and fetch them."

Benvenuto stared at the soldier with mouth and eyes open wide. He smiled in spite of himself.

"You're not related to someone called Crespino are you?"

"No I'm not! My name's Ruosi. Who the hell's this Crespino anyway?"

"Oh he's just a police sergeant I used to know in Rome. You remind me of him - he was always saying things like that."

"Was he now? To you no doubt. Always? Well I don't say it more than once, because when I fetch someone for the Duke, they stay fetched!" Ruosi pointed at Benvenuto's horse with his club. "Now, if you will be so kind ....."

Benvenuto dismounted in the courtyard of the Duke's castle and waited with three of the soldiers. Ruosi went inside and a few minutes later the Duke came out followed by Fiaschino, Ruosi, and several well dressed men and women, some of whom were holding wine goblets. One of the men pointed at Benvenuto and said something to the woman next to him and in reply she gave a shrill little laugh.

Ruosi was no longer carrying his club. Instead, coiled in his hand he had a long leather whip which he shook loose with an expert flick along the ground. The tip of the whip made a rustling sound as it slithered across the gravel.

Benvenuto was watching the Duke, but out of the corner of his eye, he saw Ruosi walk over and lean nonchalantly against a foot square tall wooden post that stood at one edge of the courtyard. Set high on either side of the post were iron rings from which short lengths of chain dangled, and at the end of each chain was a wide metal handcuff.

As the Duke slowly came towards him, Benvenuto gulped hard, while a tingling feeling crawled down the flesh of his back.

—⚜—

The Duke stood in front of Benvenuto and his guests crowded a little closer. The Duke was as tall as Benvenuto. He had a thin sharp face with a short straight black beard and almond shaped eyes which gave him look of ruthless cruelty. Clasping his hands behind him, he rocked backwards and forwards on his heels.

"What's all this about you not being satisfied with the payment for my medal. Don't you think my diamond ring's good enough for you?

"Oh no, your Grace. I mean, yes," Benvenuto stammered. "I mean on the contrary, I could not accept your magnificent gift because it was too much."

"Too much!"

"Yes your Grace. I'm flattered that your Excellency should be pleased with my work, poor though it was after my being so long in enforced idleness, but I wished to show your Excellency that I am your loyal and devoted follower and to express my thanks for your Grace's munificent hospitality while sitting for the sketches I made for your bust on the medal."

"If you have to kneel, you might as well grovel," Benvenuto thought and mentally crossed himself for describing the leftover scraps that he had been fed as "munificent hospitality."

"So you wanted to show your loyalty and devotion, did you? That's not how I heard it." The Duke turned and glared at his Butler who was cowering away in an attempt to make himself inconspicuous.

"Perhaps Messer Fiaschino misunderstood me, your Grace." Benvenuto offered an escape route.

"I don't pay Fiaschino to make mistakes." The Duke brushed his moustache with his hand. "Oh very well, let's say he did, and there's an end to it. But I don't like to accept favours from anyone. What will you take in payment for the medal?"

Benvenuto glanced down at the Duke's right hand. On his fourth finger he was wearing a broad copper band covered with engraved Greek characters. Benvenuto pointed at it.

"I see your Grace has one of those English rings that are a charm against the night cramps. I would be grateful if you could possibly get me one of those."

The Duke splayed out his fingers and looked at the back of his hand. The ring was worthless. It cost no more than a carlin - a very small silver coin. "By God, that's cheap enough," the Duke thought.

Is that all you want? Well here you are, you can have mine."

He took it off and dropped it into Benvenuto's palm. In the same movement, he waved his hand at the soldiers and his butler and the other on-lookers.

"Alright you people, Messer Cellini is leaving. You there!" he called to a sentry, "open the gate." He turned to Benvenuto. "Mount up."

He took the horse's bridle and walked with Benvenuto towards the gate and said in a very low voice that only Benvenuto could hear, "Now you listen to me, Master Goldsmith. Don't think you've fooled me. Fiaschino doesn't make mistakes. What's more, he's too frightened to lie to me, and you were too frightened not to! But you talked your way out of it very well, and you've been punished by not getting paid. Just consider yourself lucky that Ruosi isn't taking a look at your backbone right this minute."

He stopped under the archway, still holding the bridle.

"And by the way, let me tell you, I don't need any lessons in being angry. Even on a good morning I wake up in a rage that would give Satan himself the runs, and then I spend the rest of the day making it worse!"

He slapped the horse on the rump, and as Benvenuto cantered off, he could feel the skin on his back begin to crawl again.

-34-

After his arrival at Ferrara, the Cardinal kept Benvenuto waiting for several days before he sent for him. When he finally saw him, his reception was frosty.

"Show me the work you have been doing."

Benvenuto signalled to Busbacca to arrange the three pieces on a table. The Cardinal picked up the bowl that had been repaired and gave it a cursory glance, sniffed loudly, and put it down again. Then he examined the new matching vase and stood it inside the bowl, still without a word.

Finally he took his new seal from its velvet-lined box, holding it by its edge between finger and thumb. He looked first at the portrait of St. John, then, turning it over he peered closely at St. Ambrose, cleared his throat noisily, and laid the heavy disc back in its case.

"Very nice."

The Cardinal sat down and began to play with the jewelled crucifix hanging from a long silver chain round his neck. Benvenuto wriggled uneasily as the Cardinal sat there saying nothing.

After about a minute, d'Este looked up at and said, "I hear that you're suffering from night cramps."

"Me? No your Eminence." Benvenuto realised that that the Cardinal was looking at the ring he had got from the Duke. "Oh, you mean this? Well ......"

"Enough! Don't bother. I know the story. I don't think you realise what a narrow escape you had."

Benvenuto swallowed. He knew alright.

The Cardinal sighed. "What am I going to do with you?"

"Whatever your Eminence wishes. I'm entirely at your service."

"Ha!" the Cardinal snorted in disbelief. "I'll tell you what I'm going to do, or rather, what I'm not going to do." He paused. "I'm not going to take you to France."

"But your Eminence. His Majesty sent for me."

"Yes, but he didn't tell me to be your confounded nursemaid. And another thing," the Cardinal said, wagging a finger at Benvenuto, "If I throw you out of my house right away, the Duke of Ferrara won't be able to claim I owe him something for not having given you the whipping you undoubtedly deserved. I don't want to owe him any favours - they're too damn expensive to repay."

The Cardinal had to stop for breath. He leaned back in his chair he began to toy with his crucifix again.

"My major domo tells me you have been designing a salt cellar."

On ceremonial occasions, salt cellars were large, elaborate and intended to be a prominent marker on the table, where their function had nothing to do with the dispensing of salt. The custom was to judge the social status of guests at the long banqueting table by whether they had been placed "above the salt" and hence nearer the host, or "below the salt."

Benvenuto stopped sulking the moment his patron began to display an interest in his work. He snapped his fingers at Busbacca who obediently crossed the room and handed him the document case he had been holding.

"May it please your Eminence, these are only my preliminary sketches. "I am still... I am still creating the whole concept." He made some little circular movements with his hands in front of his chest as if this was some sort of mime of the artistic process.

The Cardinal pursed his lips and nodded to show he understood exactly, and began to study the drawings.

"Magnificent. Absolutely magnificent. Undoubtedly the finest piece you will ever make. Your couple of years in a dark cell may not have been wasted after all, if that's what you dreamed up in there."

Benvenuto beamed with pride. "Then your Eminence will commission it?"

"Certainly not."

"But ..."

"I couldn't afford it," the Cardinal explained. "I don't know how many months it would take to make, how many assistants you will need to do the donkey work, and I certainly can't imagine how much gold will go into a thing that size. But I'll tell you who will order it," he added, seeing Benvenuto's crest-fallen face. "The King of France!"

He clapped Benvenuto on the shoulder. "In fact that settles it! I will arrive in Paris ahead of you and when the King asks where you are, I'll tell him you are working for him on the plans of your masterpiece. And I suggest you do just that. You will travel to Florence. Since you've stolen the idea for some of your figures from Michelangelo, you might as well go and look at the originals and draw them properly."

"To Florence?"

"Don't worry. The old Chief Magistrate's been dead for years. No one's interested in you, you have my word for it. You'll be able to see your sister again - perhaps for the last time."

"Why for the last time, your Eminence? Is there something wrong with her? Is she ill?"

"No my son. In fact she left the Convent without taking her final vows just before you went to prison, and she's now married."

"Then why might I be seeing her for the last time?"

"Because you may do so well at Francis' Court that he will keep you busy there forever. **Please God!**" the Cardinal prayed silently. "On the other hand," he continued slowly, "you may misbehave yourself and annoy the King in some way, and then ..." The Cardinal left the sentence unfinished.

"And then what, your Eminence?"

The Cardinal held up his hand and ticked off the points on his fingers.

"Well, in order of probability: the King has selection of dungeons that would make Sant' Angelo look like a palace. Then he is supposed to have the finest torturer in Europe. And in France, they not only hang people, but the King is very partial to the block.

Also," the Cardinal added, "they don't always use an axe; the executioner has a big blunt two-handed sword. What's more, I hear that the King is just as likely to have someone executed just to give his headsman a bit practice as for any other reason!"

Benvenuto winced.

When they left the room, Busbacca turned to Benvenuto and asked, "Master, do you think he's right about the blunt execution sword? Do you suppose it hurts?"

"Well no one's complained up to now have they? Oh how the Hell should I know?" Benvenuto snarled.

He grabbed hold of Busbacca's ear and shouted into it, "Now listen you, there are four subjects I don't want discussed in my presence. One is hanging, one is flogging, one is prison and the last is head chopping. Do you understand?"

He pulled the boy's ear up and down, forcing him to nod his head in agreement.

"Right, you can go and start packing our things. Tell Ascanio we're leaving first thing in the morning. Meanwhile I'm going to find that Butler to see if I can get some expense money for the journey. Even if the Cardinal's given him any, he'll probably rob me of half of it. More," he added morosely, "he's probably stolen the lot."

At many of the inns spread along all the main routes a traveller in a hurry could change his horse for a fresh one provided by the innkeeper.

The innkeepers were shrewd horse dealers. They had to be in order to stay in business. Aside from trying to get the best of any strangers, they more or less knew their neighbours' stock, and whenever possible they would arrange for a horse to go back the way it had just come, so that the same animal might shuttle up and down the same stretch of road. It was therefore in their interest to see that the exchange horses were not over-exerted or ill-treated.

—ɷ—

It was Good Friday.

As the Innkeeper and his teen-age sons led out three saddle-horses and a packhorse, Benvenuto looked at the man with even more distaste than he had when he had arrived the previous night.

He was tall and heavily built, with a dome-shaped head covered with freckles, and completely bald except for a tuft of bright red hair sticking out like a brush at the nape of his neck. His round, ruddy face was pitted with pock-marks, and instead of a beard, he wore a large drooping moustache.

The Innkeeper wore an open-necked, short-sleeved shirt, once white, but now grey with dirt, under a stiff grease-spotted leather jerkin. Beneath the down of red hair covering the man's arms, Benvenuto could see his skin was another mass of freckles.

Round, green, close-set eyes stared from under thin eyebrows which framed a short snout-like nose, and Benvenuto was so fascinated by the deep dimple in the Innkeeper's chin that he nearly missed what he was saying in his strange guttural accent.

"Obviously not from round here or Tuscany or Rome," Benvenuto decided. "Maybe from the Tyrol or more likely he's some German deserter."

"Don't gallop these horses. You can't go too far today. The next post house is only eight leagues down the road and the one after that can't be reached before dark. Don't gallop them," he repeated. "Is that clear?" He tapped Benvenuto on the chest for emphasis.

Benvenuto angrily brushed the hand aside. "What's clear is that you're a most insolent fellow. Don't you know who I am? I'm Tommaso da Prato, the Pope's Chamberlain, and he," pointing at Ascanio, "is Gabriello Ceserino, Keeper of Sant' Angelo Castle.

You mind your manners or you'll be in serious trouble."

The innkeeper dropped the reins and walked away without another word. He called from the stable doorway, "Don't forget, no galloping ..... Your Excellency," he added as an afterthought.

They had only gone two or three miles when Benvenuto pulled up short and slapped his thigh.

"Damn, damn damn!" he shouted.

"What's the matter, Master?" Busbacca asked.

"I've left my bloody pillion and spare stirrups at the Inn." He pointed to the space behind his saddle where they would normally be strapped. "Be a good lad, go back and get them. Ascanio and I will follow slowly and meet you half way. Hurry now," he shouted as Busbacca trotted off.

They were almost in sight of the Inn again when they saw Busbacca coming towards them.

"Master! Master! He won't give them to me. He says I raced the horse, but I didn't. Really I didn't. I only cantered." The boy was nearly in tears. "He's going to keep them as compensation."

"Oh he is, is he? We'll see about that. Come on you two." Benvenuto dug his heels into the horse's side and galloped back to the Inn.

Benvenuto ducked his head under the low archway of the courtyard and as the horse's hooves clattered over the cobblestones, he reined it so savagely to a halt that it nearly slipped over. Ascanio and Busbacca ranged themselves either side of him. Benvenuto pulled his arquebus from its saddle holster.

"Come on you fat red pig. Get out of your sty," he roared. There was no reply. "Don't make me come in and get you or I'll smash the place to bits."

The Innkeeper emerged, flanked by his two sons. He was carrying a Landsknecht's halberd. The sight of this hated weapon enraged Benvenuto even more.

"I thought so! You're one of those thieving Huns. Well I'm no old priest or fat merchant you can rob. Give me back my stuff or you won't live long enough to regret it.""

"Fuck off!"

"Tut, tut, my man. Such language, and on Good Friday, too."

"I don't care a hat full of shit whether it's Good Friday or Bad Friday. If you don't get out of it, you'll get a bellyful of this." The Innkeeper shook the halberd at Benvenuto and took a threatening step forward.

Benvenuto lowered his gun and pointed it roughly in the German's direction. As he did so, it went off on its own. The ball missed the Innkeeper, but hit the ground in front of him and then ricocheted off one of the cobble stones. The flattened missile flew upwards catching the man under the chin, cut through his tongue and burst out from the back of his neck. He fell backwards, clutching a gaping hole on his throat through which a stream of blood came gushing out.

The innkeeper's sons looked on in frozen horror as their father lay there, making a moaning bubbling noise. After a few moments the noise stopped. He gave a few convulsive twitches, then his head lolled to the side and he was still.

The vision of the gallows flashed through Benvenuto's mind. "Christ Almighty! I've done it again. This time I'm really for it."

With a scream of rage, the older of the two sons picked up his father's lance and rushed at Busbacca and thrust it into his side. The apprentice shrieked and fell from the saddle.

Benvenuto wheeled his horse, and beating a tattoo on its flanks with his heels, he galloped off up the road without waiting to see if Busbacca was alive or dead, or whether Ascanio was also in trouble or was following him.

The horse ran and ran for about five minutes, then, it slowed down and finally stopped, panting and heaving. Nothing Benvenuto could do, no slapping with his gauntlet would make it move, and even when he viciously jabbed it with his spurs, it merely jumped and remained standing.

A little time passed, and Benvenuto used it to reload his gun. From the distance he heard the sound of approaching hoof beats.

"My God! They're after me! Well they'll have to kill me here. I'm not going to let them hang me."

He climbed on to a rock to give himself a better vantage point, but when he looked back along the road he saw that it was Ascanio and Busbacca and the pack horse, and that no one was following them. He jumped back into the saddle, and this time managed to coax his horse along the road to meet them. Still out of sight of his young men, he drew his sword, and when he came level with them, he was brandishing it fiercely.

"Hello you two! I was just coming back to rescue you. How did you get away? Busbacca, you're not hurt then."

They both started to talk at once and Benvenuto held up his hand. "You first, Ascanio."

"When the gun went off and the Innkeeper's son yelled and Busbacca screamed, my horse nearly threw me. It was all I could do to hold it."

"I know," said Benvenuto sympathetically, "mine bolted. I've only just managed to stop it."

Benvenuto lied so convincingly, and his reputation as a fighter was such that Ascanio and Busbacca really believed him.

"What about you Busbacca? The last time I saw you there was a lance sticking in you."

"It's true. I'm dying."

"You don't look badly hurt to me. There's no blood? Let me see."

Busbacca pulled up his shirt.

Benvenuto peered at the boy's side. "You were lucky, it's just a graze. I reckon the lance got caught up in your cloak and it was too heavy for the kid to handle anyway. Come on. We'd better get moving before they come after us."

"I don't think they will," said Ascanio. "A few moments after you …. after your horse ran away, the wife and daughter came out of the house and started crying and screaming; then the two lads joined in so they didn't notice us getting away, and it will take ages for them to get help."

"Yes," said Benvenuto, "and when they do, do you know who they'll be looking for? Tommaso bloody da Prato and Gabriello Ceserino!"

They turned their horses off the road. "I hope you boys like camping out and sleeping rough. Did I ever tell you about how we used to do it during the war ….?"

—⚉—

Five days later Benvenuto was standing in the Medici Chapel in Florence, his notebook and crayons poised but unused in his hands as he stared in rapt and reverent admiration at Michelangelo's magnificent sculptures on the tomb of Lorenzo de' Medici.

-35-

Benvenuto got a cool reception when he presented himself to Cardinal d'Este at Fontainebleau.

"My major domo will find you somewhere to stay for the time being, and that's what you'll do. Stay there until the King sends for you."

"Do you know when will that be, your Eminence?"

"When he feels like it. You don't ask questions of the King. And I'll just remind you, you don't argue with the King; you aren't rude to the King; you don't do anything that even mildly annoys the King. If you do ….." The Cardinal made a downward chopping movement with his hand.

"God Almighty!" Benvenuto thought. "When I get a minute I'm going to sit down and try to work out when the last time a whole week went by without someone threatening me with execution. It must be years."

The Cardinal broke into his musings. "How are the plans for the Salt Cellar coming along?"

"Your Eminence, you kindly said that it would be my masterpiece, but after I saw the actual sculptures that Michelangelo has done since I was last in Florence, I must start all over again. "

"Yes, yes," the Cardinal said impatiently, "but you'll need something to show the King. I'll lend you the bowl and the jug. You won't have time to make anything else and in any case, I can't spare you any gold. The Pope has sent me as the Ambassador to the richest Court in Europe with next to nothing in my treasury. How I'm supposed to manage, I don't know."

Benvenuto shook his head in sympathy.

"Alright, you can go. I'll let you know when the King sends for you." The Cardinal dismissed Benvenuto, but when he reached the door, the Cardinal called out, "By the way, don't forget ....."

He made a chopping movement with his hand.

—⚜—

The morning levee to which Benvenuto was summoned a few days later was the same as the one years before, with a similar crowd of princes, ministers, soldiers, artists, merchants, and a few women.

In stark contrast to the ornate clothes of most of those present, was the sinister black of the Jesuits. In the seven years since Ignatius Loyola had formed his fundamentalist "Society of Jesus," his followers, by their strict discipline and implacable, bigoted opposition to reform were already a powerful, but feared and hated sect.

Benvenuto glanced again at his own outfit. Nothing elaborate this time: a simple white pleated shirt, a brown silk overshirt. Over both of these he wore a sleeveless floor-length black velvet robe with a square neck. His hat was a matching peaked cap which he had set at a rakish angle over one eye.

He looked around the room and saw Cardinal d'Este with a group of Italian merchants and noblemen, but as he started to cross the floor to join them, the Cardinal vigorously waved him away.

There was no one else in the room that he knew, so he disconsolately stood where he was, clutching the linen bag with the Cardinal's bowl and jug in one hand, and his folio of drawings in the other. There was nothing to distinguish him from the other petitioners and artists hoping to get the attention of the King for a few moments, but before he had a chance to think too much about this humiliation, the courtiers fell silent and bowed as the Royal party entered.

King Francis was accompanied by Queen Eleanor and his daughter-in-law, Catherine de' Medici.

The forty-two year old Flemish-born Queen had a long sallow face, straight hair parted in the middle, the jutting lower lip typical of the Hapsburgs, almond shaped eyes and a broad nose. Although tall, she had the trunk of a giantess with disproportionately short legs and thighs, as a result of which she had a most ungainly gait. Queen Eleanor only came out of duty, not out of interest, and she immediately sought out some of the women, and stood in the corner, chattering throughout the whole of the morning's proceedings.

Catherine de' Medici however, was an astute politician who revelled in the affairs of State, and as the King began to circulate in one direction, she took the opposite route.

At last it was Benvenuto's turn. The Cardinal made the introduction. "May it please your Majesty, I believe Messer Benvenuto Cellini has previously been presented to you. He has come to enter your Highness' service."

"Ah yes, we recall him. Well Monsieur Cellini, here you are again. You are still welcome!" The King looked at the Cardinal and said unnecessarily, "Benvenuto - Bienvenue - welcome!"

The Cardinal and the King's entourage gave polite little titters, while Benvenuto forced his lips into a tight smile.

"Your Majesty is very kind to remember me, and your Grace's sense of humour is unaltered by the passage of time and, er, your many duties."

Benvenuto desperately tried to keep the conversation going, and to prevent the King from moving on.

"I look forward to giving my entire life and skill to your Majesty."

The King scratched his ear. "Yes, quite so. What's that in your bag? Is it for me?"

"I regret not, Sire. I have brought something to show you. It is something I made for my patron, Cardinal d'Este here."

The Cardinal flushed, and hoped that the King would not like them so much that he would be forced to give them to him, but Francis simply looked at the jug and bowl for a moment and said, "Very nice, your Eminence. I wish you joy with them.

Perhaps Monsieur Cellini will make something for me very soon. What do you have in your folio case?"

"They are the plans and specifications for a great Salt Cellar I am designing for your Majesty. They are not quite ready yet."

Francis looked at the Cardinal "Oh yes, you told me about it, didn't you? Well Monsieur, I'll look at them someday when they're ready and I have the time. My Chamberlain will make arrangements with you through his Eminence for your employment."

Benvenuto mumbled his thanks, and bowed deeply as the King made to move on, but Francis stopped to deliver his parting shot.

"By the way, I hope you find your quarters here at Fontainebleau more comfortable than those you enjoyed in Sant' Angelo as the guest of Pope Paul!"

He walked away roaring with laughter, and nudging his Secretary with his elbow as he explained his little joke.

It was late the next afternoon when the Cardinal instructed Benvenuto to call on him in the beautifully appointed suite of apartments that the King had given him in the Palace, overlooking the Garden of Diane.

"Good news, Benvenuto. His Majesty's Chamberlain will find you a house and workshop nearby where you can set yourself up. The King will be ready to discuss some commissions as soon as you're settled in."

Benvenuto beamed with pleasure.

"Did he mention a salary?"

"Dear me, no! The King doesn't talk about money. That's why he has a Chamberlain. As well as the house, you are to have three hundred ducats a year."

"And what else, your Eminence?"

"Nothing else. Don't you think it's enough? The King did rescue you from prison, after all."

"That doesn't mean I've got to be his slave. Everyone seems to have the same idea. First the Pope, now the King. Well, your Eminence, the answer to your question is no, I don't think it's enough. Sir, can I remind you that when we were in Ferrara, you told me I would have a good position with the King. If you had said that meant a measly three hundred ducats a year, I'd have stayed in Florence. I could earn more there turning out rings and bracelets and trinkets."

The Cardinal was stunned by this outburst. "My son, I don't know what to say to you."

Benvenuto calmed down. "Oh please, your Eminence, forgive me. I know it's not your fault. I can't begin to count the things you've done for me. Where ever I go, and for as long as I live, I shall always pray for you, but I'm not going to work for three hundred ducats a year - not even twice that."

Now it was the Cardinal's turn to lose his temper. "Don't you dare haggle with me! I can't do anything more for you. Do what you like! Go where you like! I can't make you let me help you."

Angrily he thrust both his hands into the wide sleeves of his robe to prevent Benvenuto from kissing his ring, and turning his back on him, stared out of the window.

"Goodbye, your Eminence, and thank you."

The Cardinal did not reply, but when he heard the door close, he shook his head.

"Benvenuto! Benvenuto," he murmured to himself, "What am I going to do with you? What are you going to do to yourself?"

Back at his lodgings, Benvenuto kicked open the door and roared out for Ascanio and Busbacca.

"What's wrong, Master?" Busbacca asked.

"Nothing's wrong. What makes you think something's wrong?" he shouted. "I've just changed my mind, that's all. I'm going straight back to Florence. I'm not staying here to work for a pittance. You know what that damned French miser offered me? Three hundred crowns a year! A year mind you! I bet he spends more than that in a day by accident!"

"Careful, sir. Someone will hear, and you'll be in more trouble." Ascanio interrupted the tirade. "So we've got to go back to Florence?"

"Not we. Just me. I won't be able to afford to pay you both for a while. I'll give you enough money to get you home, or keep you here until you find a new Master, whichever you like, but I'm off on my own."

He pointed at Busbacca. "You boy, don't stand there snivelling. Pack my things. I'll leave first thing tomorrow."

―⁂―

Benvenuto was a fair way along the road to the South-East in the direction of Sens. His horse trotting at an easy pace, followed by his pack-horse which was tied by a long lead to his saddle, when he heard the sound of several horses galloping behind him.

Glancing over his shoulder, he saw four riders with sunlight glinting on helmets and armour. Instinctively he urged his own mount to go faster, but it was obvious that the four soldiers would soon catch him up.

Hopefully he reined to a halt, and edged off the track, as if politely allowing them to get past, but when they came near to him they slowed down and finally stopped. Pointedly, two of the soldiers took up positions to his right in the direction he was going, and the other two to his left, in the direction of Fontainebleau.

Over their breast armour they wore tabards - sleeveless aprons of dark blue linen, embroidered with a gold shield with three Fleurs de Lys. The shield was surrounded by a wreath and surmounted by a crown. On either side was a letter "F". This was the King's Coat of Arms. These were his soldiers.

Their leader spoke. "Good morning, Sir. Do I have the honour of addressing Monsieur Benvenuto Cellini of Florence?"

Benvenuto was taken aback at this elaborate politeness.

"The honour?" he thought. "Why yes," he said aloud, "you do."

"Then I have to request you to be good enough to return with me to Fontainebleau."

"Are you arresting me?"

"Certainly not, sir. I am just requesting you to come back with me."

"And supposing I refuse your kind request?"

"Well then I will arrest you. But let me remind you before you make up your mind, in case you didn't know, if the King has anyone arrested, they often stay in jail for years before he gets round to dealing with them."

"I see," said Benvenuto, "then I had better accept your invitation, hadn't I? Can I ask you though, why are you taking me back? No, don't tell me. Your job is just to go and fetch people. You never ask why."

"Exactly," said the soldier. "How did you know?"

"Oh, I just guessed. I'll tell you what, though. I've never had a politer invitation to accompany a policeman, so this is what I'm going to do. If I remember rightly, I passed a quite reasonable looking Inn about half a league back along the road. The last one there can pay for the wine."

He dug his spurs into his horse and raced off, followed by his pack horse and hotly pursued by the soldiers.

—⚜—

To Benvenuto's surprise, he was taken to Cardinal d'Este's chambers in the Palace. The leader of the soldiers left him in an ante room on the first floor overlooking the King's garden with its little lily pond.

"Wait here," the soldier said, and went to find the Cardinal.

"You caught up with him then? Did he give you any bother?"

"No sir, on the contrary, he was very amiable. He even bought us all wine when he lost a race back."

"Really," said the Cardinal, "He must be getting old. You did make him think it was the King who had him brought back?"

"Yes, I did exactly what you said. He doesn't know it was really you."

"Well, let's keep it our secret then, shall we?" The Cardinal handed over five gold coins. "Here. One for each of your men, and two for you. Send him in, will you?"

"Good afternoon, Benvenuto. You look a little dusty. You've had a long ride, I hear."

"I have, your Eminence. I've been in the saddle since dawn."

"Well you're back now, and that's all that matters. If you're not too tired, perhaps you'll tell me what you make of this." The Cardinal walked to a suit of armour standing in the corner and took a long double-edged sword from the iron gloves.

Benvenuto looked puzzled. "I don't know too much about this sort of thing, your Eminence." He hefted the sword in his hands. "It's very heavy. You'd have to use it with both hands. If it goes with the armour, it's about a hundred years old, and judging by the inscription, it's English. That's all I can tell you."

"Well done," the Cardinal said. "There's just one more thing. That's the sort of sword the King's executioner uses when the block needs a bit of blood to lubricate it!"

Benvenuto snorted. "For pity's sake, your Eminence! How many more times? Isn't there any end to my being threatened with jail or torture or whipping or execution? Doesn't it occur to anyone that I might die in my bed - of old age?"

"Not the way you carry on," the Cardinal retorted. "I just wanted you to know that I've saved you once again. You needn't bother to thank me."

Benvenuto had not intended to.

"....Nor for the other thing I've done."

"What is that, your Eminence?"

"I've got you a better arrangement with the King's Chamberlain. Seven hundred crowns a year, and before you say anything," the Cardinal said as Benvenuto began to protest, "that's the same as the King used to give Leonardo da Vinci, and with all due respect, you're no Leonardo! You'll also get paid for all the work you do. If you hadn't gone mad yesterday, you'd have understood that then. The seven hundred's just a retainer."

"One more thing," the Cardinal added, "He's paying five hundred crowns as your expenses for the journey and to set up your house and workshop."

"Why that's very generous of his Majesty."

"In fact, it was my idea," the Cardinal said. "Actually, if you remember, I myself gave you five hundred crowns for the journey before you left Ferrara, so I've kept it to pay myself back."

-36-

Things were going very well. The King had given Benvenuto the largest commission he had ever had. It was for twelve silver candlesticks, each six feet high, in the form of six gods and goddesses. They were to be decorations for the King's banqueting table and would by themselves provide about two years' work for Benvenuto and several assistants. The designs and models alone would take weeks and he was still sketching ideas for the salt cellar he hoped to tempt Francis to order.

There was also the promise of more work from members of the Court, and Benvenuto could visualise himself once more being the head of a large and busy studio.

Benvenuto had also found a house - actually a small castle - called **"Petit Nesle"** or the **"Tour de Nesle"** which was an ancient bastion of the city walls, situated on the left bank of the river in a disreputable "thieves' kitchen" neighbourhood.

It was in the form of a triangle with a round tower about ninety feet high, and was reputed to have been the home, in the olden days, of a Queen who used to entice her many lovers there and then to secure their silence by having them tied in sacks and flung into the river from the battlements.

The first time Benvenuto saw the building he fell in love with it, and as Francis had promised him a permanent place to work, he had boldly asked the King's Chamberlain, Robert de Villurois to petition the King to grant him the use of it.

"He'll never agree," said de Villurois.

"Why not?" Benvenuto asked. "It's empty, and it doesn't look as if it's been used for years."

"Because His Majesty has already given it to Monsieur de Marmagna."

"Who's he?"

"He's the Provost of Paris - the Chief Administrator of the City. Why don't you look for somewhere else? I can't believe the King will want to risk upsetting him."

"But you will ask him - just the same?"

De Villurois reluctantly agreed.

"The fellow's quite right," Francis said. "It's my property, and the Provost doesn't live there. He's letting it go to rack and ruin and Cellini may as well have it."

"But your Majesty ...."

"But nothing! The Provost doesn't do anything for me and Cellini will. I've decided, and that's an end to it."

"I was merely going to point out to your Majesty," de Villurios said quietly, "that in order for Cellini to keep possession, he may have to use a little force."

"So let him," said the King, "and if a little force isn't enough, he'd better use a lot!"

De Villurois tossed a large iron key across the desk. As Benvenuto reached for it he said, "Before you pick it up, Monsieur, I want to tell you something."

Benvenuto snatched his hand back as if he had been bitten.

"I know all about your feud with the Pope's Chamberlain. What's his name?"

"Da Prato."

"Da Prato. Well, I can be just as dangerous an enemy as he was, but I'm different."

"We ought to get along fine then," Benvenuto thought.

"I'm different because I give advice only when I have to, and I don't take sides. It can be very dangerous round here if you pick the wrong one."

Benvenuto looked at de Villurois narrowly. "You're talking about not taking sides between me and who?"

"The Provost. I got the King to give you the Petit Nesle just as you asked me to, and I've warned Monsieur de Marmagna that you're going to take it away from him. So now, neither of you can be upset with me."

The Chamberlain gave Benvenuto a smug smile. "You can take the key now - if you still want it."

—⚍—

The Provost tried to forestall Benvenuto by moving some furniture into the best rooms and even began to have them cleaned up.

"Sir," Benvenuto said very politely, but through clenched teeth, "I have to tell you that His Majesty has given me this place to use in his service. The whole of it, not just bits, and I do not intend to share it with anyone. Not even an important nobleman such as Your Honour," he added to soften his words.

The Provost was not placated. "Don't you patronise me! The King gave me this building, and so far as I'm concerned, the only use you can make of it is to knock your head against the wall. Hard!"

"My permission is later than yours. The place is mine now, I tell you."

"I say you're a liar."

"And you, Sir, are a thief!"

The Frenchman's hand went to the little jewelled decorative stiletto he wore at his hip. Benvenuto's own dagger was much more business-like: over a foot long with a broad razor-sharp double-edged blade.

"One second after you draw that toothpick of yours, Monsieur, you'll be dead!"

De Marmagna had two servants with him, and Benvenuto was accompanied by Ascanio and Busbacca.

"If those two try to interfere, kill them where they stand," Benvenuto ordered.

His two assistants looked at each other. If there was going to be a knife fight, they would rather run, but they assumed ferocious expressions and half drew their own daggers.

"You take the fat one," Ascanio hissed at Busbacca and I'll deal with pimple-face."

Although he spoke in Italian, there was no mistaking his meaning. The Provost's two men shuffled backwards until they were behind their master, while de Marmagna slowly moved his hand away from his belt and clasped it in his other behind his back.

Benvenuto gave a lopsided smile. "Ascanio, I do believe our guests are leaving."

Ascanio opened the street door. As de Marmagna stamped out, he stopped and pointed his finger at Benvenuto.

"The King shall hear of this!"

"You can rely on it," Benvenuto replied. "I'll tell him myself, and when he finds out how you've tried to disobey him, I wouldn't be surprised if you found yourself a head shorter."

He felt a strange pleasure at being able to threaten someone else with execution for once. "And by the way, Monsieur, in case you were thinking of leaving any of this junk here ...." he gave one of the Provost's pieces of furniture a kick, "... may I say I couldn't possibility accept such a magnificent gift, so if you haven't collected it in an hour, you'll find it floating down the Seine!"

Benvenuto realised that he had made himself a new powerful enemy. He looked at Ascanio and Busbacca and shrugged his shoulders. "Oh well," he said. "Here we go again. It's just like being back home in Italy, really."

Benvenuto soon got his new household organised. He bought the bare essentials of furniture and cooking utensils and fitted out three separate workrooms with benches, cupboards and tools. He had taken on as assistants, two craftsmen. They were

Italians already working in Paris: Bartolomeo Chioccia from Ferrara and Pagolo Miccieri, a fellow Florentine.

Also he hired two servants: a beautiful half-Italian girl, Caterina, as the housemaid, and her French mother who would be the cook.

Benvenuto preferred to surround himself with Italians and was delighted when his new cook told him she had always made Italian food for her late husband.

"Good," he said, when he engaged her on the spot. "Then I won't be homesick. To tell you the truth, Madame, I really don't like that stuff the French eat. Their wine's not too bad though!"

Her daughter was tall, long-legged with a voluptuous figure and an elfin-like face with a delicate thin nose. Her hair was curly and she wore it like a close fitting cap. Benvenuto began to use her as a model, and soon made her his mistress with her mother's connivance.

"He's obviously very well off. Look at this house; look how many men he's got; and look who he's working for - the King himself, no less. You make him happy, and who knows …."

—⚜—

With his domestic arrangements settled, Benvenuto began to push his staff into the routine for making the set of candlesticks. He prepared the drawings of Juno, a statuesque nude in classical style, her plaited hair surmounted by a jewelled tiara, holding a flambeau in her left hand. At the same time, with the help of his assistants, he finished the clay models of three of the other figures, Jupiter, Vulcan and Mars. He even began to make a start on the silver work for the Jupiter, using some of the three hundred pounds of the metal that the King's Chamberlain had given him.

With the delivery of the silver, the King sent word that he would come to inspect progress in person on his way back from his hunting lodge. Two extra temporary maids were hired and the entire building was transformed by a flurry of frenzied activity by washing, mopping, sweeping and polishing into a state of cleanliness that it had not enjoyed for decades, while from the kitchen came the smell of the baking of little cakes and biscuits and pastry bouchees stuffed with different savoury fillings.

When the King arrived, it was in the company of the rest of his hunting party: the Queen, the Dauphin - the future Henry II - Catherine de' Medici, the Cardinal of Lorraine, King Francis' sister Marguerite and her husband, Henri d' Albret - the King of Navarre.

Included in the party was the legendary Anne de Pisseleu - now the Duchess d'Etampes - who was openly known to be the King's mistress.

Benvenuto, more used to the subtleties of Italian society, was surprised to find her in the Queen's presence. Actually, the Queen was merely a figurehead and breeder of the King's children. "Madame d'Etampes," as she was known, was firmly ensconced in the Royal household. She had her own room in every one of the King's palaces, and in Fontainebleau her bedroom was being lavishly decorated by the great Bolognese artist, Primatticio, with carvings and mouldings, gilding and paintings.

Anne de Pisseleu was already the King's mistress when in June 1530 he married, for political reasons, the thirty-two year old Flemish princess, Eleanor, the sister of the Austrian Emperor. Eleanor had been, for a short time, the third and last wife of the late Portuguese King, Emanuel I – "Emanuel the Fortunate" to his subjects - but had been a widow for the past nine years.

Eight months after her marriage to Francis, Eleanor was formally crowned Queen of France at an elaborate Coronation where she was bedecked with more than a million ducats' worth of jewels, but to her humiliation, the Queen's ceremonial entry into Paris was watched by the King and his mistress from a window where they sat in full public view for over two hours.

The King was faithful to Madame d'Etampes in his own way - which meant most of the time - but he was also aware that she too had occasional affairs. After one stormy scene at his Chateau at Chambourd, when he finally forgave her for yet another lapse, the King resentfully scratched a couplet on his bedroom window with a diamond ring:

"Souvent femme varie. Bien fol est qui sy fie."
"Woman is fickle. Mad is he who trusts her."

Despite all this, the King loved her and she was his constant companion until he died. Indeed his last kindness to her - apart from urging his son to "have pity on her" - was to send her out of the room when he was dying miserably of a combination of syphilis and tuberculosis.

After his marriage to Eleanor, he appointed Anne to be one of her ladies-in-waiting and Governess to two of his daughters of his earlier marriage, thus establishing her permanently in the King's presence.

In 1533 he arranged a marriage of convenience for her with Jean de Brosse, who was prepared to allow himself to be used in this way so as to recover his family's estates which Francis had confiscated because of de Brosse's father's involvement with the rebellious Constable Bourbon. One year after the marriage, the King made her husband Duc d'Etampes and Governor of Brittany - a post which conveniently took him well away from Paris.

Madame d'Etampes' power at Court and over the King was enormous, not just because of her beauty and the sexual attraction she had for him, but because of her considerable intellect. Even the courtiers, many of whom had no reason to like her, paid her the compliment of being "La plus belle des savantes et la plus savante des belles" - "The most beautiful wise woman, and the wisest of the beauties".

Francis sometimes resented her influence over him. His death-bed advice to his son, who would in a few hours become

King Henry II, was not to allow himself to be ruled by others - as he had been by Madame d'Etampes.

—⁂—

The Duchess was petite, with a heart shaped face, crowned by rich red hair, pale arched eyebrows and eyelashes so fine that they were almost invisible. Her dress was cut square at the bosom and at the tops of her arms, revealing delicately curved shoulders, a slender neck and a skin the same creamy colour as the flawless complexion of her face.

The top of her black velvet dress, embroidered in gold thread was framed by a wide band of lace appliquéd with poppies and blue flowers, and a row of the same lace was repeated in her hair-piece.

She wore no jewellery except for a plain gold wedding ring and a large gold letter "A" hanging from necklace which reached almost to her narrow waist.

Benvenuto stared at Madame d'Etampes and stood frozen in half a bow, his hand across his breast. He found himself almost tottering towards her, and he consciously had to restrain an urge to reach out and touch her. He had felt himself attracted to many women before, but never like this, never so violently, never so quickly, and never so dangerously.

The Duchess knew at once what effect she had on this tall dark Italian. She did nothing to relieve his embarrassment as, with the corners of her mouth dimpled in a smile, she stared at him through green, almost lidless eyes.

Benvenuto straightened up, blushing, and took two steps backwards, but cannoned into Busbacca who had been standing close behind him. Humiliated by his own clumsiness, he angrily kicked and then cuffed the boy, sending him staggering against the King to whom Busbacca first clung for support to prevent himself from falling, and then dodged behind to avoid further blows.

Benvenuto looked fearfully at the King, but Francis started laughing and then Madame d'Etampes joined in, followed by the Queen and the rest of the visitors.

Benvenuto managed to force a wan smile, and turning to his assistants, clapped his hands together.

"Ascanio! Pagolo! Bartolomeo! Come on. His Majesty isn't here to see what's his name clowning around." He glared at Busbacca. "Let's show him what we're working on, and then perhaps His Majesty will honour me by taking some light refreshment."

—⁂—

It was while Benvenuto was showing the Royal party his sketches of the great salt cellar that Madame D'Etampes unobtrusively began to titillate him again - deliberately ….

He had spread the drawings on a table. The King and Queen stood on his left and Madame D'Etampes on his right, with the others crowded behind peering over their shoulders. Benvenuto felt something pressing against his leg. He shuffled an inch or two to the side but the pressure continued. Again he moved. There was no mistaking it: there it was again. Madame D'Etampes was grinding and rubbing her knee against his thigh!

As if to emphasise what she was doing, the Duchess leaned across him, the bodice of her dress falling forward revealing small round unbound breasts. Benvenuto reluctantly drew his eyes away as she lightly but sinuously brushed the back of his hand with the palm of hers, and pointing to one of the sketches, asked a totally trivial question.

"Monsieur, why is all this writing in Italian? Surely if you hope to sell it to His Majesty, it should be in French."

"Your Grace, these are only rough sketches. The final perfect drawings that His Majesty will approve will have descriptions in French."

"Oh what does it matter?" the King said testily. "I can see what he means." He clapped Benvenuto on the back. "Now what was that you said about refreshments?"

"There is something that Monsieur Cellini can do for me," Madame D'Etampes interjected.

The King looked at her sharply, but she pretended not to have noticed.

"I have an artist working for me who is in need of a small studio. I wonder if he can find a corner of one of the basements for a fellow sculptor."

"I am at your Grace's command," said Benvenuto politely.

"Are you, indeed?" she replied in a low husky voice, "We'll see."

The King took a swig of Benvenuto's best wine, made an elaborate grimace of distaste and set the goblet down on the drawings with such a thump that some of the contents splashed out and stained the paper.

A few days later the invitation that Benvenuto knew would come, duly arrived. It came by word of mouth from a messenger.

"Her Grace is giving a small soiree at six o'clock at the Rue de l' Hirondelle."

This was a town house on the Left Bank, opposite the Isle de la Cite which Francis had bought for the Duchess in addition to the two splendid chateaux that he had given her at Etampes and Limours.

The King himself was at that time away on one of his regular hunting trips at Chambourd, his lodge in the Loire Valley.

"Her Grace suggests that you bring with you anything you wish to show her."

"I'll do that alright," Benvenuto thought to himself as the messenger continued, "Drawings or models perhaps. Supper will be served, of course."

"Of course," Benvenuto echoed.

Benvenuto carefully dressed himself, this time not in things borrowed from Ascanio, but in his new best clothes bought with the money he now had jingling in his purse. To complete his outfit, he selected from his trading stock an unostentatious, very tasteful double chain of gold links.

While he stood at the door buckling on his sword belt and waiting for Busbaca to bring his horse, Caterina came out. In contrast to her elegantly dressed employer, she was tired and bedraggled after a long day of housework. There was a smudge of ash from the kitchen fire on her jaw.

"I know where you're going. You're going to that skinny doxy you've been mooning over for days."

"If there are two things I can't stand," Benvenuto said in a quiet conversational tone, "it's a nagging woman or one who's crying."

"I'm not nagging."

"Oh yes you are!"

"And I'm not crying either."

"You are now," said Benvenuto. He slapped her viciously on both cheeks, snatched the reins of his horse from Busbacca and galloped off.

Benvenuto was disappointed to find there were at least fifty or so other guests, a dozen servants and three musicians to whom nobody was paying any attention whatsoever.

Madame D'Etampes greeted him perfunctorily, and with a gesture invited him to help himself from a large buffet set against one of the walls, after which he was left to wander round the room, attaching himself first to one group of guests and then to another, while she totally ignored him.

Benvenuto was getting quite irritated. He wanted to walk out, but he knew that it would be insulting - and hence dangerous - for him to do so. "Besides," he thought to himself after his third brimming goblet of the heavy red wine, "I might as well stay to see what happens. After all, presumably she didn't ask me here just to try the chicken in aspic!"

At about nine o'clock one or two of the guests began to leave, and Benvenuto perked up as the Duchess purposefully crossed the room, and took him by the arm.

"Ah Monsieur Cellini, I'm so glad you were able to come, even though you have to leave so soon. What a pity there is no time to look at your work, but some other time perhaps."

Benvenuto's felt his stomach knot with disappointment, and just in time he stifled a sarcastic retort as she whispered, "Up the stairs. Second door on the right. Wait."

Responding to the cue, Benvenuto gave a deep bow. "I shall look forward with great impatience to my next meeting with your Grace."

Madame D'Etampes turned back to her remaining guests, leaving Benvenuto to leap up the stairs three at a time and furtively race along the corridor.

He flung himself into the room, leaned against the door and looked round as he caught his breath. He was in a dressing room: there was another recessed door to his left, while the wall to his right was filled with cupboards. Heavy red and gold brocade curtains were drawn across the windows which took up most of another wall. There was a long sofa, three high backed chairs and, in the centre, a long carved gilded table on which stood a five branched candelabra which gave a bright flickering light.

Benvenuto crossed to the table where there was also a silver wine jug, some goblets and a fruit bowl. He started to pour some wine, but stopped and shook his head.

"I've had enough already."

Instead he picked a few plump grapes from the bunch and looked around for somewhere to put the pips: there was nowhere, so he crunched them up with his teeth, wrinkling up his nose at the bitter taste.

He tiptoed across to the other door and gingerly tried the handle. It turned. He gently pushed. The heavy door swung open a little and he peeped into the next room. All he could see through the crack was a high four-poster in the centre of the polished wooden floor. It was a bedroom. Her bedroom!

Hastily he shut the door again, ran the few steps back to the table and stood there drumming on it with his finger tips. Then he picked another few grapes. He gave each a couple of hard chews and swallowed them whole, pips and all.

He went to the window, drew back the edge of the curtain and looked out. Down in the street he could see some of the guests leaving. At that moment the bedroom opened. Anne D'Etampes stood there, the candle light glinting in her red hair and making her smooth bare shoulders gleam with a creamy glow. Benvenuto just looked at her.

"Well, if you won't come to me, I suppose I'd better come to you," she said.

In half a dozen steps she was standing provocatively close in front of him - a tiny figure, her head just level with his chest. Without any hesitation or even a hint of bashfulness, she reached into his tunic and rummaged under his shirt until, in an instant, she found what she was looking for.

"Let's see what you're made of. Hum! There's no doubt about that, so now we'll find out if you deserve that reputation of yours."

Still holding him tightly, she led him like a puppy on a leash, through into the bedroom. When she did let go, she turned her back on him and pointed to the fastenings on her dress.

"Are you going to undo it, or are you going to tear it off me?"

At last Benvenuto found his voice. "Am I supposed to be a ladies' maid then?" he said thickly.

"And that's the other thing we're going to find out tonight, isn't it?"

—⚊—

Benvenuto awoke at the first tinges of dawn feeling as if he had been buffeted and mauled in some gigantic storm.

As he lay there on the great bed, amid the rumpled sheets, still damp from their sweaty exertions and speckled with the little curls of black hair that had torn loose from his chest and arms and legs when her body had ground against his, Anne too stirred and woke. Not realising Benvenuto was already awake, she gently shook his shoulder.

"Oh God!" he thought, "not again. I simply can't."

"Come on, it's time for you to go," she said.

"To go?"

"Yes, you weren't thinking of moving in were you?"

She lay there, the sheet up to her chin, watching him dress and smiling.

"What's the joke?"

"Nothing. I just think there's nothing more undignified than a man dressing to go home."

"Thank you very much," Benvenuto replied indignantly.

"Oh it's nothing personal. It's only that I've seen more of it than most women." She changed the subject. "Tell me," she said as he struggled to pull on his hose, "is there anything I can do for you?"

"Do for me? I reckon you've done all you can for one night."

"Not that, stupid! I mean at Court. With the King. Is there anything you want from him?"

Benvenuto looked down at her, not knowing whether to be insulted or grateful. He chose his words carefully and spoke quietly.

"I only want one thing of the King's."

"What?"

"You."

"Being practical, is there anything else?"

"Yes, I desperately want him to commission the salt cellar. I know it will be my masterpiece - the greatest piece I have ever done."

"A salt cellar?" she echoed. "Is that what I've come down to? Others ask me for titles, for loans, for every possible privilege under the sun that the King can grant, and all you want is a salt cellar. Procurer of the Royal Condiment Sets, that's me," she laughed. "Alright, I'll try for you."

"When will I see you again?"

"I'll let you know. The King doesn't often go off hunting alone. Alone?" she added almost inaudibly, but just loud enough for Benvenuto to hear. "That's a laugh. He thinks I don't know that he's taken that Marie de Canaples with him!"

Dame Marie de Canaples was another of the King's mistresses and Benvenuto suddenly realised that it was not merely because Anne D'Etampes had wanted him that it had happened: she had also wanted to revenge herself on Francis.

"I'll be off then," he said sullenly. He bent to kiss her cheek. She caught his head in her hands and her tongue darted in and out of her mouth just once.

"Yes, off you go. Get some rest. You look very tired." She giggled and pulled the sheet over her head.

-37-

Benvenuto was like a man demented, rushing from one project to another and employing more and more staff to help him and Ascanio and Busbacca and his two newest Italian assistants Pagolo Miccieri and Bartolomeo Chioccia in all the work he was undertaking.

Two silversmiths were noisily beating out and shaping sheets of silver for the head arms and body of the Jupiter candlestick; there was a silver gilt bowl and jug for the King; clay models were being worked on for three more of the candlesticks and several small pieces of jewellery were being made for members of the court. At the same time Benvenuto was working on grandiose schemes of his own for two sculptures for the Chateau of Fontainebleau.

He had not had another visit from the King, nor had he been invited to the Palace. Neither had he heard from Madame D'Etampes, but then he had not expected to.

Then, in the middle of all this frenzied activity, he received a summons to go to Cardinal d'Este's quarters which were now, in effect, the Embassy of the Vatican. The Cardinal embraced him warmly.

"My son, it's good to see you. Why have you kept yourself so strange? I'm sure a friendly face from home is as welcome to you as it is to me."

"Well, er...." Benvenuto began.

"No, it's alright. I understand you've been very busy. Working hard I'm sure. I've been hearing very good reports about you. But I rather think you've been up to one piece of mischief. Stupid mischief. Dangerous too."

"What do you mean?" Benvenuto asked.

"You know exactly what I mean. I can't prove anything, but luckily neither can anyone else - especially the King."

"The King?"

"Yes, the King. Don't play the innocent with me. You went to a supper party at Madame D'Etampes' and were supposed to have left early. Suddenly she's asking favours for you."

"For me? What favours?"

"We'll come to that later. Meanwhile you had better understand that the King is no fool. He knows that for her to ask for something for you, she must have seen you at some time. For the moment he believes it was while she was visiting that tenant she planted in your basement. But make no mistake about it, if he gets suspicious, he'll have you watched, and if you give him half a reason you'll finish up in jail again, or more likely in two pieces." The Cardinal's made the familiar chopping motion with his hand.

"Now listen to me, Benvenuto. You've got quite a beauty living with you, so they tell me. The ladies of the Court are more than averagely willing. Paris is full of women, and in case that's not enough for you, there's the whole of France. But for your own sake, stay away from the King's Mistresses - all of them. Do I make myself clear?"

Benvenuto nodded glumly, but the Cardinal was not satisfied.

"I asked you if I made myself clear. I didn't quite hear your answer."

"Yes, your Eminence."

"See you do as I say, or you'll live to regret it - but not for long."

"Um - did your Eminence say that her Grace had obtained a favour for me from the King?"

"Not one. Two. Only one of them may not turn out to be such a favour if you don't behave yourself. The King is going to give you your naturalisation papers. He's going to make you a Frenchman.

"What sort of favour is that? I can't eat naturalisation papers, can I?"

"No, but it's a great honour which may do you some good. It may also do you a great deal of harm."

Benvenuto looked worried. "How, your Eminence?"

"Because Monsieur Frenchman, if you stupidly get yourself into trouble with the King, I won't be able to help you. Those naturalisation papers could also be your death warrant. Anyway, I'm telling you all this in confidence. When you are told officially, you will pretend to be surprised; you will accept without hesitation and express yourself as being absolutely overwhelmed by the great honour. Is that clear too?"

Benvenuto nodded again.

"Now the other favour. His Majesty thinks you haven't got enough to do and that you're not working hard enough."

"What!" Benvenuto shouted. "I've never been so busy in all my life. I'm even thinking of fitting a chamber pot under my bench because some days I can't even spare the time to go for a pee! Who's been telling the King I'm not working?"

The Cardinal let out a bellow of laughter and placed a pudgy hand on Benvenuto's shoulder.

"Come on, don't take it so seriously. All I wanted to tell you was that the King is giving you another commission. He said something about a salt cellar."

"He wants my salt cellar. He's going to let me make it!"

Benvenuto stood with both hands covering his mouth as tears started in his eyes.

The Cardinal looked at him quizzically. "Benvenuto, it's only a …. it's only a thing."

"Eminence, it's going to be the greatest thing, as you call it, that I have ever done."

"Let us hope so. I wish you success with it. Tell me, how much gold will it take?"

From years of thinking and hoping, Benvenuto could give the answer without hesitation.

"I will need one thousand crowns."

Cardinal d'Este pursed his lips. "Phew. I was right when I said I couldn't afford it. I can't imagine how you got Madame D'Etampes to persuade the King to spend all that on the gold alone!"

He leered at Benvenuto, snapped his thumb against his front tooth and crossed to his desk. He searched among his papers until he found the one he was looking for. Dipping his pen in the ink, he wrote a figure in a blank space.

"Here," he said. This is an order from the King to his Chamberlain. I've filled the figure in. De Villurios is expecting you.

Benvenuto looked at the paper with the King's seal, the spiky writing of the scribe and the still damp figures that the Cardinal had just inserted.

"Your Eminence...."

"Before you thank me, here's another piece of advice. De Villurois tried to talk the King out of giving you this job just yet. He said it was too big a project. 'A whole life's work,' he called it. He told the King you already had too much to do as it is, and that you would neglect your other work for this pet dream of yours."

Benvenuto started to protest but the Cardinal persisted.

"No - just you listen. He's not the first one to say that about you. What's more, it's true. It was the same in Rome. You rush from one thing to another as you find a new enthusiasm."

The Cardinal's voice fell to a whisper, as if he was frightened of being overheard. "The King can be a real tyrant when he wants to. Please, I beg you for your own sake - you can be settled here for life. Rich and famous too. Another Leonardo da Vinci. Don't do anything to spoil it."

He held out his hand. "Alright, you may go."

As Benvenuto knelt to kiss his ring, the Cardinal added his final word. "And don't forget. Stay away from that woman."

—◆—

Benvenuto hurried home, alternately running forty or fifty yards and then walking when, unused to such strenuous exercise, he became breathless. Without a word to anyone, he rushed into the kitchen and searched around for something to carry the gold in. He picked up a wooden bucket and discarded it.

"Too small," he muttered.

"Too small for what?" Caterina asked.

"Too small for what I want," he shouted. Angrily he gave it a kick and Caterina had to duck as it flew past her ear and crashed into the pots hanging in the fireplace, bringing them down to the floor with a clatter.

"If you'll tell me what you want, I'll help you find it," Caterina said mildly.

"If I bloody well knew what I wanted, I'd find it myself."

The girl flounced out of the kitchen in disgust, leaving Benvenuto opening cupboards and slamming them shut. Then in the corner near the street door, he spotted Caterina's wicker shopping basket. Deep, narrow and rectangular, it had a handle on either side and a hinged lid that ran along the whole length, so that when an arm was thrust through both handles, the lid was held down, closed tight.

"It's alright, I've found it."

Caterina poked her head round the kitchen door. Benvenuto smiled at her.

"I'm going out again. Thanks for your help," he said sweetly.

In his excitement, he forgot the elementary precaution of taking some of his men with for protection.

—⚉—

De Villurois was not ready when Benvenuto rushed into the King's private treasury and presented the warrant for the gold.

"You didn't waste any time did you?" he grumbled. "Why didn't you give me a little notice?"

"Because some people" - how easily the old venomous phrase jumped to his lips - "some people might tell His Majesty that I was not diligent enough in attending to his business."

De Villurois looked up from the document. "Some people? Well I'm not 'some people.' I'm the King's Chamberlain." His voice hardened. "And he needs me more than he needs you, so don't get snotty with me. I can make things easy for you round here, or hard. It's up to you. I've told you once before, I give His Majesty whatever advice I think is right, and if and when I think you need anything, then I'll be the first to tell him."

Benvenuto cleared his throat, "Well thank you." He wisely chose to ignore the first part of De Villurois' remarks.

The Chamberlain re-read the warrant. "A thousand crowns it says here. A thousand old crowns will do, I think."

This was not because the coins would be worn and contain marginally less gold, but because he knew that Benvenuto would melt most of them down and could just as well use battered, bent and damaged coins for the purpose.

Benvenuto was anxious to mollify the Chamberlain. "Yes, that will be very satisfactory," he paused, "If it's not too much trouble that is."

—⚜—

It took over two hours to select and count the coins from the sacks in the Chamberlain's custody. As they neared the end of the task de Villurois, now mellower, was suddenly struck by a thought.

"I say, you didn't come here alone, did you?"

"I certainly did. Why?"

"Well, apart from the fact that this lot," he pointed to the stacks of coins, "will be damn heavy, wouldn't it have been a good idea to have an escort?"

"I don't think that's necessary."

"Well I do. You're just asking for trouble carrying all that alone. Especially where you live. You see you might be attacked and robbed, and unlucky enough not to get killed in the process. If you didn't die bravely defending his gold, I think the King would be extremely angry."

—⚜—

The streets of Paris were not safe, even in daylight. Robbery and violence were commonplace. No one would go to the assistance of the victim of an attack. Drunks and beggars would brawl anywhere and woe betides anybody who accidentally got in the way. Even members of the Guet - the Watch - were liable to be beaten up if they tried to interfere.

Parisians were supposed to have a lantern in front of their houses and candles in their windows at night. They only gave the poorest of light and always burned out before dawn. Only the very brave - and the very foolish - ventured out alone and in darkness, and certainly no one with more gold than the average workman would see in two lifetimes!

Benvenuto therefore allowed himself to be persuaded to send one of the Chamberlain's servants to his home with a message that his four Italian assistants should come and act as bodyguards.

What neither he nor de Villurois knew was that the man did not go to the Nesle, but to a nearby inn where he found a villainous looking character dressed in clothes that hung in tatters from his body, and began to whisper earnestly in his ear.....

—⁂—

The gold coins were put in the basket and the empty spaces packed out with rags to stop them rattling. Benvenuto signed the receipt with a flourish.

"A little wine perhaps while we're waiting for your men?" the Chamberlain suggested.

"Why yes, that's very kind of you."

De Villurois raised his goblet. "To the successful completion of your work," he toasted.

They stood for a few minutes sipping their wine and awkwardly trying to think of some small talk until the Chamberlain detected the aroma of cooking coming from his kitchen. It was nearly dinner time.

"It doesn't look as if your people are coming."

Benvenuto took the hint. "No it doesn't. I think I'd better be off then."

"Well, if you must. I'll lend you a chain mail shirt and a set of gauntlets and a soldier's cloak. I see you have your own sword - let's hope you don't need it."

Benvenuto made his way homewards as fast as he could. His left arm ached from the strain of holding the heavy basket concealed under his cloak. He did not dare risk transferring it to his right hand except for a few moments at a time, in case he needed his sword.

He had crossed the river and was nearing the Augustinian Monastery about five hundred yards from the Nesle, and was about to heave a sigh of relief when he heard a faint scraping sound, and caught a gleam of light on something shiny and a glimpse of a slight movement in the deep shadow of the monastery wall.

There was no doubt what it was. Someone had just drawn a sword. Benvenuto's hand surreptitiously dropped to the hilt of his own weapon, but he did not take it from its scabbard. Two could play at the game of surprise.

Two? It was four men who stepped in front of him in a line across the road. He tried to talk his way out of trouble.

"Hey, you lot! You wouldn't try to rob a poor soldier of his cloak, would you? That's all you'll get this side of pay day."

The four men shuffled to a halt. No question about it, it was a soldier's cloak. But they were looking for an Italian, and from his accent this was obviously an Italian. They briefly conferred amongst themselves. There was only one way to find out if they had made a mistake.

They came forward again and Benvenuto edged sideways until his back was against the wall. There was no use in his calling for help. At that distance it was unlikely that anyone in the Nesle would hear, and even if they did, they would assume that it was one of the local drunks.

Two of the men rushed forward and Benvenuto caught one a stinging blow, but only with the flat of his sword, but the second - Benvenuto recognised the Chamberlain's treacherous servant - got in with a vicious thrust which slipped under his arm. It would have killed him there and then if it had not been for the basket of gold which had actually been impeding his sword play.

The tip of the sword penetrated the wicker work, and the force of the robber's lunge made the blade snap off a few inches down. Benvenuto swung his right hand round and smashed the hilt of his sword like a knuckle duster downwards against the bridge of the man's nose. The fellow reeled away, screaming.

One less.

The other three drew back for a moment and Benvenuto edged crabwise along the wall, still waving his sword, and still hiding the basket under his cloak.

"I'm telling you," he shouted, "if you want my sword, you'll have to take it from me, and you may get it in the guts instead."

Warily, the three of them continued to follow him just out of range of his circling blade. They covered a hundred yards this way, and Benvenuto thought that his left arm was going to drop from its socket with the strain of holding and concealing the gold. He stopped and again tried to persuade his attackers to leave him alone.

"Go on! Be off with you. I've killed better fighters than you before now. Go and help your friend."

He pointed with his sword at the first man who was leaning against the wall, retching.

"Aaaah!" Benvenuto let out a loud yell and took a couple of menacing steps towards the men who retreated several yards.

Benvenuto seized the opportunity to get about half way towards his own doorway before the three robbers plucked up courage to come after him again, but by the time they caught up with him he was only a hundred yards from home, and well within sight of it.

"Right you bastards," he hissed. "I've given you a chance. Now you're for it. Which of you wants to die first?" He raised his voice to a shout. "Help! Help! You in the Castle! It's me. Benvenuto."

Again the men paused, nonplussed. Was he bluffing? Would anyone come to help him? Benvenuto gained a few extra yards.

"I'm being attacked. To arms! To arms!"

The street door flew open. Ascanio stood silhouetted against the light.

"Come on," Benvenuto shouted, "Hurry. Bring the others."

Ascanio disappeared inside, and in a moment came rushing out again with a pike levelled in front of him, closely followed by Busbacca, Pagolo, Bartolomeo, two with pikes and one with a sword. The three would-be thieves turned tail and fled down the road. Benvenuto stopped his workmen from chasing them.

"Never mind about them. Just let me get inside. This is what they were after."

As he reached the safety of his own doorway, he turned and held up the basket.

"There's a thousand crowns in here," he jeered, "but you weren't good enough to get it. Next time, try it with six men - ten if you like!"

He turned to Busbacca and shouted loudly, "go and get my gun. Let's find out if they're bullet proof."

He glanced over his shoulder, but the robbers were gone.

—⚏—

Busbacca slammed the door and shot the bolts.

"I ask you, have you ever seen anything like that?" Benvenuto panted, "Four against one, and I beat them. Single handed, and I do mean single handed. Look, I had one arm useless - weighed down with a quarter of a ton of gold," he exaggerated.

His eyes were gleaming with exhilaration.

"That was great, really great. I haven't been in such a good fight since .... since the Siege of Rome. By the way, did I ever tell you ....?"

Ascanio and Busbacca looked at each other. He had told them. Many times.

"Let me take your sword and cloak master, and here, have some wine," Busbacca interrupted. "Have you eaten?"

"No I haven't. That skinflint of a Chamberlain shooed me out to save himself offering me supper. Yes, by God, I am hungry. There's nothing like a good fight to give you an appetite. Caterina!" he roared, "Food!"

He seated himself at the kitchen table. Caterina's mother, Madame Leone, gave him some soup from the stockpot hanging over the kitchen fire. Benvenuto held the bowl level with his chin and greedily spooned the thick mixture of vegetables and meat into his mouth. When the bowl was empty, he tore a lump off the loaf that lay on the table and wiped it clean and swallowing, the sodden piece of bread, belched noisily.

"What's next?"

Madame Leone brought him the remains of the leg of mutton that the others had eaten for their dinner. Benvenuto eyed it with disgust.

"What's the matter? Wasn't the dog hungry?"

"If you can eat that, I'll cook you another one. There's also a torta di vitello."

"Veal pie. Good, I'll have that for dessert."

Benvenuto drew his dagger and carved a thick strip of meat from the bone, chewed on it and banged an empty goblet on the table. "Don't tell me you guzzled all the wine too!"

Satisfied at last, he leaned back in his chair. "Well, aren't you going to ask me what the gold is for?"

"Alright. What's the gold for?" It was Pogolo Miccieri who spoke.

"The salt cellar. His Majesty Francis the First, King of France and God knows where else, has finally ordered it."

The four workmen crowded round to offer their congratulations with genuine enthusiasm.

"I suggest, gentlemen, that you all have an early night. We're going to be very busy tomorrow. Very busy indeed."

After the others had gone, he sat for a while, dreaming and half watching Caterina clearing away the plates. She came and stood close by him.

"You weren't hurt in the fight?"

"Of course not."

"But you could have been."

"Oh pooh! By those farmers? I could have managed a dozen of them." Benvenuto rubbed his chin reflectively and nuzzled her with his head. "You know when you win a fight like that, it doesn't make you feel tired. I feel as fresh as if I've just got up."

He gave Caterina a slap on the bottom. "I'll tell you what, we'll go and play rumple-bed! Come on," he said and led her by the arm up the stairs.

-38-

Benvenuto woke well before dawn and nudged Caterina.

"Go and wake your mother and the men. We want breakfast in half an hour. Less."

Muttering to herself, the girl did what she was told, and in the thirty minutes ordered by Benvenuto, the whole household was seated on benches on either side of the long kitchen table, while Benvenuto, ceremonially, took his place at his high-backed chair at the end.

The table was set with hot bread fresh from the baker, cheese, fruit, the ragged remains of the mutton, the large veal pie that Benvenuto had been too full to try the previous night and some dark salami-like sausages. To drink, there was ale in large earthenware pitchers, with pewter tankards neatly lined up in front.

Benvenuto swallowed the last of his meal, washed it down with a draught of beer and tapped on the table for attention.

"I hope that you all had a good night's sleep."

They all nodded with different degrees of enthusiasm.

"Fine. I suggest you make the most of it, because it's the last one you're likely to have for months!"

The response was a shuffling of feet, a few coughs and sickly grins.

"Now look," Benvenuto continued, "we've got a lot to do and precious little time to do it in. Here's what's going to happen. You two, Monsieur and Monsieur ...." he pointed to the two French silversmiths - he could still not remember their names, ".... you two will get on with the Jupiter and by the time you're finished, I'll have some gold ready for you to beat into sheets."

He turned to Pagolo. "You can get on with the King's bowl and vase. Just carry on with the decorations and don't bother me unless you get stuck. When that's finished, I'll be ready to talk about some figures for the salt cellar. Bartolomeo, we've got a few bits and pieces of jewellery on hand. Keep them moving, but only enough to see the customers don't nag. I want you on the salt cellar too."

Busbacca looked up expectantly.

"Ah! I've got a lovely job for you. Your favourite."

"Oh no, not ...."

"Oh yes! Build a new furnace and melt the gold. Ascanio, you supervise him. See he pours it into flat moulds, the thinner they are the less beating we'll need to do. Also you can help the others if they need it." He waved his hand in the direction of the two Frenchmen.

"You two, Madame Leone and Caterina, you can also both help." They looked puzzled, and Benvenuto explained.

"We'll take meals as normally as possible, but work comes first." He repeated himself, slapping the flat of his hand on the table for effect. "Work comes first! So, Madame, I expect your stock pot to be kept full and a good supply of cold meat, cheese and tortas in case we have to eat at odd times. That doesn't mean that any greedy little pig can keep sneaking off at all times to stuff his fat belly though, does it?" He pinched Busbacca's plump cheek so hard that the boy squealed with pain.

"Caterina, go and get the cabinet maker right away. If he's not up, knock on his door until he is. Tell him it's urgent and that if he comes now, I'll give him breakfast while we're talking. Have you got that?"

"Yes, you want the carpenter, right away."

"No, damn it. Not the carpenter. The cabinet maker. I'm making a work of art, not a bloody coffin!"

He stood up. "Alright everybody. You all know what you have to do." He clapped his hands. "GO!"

With a sweep of his arm Benvenuto cleared a space for himself on the table and swiftly began to sketch the working drawings of the base of the salt cellar. By the time that Caterina returned with the cabinet maker, they were ready.

A thin, round shouldered, bleary eyed man with large hands scarred from many slips of the saw and the chisel stood in the doorway, scowling belligerently.

"Your Excellency," he said with heavy sarcasm, "I have received your gracious command, and here I am, eager to meet your slightest whim."

He rubbed a stubbly cheek while Benvenuto smiled benignly.

"Monsieur, I am very grateful to you for putting yourself out for me. Please! Take a seat. Let me offer you some breakfast while we talk." He snapped his fingers. "Caterina, a plate and a tankard of ale for our good friend."

Benvenuto continued with the soothing process.

"You were quite right to wonder what the urgency is. I have just been commanded by His Majesty …" He paused for effect "…. I have been commanded by His Majesty to create a major work of art. A masterpiece. One of the greatest the world has ever seen."

The cabinet maker paused with a lump of meat in his fingers, half way to his open mouth.

"Yes," Benvenuto repeated, "it will be absolutely magnificent, and the whole process begins with you."

"With me?" the cabinet maker mumbled through a mouthful of mutton.

"Yes sir, with you. You have been selected to make the plinth. The base."

Benvenuto's tone inferred that the selection had been made by the King himself, As the man preened himself, Benvenuto moved his plate away and put the drawings in front of him and with a finger traced the details on the plan.

"Up here in the corner is a rough sketch of what it will look like when it's finished."

"What's it for?"

"It's for a - what's it matter what it's for? It's got nothing to do with you." Benvenuto was irritated by the interruption.

"Just pay attention. Now this is a view looking downwards."

The cabinet maker sniffed and reached past Benvenuto for the nearest food to hand - the end piece of sausage. He peeled off the skin, which he dropped on the floor and began to chew noisily. Benvenuto was too engrossed in what he was saying to take any notice.

"Now here's what you'll make."

His finger flicked backwards and forwards between three large scale drawings, the top and side view and a section through the base. It was oval shaped, about ten inches long, eight inches wide and two inches high. The edges were deeply scooped out so that the fluted top and bottom were like frames for the figures that Benvenuto planned to set round the edge.

"And finally," Benvenuto said, "underneath there will be four sockets, in each of which you will set an ivory ball so that the salt cellar can be moved about the table and rolled to where it's wanted."

"A salt cellar," the cabinet maker thought. "So that's what it is."

Benvenuto waited. "Well, what do you think?"

"What do you want me to think? You want a simple oval block of wood, scooped out at the edges and with a beading running round the top and bottom. For that you could have waited 'till daylight, instead of dragging me out of bed."

"It's going to be the base for the finest goldsmithing the world will ever see!"

The cabinet maker was unimpressed.

"What do you want it made of?"

"Ebony."

The man sucked his cheeks in and scratched his nose between thumb and forefinger.

"That will be expensive, and it will take me a while to find a piece that big. Ebony's a hard wood to work with. I'll need time to shape it properly. I suppose you want it polished.

"I want every bit of it as smooth as - I want it to feel like a girl's cheek when you touch it." The fingers of both of Benvenuto's hands rapturously caressed the air as he stood there, head tilted back, eyes half closed.

"Is that all?" The cabinet maker stood and rolled the drawings up.

"No. I want three extra exact copies."

"Not in ebony, for God's sake?"

"No of course not!" The veneer of politeness was fast disappearing with Benvenuto's mounting impatience. "You can make them in pine or anything. I just need them for trying out the figures for size - to see how they'll fit. I don't want the men spoiling my piece of ebony by making holes in it."

Already it had become Benvenuto's own block of wood.

"How long have I got?"

"For the copies, tomorrow will do. For the real thing, take your time. It may even be a year. I don't know how the gold work will go. Just find a perfect piece of wood, that's all."

The cabinet maker shook Benvenuto's hand. A little of his enthusiasm had worn off on him.

"I wish you luck."

Benvenuto was touched. "Why thank you."

The man made for the door, opened it, but before stepping out, came back into the room, grabbed the mutton bone and went out munching it. A little way up the road he stopped, turned and seeing Benvenuto still standing there, cheerily waved it at him and went on his way.

—ᗯ—

Benvenuto had the men carry a long table into one of the empty rooms in the tower of the little fort. A chair, a stock of paper, pens, ink, charcoal, crayons, water colours and brushes, a mattress and blankets and a large supply of candles completed his equipment.

"He stood at the top of the stairs and shouted down, "I don't want to be disturbed by anyone. Nobody's to come into this room for any reason - not unless the building's on fire. Do you hear?"

"What about your food?" Madame Leone was always practical.

You can leave something out on the landing. If I want it, I'll take it. Now you've all got work to do. Let me get on with mine - in peace!"

The door slammed shut, and no one saw him again for two days.

—⚬—

On the morning of the third day Benvenuto was sitting in the kitchen when the others came in for breakfast. His eyes were red rimmed, but he was leaning back in his high chair with a triumphant expression on his face. The workmen looked at him warily, and waited for him to speak.

"Come on. Get your breakfast down. I've something to show you."

"What is it, master?" Busbacca could not restrain his curiosity.

"You'll see." Benvenuto gave a mysterious smile and thumped the table with his fist. "Eat! Eat! I've never had to tell you that twice before, boy. The same with the rest of you. We haven't got all day."

He was soon leading a small procession up the winding stairway to his studio. Pinned round the walls were his final working drawings, the product of his two days and nights alone while he had transferred to paper the images and ideas he had been carrying round in his head for more than three years.

He stood in the middle of the room.

"There you are. See for yourselves."

The men wandered about the room, looking at the sketches, some in plain ink or crayon and some coloured. Pagolo Miccieri, the most experienced of the workmen, occasionally pointed something out to the others. Eventually he turned and looked at his employer.

"Congratulations, sir. If the piece comes out like these," he pointed to the diagrams, "it will be marvellous."

Benvenuto fluttered his hand modestly. "So it will," he said. "And now I'll explain it all to you. Gather round."

He picked up a long thin paint brush by the bristles and held it between thumb and forefinger. Using it as a pointer, he tapped the first of the drawings. This was the roughest and crudest of them all, drawn with a few strokes of charcoal stick.

"Here is the base. Just a sketch to give you a little idea, because the cabinet maker's already working on it."

"We know what it's like, because he brought in the dummies yesterday," Ascanio interjected.

Benvenuto fixed him with a hard stare, and kept on staring until Ascanio turned his head away, blushing.

"I hope, my dear sir, that you don't mind my talking while you're interrupting? Do I have your permission to continue?"

Ascanio insolently extended his hand, palm upwards in the direction of the drawing. "Please do."

"Shut up will you, or I'll pull your bloody tongue out and strangle you with it," Benvenuto snarled.

He tapped on the next sheet with his knuckles. On it were two series of sketches of little figures.

"These are the decorations of the base," he announced. "Four cherubs: one at each end and one in the centre of each side. As you can see, they represent the four winds. Then on each of the corners of the oval I'm going to put these reclining figures in gold and enamel. Those with blue enamel represent water and those with green, earth. Do the figures look familiar?"

Without waiting for an answer he continued, "Well they should be. I've copied them from the tombs in the Medici Chapel in Florence. They are Day and Night, Twilight and Dawn."

He paused, looking from one man to another. Obviously he was waiting for some comment. Timidly Bartolomeo Chiocca raised his hand and gave a little cough.

"Yes?" Benvenuto asked.

"If I might make the smallest possible suggestion, sir? No doubt you've already thought of it yourself," he added hastily as Benvenuto's eyebrows began to close together.

"Those eight figures of yours, the cherubs and the gods and goddesses will still leave a lot of space round the edge of the base. I'm sure you'll want to show more gold than wood. It's only a comment ...." His voice trailed away.

They all waited for the inevitable outburst. There was a moment of silence then Benvenuto snapped his fingers and pointed at Bartolomeo.

"Excellent! Very good! I was going to say the very same thing myself, but I was waiting to see if any of you are awake yet. And the reason why I have not already designed the other decorations for the base is because ...." he thought for a moment, "... is because I want to give you all a chance to do something creative. Yes, that's it. You can all have a chance. Come on, you first, Bartolomeo."

"Gold and enamel, I suppose?"

"Of course. What else?"

"So, to go with the four winds, what about some anchors and tridents?"

"Good. Anything else?"

"Some sails."

Benvenuto nodded, looked towards Pagolo Miccieri and cocked his head on one side in a silent question.

"Some agricultural instruments - scythes, sickles, mattocks and such like perhaps."

Benvenuto gave him the "thumbs up" sign.

"Ascanio, you had a lot to say for yourself before. What about it?"

"Er. Er. Um. Yes, how about a cornucopia?" Ascanio let out a sigh of relief as he finally found some inspiration. "And some spears and arrows and a shield," he gabbled.

Benvenuto's raised hand stopped him. "That's enough, I think."

"If you please, master," Busbacca piped in a tiny voice, "I would like to suggest some musical instruments in your honour as a musician."

Benvenuto took a few steps towards the boy and raised his hand. Busbacca cowered away, expecting a blow, but instead Benvenuto patted him on the shoulder.

"That is the best idea of them all. But not in my honour as a musician, but for my dear father. I haven't played my flute for ages, but tonight at supper, I shall."

He wiped his suddenly moist eyes with his sleeve.

"We'll have his favourite instruments: a flute, a viola, a sackbut, a recorder and ... well we can see how it looks." He patted the boy's head again. "Thank you Busbacca, you can make them for me. And you others: you can make - you can have the honour of making - the bits you suggested."

Benvenuto stuck the paint brush he had been using as a pointer into his belt like a dagger.

"There. That, gentlemen, was just the 'ante pasta'. The 'hors d'oeuvres', as our French friends here would say." He rubbed his hands together. "And now for the main course."

He crossed to the largest drawing of all. "I don't want any interruptions - from anyone." He stared at Ascanio. "I'll answer questions later."

He gestured again with the pointer.

"The two large figures, male and female represent Sea and Land. They will be seated facing each other. Their knees will be raised like the mountains, and their legs and feet will be intertwined, just like the land juts out into the sea and the sea into the land. These two figures are again based on 'Dawn' and 'Dusk' from the tomb of Lorenzo the Magnificent. In other words, gentlemen, the work of the world's greatest sculptor, Michelangelo Buonarotti, will be honoured by the world's greatest goldsmith, Benvenuto Cellini. The whole piece will be seven inches high over the base."

"Seven inches on top of a two inch base," Busbacca muttered to Ascanio. "Phew, that's nine inches – a whole cubit."

Benvenuto flicked the boy's forehead with his thumb and middle finger. "Silence," he hissed.

He turned back to the drawing, leaving Busbacca to rub the angry red mark which appeared between his eyes. Benvenuto put his pointer down and stood with his thumbs tucked into his belt.

"Now I'm going to tell you about the male figure. He's Neptune, the God of the sea. He is going to have four horses - very fierce, wild horses, with flared nostrils, open mouths and eyes of black and white enamel. But they won't be ordinary horses, because they'll have webbed feet, tails and scales. Pagolo, you'll etch and punch out the scales."

Pagolo Miccieri bobbed his head and grinned with pleasure as Benvenuto went on, "The middle horse, the one on which Neptune will actually be sitting, is going to have a saddle cloth of blue enamel with gold fleurs-de-lys, and on top of that a white enamelled cloth."

The men all nodded wisely, pursed their lips or made other gestures of approval.

"Round him," Benvenuto made little swimming motions with his hands, "will be some sea creatures: dolphins, sea serpents, a turtle and some fish. His left elbow can rest on the head of one of the horses. He'll also be holding some seaweed, and he'll have a crown of it on his head. His Trident will be in his right hand of course; about five and a half inches long, and I'll enamel the end in blue as well. For balance, I'll make him hold at forty-five degrees - parallel with the woman's body."

Benvenuto smacked his lips, walked over to the door and shouted down the stairs, "Caterina! Bring wine. I'm thirsty."

He waited until the girl came up with a jug and some pewter goblets and in the meantime ignored the men who gathered in a little group whispering among themselves. He poured out a generous measure for himself, but did not offer any to the others.

He drank down the thin, sour white wine in one long draught and pulled a wry face.

"Ugh! Gnats' piss. Right, let's get on."

Again he took his pointer. "I was just going to describe the female figure. I told you she comes from Michelangelo's 'Dawn,' but to me she is 'Earth.' She is holding her left breast, or rather her nipple to symbolise how she feeds all her children."

He beamed at the others, but there was no reaction from them. Disappointed, he waited, looking intently at his drawing. Suddenly he picked up a black crayon from the table and with a few fluent strokes scribbled out and re-drew the figure's right hand.

"You can see that I had her holding a Cornucopia. Well, I've changed my mind. It interferes with the composition. She'll just have a few pieces of fruit in her hand instead.

He pointed the crayon at Bartolomeo Chiocca. "You can make the fruit and stuff. I'll enamel them. Mind you, I'll want every tiny line on the husk of every acorn clearly etched. Can you do it?"

The workman nodded.

"Now round this figure I'm going to put other creatures, land animals of course, dogs and lions and she's going to be sitting on another one - an elephant."

This caused raised eyebrows among his audience. An elephant was a real rarity. None of them had actually ever seen one.

"Busbacca, my fat little friend, you can make the elephant because you remind me of one."

Benvenuto would come to regret this little joke because the elephant took on something of its youthful maker's permanently bewildered expression. It was also anatomically incorrect, but Benvenuto later would not be able to spare the time at a crucial stage of the work to change it. He just hoped the King knew as little about elephants as his apprentice did.

"The saddle cloth."

The men looked up.

"The saddle cloth will be green, like the Earth. Neptune's is blue for the Sea. And for the decoration it will have a gold border and gold fleurs-de-lys again. That should please the King - I hope."

He poured himself some more wine.

"Now I can hear you saying, 'this thing's supposed to be a salt cellar, so where does the salt go?' "

In fact no such thought had yet crossed any of their minds, but they all nodded vigorously and Benvenuto moved on to the next drawing.

"Ascanio, you'd better start paying attention now, because I'm going to let you help with this bit. The salt holder will be a fat galley boat - a man of war. The sea is salt; Neptune's the Sea God. The salt is at his right hand.

The port holes for the oars will be in white and red enamel, and there'll be enamel on the bows and on the decorations worked in the gold sides of the boat itself. "

He beckoned the men forward with both hands. "Look closely. The sides will be battle scenes and weapons. Nice, eh? Right, I'll go on. The figurehead will be Neptune again. A really fierce face with a beard and big mustachios. He'll have a crown with white enamel spots - pearls - jewels of the sea. Then at the bow and stern will be a couple of rams, horns and all, looking into the boat."

Another sip of wine and Benvenuto stuck his finger on the sketch.

"Oh, and while I'm talking about enamelling, the sea which will be shown on this side will be dark blue with little white waves - the other side will be green and covered with all that fruit."

Benvenuto put his goblet down.

"So what's left? Here's the last drawing. A Roman triumphal arch with Greek columns - a bit of a mixture, but who cares? If anyone asks we'll say it was an Ionic Temple. There will be another of Michelangelo's reclining figures about two inches high on the top, and two tiny male figures and two tiny female ones diagonally from each other on the top corners. Then at each end there will be a niche, one with a female figure and one with a male. And do you know who the male is?"

They shook their heads. Benvenuto tapped the sketch at the bottom of the sheet. "It's Michelangelo's 'David' from the Accadamia in Florence. It's the first thing I remember my father taking me to see when I was a little boy. Anyway, over these two figures I'm going to have a blue enamel plaque; the one over the 'David' will have a crown and fleur-de-lys and the one over the woman will have a crown and Francis' personal monogram, 'F'."

Again he looked round

"You think I've finished. That's all, is it? No, well what's missing?"

The workmen looked puzzled.

"Come on, think! What's missing from my salt cellar? From my **salt** cellar," he emphasised.

"Pepper!"

"Right, Pagolo. I'm glad you've got some sense. Pepper."

He took up his paint brush again and pointed to the roof of the temple. "That will have a concealed hinge. The pepper will go in here and won't get spilled when the piece is pushed all round the table. We don't want the King's guests all sneezing into their soup, do we?"

He straightened his shoulders. "Gentlemen, that's it. My masterpiece." He threw his arm across his waist and bowed. "Thank you."

On this cue they dutifully applauded, and then crowded round to shake his hand.

"I think there's some wine left," Bartolomeo hinted.

"So there is. Fill your goblets and we'll have a toast . to the Salt Cellar."

"To its creator, Benvenuto Cellini," added Pagolo.

"Not to mention Michelangelo," Ascanio muttered into his drink so quietly that no one could hear him.

-39-

Benvenuto soon found that his plan to leave himself free to get on with the salt cellar was not going to work because of interference from Francis himself.

The King had given Benvenuto the commission to make the candlesticks because the local French craftsmen did not know the technique of disguising the ugly joints where large pieces of silver were connected. Benvenuto did, and this meant that he had to be more personally involved in the work than he wanted.

Benvenuto's method was similar to that used by goldsmiths for making medium sized gold figures. He began with a full size clay model which he cut into pieces. The trunk was cut in two vertical slices, back and front; the head was also in two halves and each leg and arm was disjointed at knee and elbow. He then made a plaster mould of each part which he covered, first with wax and then with more plaster. When he melted out the wax, the hollow space thus formed could be filled with bronze.

Then the sheets of silver, thin enough to be cut with scissors, which his French workmen had been making, would be carefully beaten with wooden mallets over the tough bronze foundation until they took the shape of the metal underneath and to which they were to be fused by heating.

Next would come the tricky part; to join the pieces without the seams showing, and this was where Benvenuto's special skill was called for. He would expand the edges into an extra degree of thinness by beating them some more and then make one section overlap its neighbour, cutting jagged, matching indentations so that each piece would fit snugly into the other.

Firmly supporting the back of each joint with a piece of wood, they would then be carefully beaten again until they were tight, and then everything was soldered together, and smoothed and polished until it became a silver replica of the original clay model.

—⁂—

The King was always interested to watch his craftsmen at work, but every step in the making of the first candlestick positively fascinated him. He took to calling into the workshop at all hours.

Whilst Benvenuto characteristically boasted about how "my friend, His Majesty, can hardly bear to tear himself away from my workshop," he was also irritated at the disruption that these visits caused, because Francis was usually accompanied by distinguished guests to whom Benvenuto was expected to give a personally guided tour and a detailed explanation of the work in progress.

Strangely, whoever else the King brought with him, Madame D'Etampes, normally his constant companion, never came.

It was on one of these visits that the King was amused to find that he had walked in on the middle of a clash of artistic opinions between Benvenuto and his two French assistants.

The King had especially come to see the casting of the bronze foundation of the Jupiter, and when Francis arrived, Benvenuto and the two Frenchmen were arguing over the best method.

Benvenuto barely took the time to give Francis a perfunctory greeting before returning to the fray.

He thrust his face close to that of the older of the two workmen and spat out venomously, "Now look here, Monsieur 'what's-your-name?' I'm not interested how you've been doing things for the last fifty years. It's because you've been doing them wrong all that time that I've been given the job by His Majesty."

"But sir," the Frenchman said, "I think …. "

"What you think doesn't matter. It's what I say that counts. If you knew more than I do, then it would be me who was working for you, not you working for me!"

Benvenuto looked appealingly at Francis who realised that, like it or not, he would have to give a ruling. There could only be one - to back up Benvenuto.

"Monsieur er. Monsieur" - the King did not know his name either. "Your master has been personally chosen by me to carry out this work. I don't think you should argue with him."

"But Sire, we are only discussing the best method of casting the bronze and, your Majesty, we can easily make a new casting if there is an accident. There's no harm done if we do it our way and it goes wrong like Monsieur Cellini thinks."

"Just a waste of time and money and risking a valuable mould, that's all," Benvenuto interjected. "Your Majesty, there is only one way to teach these fellows a lesson. If you agree we'll cast the piece their way, and at the same time, I have a couple of pieces of my own we can cast by my method in the same oven."

"A couple of pieces of your own?" said the King. "Why are you working on your own things? Do you know how long you've been working for me, and not a thing have I seen for your salary?"

Benvenuto flushed. "Your Majesty, the pieces are for you. Or rather one of them is. The other is a piece I made just to test the quality of the clay. It's a bust of Julius Caesar."

"And what have you made for me?"

"A bronze piece in relief to fill one of the Lunettes over one of the doorways at your palace of Fontainebleau. I'll go and get the drawings."

The King stopped him. "You can show me later when the bronze has been poured. Let's get on with the work. And gentlemen," the King looked from Benvenuto to the two French workmen, "aren't you going to have a wager on it?"

"I don't need to," said Benvenuto. "I know I'm right, but I'll tell you what, if I'm not, the Lunette will be my gift to Your Majesty."

"And if they lose?" The King jerked his head in the direction of the two workmen.

Benvenuto bared his teeth. "Then they can bloody well pay me for the wasted fuel and the cost of a new mould. Oh, and three day's pay."

"Is that alright?" asked the King. The two workmen nodded glumly, their confidence evaporating in the face of Benvenuto's brash assurance.

Even before the King arrived, the bronze was being melted. It was only now that Benvenuto put his moulds into the pouring pits alongside those that his workmen were going to use. This was his first point of disagreement with them. Benvenuto believed that if you left the unfilled moulds in the earth too long they could become damp and weakened. Another dispute with the workmen was the number and placing of the vent holes.

"You see Your Majesty, if you have too few vent holes in these larger pieces, the air and the noxious fumes and vapours all accumulate in the bends and corners, and stop the mould from filling perfectly."

The King nodded.

"And then," said Benvenuto, ticking his fingers, "I take exceptional care when melting out the wax, not to heat it so much that it boils and leaves little bumps. Also I reheat my mould just a little before firing to get rid of any moisture, and I avoid green wood, oak or charcoal because they make the clay too hard. The last difference between me and these fellows…," he gestured contemptuously in the direction of the two workmen who were standing out of earshot, "… is the method of pouring the bronze. They are far too impetuous. They just open the plug of the furnace, and in it goes."

"What's wrong with that?" the King asked.

"Your Majesty, the first tool of a craftsman is patience.

"Now we" - Benvenuto corrected himself, "I mean, I hold an iron crook in the mouth of the furnace so that the first of the metal is spilled. I don't want it to get into the mould because at first it comes out of the crucible in fierce splashes and spurts. I wait until it is flowing smoothly and makes no air bubbles."

The King nodded.

"That seems to make sense. I don't know why every craftsman doesn't use the same refinements, but as you said, that's why you got the job and not them. You also began to say 'we' do so-and-so. Who are 'we'?"

"Why the great Florentine craftsmen," Benvenuto said with some pride. "Your Majesty, I am not just a goldsmith. I have learned every kind of metal work, right down to iron smithing. I paint, I can work in gems, in stone, in marble. Look at Leonardo da Vinci, may he rest in peace, and Michelangelo, not that I presume to compare myself to either of them. In how many crafts have they produced masterpieces?"

Without waiting for an answer, Benvenuto continued with his catalogue. "All the greatest bronze workers are Florentines, Michelangelo himself has told me his secrets. Does Your Majesty know that they melted down his statue of Julius II? He wasted two precious years when he could have been carving another "Pieta," and some barbarian melted it down a couple of years later. That was Michelangelo's own fault. I told him so, and he agreed I was right. He used nearly eight tons of bronze. Eight tons! Statues should be no thicker than the blade of a knife."

All the time he had been talking, Benvenuto had been filling his moulds, leaving his workmen to do their own. The King licked his thick lips.

"Thank you for the lecture, Monsieur. I suppose that all that talking and the heat of the furnace and all that talking has made you dry."

Benvenuto took the hint. "Please excuse me, Sire. May I offer you some wine?"

"Exactly what I had in mind." The King as a frequent visitor had no difficulty in finding his way to the dining room. He put his arm round Benvenuto's shoulder and led the way.

"Now tell me about this bronze Lunette you've made for me without my asking. The one you're going to have to give me if you lose your bet."

Benvenuto poured the King a generous goblet of dry white wine, and crossing to a chest of drawers, took out a long roll of paper which he laid out on the table, weighting the corners down with a fruit bowl and some plates.

"This is what it will look like. You will see the real thing when we break open the moulds."

"If you've got your casting techniques right, that is," the King interrupted unkindly.

Benvenuto ignored him.

"If it pleases you, I've called the piece - 'The Nymph of Fontainebleau'. That's where I intend it should go. As you see, it's a beautiful reclining female nude with her right arm flung round the neck of a stag. Under her left arm are vases from which water is flowing, symbolising the rivers, while all round her are boars, deer, dogs and similar animals to represent Your Majesty's great interest in hunting. It's all done in half relief except for the stag which is in full relief, facing outwards."

The King studied the drawing. "Who was the model?"

"Why, Caterina here." Benvenuto affectionately slapped the rump of the girl who was standing at the side of the two men, waiting to serve some little cakes.

The King looked at her admiringly. "Very pretty. Well, if she's the Nymph, who's the Stag then? You I suppose." He punched Benvenuto's arm and laughed coarsely. Suddenly he stopped and looked at Benvenuto sideways.

"Have you still got your tenant here. The old chap Madame D'Etampes had installed in your basement."

The familiar lump of iron began to rise in Benvenuto's throat. "Why, Your Majesty, I've been so busy, I've forgotten all about him." Benvenuto genuinely had. "I never see him. I'm not even sure what he's doing down there." He turned to Caterina. "Do you know?"

The girl shook her head.

"No? Well remind me that I must go down there some time and take a look."

"Does the Duchess ever come to see him?"

Benvenuto realised that the King was checking the story that Madame D'Etampes had told him. Mentally he thanked Cardinal D'Este for the tip. He snapped his fingers. "Yes, as a matter of fact she has been here to see him. Her Grace has visited my workshop since you last brought her. Once. Maybe she has been other times when I was out. Shall I ask my men? Is it important?"

"Hurrump!" said the King. "I must be going now. When will the bronze be cool?"

"By tomorrow morning, Your Majesty."

"I will be here at noon. Don't open the moulds 'till I come. And you child," the King said to Caterina, "will pour my wine for me and tell your mother I'll sample some more of those delicious hot beef pasties of hers." He pinched the girl's cheek and strutted out of the door.

Benvenuto was impatiently pacing up and down in the hot sun in the roadway outside the front door. He was anxious to get started on opening the moulds, but the King had not arrived.

He mopped his forehead with his sleeve, and muttered angrily to himself. Screwing his eyes up against the strong light, at last he saw a carriage and a group of riders.

Benvenuto groaned. "Here they come. A plague of locusts. When the King fixed my salary he didn't tell me I'd have to keep him and his hangers-on fed. 'Some of your excellent wine Monsieur Cellini. Tell your mother I'll sample some of her delicious beef pasties'," Benvenuto mimicked.

The carriage rattled to a halt and the King stepped out.

"Your Majesty. Two days in succession; you do me too much honour." Benvenuto peered past the King's shoulder and saw Madame D'Etampes.

"Your Grace! Er - welcome to my humble workshop," he stuttered.

"Sire!" He bowed to the King's brother-in-law, the King of Navarre. "My Lords." This to two other noblemen whose names Benvenuto did not know.

"If your Majesty's escort would care to go round the back to the kitchen, I'm sure there will be something for them."

There would be. Bread and ale. The King dismissed his six soldiers with a wave of his hand.

"Very kind of you. A few scraps from your table will do," he said.

"Scraps from my table!" Benvenuto thought. "Doesn't he know that's all we have to feed ourselves on when he's more or less a permanent house guest?"

Out loud he said, "May I lead the way, Your Majesty?"

Yes, let's open the moulds. I've made a couple of wagers myself." He looked at the King of Navarre and the two courtiers.

"Who did you bet on?" Benvenuto could not restrain himself from asking.

"On you, of course. Did you doubt it?"

—m—

The first castings out of the pit were the two halves of the bust of Julius Caesar. They broke the moulds open and Benvenuto ran his fingers over the still-warm metal. It was smooth; a few barely noticeable bumps and pits that skilled hands would soon make vanish, but otherwise a perfectly filled mould.

Benvenuto pronounced his verdict."First class. Excellent."

The two French workers silently nodded their agreement.

Next came the pieces of the '"Nymph": the stag's head, the girl's head, the torso, the legs, her right arm and five large sections of the background. Ten difficult mouldings, each one an outstanding example of the sculptors' art. As the pieces lay on the ground, glinting dully in the sunlight, the visitors broke into spontaneous applause, accompanied reluctantly by the two workmen.

The King nudged his brother-in-law in the ribs with his elbow, grinned at him and rubbed his thumb and first two fingers together in the time-honoured sign for "pay up!"

With both hands Benvenuto silently signalled for the sections of the Jupiter candlestick to be lifted from the pit.

Even before they were opened, it could be seen that something had gone very wrong. The two largest pieces which contained the trunk were broken and had large stains of spilled metal, with jagged lumps hanging down like melted wax on a candle.

Out of the eight moulds, only two had been completely filled. In the other six, the extremities - the tops, bottoms and ends - had gaps and areas of thin metal.

The older of the two French workmen wrung his hands in despair. The younger one was more animated. He gave the front half of the head a kick which sent it bouncing and rattling across the courtyard until it stopped at the King's feet.

Francis nudged it with his toe and turning to his companions held out his hand. Each of the men dropped a small but heavy purse into his outstretched palm.

―⚋―

Benvenuto hid the look of triumph on his face by arranging the segments of the Nymph on the ground so that they roughly fitted together and gave an impression of how the finished work would appear. Then he stood well back and invited his visitors to look.

He saw Madame D'Etampes point with her finger along the length of the naked figure of the girl and ask the King something. Francis looked round and jerked his head in the direction of Caterina who was standing against the doorpost of the kitchen, her hands in the pockets of her apron. Then the King leaned over and whispered in the Duchess' ear and gave a loud chuckle.

Whatever it was that amused the King did not please his mistress. She drew her lips in a taut thin line and frowned.

Francis however, was too busy repeating his witticism to the King of Navarre to notice.

—⁂—

Two days later Benvenuto was working on the model of Neptune for the salt cellar when he heard a carriage and horses in the courtyard. With a sigh of exasperation, he threw his long bladed chisel down on the bench and brushing the fine shavings of wax from his robe, crossed over to the window and peered out.

It was Cardinal d'Este. Benvenuto hurried out to greet him. "Your Eminence. What an unexpected pleasure. It's been a long time since you came to see me."

"Yes, but people might think that since I'm a Cardinal and you're an artist, it ought to be you calling on me. However, it is very good of you to grant me an audience."

"I'm sorry your Eminence. I really am. It's not neglect. I've been so busy."

"So I hear. Aren't you going to ask me in?"

Benvenuto swept his arm in the direction of the door and followed the Cardinal and the chaplain inside.

"A little wine, your Eminence?"

"Thank you, but no. Just some lemon juice in water, if I may. My physician's orders," the Cardinal explained.

Benvenuto tried to think of something to say. "Your physician? I hope you are in good health."

The Cardinal ignored the remark. "I saw the King yesterday evening," he said.

"Did you?" Benvenuto replied. "He was here the day before."

"I know." The Cardinal took slow sip of his lemon juice and grimaced. "Actually the King spoke very highly of you. He's very pleased with you for the moment."

"Pleased with me? Spoke highly of me? What did he say?" Benvenuto begged.

"I don't know if I should tell you; You're conceited enough as it is." Then, seeing Benvenuto's crestfallen expression, the

Cardinal drained his cup and went on, "Well, he just said that you were an excellent technician, and that you had won some tremendous argument with the artisans you employed."

Benvenuto sniffed and diffidently shrugged his shoulders.

"So I did. Would your Eminence care to come and see?"

"That's one of the reasons I'm here."

After he had inspected the castings of Caesar, the Nymph and finally the ruined pieces of the Jupiter, the Cardinal. Still standing in the courtyard with Benvenuto said, "The King was also pleased with the way you dealt with the two workmen. He said you didn't punish them for their mistake."

Benvenuto let out an explosive puff of air.

"Pah! First he forced me into a ridiculous bet with them, and then, no sooner I had won, than he made me let them off. 'Now that you have proved your point, Monsieur Cellini, I suppose you'll be merciful, won't you?' Did you hear that, your Eminence? Him talking about mercy. He's got enough men locked up in his dungeons for no reason to make a small army - and what about all that head chopping that you said he goes in for? If I'd have lost, he'd have damn well grabbed a couple of thousand crowns' worth of sculpture for free, you can be sure!"

The Cardinal was taken aback by this outburst. He thought he had paid Benvenuto a compliment.

"He won some bet or other, didn't he?"

"Yes, ten crowns each from the King of Navarre and his other two friends. Thirty crowns? It must cost that much every week to feed his hunting dogs."

"Anyway when I told him I was coming here, he sent a little gift for you."

It was an antique ring made from three twisted strands of thick gold wire and set with a few tiny stone chips. Benvenuto's professional eye quickly appraised it. "About fifteen crowns. Ah well, decent of His Majesty to go halves with me on his winnings, I suppose," he thought as he slipped the ring on his finger.

Just as Benvenuto and the Cardinal were about to go back into the house, a young man strolled into the courtyard. He was dressed in a livery of dark green doublet with pale green hose and a matching green velvet beret with a large black feather hanging from it.

Seeing the Cardinal, and recognising either him or his robes, he bowed to him politely before addressing Benvenuto.

"Sir, are you Monsieur Cellini?"

"I am. Who are you, and what do you want?"

"My mistress is Her Grace, the Duchess of Etampes. Her Grace sends her compliments and requests that you join her at a supper party at six o'clock tonight."

Benvenuto's heart seemed to give a great thud in his chest.

"Why thank ..."

Before he could complete his reply he saw that behind the messenger's shoulder, the Cardinal was wagging his forefinger from side to side and simultaneously shaking his head. D'Este must have detected some obstinate look on Benvenuto's face, because the gesture changed to a chopping motion, and the Cardinal's clenched his lower teeth over his upper lip.

Benvenuto gave a resigned shrug of his shoulders.

"Listen," he said, "if I give you a message for your mistr ... for her Grace, will you remember it, word for word?"

"Of course," the boy said scornfully. "That's my job."

"Alright. Pay attention. 'Monsieur Cellini presents his humble respects to Her Grace'." Benvenuto paused. The messenger looked at him waiting for him to continue.

"Well?" Benvenuto asked.

"Humble respects. Go on."

"Monsieur Cellini presents his humble respects to Her Grace, but unhappily regrets that he will be unable to accept her very kind invitation."

Again he paused.

"Humble respects - unhappily regrets - unable to accept - kind invitation." The boy looked at Benvenuto. Obviously he still expected Benvenuto to say more.

"Er yes. Because er - because his duties to His Majesty prevent him from doing so."

"Duties to His Majesty," the boy said.

Benvenuto dismissed him with a backwards flick of his wrist, but as he reached the gate, Benvenuto called him back.

"Just to be sure, tell me the message again."

The boy repeated it perfectly and Benvenuto patted his arm. "Good lad. Well done. Here this will help you remember it all the way home." He dropped a silver coin into the boy's hand.

"Thank you sir. Humble respects - unhappily regrets - unable to accept - kind invitation - duties to His Majesty," the boy mumbled to himself as he ran off.

As soon as he had gone, the Cardinal walked over to Benvenuto.

"As you said, 'Good lad. Well done.' You did the right thing. You won't regret it."

For once, the Cardinal was wrong. Benvenuto had insulted one of the most influential persons in the country. He might have been better off to have relied on Madame D'Etampes certain knowledge of when the King would not catch her out in one of her adventures.

None of these thoughts was in Benvenuto's mind. Instead he grumbled to himself, "Just my luck that the old fool should be here when she sent the invitation. I'm sure she won't ask me again. I know what I'll do. I'll make her a piece of jewellery and then perhaps…."

As it was, he was so busy that he kept on putting it off, first for days, then for weeks and then for months, until finally it was too late.

That was his next mistake.

He was now irretrievably in Madame D'Etampes' bad books.

-40-

As well as making progress with his commissions from Francis, Benvenuto was getting a flood of work from new customers now that the King's stories about his skill were once more making him the fashionable court goldsmith.

He had made a great silver vase for the Cardinal of Lorraine, There were even a few minor pieces for Cardinal d'Este who was not going to allow himself to be out-done in patronising his popular protégé.

During this busy time the pieces of the salt cellar were being painstakingly and delicately assembled ready for enamelling; the silver overlay for the Jupiter was slowly being shaped over the now perfect bronze and Benvenuto was also making the model of the plinth of the candlestick. This was to be, as he himself described it, "very elaborate and intricately ornamented".

On one side there would be a scene in low relief showing the Rape of Gannymede, and on the other his old favourite, "Leda and the Swan". He was also designing the plinth for the as yet unmade Juno candlestick.

In case all this was not sufficient, he persuaded the King, who wanted a simple fountain for his courtyard, to allow him to design a new and utterly impractical project, which would have taken years to complete - a giant, fifty four foot high statue of the god, Mars, with a life-size figure in each corner.

"Sire, they represent the Arts and Sciences which Your Majesty so generously supports: 'The World of Learning', 'Music, 'Liberality' and 'The Art of Design', that is, 'painting sculpture and architecture'."

Benvenuto simpered and gave a courtly bow. "The giant statue in the centre represents Your Highness - Mars, the great God of War himself; unique in the valour you employ in defence of the honour of France."

The Chamberlain, Robert de Villurois coughed apologetically. "Excuse me Your Majesty, and you too, Monsieur Cellini, but a statue fifty-four feet high? Isn't that rather large? Won't it be too heavy or if it's hollow, won't the wind blow it down?"

Benvenuto breathed heavily through his nose. "Tell me Monsieur de Villurois, are you an expert on sculpture as well as everything else?"

"No," said the Chamberlain mildly, "far from it. That's why I asked."

"Go on, Monsieur Cellini, explain it to him." The doubt had been instilled in the King's mind, and he wanted an answer too.

Benvenuto tucked his left thumb in his belt and put his right hand behind his back.

"Collossal statues," he began, "have been made for centuries by artists - by great artists who have courage and boldness ..." He tapped his chest.

"Sometimes," he continued, "they are cast from the base upwards, new mouldings being added as each part cools, but mostly they used my method - casting the thing in sections and assembling them later. The Chinese Emperor, Shih Huang Ti, the one who built the Great Wall of China, had twelve, fifty foot statues made."

"A heathen?" asked the King with some disgust.

"What else could he be, Your Majesty? He died two hundred years before Christ was born. Round about the same time Charos made a statue of Helios - we call him Apollo, the Sun God - at Rhodes. It was one of the Seven Wonders of the World. A hundred and twenty feet high. Pliny said that a man couldn't encircle its thumb with two arms."

"You're talking about 'the Colossus of Rhodes'. Didn't it fall over?" the King asked with some interest.

"Er. In an earthquake."

"Perhaps the wind blew it down," de Villurois suggested.

"Or maybe some damned book-keeper had it melted down for the cost of the metal," Benvenuto snarled.

The King clapped his hands with pleasure. "Touché, Monsieur Cellini!"

Benvenuto turned to the Cardinal Lorraine who, as usual, was with the King.

"Your Eminence, doesn't it say in the 'Book of Kings' that there were two brass pillars at the porch way of King Solomon's Temple, each thirty feet high?"

The Cardinal nodded and added his own contribution. "In Rome, the Emperor Nero had a statue made of himself, one hundred and ten feet high. The Colosseum was actually named after it, and Hadrian had to use twenty-four elephants to move it. Then the Apollo in the Capitol was forty-five feet high and the Tuscan Apollo on the Palatine Hill was fifty feet."

"Bout to Monsieur Cellini," announced the King.

Nevertheless, it was de Villurois who won the bout, because when Benvenuto submitted his estimate of the cost of the work, the King needed no persuading that he could not afford it, especially at a time when the State funds were steadily being drained by yet another round of the King's seemingly endless series of wars with Charles V.

In June 1538 Francis and Charles had signed a ten year truce under the Pope's aegis, and in January 1539 at Toledo they entered into a further pact, in which they each promised not to enter into any agreement with Henry VIII of England without the consent of the other.

Henry VIII realised that a Catholic Crusade against him was being plotted, especially as the Pope had just excommunicated him and pronounced him "deposed from the English Throne". The Pope had also absolved Henry's subjects from serving him, while the English Cardinal, Reginald Pole went on a mission to rally the Catholic powers against "that most cruel and abominable tyrant, the King of England."

Henry's revenge was to have Pole's aged mother executed at the Tower of London, his older brother having already been judicially murdered in 1538.

On July 10th 1542 - after only four years - the "Ten Year Truce" was broken when Charles again went to war with Francis with Henry's encouragement and his secret promise to join in a two-pronged invasion of France. Each King was to put an army of forty-two thousand men in the field, Henry through the Somme in the North East, and Charles through Champagne on the Belgian border.

By 1544 Henry had captured Boulogne and was besieging Montreil, but Charles had been virtually defeated. In September he treacherously made peace with Francis at Crepy, leaving Henry alone in the lurch. Later the same year therefore, Henry too was forced to begin to negotiate peace terms with Francis.

Apart from the King's preoccupation with the war and the peace negotiations and his acute financial problems, another obstacle stood in Benvenuto's way. Madame D'Etampes lost no chance to support every doubter, every scoffer and every opinion adverse to his plans. She had patiently waited for her opportunity.

Her revenge had just begun.

Benvenuto was seated at Cardinal d'Este's wide dining table, with a morose expression on his face. Idly, he twirled a long-stemmed pewter wine goblet between his fingers, viewing it with some disgust.

"Too heavy," he thought. "Too thick, the pattern's crude and badly done, and what's more it makes the wine taste like it's come out of a cooking pot! Surely the mean old bastard could use the silver ones I made for him. What's he saving them for? The Second Coming?"

His irritable mood was not helped by the fact that his polite request for an audience had been answered by his being told to come just after the Cardinal would have dined.

When Benvenuto arrived he found that the Cardinal had taken longer than usual over his meal. He still had his mouth full of jam tart. Benvenuto looked at the plate enviously. Sugar was a new, exotic and expensive luxury that could only be afforded by the very rich. The Cardinal pointedly helped himself to the last piece of tart, allowed Benvenuto to kiss the ring on his free hand and had then gestured him to take the seat opposite.

The Cardinal swallowed hard. "I suppose you've already eaten. Pour yourself some wine." As Benvenuto did so, he added, "What about some fruit?"

Benvenuto shook his head.

"Alright, my son," the Cardinal said through a mouthful of pie. "Tell me your troubles. I'll listen while I finish." He patted his stomach. "My one weakness," he confessed.

While Benvenuto began to speak, the Cardinal dipped into a bowl of nuts - Spanish filberts. He grudgingly held out his hand towards Benvenuto and offered him some while still holding on to the wooden nut crackers.

Benvenuto again shook his head. He knew that he could not crack them with his rotten teeth, and he was not going to try to break them between a table and a plate - although the scarred table top showed that it had already suffered considerable abuse. He carried on talking while the Cardinal carefully lined up some nuts like soldiers and stuffed them in his mouth one at a time, cracking the next while he was still chewing the last one.

Benvenuto finished speaking and waited for the Cardinal to answer.

D'Este swept the nut shells into a little heap and leaned back in his chair, his pudgy hands interlaced across his belly. He sucked noisily on his teeth, making a bird-like cheeping sound, ran his tongue under his lips to clear the last fragments of nut, and took a large gulp of his wine which he swished around his mouth before speaking.

"Look, what you're complaining about is that the King is neglecting you. Isn't that right?"

Before Benvenuto could reply, the Cardinal half stood, and with the palms of his hands flat on the table, leaned across and pretended to peer closely at Benvenuto.

"You are Benvenuto Cellini, aren't you?"

"Your Eminence is pleased to jest."

The Cardinal sat down again.

"The same Benvenuto Cellini who was recently complaining to me that the King was stopping you getting on with your work by dropping in on you at all hours, and that he was eating up all your profits by constantly bringing visitors for you to feed? Now you're upset because he's stopped coming?"

"There is a happy medium."

The Cardinal mockingly crossed himself. "Dear God! That I should live to hear you, of all people, say that. Truly, 'Joy shall be in Heaven over one sinner that repenteth'."

Benvenuto flushed with fury, but had enough sense to control himself as the Cardinal continued, "First the King's at war with Charles and Henry, as if one of them at a time's not enough." He held up his thumb. "Then he's trying to negotiate a peace treaty." He held up his forefinger too. "And he probably hasn't got too much money either - just like me."

The cardinal showed Benvenuto his thumb, forefinger and middle finger.

"Talking about money, the King is still paying you your retainer, isn't he? And you're still doing work for him, aren't you?"

"Yes," Benvenuto said truculently, "but he hasn't ordered anything new."

The Cardinal slammed his fist down on the table, making the plates rattle.

"I should think not! He's probably as tired as the rest of your customers of ordering things you never finish because you try to do too much at the same time."

"Sir, you don't understand," Benvenuto protested. "When an artist is relying on inspiration, he can't concentrate on one subject for too long, otherwise his mind goes blank."

"Tell me, has it ever occurred to you that the King is keeping away from the Nesle is because of its terrible notoriety?"

"Terrible notoriety? As what?"

"As the worst disorderly house in the whole of Paris, which believe me is no mean achievement!"

"Your Eminence, I swear that I don't know what you're talking about!"

"They say you've got a house full of loose women; that there are orgies there every night that would make Sodom and Gomorrah look like a convent and that they indulge in flagellation and - er - and other perversions that I've never even heard of."

"You could ask the Pope. He's an expert," Benvenuto muttered, but not quietly enough.

"I heard that!" said the Cardinal. "No wonder you spend half your time in jail or dodging the executioner."

"Your Eminence, I have a big staff and a large house. If I didn't let them live in, I'd have to pay them more wages than I can afford. They're mostly young men, and I can't help what they get up to after work. If they do have any orgies, they don't invite me. Even if they did," he added with a sigh, "Caterina wouldn't let me go."

"Your Eminence," Benvenuto added entreatingly, "if they didn't stay with me, where would they live? The whole city is absolutely packed."

Benvenuto was right. Paris was less than three square miles in area and contained only about ten thousand houses. Many of these were subdivided floor by floor. Accommodation was hard to find and very expensive; the inns were always full and important visitors would have to beg hospitality from the residents. Even the nobility would let their houses when the court was travelling or when they went to their country estates. Sometimes the caretakers would secretly rent out their masters' houses, and would have to get them hurriedly vacated again when they learned their employers were returning unexpectedly.

"Your Eminence, if I may respectfully say so, my problems with the King have got nothing to do with wars, peace treaties, money, how I do my work, or the notoriety of my house Those are all the theories we covered are they not?"

"What is the reason then?"

"It's that woman."

"What woman?"

"Her Grace the Duchess of Etampes of course."

The Cardinal chuckled. "Madame D'Etampes? What have you done to upset her?"

"You were the cause of it, I am afraid. She invited me to her place. For one of her supper parties - you know what I mean. You warned me off. You forbade me to go," Benvenuto said accusingly.

"So what do you want me to do? I've no influence with Madame D'Etampes. Far from it!"

"I just want to know if the King has said anything bad about me to you. Something like this happened to me once before. Someone influenced the ruler against me for no reason, and I spent two years in a dungeon, as you are often kind enough to remind, me usually in the same breath as you tell me about the King's executioner."

"The King hasn't said a single thing, but if he does, I promise I'll warn you."

"Thank you. And I promise you that at the first sign of trouble, I'll be off so fast that I'll leave my shadow behind!"

"My boy, I've only got one piece of advice for you. That is not to ask me for any advice about how to deal with women. Send her a present, or something, that's all I can suggest."

This had been Benvenuto's intention when the incident had first happened and he suddenly realised that it had slipped his mind for months.

"I'll do it as soon as I get back to my studio, your Eminence."

"Then I expect that you'll want to be excused right away. Do come and see me again soon."

When Benvenuto left, the Cardinal greedily rummaged in the bowl of nuts and selected the shiniest and largest one, cracked it and popped it into his mouth and crunched hard.

Immediately he pulled a face and spat it out, and stared angrily at the pieces lying in the palm of his hand.

The nut was bad.

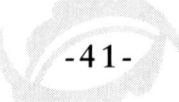

-41-

Benvenuto knew that if he was going to send Madame D'Etampes a peace offering quickly, it would have to be taken from stock. Benvenuto, as a conscientious teacher, would set his apprentices on to a wide range of jobs to ensure that they learned their trade. He himself, had spent a great deal of time learning the ancient Byzantine craft of **niello**. This is the art of filling engraved or etched patterns on gold and silver objects with a black compound of copper, silver and lead so that the design stands out strongly.

Benvenuto's recipe was to take an ounce of pure silver, two ounces of copper and three of lead, and having melted them together, to shake them up in a small earthenware flask half filled with sulphur and a pinch of borax until the alloy cooled into little grains - a process which had to be repeated two or three times.

The grains would finally be crushed to a coarse powder, washed clean and spread evenly over the heated surface of the ornament and after being dusted with a little more borax, the paste would be slowly and carefully melted until it fused into the design.

The whole procedure required considerable skill and, above all, patience, because otherwise the piece could be ruined beyond repair, and all the time and work wasted.

—❦—

Busbacca had early on shown an aptitude for this painstaking work. He had been making a delicately engraved silver vase, and Benvenuto selected this as his gift for Madame D'Etampes.

But first it was necessary to give it the final touches.

Busbacca watched while Benvenuto examined the vase which was covered with about two millimetres of the black compound.

"Now follow what I'm doing. You've got to get most of the metal off with a very fine file, right down to the silver, but make sure you don't scratch the vase itself. Like this - you see what I mean?"

The young man - he was no longer a boy - nodded.

"Well, get on with it then, and when you've finished, make up a small charcoal fire and call me. Be careful, if you scrape the vase, I'll file the skin off your backside!"

Three hours later Benvenuto was taking the cleaned vase from the hands of his apprentice, who was so covered with a film of metal filings that he looked as if he was wearing elbow length gloves.

Benvenuto went to the window and turned it this way and that, examining it closely.

"Hum," he said.

Busbacca recognised this as a trick that Benvenuto had learned from his customers. So far as Busbacca was concerned, "hum" from Benvenuto was the same as the highest praise.

"Now," said Benvenuto, "put the vase in the charcoal and warm it up. Not too much, just a bit too hot to hold."

They waited.

"Try it now."

Busbacca reached out to pick up the vase, and immediately dropped it on the bench with a yelp.

"Good," Benvenuto said. "That seems to be about the right temperature." Busbacca sucked his burnt fingers and glowered at him, balefully.

"Watch closely again. I'll put a little oil on a steel burnisher and brush the surface, very carefully, or we'll scratch out the filling. What I'm trying to do is to seal up any little bubble holes in the niello. Patience, that's all that's needed. And a light touch."

Benvenuto worked silently for a while with Busbacca stood behind him, his eyes never moving from his master's hands.

"Don't hover over my shoulder like the Angel of Death. Go and get me some of that fine sand - 'Tripoli' we call it in Italy; God knows what these heathen French call it - and some crushed charcoal and a cabbage stalk or something like that and we'll rub the vase all over until it's smooth and shiny. Then you can have the pleasure of polishing it."

As his apprentice went off in the direction of the kitchen, Benvenuto called after him, "And ask one of those French workmen to come in - the one who can translate Italian. I've got a letter I want to send, and I don't think I'd better trust myself with that ridiculous language of theirs."

—⚒—

Benvenuto wrote out a fair copy in his own handwriting.

> *"Benvenuto Cellini, Master Goldsmith and Sculptor in the service of His Majesty Francis I, by the Grace of God, King of France, extends his humble duty to Her Grace, the Duchess of Etampes, and begs her kind permission to call on Her Ladyship at 2.30 tomorrow afternoon when he hopes to have the honour of presenting her with an example of his work as a token of his respectful devotion."*

There was nothing in the letter that the King could take exception to. It was typical of the many similar ones Madame D'Etampes received every week from people wanting her to use her considerable influence at Court on their behalf.

"Busbacca, put on your best suit - wash your filthy hands and face first, and deliver this to Madame D'Etampe's house. Wait to see if there's a reply."

Benvenuto tried to get on with his work, but impatiently kept crossing to the window to see if there was any sign of the youth. It was past noon when Busbacca got back, tired, hot and dusty. As he came panting into the work room, Benvenuto stood up.

"Well?"

"I'm sorry, master. The butler took the letter. I asked him if there was a reply and he left me standing in the street for ages. He never even gave me a drink of water. Then he came out and he said there was no reply."

"Exactly what was it he said?"

Busbacca hesitated, "He said, 'There's no point in your hanging about, buzz off'!"

"I told you to bring back a reply," Benvenuto shouted unreasonably. "What kind of bloody answer is that?"

He picked up a wooden mallet and flung it at Busbacca, but he had been with Benvenuto long enough to know what was coming. He was out of the door before the hammer hit it.

Benvenuto decided on an outfit of dark green velvet. "Green is her favourite colour," he reasoned. "At least she dresses her servants in it. No harm in trying to please her right from the start."

The page boy who opened the door was certainly dressed in Madame D'Etampe's green livery, but the butler who stood a few steps behind him in the dim hall was wearing a severe black robe relieved only by a white collar and a gold chain from which hung an enamelled letter "A" - for Anne in a script which resembled the "F" in Francis' Coat of Arms.

"I am Benvenuto Cellini. I am here by appointment to see Her Grace."

The Butler gave a little jerk of his head. "This way. I'll see if Her Grace is in."

Benvenuto went into the waiting room with a sigh. From past experience he recognised the signs of being in for a long wait.

He put the tooled leather box which held the vase on the table in the centre of the room, next to an earthenware fruit bowl which he flicked with his finger. It gave out a dull "clunk". Benvenuto wrinkled his nose with scorn and began to walk around the room, poking the furnishings and picking up and inspecting the ornaments; standing up, sitting down and staring out of the window.

When he judged that about an hour had passed, he opened the door and peeped out. The butler, who was standing in the hall talking to one of the maids, looked up.

"Her Grace is not yet available. Are you still going to wait?"

Benvenuto closed the door. Angrily he pulled a few black grapes off the bunch in the fruit bowl and crammed them into his mouth. Then he looked round furtively, swallowed the pips and tore off the soggy stumps which he stuffed down the edge of one of the chairs.

He leaned back in his seat and began to clean his finger nails with a cutter which he took from his pouch and restlessly paced about the table, rehearsing what he intended to say to the Duchess, smacking the fist of one hand into the palm of the other for emphasis.

He stopped short and tore off a few more grapes, snatched up his presentation box and stamped out into the hall. The Butler was still there, obviously guarding the staircase to the upper floor. He looked at Benvenuto with raised eyebrows.

"Does she usually keep people waiting like this?"

"Not when she wants to see them, or when they really have an appointment."

"I see," said Benvenuto. "In that case, I'll be off then."

"May I give Her Grace a message for you?" the butler asked politely.

"Yes. Tell her I couldn't wait any longer. The grapes in there," he pointed to the room, "are sour. And besides, my bladder is bursting. Good day to you!"

—m—

When Madame D'Etampes got Benvenuto's note, she decided to forgive him for his slight in turning down her invitation, and for the rebuke about "his duties to His Majesty." Not only was it beneath her dignity to be seen quarrelling with a mere tradesman, but the King might begin to wonder what this Cellini person had done to incur her displeasure. Besides, the note promised a present, and a present from a goldsmith, was not to be lightly rejected.

She would stop actively trying to turn the King, but that was all. Benvenuto would be made unmistakably aware that he was permanently out of favour with her. Keeping him waiting was part of the treatment, but she carried it on far too long, and she underestimated Benvenuto's explosive temper that had got him in trouble all his life.

She would even have pardoned him for storming out of her house without waiting for her to see him - she was used to her frustrated lovers doing that, but when Benvenuto got home, still in a rage, what he did there made sure that Madame D'Etampes would become his implacable enemy.

Benvenuto flung open the door of his big communal living room. Ascanio, Busbacca, Pagolo and Bartolomeo, politely rose to their feet.

"I want you lot. Now. Bring a sword, each of you, and Busbacca get an axe. There's something I'm going to do down in the basement."

"Catch rats?" suggested Busbacca.

"You could say that," Benvenuto replied. "I'm going to get rid of a pest."

The Nesle was big enough to have an indoor tennis court. This was a large galleried room in which "Real Tennis", the game which is the fore-runner of modern tennis was played. It was a favourite pastime of the nobility during that period, especially in France where the game originated. The name came from the Old French word, "tenetz", (now tenez), meaning "catch" which would politely be called to the receiver before the ball was served.

The game was already old in the sixteenth century. King Richard III had passed a law in 1389 forbidding "all playing at tennis, football ..... and other such importune games."

Like King Richard, Benvenuto had no time for this sort of frivolity. He had therefore converted the court itself into his main workroom, while the gallery had been turned into a series of little studios, some used by his own craftsmen and some which he let, the rent being a useful contribution to his household expenses.

Occupying the entire basement beneath the tennis court was the workman who had been installed there by Madame D'Etampes. Benvenuto did not even know his name, and he could only recall having seen him now and again as he went about his mysterious business. Benvenuto did not know what that was either, because although Madame D'Etampes had said he was a "fellow sculptor," there was no sign or sound of that sort of work going on.

He only entered and left by a trap door leading into the courtyard, by which his materials and goods also came and went.

Benvenuto and his quartet of helpers used the main entrance leading directly from the workroom, stamping across it with military precision, much to the surprise of the labourers who were still there clearing up from the day's work and preparing for the next. They crowded behind to watch and it was therefore quite a small army that clattered down the stairs and confronted the startled occupant.

Benvenuto glanced round. The large room was unusually dimly lit, and not by ordinary candelabra, but by metal lanthorns such as were usually carried in the open, with glass windows to prevent the wind from blowing them out.

He could hardly make out the features of his tenant, an elderly man, tall, but stooped with a thick fringe of grey hair round the sides and back of his balding head. The man screwed up his eyes and squinted at Benvenuto in the gloom.

"Why, it's Monsieur Cellini, isn't it? My name is Galland - Armand Galland. How nice of you to come and see me after all this time. And who are these gentlemen? Never mind, it's a pleasure to meet you ….."

"You won't think it's a pleasure in a minute. Why is it so dark down here?" Benvenuto called over his shoulder, "Hey! One of you up there, bring some more candles."

"No! For the love of God, no! No naked flames," Galland shouted.

"Why on earth not?"

Benvenuto looked around again. The room was practically bare. There were three barrels, two near to one wall and one on the opposite side. There were also several wide necked half-barrels of water, each with a wooden bucket standing next to it. A wooden bench, also with a water container handy, was underneath the trapdoor leading to the outside. A large pestle and mortar stood on the bench, together with a wooden scoop, a few little linen bags, some full and some empty, a few small wooden boxes and a set of scales. Nothing else.

Benvenuto noticed that the floor seemed to have been meticulously swept clean. Forming little pathways between the three barrels and the bench were raised wooden slatted duckboards, which, in view of the dryness of the cellar floor were obviously intended to keep Galland's feet off the ground and away from anything that may have fallen or have been spilled.

This thought drew Benvenuto's eyes to Galland's feet. He was wearing cloth slippers with felt soles. A terrible suspicion dawned in Benvenuto's mind and he grabbed the front of Galland's robe and dragged the man towards him.

"What the hell are you doing down here? What are you making? What's in that barrel over there?"

"Charcoal."

"And that one?"

"Sulphur."

"And the last one?"

Galland did not answer, so Benvenuto shifted his grip the man's shoulders and shook him.

"Answer me at once you bastard, before I kill you!"

"It's saltpetre."

"Charcoal, sulphur and saltpetre. You're making gunpowder."

He flung the man away from him. "I don't believe it! You're really doing it. Making gunpowder down here, right under my workshop. You could kill us all!"

"I'm only making fine priming powder - and look, it's in tiny lots, all in separate bags, and every bag in its own box."

"Don't tell me about gunpowder!" Benvenuto roared. "I've exploded more of it than you could ever make if you live to be a hundred, which you won't. Not when I've finished with you. Now I'll tell you what I'm going to do. I'm an exceptionally reasonable man. No one can say I'm not, can they?" He looked round, inviting his workers to disagree with him. Nobody did.

"I'll tell you what I'm going to do," he repeated. "I'm not going to turn you out of here ....."

Galland's face brightened.

".... so long as you move out of here on your own in - oh, let's be generous - in say five minutes."

"Five minutes?" Galland protested, "Where can I find in five minutes? You can't put my stuff outside. It's raining. It'll get wet."

"Not as wet as it will be if I chuck it in the Seine," He turned to his workmen. "Help him shift that stuff through the hatch, but don't drop anything, and don't make any sparks or they'll be burying you in a bucket."

Galland looked on helplessly while his belongings were dumped outside. "Monsieur, you're a fool," he snarled. "You know I'm under the protection of Madame D'Etampes. She will hear of this within the hour."

"To be sure." After all the shouting, Benvenuto's voice was quiet and mild. "I'm absolutely counting on it."

—⚂—

Benvenuto was again in Cardinal D'Este's house: in the study this time.

"Lucky for you that Madame D'Etampes couldn't tell the King the real reason for your outburst."

"What did she say then?"

"According to my informant, she said you had dispossessed one of her protégés using foul and disrespectful language."

Benvenuto shrugged.

"Your Eminence, I don't know how to kick someone out into the street politely. Didn't the King ask why I did it?"

"That was the one thing in your favour. When the King heard the fellow was making gunpowder right under your workroom, he was furious. He said he didn't blame you in the least. You know, you were very lucky you actually had a genuine excuse."

"So it's alright then?"

"No-o I wouldn't go so far as to say that."

"Why not, Your Eminence?"

"It seems that Madame D'Etampes has someone else she wants to install in your basement."

"Oh yes, and what does he make? Poison?"

"No. Perfume."

"Perfume! All that alcohol right near my furnaces? Is the woman mad? Why doesn't she just come round and burn the place down? I'll go and see the King. He told me to look after the place, and I will. Anyone who puts it in danger will get flung out the nearest window."

The Cardinal tried to soothe his visitor. "Don't worry, it won't happen. The King's not stupid. He turned her down. He said he'd find a workshop for Monsieur Galland and the perfumier, whoever he is. If he puts them both in the same place, there could be quite a bang one day!"

"Thank you, Your Eminence. If you say, 'don't worry,' then I won't."

"My son, I don't want to deceive you; there is just one thing. When Madame D'Etampes kept on at him, the King told her that if Galland had any complaint, then he should sue you."

"And?"

"And that's what he's going to do."

Benvenuto could not believe it. "He's going to sue me? What for? I never laid a hand on him - well hardly. It was more like helping an old man up the stairs."

Cardinal d'Este shook his head sadly.

"Benvenuto, you've lived in this city as long as I have and yet you know nothing about the people. They sue each other for anything. What's more as you're a foreigner, the judge will be biased against you from the start, although working for the King may cancel that out - unless they bribe him that is. And if they can't bribe the judge, they'll try to get at your lawyer. What's more, it's considered quite usual to bring along a few witnesses to commit perjury. They even buy and sell shares in law suits. 'Champerty,' they call it."

"God help me! What shall I do then?"

"Well, it pains me to say so, and I'll do a penance for it tomorrow, but just make sure you're a better liar than they are."

"But truth and justice are on my side," Benvenuto protested.

"Hah!" The Cardinal snorted. "If that's all you've got to rely on, then as you said, God help you!"

"You still haven't told me what he's going to sue me for."

"My dear fellow, that I can't say, but in inventing law suits, the French display their amazingly fertile imaginations in their fullest splendour!"

―∽―

The Judge read from a sheet of paper: "Breach of Contract; unlawful ejectment by a Landlord; assault and battery; causing bodily injury; defamation; insulting behaviour; aggravated personal affront; damage to and destruction of personal property; threats; molestation; intimidation."

The Judge was impressed. He looked at Benvenuto with small, pig-like eyes sunk into fat face. Several chins hung in layers on his collar, and his cheeks quivered as he spoke.

"Monsieur Cellini, do you admit all of this?"

Benvenuto looked around the huge noisy courtroom. Litigants waiting for their cases to be heard were standing in groups, arguing with each other or their lawyers, or discussing their evidence with their witnesses. Some were excitedly haggling.

There is nothing like reaching the door of the Court to induce parties to reach a compromise that common sense should have dictated right at the beginning.

The Judge was seated midway along a table. Benvenuto and his witnesses were facing him at one end and Galland and his witnesses at the other, both sides being separated by another table forming a "T" with the Judge's.

"Monsieur Cellini! Did you hear what I said? Don't you understand the claim, or are you just not paying attention? I've got a lot of cases to get through today you know."

Benvenuto had decided against employing a lawyer in view of Cardinal d'Este's warning about how easily they would take a bribe. Instead, he brought with him his French workman who spoke fairly good Italian. With that and his own reasonable command of French, he felt he could get by.

"Tell the Judge it's a pack of bloody lies from start to finish."

"Sir, Monsieur Cellini refutes the allegations."

Benvenuto dug his elbow into the interpreter's ribs.

"Er, Monsieur Cellini emphatically and indignantly rejects the allegations."

The Judge sniffed disdainfully.

"Monsieur Galland, tell me what happened. Slowly, so that this gentleman can translate."

"I am an old family retainer of Madame Anne d'Heilly, Her Grace the Duchess of Etampes - the King's - er, the King's - um, friend."

"I know who the Duchess of Etampes is," snapped the Judge testily. "Do get on!"

"At her request, Monsieur Cellini granted me a ten year lease of the basement of his tennis court."

"Liar!" Benvenuto shouted. "I hold the Petit Nesle by the King's grace - out on a minute's notice. How could I grant a ten year lease on something I don't own?"

"I don't know," said the Judge. "Maybe Monsieur Galland wants to add 'false pretences' to the Complaint."

"Ask him where the lease is, then," Benvenuto pleaded.

"You stole it with my papers when you threw me out."

The Judge pounded the table with his fist.

"Stop this arguing both of you. I'm listening to what Monsieur Galland has to say. You, Monsieur Cellini, will await your turn."

"Last Wednesday, Monsieur Cellini came down to my basement with a whole gang of workmen, all armed to the teeth. Without any provocation they attacked me, threw me out into the street, smashed up some of my property and stole several valuable pieces of furniture, some paintings and my strong box with all my life's savings and a pearl crucifix - the very one my sainted mother was holding as she lay dying."

Benvenuto could not contain himself. "Liar! Liar!"

The interpreter had to prevent Benvenuto from climbing over the table to get at Galland, who cringed back in fear.

"You had a table, three barrels of gunpowder and two lousy pots. The whole lot wasn't worth two sous."

"Monsieur Cellini, I won't warn you again! One more interruption and I'll put you in prison. As it is, I can see the Plaintiff may have some reason for saying you attacked him. If your conduct here is anything to go by, I think you've almost proved his case for him. I'm going to adjourn this matter for two hours. I suggest you have a quiet word with Monsieur Galland and see if you can't offer him a settlement. A generous one."

Benvenuto left the Courtroom in disgust. Outside the door he said in rapid Italian to Busbacca, Ascanio, Pagolo and Bartolomeo, "Keep that lot back." He jerked his head at Galland's witnesses while, with a forced smile, he linked his arm in Galland's.

"Come Monsieur, let's go somewhere private and talk this thing over like gentlemen."

He led Galland along an alleyway at the side of the court building. Galland began to resist, but Benvenuto reassured him.

"We don't want your witnesses to know what you're getting, do we? Otherwise they'll all want a share."

When they were out of sight of the road Benvenuto suddenly turned and pinned Galland to the wall with his forearm against the man's throat. Drawing his dagger he pricked Galland hard in the shoulder and biceps and then deeper in the thigh. Galland gave a throttled yelp.

"Please Monsieur Cellini. In God's name, what are you doing?"

Benvenuto showed him the point of the dagger on which there was a tiny red smear, and then pressed the blade against the tip of Galland's nose.

"If you as much as cough, you'll wear that long beak of yours on a string round your neck."

"For pity's sake, what do you want?"

"I want you to stop lying about me. Now listen, I'm going to give you a chance. If you go on with the case and lose, I'll cut your nose and ears off, and stab you in the arms and legs. If you go on with the case and win, I'll cut your throat." He pressed the blade against his victim's bobbing Adam's Apple.

Galland found a little courage. "What sort of chance is that? Either way you cut me up."

"Well, there is another alternative. You stay out of the court-room. You don't come back. I'll tell the Judge we've reached an amicable understanding, and that will be that."

Galland hesitated. Benvenuto pressed a little harder on his knife.

"Alright! Alright! Just leave me alone."

Benvenuto released him and playfully pinched his cheek.

"There! I told you we could settle this like gentlemen."

―∞―

"An amicable understanding," said the Judge. "Congratulations, Monsieur Cellini. You did the right thing. I knew that with a little hint from me, you'd see reason. But do take one word of advice: try to avoid violence in the future. That way you won't get into any more trouble."

-42-

Benvenuto's business affairs were getting more complicated, and he simply did not have the time to handle them properly.

There were an increasing number of employees, labourers and skilled craftsmen alike, whose work had to be supervised. Supplies of materials, from charcoal to precious metals had to be organised and checked. It was simply no longer possible to send a boy up the road every time some small item was needed.

The master craftsmen worked for Benvenuto on the usual arrangement under which they shared with him the profits on the commissions they brought in. Customers had to pay money on account, outstanding bills had to be collected and Benvenuto discovered he was getting into a muddle about paying his own debts. Some he paid twice; some he did not pay at all, and found himself being dunned by tradesmen who were then reluctant to give him further credit. He also had to handle the expenses of his growing household.

Benvenuto decided he needed a steward to manage his finances, and chose one of his own craftsmen, Pagolo Miccieri.

Although Pagolo was skilful in his work, he had no interest in it and was too impatient to take the hours that were required on the fine and sometimes repetitive detail. Benvenuto was sure that the man would be happier spending most of his time attending to his accounting, so he picked an opportune moment to offer him a change of position.

Pagolo was flattered. "Of course I'd like the job, but why me?"

"I'd sooner trust a fellow Florentine than a Roman, or worse still one of those thieving Frenchmen. By the way, you do speak a bit of French, don't you?"

Pagolo nodded. "Enough to get by."

"Good. And wasn't that brother of yours - what's his name? - oh yes, Gatti - the manager of some of Messer Chigi's properties?"

"That's right. He taught me bookkeeping. I used to help him."

"So you told me. That's the other reason I picked you. You always carry a rosary, don't you?"

"Certainly." Pagolo was puzzled by the change of topic.

"I say my prayers every time I have a spare moment. Why do you ask?"

"Because I believe that a religious man must be an honest one."

Benvenuto reached out and shook Pagolo's hand.

A week after this conversation took place was a feast day, and Benvenuto and his Italian workers were invited to a midday garden party at the home, just outside the city, of a Bolognese sculptor, named Matteo del Nazaro.

Benvenuto, Ascanio, Busbacca and Bartolomeo, all dressed in their best clothes set off together, but Pagolo said he would not go with them.

"I must stay behind. Your accounts are absolutely chaotic. It will be ages before I can get them straight. And then, with all the men on holiday, somebody's got to guard the gold and jewellery. Another time, someone else can do it, but I can use the peace and quiet to get on with my book work and when I'm finished I can say my prayers."

He stood at the gate, looking after them as they rode off. "Don't worry, I'll look after the place." He patted the sword at his belt. "Enjoy yourselves. Don't even think of me slaving away here while you're all having a good time."

He gave a little wave and went back inside.

The lunch had been first class; a variety of cold meats, vegetables fruits and cheeses, all served from a big buffet in Matteo del Nazario's garden - a garden on which he spent almost as much time as he did on his work in his studio, so that, at this time of the year, it was full of flowering shrubs and plants as well as bushes that Matteo had sculpted into the shape of birds and animals.

There had been plenty of good wine too, and afterwards an entertainment provided by the guests themselves. Even Benvenuto had been prevailed upon to play his flute.

It was about half past two when Benvenuto started to think about what Pagolo had said to him, and a gnawing suspicion began to make him feel restless.

"He was never so conscientious before. Why should he want to work on a holiday when up to now I've always had to chase him to get on with his job? I don't trust this sudden enthusiasm."

He found his host.

"Matteo, will you excuse me if I slip away? I'll do it quietly. Nobody will notice and it won't break up the party."

"Why? There's nothing wrong, is there?"

"Of course not," Benvenuto reassured him. "It's only that I'm in the last stages of finishing my salt cellar, and there's something that I've just thought of that I must see to."

"What a pity. We've got some girls coming soon?" Matteo winked suggestively. "Are you sure you can't stay?"

Benvenuto hesitated "No, I must go. I'll tell you what though: if I'm through quickly, I'll come back."

"Then I'll see if I can save you a little desert!" Matteo winked again, and this time leered too.

—⁂—

Benvenuto galloped his horse through the unusually empty streets.

Instead of the crowds in the shops and around the market stalls or haggling with street traders and farmers selling their wares from loaded carts, barrows, or even from trays round their necks, a large part of the population was either at home or drinking in the inns. Most of those who were out of doors were at the many little fun-fairs that had sprung up for the day with side shows of conjurers, acrobats, performing animals and pedlars selling cakes and pies, sweets, wine and fruit.

Benvenuto reined up at the blacksmith's shop that stood fifty yards from his house. For once, instead of the noise of hammering or the hiss of the bellows or the roar of the furnace, it was completely silent.

The smith was seated in the shade of the awning covering his open air shop. On a table next to him was a tankard which he had been filling from a brown earthenware pitcher that had once held a gallon of beer, but which was now nearly empty. He had a grinding wheel between his knees and he was busy sharpening a large box of kitchen knives.

"Good afternoon," Benvenuto said casually. "Working today? Don't you ever take a holiday?"

"Hah! When it's a holiday my wife can find more for me to do than on my busiest day. She had me repairing the roof this morning. Then I had to put new handles on her cooking pots. Now it's the knives, and then there's the blasted chicken coop to fix." He took another mouthful of beer and smacked his lips. "I can tell you, I'll be glad when it's tomorrow!"

A thin piping voice came from the house. "Who's out there? Who are you gossiping with, husband? Have you finished the knives already? You can't have made much of a job of them!"

Benvenuto smiled. He had never met the blacksmith's wife and it amused him to hear this giant of a man being henpecked by what he assumed, from the sound of her voice, to be a little sparrow of a woman, but his eyebrows nearly disappeared into his hair when she came out of the house, wiping her hands on her apron. She was as tall as her husband, and nearly as broad, with muscular arms and thick wrists which would have done justice to any of his assistants.

"This is Monsieur Cellini, our neighbour from the castle up the road. A very good customer of ours," he stressed meaningfully.

"I would offer our guest some beer," she said glancing into the pitcher, "but I see you've already swilled it all down, you great pig." She gave her husband a playful push that nearly knocked him from his stool.

"Thank you, Madame," Benvenuto said politely. "Another time, perhaps. I was just wondering if your husband could have a look at my horse. I think he's picked up a stone in his foot," he lied. "I'll leave it with you; there's no hurry, but I don't want him to suffer until tomorrow. Now if you'll please excuse me, I must get home - there's something urgent ...."

Benvenuto gave a hurried bow and half ran and half walked up the road to the Petit Nesle.

Benvenuto went through the gate, but instead of crossing the courtyard, he sidled round the edge of the house and quietly opened the kitchen door. Madame Leone, Caterina's mother was preparing some vegetables, stood up.

"Why it's Messer Cellini come home early!" she shouted loudly. She went to the door. "Caterina dear!" she called up the stairs, "the Master's home. Do you hear me? The Master's back."

"Shut up, you old cow!" Benvenuto snarled, and swinging his arm round, he sent her staggering across the room and went racing up the stairs.

He burst into his bedroom and found Pagolo with his shirt half buttoned trying to tuck it into his breeches, while Caterina was still wriggling into her dress, and at the same time kicking layers of petticoats.

"Got you!" Benvenuto shouted. He drew his dagger. "By God there's going to be some blood spilled here in a minute!"

"No! Christ! Have mercy. No!" the girl shrieked. She dodged past him and fled down the stairs, screaming for her mother.

Benvenuto turned his attention to Pagolo who was cowering on the side of the four-poster bed. As Benvenuto edged his way round the end to get at him, Pagolo scrambled on to the bed and rolled over to the other side, but Benvenuto grabbed his hair as he landed, and, pulling his head back, raised his dagger.

"No! No! Wait!" Pagolo pleaded. "She's not your wife! The law won't protect you. If you kill me, you'll hang!" Pagolo played his only card - Benvenuto's fear of the hangman.

Benvenuto hesitated.

"Please let me go. I'll leave the city. I'll do anything you ask."

Benvenuto slowly put his dagger back in its sheath and Pagolo let out a deep breath.

"Get up."

He put the flat of his hand in the small of Pagolo's back and pushed him out the door and on to the top of the landing.

"You said you'd do anything I ask?"

"Yes master, anything."

"Well let me see you fly then," Benvenuto gave Pagolo a vicious kick sending him crashing head over heels down the stairs.

Benvenuto leaped down after him and dragged him to his feet, dazed and trembling.

"Dear, dear! You didn't do that very well, did you? You bounced half way down, and then hit most of the stairs to the bottom. Alright, if you still want to do anything I say, let's see if you can knock the wall down with your head."

Pagolo wrenched himself out of Benvenuto's grasp and ran out of the door.

"You're mad! Absolutely mad!" he shouted. over his shoulder. "Why pick on me? There isn't a man in the house she hasn't been to bed with except for Ascanio and Busbacca, and you know why they're not interested. The workmen used to stand in line for it. Will you kill them all as well?"

Benvenuto turned his attention to the two women, clinging to each other in the kitchen, the younger one still sobbing.

"Right you pair of whores, now it's your turn."

"How dare you speak to me like that? I'm a respectable woman!" Madame Leone was indignant.

"Respectable? Then why were you standing guard while your daughter was betraying me? It wasn't the first time, was it?" Benvenuto bellowed. "Is that your side line? When you're not stealing from me, you pimp on your daughter. Now get out, the two of you. If you're still here in one minute, I'll kill you both."

The older woman turned towards the stairs.

"Where the hell are you going? I said, 'out'!"

"I'm going to get our things."

"What things? You had nothing when I picked you out of the gutter - or was it the brothel? - I forget which, and that's what you'll leave here with. Nothing. And that reminds me..."

He walked over to Caterina, grabbed hold of the gold chain and pendant she was wearing and snatched it off with a jerk of his wrist. The girl screamed with pain and a deep weal on the side of her neck began to ooze tiny drops of blood.

"Now, you heard me. Out! MOVE!"

Mouthing a stream of profanities, Madame Leone grabbed hold of her daughter's arm and ran, dragging her up the street in the same direction that Pagolo had taken.

If Benvenuto had contented himself with throwing Caterina and her mother out of the house, they would have philosophically accepted it as being only just. They would not have even worried about their few belongings that they had to leave behind. Madame Leone had a little nest egg salted away from what she had stolen from the housekeeping.

But Benvenuto, not content with hurting and frightening Pagolo, lost no opportunity to ridicule him by spreading a highly embellished version of the story around the town.

"When I came in this bastard was hopping around on one foot, trying to get the other one into his drawers .... I only showed him my dagger and he began wetting himself.....kicked

his arse so hard, he must have been sneezing shit for a week .....
running up the street with his shirt flapping and his backside
full of lead pellets...."

It was inevitable therefore, that they should plot to get their
revenge, and it was Pagolo who put Caterina up to it ....."

—⚏—

The Judge to whom Caterina made her complaint was the same
one who had presided over Benvenuto's last case. He issued a
summons for Benvenuto to appear before him in two day's
time, and also made sure that Cardinal d'Este knew what was
going on.

The Cardinal took the hint, and wrote a letter to the Judge.

> *"Your Excellency,*
>
> *I regret that my duties on behalf of His Holiness at the Court of His Majesty, King Francis, prevent me from appearing before you to testify as to the noble character of the defendant, Benvenuto Cellini, but I would like to inform you that he is a devout, practising Christian. In my opinion, he could not be guilty of the abominable crime with which he has been falsely charged by the debased person whom he rightly dismissed from his household for grossly immoral conduct.*
>
> *I am enclosing by way of corroboration, on loan to your Excellency, two examples of the defendant's skill as a Master Goldsmith, and I am sure you will agree that no one who was able to execute such delicate work could be capable of committing the bestial acts which this woman alleges.*
>
> *No doubt, at your Excellency's convenience, you will return these exhibits to me having seen that justice is done by his acquittal."*

The two samples of Benvenuto's work were the silver niello vase that he had been unable to give to Madame D'Etampes and the gold necklace and pendant, now repaired, that he had torn from Caterina's neck. The last thing that Benvenuto or the

Cardinal expected was for either piece to be returned by the Judge.

"Everyone does it here," the Cardinal excused himself. "After all it's not really bribery when the charge is false. I'll do a penance just the same. A little one."

Benvenuto carefully dressed himself in a black velvet suit with white lace collar and cuffs lightly trimmed with silver thread. Ascanio, Busbacca and Bartolomeo, who were coming to give evidence about Caterina's bad character, also wore sombre clothes.

It was the same courtroom as before, but because the judge was today trying criminal cases, the atmosphere was subdued. The little groups of people mostly stared at each other in silence. When they did speak, it was in whispers. In many instances they were waiting for the first glimpse of a friend or relative who might have been locked in a dungeon for weeks or months.

Those who took the trouble to listen to cases other than their own did not do so out of idle curiosity, but out of anxiety, hoping to find some clue as to the Judge's mood, or how he would behave in their case.

At the conclusion of a trial there were no ribald comments or good humoured teasing. If someone was found guilty, the spectators would turn their heads away, unable to meet the defendant's eye, especially if, as often happened, the sentence was death. At best, if someone was acquitted, they would nod their congratulations, trying to hide their own envy at his good fortune.

Benvenuto's was first on the list, preference having been obtained by the "evidence" that the Cardinal had "lent" to the Judge. Benvenuto took his place on one side of the "T" shaped table without so much as a glance at Caterina and her mother on the other side. The girl was wearing a long rough wool robe.

She stood with her head bent, her hood hiding her face. Pagolo was not there.

—⚏—

"Well, well. So here you are again, Monsieur Cellini. What have you been up to this time?" The Judge pretended not to know. He picked up a paper from in front of him.

"Caterina Leone?"

She nodded.

"Speak up!"

"Yes."

"Is this your mark?"

She nodded again.

"I won't keep telling you. When I ask you a question, you answer out loud. You're not dumb, are you?"

This time Caterina shook her head and the Judge smashed his fist down on the table, making her flinch. Even Benvenuto jumped.

"No sir," she said.

"You call me, 'Your Excellency'," the Judge growled. "Now, is what you say here all true?"

Benvenuto interrupted. "Excuse me, your Excellency. Before we begin properly, may I ask you a point of law? As you will see, I have no lawyer here to defend me."

"What is it?"

"This woman has charged me with sodomy, has she not?"

"That's what it says here. What's the point of law?"

"She accuses me of perpetrating this vile act on her by force, not just once but many times. So, if she is telling the truth, as she did not complain to the authorities the first time, that would make her an accomplice to the filthy practice. And the law punishes the active and passive partners in the same way - death at the stake. She would have to burn too."

The Judge rapped his knuckles on the table. "I decide who's to burn." He looked at Benvenuto thoughtfully. "But you've raised a very interesting point, you know."

The Judge feigned surprise, although it was he who had secretly advised the Cardinal to tell Benvenuto what to say. He rubbed his forefinger along his thick lips.

"Young lady, do you understand what you've let yourself in for? If I believe what you say here," he tapped the paper, "then you will be guilty of sodomy too, and you'll be burned alongside this man. But if I don't believe you, then you'll be guilty of perjury, and the penalty for perjury in a capital case is hanging.

So which do you prefer? Do you want to be burned or hanged?"

The girl stuffed her fingers into her mouth, and her mother began to moan and wring her hands.

"I didn't hear your reply," said the Judge. "Now I can understand that you're upset with Monsieur Cellini." He stood, leant over the table, and pulled the hood off the girl's head. "If you had just accused him of assault for giving you that nasty mark on your neck, I might have been very severe with him. I've warned him about his violence before. But this case hasn't begun yet, so you've got just one last chance. Do you withdraw the charge?"

The girl clung to her mother and began to cry.

"I wish to hell you'd answer me when I talk to you, girl," the Judge said," but I suppose that means you do. The charge is dismissed."

Without looking at Benvenuto, the Judge picked up another sheet of paper and held it at arm's length."Next case, please," he announced.

Benvenuto stood on the steps of the court house and took a deep breath of fresh air. He turned to his men. "I still think he should have had her burnt."

He strode off in the direction of home.

-43-

"That cursed woman must have been brought into the world just to destroy me!"

Benvenuto rushed into the work-room, shaking his clenched fists at heaven. The workmen stood in frozen attitudes, staring. Even those who did not speak Italian realised that for a change his rage was not with one of them.

It was Busbacca who, as usual, could not let things be. "Which woman Master, and what has she done?"

Benvenuto grabbed the youth's shoulders.

"That whore-the King's strumpet - Madame D'Etampes. I ought to feel flattered she thinks I'm so important that she spends so much time and effort trying to ruin me," he shouted. "She's trying to get the King to take my commissions away from me."

"What commissions?"

"What commissions do you think, you fat fool?" Benvenuto spat at Busbacca. "The silver candlesticks and the Mars Fountain - what else is there?"

"The salt cellar," Busbacca suggested.

"The salt cellar?" Benvenuto went pale. "God no! Even she wouldn't dare. I'd melt it down first! And I'd burn the plans in the same furnace."

"I thought the King had dropped the statue idea entirely," Ascanio said.

Benvenuto shook his head impatiently. "Only temporarily on account of the war. He's just short of money. That's why I've been carrying on with the preparatory work at my own expense. When I can afford it, that is, which means when my so called workers actually help me to make a few crowns instead of my having to grub for a living all the time."

"Is the Duchess just trying to get the King to drop the jobs, or does she want him to give them to someone else?" Bartolomeo asked.

"Give them to someone else, of course. It wouldn't be enough for her unless I was publicly humiliated at the same time. The bloody red-headed trollop! Why the hell doesn't she stick to what she does best, and keep her nose pointed at the ceiling and right out of my business?"

Bartolomeo persevered doggedly. "Who's she trying to get the work for?"

"Francesco Primaticcio."

"Il Bologna!" Ascanio pronounced Primaticcio's nickname the natural contempt of a true Florentine for any other Italian, especially one from the rival city of Bologna. "But he's a painter. What sculpting has he done?"

"None, except those stuccoes in the Great Gallery and in her bedroom at Fontainebleau."

"But why Primaticcio?" Ascanio asked.

"Because with all the time he's spent decorating her bedroom, he's just another of her poodles - no offence to poodles intended."

"In other words, she's trying to get him the job because he's one of her bedfellows."

"Not in other words. In those words. The King's Chamberlain, de Villurois, who hates her more than I do, told me. He says she keeps nagging away day after day."

"Why don't you go and see him and try to reason with him, Master?" Busbacca still could not keep quiet.

"Yes, I'll do that," Benvenuto sneered. "I'll go and argue with the King, just as soon as I go out of my mind."

"Not with the King," Busbacca stubbornly insisted. "With Il Bologna - Primaticcio."

"Go and reason with Bologna? Ha!" Benvenuto went silent.

"No, wait a minute. Maybe that is an idea." He patted Busbacca on the arm. "You know, sometimes you're not as stupid as you look."

—⚍—

Benvenuto rode out to Fontainebleau and stopped first at the little workshop the King had provided for his use. He brushed the dust of the road off his clothes, combed his fingers through his beard and, smiling appreciatively at his reflection in the mirror, adjusted the angle of his hat before striding off purposefully in the direction of Primaticcio's quarters.

He lifted his sword a few inches out of its scabbard and let it drop back again to make sure it would slide out again easily, tapped politely on the door of Primaticcio's studio and waited for the man to invite him in. The painter rose to his feet, and with his hands held out, greeted Benvenuto enthusiastically.

"Messer Cellini! What an unexpected pleasure. What business brings you here?"

"Important business," Benvenuto replied curtly.

Primaticcio ignored Benvenuto's coldness and called out to one of his assistants, "Emilio, go and bring some wine for our guest." He turned to Benvenuto, "Messer Cellini before we discuss anything let us have a drink together."

"Messer Primaticcio. What I want to discuss with you doesn't call for drinking beforehand. Perhaps we'll be able to afterwards. And it's private." Benvenuto looked pointedly at the assistant and Primaticcio dismissed him with a flick of his hand. Benvenuto crossed the room and firmly closed the door.

"You have a reputation for being an upright man."

Primaticcio acknowledged the compliment with a little bow as Benvenuto continued,

"It's hard enough to get a reputation like that, and you have to work hard to keep it. It's too easy to lose."

Primaticcio pursed his lips. "What's the point of all this?"

"The point is that the King has commissioned me to design the Colossus - the Mars statue." He tapped his chest. "It took me eighteen months to sell him on the idea and to plan it, all at my own expense, and no one contributed one damn thing to it, before, after or since."

Primaticcio shrugged his shoulders. "So?"

"So what's this I hear about you trying to filch the job from me."

"But Benvenuto," Primaticcio protested, "everyone has to look after himself. If the King has really decided to give me the job, what can you do about it? You're just wasting your time arguing."

"Francesco," Benvenuto said in a carefully assumed moderate voice, "the job is already mine, but I'll tell you what: you make a model and I'll make one. We'll show them to the King together, and if he picks yours in preference to mine, I'll step aside with no argument or fuss. I'll even help you if you like, and we'll still be friends."

"That's extraordinarily generous of you! You believe the job has been given to me, and now you want me to take a ridiculous bet where I can lose it again and you risk nothing, because that's what you've got. Nothing - nothing at all."

"So it's true then. You're trying to get the candlesticks from me as well."

"Not 'as well'. Just the candlesticks. Nobody's said anything about your stupid Colossus. I heard the King has scrapped the idea, and no wonder. It was completely impractical if you want my opinion. Maybe the King has got tired of waiting for the candlesticks."

Primaticcio started to get up from his chair, but Benvenuto held him down with a hand on his shoulder, half drawing his sword.

"I offered you a fair way out. You won't forget that, will you? Now I'll tell you the alternative. If you take on the candlesticks or if you tell the King about this conversation, I'll kill you. So which is it to be, the candlesticks or a ripe old age?"

"Ha! Cellini, you make me laugh. Where do you think you are? Florence? Rome?" Primaticcio tapped his chest. "I'm not some little workman you can terrorise like you did Galland. Oh yes, everyone in Paris knows why he dropped his law suit. You think you're someone special to the King? Let me remind you, I was in his service ten years before you got here. The King put me in charge of the decorations while you were still sitting in prison. And I've got something you haven't."

Benvenuto let go the hilt of his sword which made a hissing, slithering sound as it slipped back into the scabbard.

"What?"

"A good friend. Madame D' Etampes is her name. One word from that lady and you could finish up with no fingers."

"You don't frighten me," Benvenuto retorted. "I've been threatened by real experts."

"So, as neither of us frightens the other, let's be friends anyway." Primaticcio stood up. "Come on, we'll have that drink together now."

Benvenuto made one of his dramatic exits.

"I wouldn't drink your wine. You probably stole it at Holy Communion."

"Well Busbacca, have you got any more brilliant ideas?" Benvenuto snarled.

"I still think it was worthwhile trying," the young man insisted with unusual spirit.

Ascanio gave a little cough. "What about the King?"

"What about him?"

"He hasn't actually told you you've been dismissed. He owes you at least that. Only …."

"Only what?"

"Only watch your tongue. Otherwise ….." Ascanio grasped his throat cocked his head sideways, and stuck his tongue out.

"For Christ's sake shut up! You sound just like Cardinal d'Este."

The Chamberlain, de Villurois, arranged for Benvenuto to attend one of the King's levees in the State Apartments in the Louvre. This time it was not a social occasion, and those having business with the King, waited at one end of the hall until de Villurois brought them to Francis one at a time. Benvenuto was the last.

"My dear Monsieur Cellini," the King was saying, "your customers are your bread and meat, and yet the whole lot of you artists treat us with such arrogance that you'd think you were doing us a favour by taking our money."

The King slumped down in his chair, holding both hands out at arms' length and peering through a circle which he made with his thumbs and forefingers.

Benvenuto puffed his cheeks and slowly let out a long, silent breath. "Holy Mother!" he thought. "These fellows all have exactly the same mannerisms. I wonder if there's some special school where they go to learn what gestures to make when they're kicking someone in the crotch."

"I gave you express orders to make twelve candlesticks, that's all." the King said petulantly. "Two or three years' work at least. I didn't want anything else, but you set your mind on making me a salt cellar, and a colossus, and a bronze doorway, and busts and more things than I can remember. And how much work have you done for other people while you were supposed to be working for me? You don't ever finish anything. How many half-started jobs have you got on at this minute?"

Benvenuto theatrically dropped to one knee.

"Sacred Majesty, how can I answer? Everything you say is true. With all my heart and soul, all I want to do is to serve you. Life is so short that I wanted to give you everything I could create all at once."

The King looked unimpressed.

"The salt cellar was specially commissioned - you gave me the gold for it. As for the doorway - the Nymph - how many times have you honoured me with visits to watch its progress?

The bronze busts were only exercises to test the qualities of local clays. And everything that's been done on the colossus has been at my own expense and for Your Majesty's glory ...."

Benvenuto's voice tailed off as the King lolled back in his chair, interlocked his fingers, twisted his hands and made his knuckles crack loudly.

"Alright," he said wearily, "I've heard what you've had to say; now you listen to me. Carefully." Francis shook a jewelled finger at Benvenuto. "I am not, not, not going to have your Colossus. I don't want it. You may as well finish the salt cellar since I've got a thousand crowns of gold invested in it already, although," he mused with a glance at his Chamberlain, "I'm so short of money, I've been advised to melt it down again. Yes, I do like the doorway, but get it finished, for God's sake!"

Benvenuto winced as the King thumped the arm of his chair with his fist in time with the last few words, but then he lowered his voice.

"Monsieur Cellini, there is one matter where you are absolutely right. You are entitled to learn my intentions about the candlesticks directly from me, not from people who should know better than to gossip about their monarch's business." Another look at de Villurois. "I'm sending Monsieur Primaticcio to Florence for three months. He's been in France for so long that he's out of touch with what your idol, Michelangelo is doing there. As you use his work as your inspiration, he had better do the same. When he gets back, he's going to make some of the candlesticks. How many he makes and how many you make will depend on how fast the pair of you can work."

"But Your Majesty ....," Benvenuto began to protest.

"Silence!" Francis shouted. "I told you to listen. I know all the objections, but you can leave it to me not to approve designs that clash in style or proportion. It's up to you now. Get something finished!"

Benvenuto's whole body sagged in despair and his arms hung loosely at his side.

"What does he know about metal sculpture, Your Majesty?"

"About as much - or as little - as you did when you first came here, I'll wager. But you'll help him with your special method of putting on the silver, won't you?"

The King made a little circle in the air with his raised forefinger. "There is one thing though. I'm going to have some new coins made. You can submit designs for them if you like. Ask Monsieur de Villurois to give you the details. That's only the designs, mind you, not the dies. I don't want crown pieces with more than a crown's worth of gold in them like you did for poor old Pope Clement. No wonder he got poor with you making overweight coins for him!"

At that moment a messenger arrived and diverted attention from Benvenuto's discomfort.

A small boy about eleven years old, dressed in the King's household uniform, went to de Villurois who bent over so that the child could whisper in his ear. The King tilted his head to the side and de Villurois in turn passed on the message.

Francis clapped his hands twice and stood up.

"That's it, my Lords, gentlemen. Our Marshall, Monsieur Blaise de Monluc is here to report on how the war is going. Badly, I fear. Monsieur Cellini, you have my permission to withdraw. Just now I have more need of generals than of goldsmiths."

—⚏—

Benvenuto was too distressed by his interview with the King to want to go back to work right away. He got on his horse and, holding the reins listlessly in his hands, he let it slowly wander where it wanted.

The narrow roadways were like tunnels, and the overhanging upper stories of the buildings often almost shut out the sky. In the gloom, the other hazard that Benvenuto had to avoid were the street signs.

The houses did not have numbers, but hanging boards, either with the name of the owner or with some other fanciful name. They were made of wood, metal, plaster, terra cotta, or ceramic and were often in the shape of animals, saints, musical instruments or household utensils. The streets themselves often took the name of the most prominent sign - hence there are still to be found the Rue du Chat qui Peche - Fishing Cat Road - and Rue de la Harpe.

Those signs which were not placed flat on the wall were attached to metal arms or chains and constantly flapped in the wind. The more an owner tried to get a prominent position for himself, the further he made his sign project out into the road so that the heavier ones sagged down, to the danger of passers-by.

Being tall, Benvenuto always preferred a big horse, so he rode hunched down with his shoulders bowed to prevent the signs from hitting his head.

As usual, the streets were crowded with pedestrians, hawkers, barrows, carts, and the five thousand licensed porters who, for a few coppers, carried goods of every description and the household water supply. Only a few homes had wells - the rest depended on sixteen public fountains. During the day the noise was incredible: the cries of the vendors and the sound of horses, sheep and cattle were mixed with the almost continual ringing of church bells.

Benvenuto's horse stopped when it got caught up in the throngs of people going about their business in a street which ran ankle deep in mud along the side of the River Seine.

This was Wednesday and one of the two busiest market days - the other being Saturday. Two thousand horses had come to Paris loaded with poultry, game and rabbits. There was a wine market that day too. On Saturday there would be a whole herd of horses for sale, while every day there were four bread markets.

Benvenuto leaned down from his saddle, picked two apples from the basket on the shoulder of a pedlar and gave him a small copper coin.

His horse craned his head round and Benvenuto reached out and gave it one of the apples, while he sat there chewing the other and moodily staring out over the water. He flung the core into the stream and watched two ducks squabbling and flapping their wings as they fought over it. Benvenuto mentally urged the green and black mallard on, but it was his mate, a dull-brown feathered bird which won the prize and swam off, leaving the other to poke amongst the floating rubbish for some other morsel.

"Hah! I bet that greedy, ugly one is called Primaticcio," he thought, smiling grimly as he dismounted and began to walk, pulling the horse along by its bridle.

Just where the crowds began to thin out, he felt his sleeve being tugged from behind. He whipped round, his hand flying to his dagger, but he relaxed when he saw it was only a girl, about sixteen years old, with a pale bony face surrounded by straight, lank hair the colour of old damp straw. She wore a long red skirt, a dirty blouse. Her feet were bare despite the cold and the mud and the dirt through which she had to tread.

"Are you looking for someone? Me, perhaps?" she said in a little voice that she was trying to make sound husky.

Benvenuto shook his head.

"Are you sure you don't want to come me with me? I'm very good."

Benvenuto shook his head again. The girl's eyes began to fill with tears. Benvenuto patted her shoulder.

"What's your name?"

"Claude, Your Honour."

"Well I'm sorry, Claude. I just don't feel like it. Some other time I'll come back and look for you. Meanwhile, here, take this." He took a silver **teston** from his purse and pressed it into the girl's grimy hand. "Go on," he said gruffly, "get yourself something to eat."

He swung into the saddle and rode away towards the Petit Nesle.

"Even the horse is better fed than she is," he thought.

By the time he got home his mood of self pity had vanished. The new challenge to his skill made him almost bounce into his living room, which was now the exclusive club room of his Italian workers.

The men rose to their feet politely, and it was left to Ascanio to ask the question.

"What did the he say?"

"You know, next to Busbacca's idea about trying to beg Primaticcio off, talking to the King was probably the most stupid suggestion in the whole history of the world."

"But what did he say?"

"Primataccio's being sent to Florence to learn how to be a sculptor. In three months, if you don't mind. Then it's a race between him and me as to who can make the most candlesticks - except that I've got to teach him at the same time. I'm to finish the Nymph. The Mars Colossus is off - forever."

"And the salt cellar," asked Busbacca.

Benvenuto snorted. "You don't give up do you? Of course I'm going to finish the salt cellar. Even the King himself wouldn't dare stop me. I said to him, 'Sire, I'll finish my masterpiece even if Your Majesty says nay'."

"My God! What did the King say to that?"

Benvenuto felt that a little fantasising was justified to offset the humiliation that he had received from Francis.

Busbacca was impressed. "Gosh! Then what happened?"

"He had my bloody head chopped off. What do you think happened, you stupid oaf?"

Benvenuto sat down and drummed his fingers on the table. "What we've got to do is to finish."

"Finish what, Master?" asked Busbacca.

"God's blood! Can't you keep quiet boy?" Benvenuto snarled. "What we're going to finish is everything. Every damn thing we're working on. The Nymph's all but ready. The French workmen can take it down to Fontainebleau and assemble it. I'll have to be there for that. I'll want scaffolding and screens - I'm not having gawping and peeping while it's going up."

"Next, the Jupiter candlestick is also nearly ready - it's the pedestal that held me up. That's what comes of being a perfectionist. Give the King the most beautiful decorations, and does he appreciate them? No, he complains about the delay.

"Bartolomeo, you'll do the polishing and get rid of the joints. Ascanio will help you, but I also want him and Busbacca to assist any of the workmen to finish all the private jobs. We've got to get some money in from somewhere."

Benvenuto turned to Busbacca and ruffled his hair. "And fatty, since it seems to be your main worry in life, I shall see to the salt cellar myself and when I've finished the enamelling, you can fit all the pieces on the base."

"Excuse me, Master." Ascanio looked worried. "With all respect, you're going to travel to Fontainebleau, a good day's ride each way, to put up the Nymph; you're going to supervise the candlestick, and you've still got the next ones to design. Then it's easy for you to say the workmen have got to finish their commissions, but you'll have to chase them - they won't hurry for me. And the salt cellar. God alone knows how many hours - weeks - of work are left on it. You can't do it all."

"Can't I?" boasted Benvenuto. "I can work like any three men, and what's more, until Primaticcio gets back from Florence, I don't suppose I'll get two hours' sleep a night."

Suddenly remembering that he had not eaten anything for hours except the apple, he walked towards the kitchen, but then faced his men again.

"You've forgotten something. I've also got the Colossus."

It was, naturally, Busbacca who fell into the trap.

"I thought the King doesn't want it."

"Of course he wants it," Benvenuto smiled sweetly. "He just doesn't realise it!"

—⚒—

Francis was the first to see the Nymph after the workmen had finished installing it, and ordered that it should be kept hidden behind its canvas screen until it was ceremonially unveiled.

The King invited the whole Court to Fontainebleau and laid on an elaborate buffet with a troupe of musicians for entertainment. It was only when everyone had eaten and drunk that Francis strode over to the dark blue curtains that had replaced the rough tarpaulin. Clapping his hands for attention, he tugged on a tasselled cord to reveal the sculpture and stood back to listen to the buzz of comment.

As the voices got louder and more excited, the King began to strut up and down, from group to group, accepting their congratulations, while Benvenuto stood discreetly in the background, modestly acknowledging the few people who took any notice of him, and explaining the finer parts of the work to those who troubled to ask him any questions.

The greatest satisfaction he got that afternoon was from the unwilling presence of Madame D'Etampes, who had only come with the rest of Francis' party because there was no way she could avoid it.

At first, she and her personal friends had kept well away from the guests clustered round the Nymph, but when Francis spotted her at the edge of the crowd, he took her by the arm and led her to the front.

"So Madame, how do you like my newest acquisition, now that it's finished? Don't you agree that it's magnificent?"

"I think it's disgusting, Sire."

"Disgusting? What do you find disgusting?"

"Look how she's lying there. I don't mind her nakedness, but the pose. It looks like she has just - as if she has just ...."

Francis roared with laughter. "You're right! Knowing who she is, she probably just has! Cellini is quite a ladies' man." Francis nudged the Duchess with his elbow and whispered in her ear, "They say there's hardly one of his customer's wives he hasn't slept with."

Madame D'Etampes gave a sniff of disdain. "The man's lechery simply shows in his work. And what about that stag she's holding - no, cuddling." She clapped a hand to her mouth. "You don't suppose he means that she ....."

"No I don't," Francis interrupted. "The stag is a sort of symbol. You see its antlers up there? Well, in his language, 'giving horns' to someone means cuckolding him. I dare say he's done it to enough husbands. I don't know if he's just boasting, or whether it's his sense of humour."

"Yes, and you don't realise that the joke's on you," Benvenuto thought to himself.

He furtively glanced at Madame D'Etampes, and as his eye caught hers, he saw her lips tighten into a thin line.

Benvenuto watched in despair while Ascanio counted out the coins from the thin purse that the King's Chamberlain had given him as payment for the Nymph.

Ascanio pointed in turn to each little pile of coins with the feathered end of his quill and ticked each one off on the list in front of him.

"I'm sorry, Master. I've checked it twice. That pile is the wages for the workmen." He cleared his throat. "Excuse me, may I take mine while I'm here?" Without waiting for a reply he picked up four coins and went on with his account.

"Then you have to pay the blacksmith, and you owe that to the carpenter." He indicated two more little piles. "Also the housekeeper. And you borrowed something from the banker, what's his name? Oh it doesn't matter, and if you don't pay him you won't be able to ask him another time."

"So what's left?"

"Here." Ascanio swept up the last few coins and dropped them into Benvenuto's palm.

Benvenuto eyed them with disgust. "Five crowns! Is that all that all I've got for myself for the Nymph? Three years work."

"Well, you had quite a bit on account, didn't you? And you are up to date with your bills, so there should be quite a lot left over when you get paid for the candlestick and the salt cellar."

"We've got to finish the bloody things first," Benvenuto grumbled.

A thought struck him. "I've also got my private jobs and my share of the ones the craftsmen are doing on their own account. Which reminds me, you've been paid for the necklace you made for Madame de Canaples, haven't you."

"I worked very hard for it," Ascanio admitted grudgingly.

"So long as you work for me and use my studio, you know what the custom is. When you've built up a big enough clientele, you can go and start your own business and keep all the profits for yourself. My old master, Meanwhile, ..."

Benvenuto held out his hand and rubbed his thumb and two fingers together. Ascanio reluctantly gave him back his wages.

-44-

The salt cellar and the Jupiter Candlestick were finished at the same time, due to a final spurt of effort when Benvenuto heard that Primaticcio had returned from Florence and was busily preparing his own wax models for several of the Candlesticks.

King Francis never needed an excuse for a celebration, so the completion of two major pieces by Benvenuto, and the chance of witnessing what promised to be a major row between two highly temperamental Italian artists was too good to be missed.

The banquet was to be at Fontainebleau, where the salt cellar was to be displayed and used on this and future State occasions. This would be followed by the unveiling of the Jupiter candlestick and an exhibition of Primaticcio's models in the Great Gallery.

This time, Ascanio, Busbacca and Bartolomeo were also invited as a reward for the work they had done on the salt cellar, and Benvenuto decided that they would all make the forty mile journey to Fontainebleau two days before Francis was due to arrive. When the Court travelled it was in a vast procession, and by getting there in advance, Benvenuto could use the time in his workshop in the Chateau for any last minute finishing touches that were needed to the two pieces.

A cart was brought into the yard of the Petit Nesle; its floor was covered with sacks loosely filled with wood shavings and clean straw was piled on top. Then some blankets were laid over that, and finally the Jupiter, thickly swathed in linen to prevent it getting scratched, was gently placed inside, covered with a tarpaulin and tightly lashed down.

A labourer and Busbacca sat in the open cart with strict instructions not to let the statue jog about, while Bartolomeo nervously rode Benvenuto's horse - the truth was that he was afraid of the huge animal. Ascanio drove the cart with Benvenuto sitting alongside clutching the box which held the salt cellar in both arms, bracing himself against the lurching of the cart by pressing down against the foot board.

By the time they had gone half way, Benvenuto was bruised and sore; his arms and the calves of his legs ached and he wished that he had fixed the salt cellar inside the cart. Determined not to show any weakness before his men, he gritted his teeth and curtly told Ascanio to pay attention to his driving and to see if he could miss at least one pot-hole in ten instead of hitting every one.

With a sigh of relief he called a halt at an inn for their midday meal. The labourer was left outside to guard the cart and a plate of bread and meat and a mug of beer were sent out to him.

After this short break, Benvenuto said, "We'll change round. I'll ride the horse, Bartolomeo can drive the cart, and Ascanio can sit up front and look after the salt cellar."

"What about me, Master?" asked Busbacca. "If we're going to change, where shall I go?"

"God help me!" said Benvenuto. "I don't know. Ask one of the horses. Maybe he'd like to sit in the cart while you take a turn at pulling."

For the twentieth time, Benvenuto got up from his chair, peered out of the workroom door, and decided it was still too early to go to the main building of the Chateau and join the other guests, strolling in the gardens, waiting to be summoned in for the banquet.

He paused in front of the mirror and looked at himself admiringly. Despite being short of money, he had bought another new outfit for the occasion: a crimson shirt with slashed sleeves, matching velvet pantaloons tied off in large frills at the knees showing red stockings, black shoes with silver gilt buckles in the shape of what he claimed were his family's coat of arms.

His hair was carefully combed and his beard trimmed to a fashionable point. He stared at his reflection more closely and prodded at his temple with anxious fingers. There was no doubt about it, grey hair and nothing to show for it! He sighed. Ah well, tonight would see his great triumph. His two masterpieces would astound the whole court; Francis would realise that he had been doing him an injustice; he would be reinstated as the King's leading artist, and the whole of the French aristocracy would flock to his studio, begging him to take on their commissions.

Ascanio broke into his day dream. "Master, I think we should go."

Benvenuto jerked his head, at the salt cellar standing on the table and then at the box that the carpenter had made to hold it: one with sides that were heavily padded with down-filled velvet and which hinged open flat when the lid was removed.

Ascanio lifted up the salt cellar and began, reverently, to set it in the case, when Benvenuto suddenly shouted, "No! Leave it where it is! Francis doesn't deserve the honour of being the first to use it." He pointed his thumb at his chest. "I'm going to. Who's got the salt and pepper?"

Bartolomeo produced two draw-string linen bags that he was supposed to take to the Chateau. Benvenuto lifted the hinged roof of the Temple at the female figure's right hand and poured in the pepper, and then emptied the salt into the galley boat.

"Busbacca, see what food we've got left."

While they were at Fontainebleau, they could have had their meals in the kitchen, but on this occasion Benvenuto had preferred not to. Experience told him that it was better to eat at any of the King's palaces on the day after a banquet, rather than on the day before.

They had bought some ready-cooked meats and pies when they had set out from Paris. In the city there were a large number of master roasters, bakers, and pastry makers. Pastry was a favourite, and food could be bought at any hour day or night, oven-ready or ready-cooked. Every district had delicatessen shops called **cuisines** -kitchens - and you could purchase a single dish, a simple meal, or an elaborate banquet to be served at your home or even cooked there if that was what you preferred. Meat, tarts, pies, stews - anything, were always there to be had. The only limitation on what you could order was the price you wanted to pay.

Busbacca came back from the kitchen carrying five pewter plates, on the top one of which was the last of the beef pie they had eaten for their midday meal. A thin piece of meat was clinging to thick, and by now stale pastry, held in place by some amber coloured jelly. This unappetising scrap had been put outside to feed Benvenuto's dog, but now as Busbacca placed it in front of him, Benvenuto looked at it with feigned relish.

With a flourish, he cut a triangular piece from one corner and delicately sniffed it.

"It could do with a little seasoning, I think."

Ascanio stepped forward to join in the game and rolled the salt cellar towards Benvenuto.

"A little salt, Your Majesty?"

"A soupcon, as we French say." Benvenuto dropped a pinch on the meat.

"And some pepper perhaps, Sire?"

"A grain or two," Benvenuto replied, opening the lid of the Greek Temple. He put some on his wedge of pie and popped it in his mouth with a grimace and began to cough as the salt and pepper combined to burn and tickle his throat. Wiping some tears from his eyes he offered the plate to Ascanio.

"Will your Eminence partake?" he croaked.

"It will be an honour, Your Majesty." He took a little of the pie, added salt and pepper and waited while Benvenuto cut off a piece for Bartolomeo.

"How about Your Grace?"

"With pleasure, Sire"

"What about me?" Busbacca's voice was an indignant squeak.

"If you're the King, and Ascanio's a Cardinal, and Bartolommeo's a Duke, what can I be?"

"You? Well you're so fat, you could be the rest of the Court rolled into one. Here, help yourself." He gave the young man the plate. "Don't eat it all, or even you won't have enough room for the feast."

—⁂—

The banqueting tables were set out in the shape of a letter "E", the upright being reserved for the King and the more important guests. They would enter in procession when the others were seated, and would take their places alongside Francis in accordance with their order of precedence.

For those on the arms of the "E", seating was more haphazard, although those with the greater claims of power and dignity always managed to be in the most favourable position near the top table. That is how Ascanio, Busbacca and Bartolomeo found themselves at the bottom of the remotest sprig.

By the King's command, Benvenuto had a place of honour at the top of the centre arm, which put him within a few feet of Francis. To his disgust, when he got there, he discovered that the King had mischievously put Primaticcio facing him.

Primaticcio bowed, smiled and extending his hand across the table said in Italian, "Good evening, Messer Cellini, I'm looking forward to seeing your great masterpiece."

Benvenuto did not reply and refused to accept the proffered hand which Primaticcio was forced to drop angrily, while Benvenuto pointedly turned to his immediate neighbour on his left and said,

"Good evening, sir. Whom do I have the honour of addressing? I am none other than Benvenuto Cellini," he patted his chest. "I am the guest of honour this evening!"

At that moment the doors at the end of the room were flung open and Francis and his party entered. The guests stood and applauded politely until the King, raised his hand and pointed to Cardinal d'Este who was on his right.

"Before His Eminence says Grace, I would like you all to meet tonight's guest of honour."

Benvenuto half rose to his feet, but hurriedly sat down again, flushing with embarrassment when he saw the King beckoning to his Butler who advanced carrying the salt cellar which he set in front of Francis.

The guests craned their heads to see but for those furthest away it was impossible, and etiquette prevented them from leaving their seats and crowding round.

Again Francis raised his hand. "Patience, my friends. You shall all have a chance to look. Meantime, God be praised that there are men born in our own day who can still create works of art like this."

"Amen," said the Cardinal, with which he crossed himself and gabbled off the Benediction.

—⚘—

Grace over, page boys came in with bowls of scented water. The rules of good manners were just beginning, and the whole company were expected to wash their hands at table.

Fingers were still used in place of forks, and it was the custom to have a napkin placed on the left arm or over the shoulder - in cold weather they might even be warmed first - and in wealthy homes, they would be changed after every course.

Then the food was brought in by long lines of servants.

They kept returning with fresh dishes: mutton, beef, veal, venison, kid, and lamb; platters heaped high with baby chickens, duck, pheasant, partridge, pigeon, woodcock and even turkeys, newly introduced from America; there were also rabbit, wild boar, hare and all kinds of exotic game including heron, lark, plover and teal.

The less than two hundred thousand population of Paris used to consume vast quantities of meat - as many as two hundred bulls, two thousand sheep and seventy thousand or so chickens and pigeons every single day. It was therefore not unusual for perhaps three or four dozen kinds of meat dishes, many of them heavily spiced and flavoured, to be served at a banquet.

When the first course was put in front of the King, he rapped the table for silence.

"I intend to be the first to use my magnificent new salt cellar."

Benvenuto exchanged knowing grins and winks across the room with his men.

"A little salt, Your Majesty?"

As the Cardinal offered the King the salt cellar, Busbacca clapped his hands across his lips, and when the King replied, "And what about Your Eminence?" the young man had to stuff his napkin into his mouth, his eyes bulging and running with tears of laughter, and while his neighbours stared at him in puzzlement, Ascanio and Bartolomeo also had to pretend to have fits of coughing.

Fortunately the noise was hidden in the polite applause from the other guests, and Benvenuto was too busy watching the King's reaction to notice what was going on.

The King pushed the salt cellar on its ivory castors along the table, first to the Queen and then in the direction of the Duchess of Etampes who was sitting a few places away.

"Will Your Grace take some seasoning too?"

"If Your Majesty will excuse me, no thank you. I think that thing is disgusting?"

"First the Nymph and now this. How so, Madame?"

"Look at the poses, Sire, especially the two big figures. They're erotic. Lewd in fact. The man is positively obsessed by sex!"

"What do you think, Monsieur Primaticcio?" the King asked.

"I agree with Her Grace."

The King turned to Benvenuto. "What do you have say to that, Monsieur Cellini."

"The two main figures are based on those by the great Michelangelo at the Medici Tombs - as anyone with the slightest knowledge of art would know." He paused and looked first at the Duchess and then for a moment longer at Primaticcio.

"You know, Sire," he added, "I hear that that idiot Biagio da Cesena, the Pope's Master of Ceremonies, even complained about the nudes in Michelangelo's 'Last Supper'."

"And got himself lampooned in the fresco with a pair of asses ears for his trouble," Cardinal d'Este interjected.

"And are you 'positively obsessed by sex,' as Her Grace says?" asked the King.

"I get my fair share, Your Majesty, but unlike some people ...." Benvenuto subconsciously used the old phrase, and a Tommaso da Prato's face flashed into his mind as he glanced sideways at Madame D'Etampes. "..... I don't confuse quantity with quality. Enthusiasm is alright, but it's no substitute for ecstasy."

The King jabbed the Cardinal in the ribs with his elbow.

"Did you hear that Your Eminence? Your man here is quite right, you know. Sorry, I beg your pardon, you don't know, do you? Well that's your loss." He started to laugh with his head thrown back, and his eyes closed so that he did not see Madame D'Etampes tear off a leg of chicken, and with a gesture whose meaning was unmistakable, viciously bite into it.

—⚭—

The meal was finished at last. The many meat dishes, accompanied by cabbage and beans for those who wanted them, had gone, followed by fresh fruit and jellies and mountains of fraises du bois - the tiny wild strawberries that were, even then a delicacy, all washed down with rather poor local wine from Argento - a surprising piece of meanness on the part of the King who had a cellar full of fine wines from Orleans and Burgundy.

As soon as the servants withdrew, the King who was slightly drunk, nudged the Cardinal again, and put the palms of his hands together as if praying. D'Este took the hint and hastily recited Grace. As soon as he had finished, the King stood up.

"We will now go to the Great Gallery to inspect the sculptures of these gentlemen." He gestured in the direction of Benvenuto and Primaticcio "You will both accompany us. Everyone else too, of course, but don't crowd too close."

The Great Gallery, now known as the Francis I Gallery, which connects the two wings of the Chateau, was the work of Giovanni Battista di Jacopo, nicknamed "Il Rosso" by the Italians.

The Sack of Rome had shattered his world and had left him wandering round central Italy, frightened and argumentative and dragging unfinished pieces of work from place to place until he finally settled down in the King's service.

Francis had been impressed by Rosso's drawing of "Mars being disarmed by Cupid," which allegorically depicted Queen Eleanor persuading Francis to make peace with Charles V, and in 1530 he invited the artist to come to Fontainebleau. From 1534 to 1537 he had worked on the Gallery.

Under a carved and gilded ceiling and above a six foot high wainscot of elaborately carved walnut, he created twelve frescoes symbolically telling Francis' life story with exaggerated romantic figures painted in startling and sometimes clashing colours.

Each of these scenes was surrounded by stucco work - fat cherubs and tall, slender half-draped females, and garlands of fruit mixed with strange mythological figures, medallions and masks.

It was this corridor that Francis chose for the exhibition by his two rival artists Benvenuto Cellini and Francesco Primaticcio.

Benvenuto's heart sank when he followed Francis into the Gallery.

Earlier in the day he and his men had carefully placed the Jupiter in a prominent position, but since then, Primaticcio had put his reproductions of antique roman statues in the most favourable places, and had relegated the Candlestick to the back.

The King who had passed through the Gallery earlier in the day, saw at once what had happened and rounded on the infuriated Benvenuto with forefinger upraised,

"Don't say anything," he ordered, "and don't worry."

Benvenuto bit back his protest.

The King and Queen, accompanied by Prince Henry and Catherine de' Medici, and the King's sister and her husband the King of Navarre and Cardinal d'Este inspected Primaticcio's bronzes gleaming dully in the candlelight.

Francis spent no more than a minute in front of each one, and when he reached the last he simply said, "Hum. These are all copies I believe, not original sculptures. Very nicely made. And now Monsieur Cellini, you have your Jupiter finished at long last."

Benvenuto had used the time when Francis was preoccupied with Primaticcio's work to execute his own counter-attack. He had put a candle in the middle of the thunderbolt that the figure was holding, and on his signal, Ascanio lit it with a taper and gave the statue a very gentle push so that it slowly rolled forward on concealed castors over the highly polished wooden floor, and came to rest in the middle of the semicircle of bronzes.

Primaticcio's pieces then seemed to be a frame for Benvenuto's work, while the flickering candle it held made it seem alive as it glided across the floor.

The King winked at Benvenuto. "Whoever tried to do you a bad turn has done you a favour instead," he whispered. He stepped over to get a closer look at the statue and walked round it several times.

"Beautiful, absolutely beautiful. I'm a connoisseur, and I say it's absolutely beautiful."

Madame D'Etampes did not agree. "These bronze sculptures are works of genius. You can't compare them with this modern rubbish!"[1]

"Modern rubbish, Madame? You can complain about 'rubbish' if you like. That's a matter of opinion, which I don't happen to share." He glanced at Benvenuto apologetically. "But to criticise style for being 'modern' is, if you will pardon me, nonsense. Even the oldest antique was modern once."

There was a murmur of approval from the King's party, none of them friends of Madame D'Etampes, as the King rubbed the lesson in.

"I personally like the style. Why, your friend Monsieur Primaticcio here even decorated my bedroom in it. And the Queen's.

Yours too," he added coyly.

"If Cellini's work is so perfect, then why did he have to hide it under a drape? To cover up his mistakes and all the blemishes, I'll wager."

Madame D'Etampes pointed to a strip of white linen draped diagonally around Jupiter's loins.

Benvenuto could not control himself any longer. Angrily, he trundled the statue over until it stood only inches from the Duchess' face.

---

[1] Both the salt cellar and the Jupiter were in the new 'Mannerist' style developed early in the 16th century by young Roman artists, including Giulio Romano, Parmigiano and Rosso himself. It called for elaborate fantasy concentrating on nude, muscular figures often in strange twisted poses.

The subject would either be made obscure or difficult to understand by being pushed into the background or by being swamped with irrelevant figures and rich decorations intended to show off the artist's skills.

Unlike the simple 'High Renaissance' style of sculpture that only needed to be viewed from the front, Mannerist work had to be looked at from all angles.

Considering that the Fontainebleau school of artists were the leading proponents of this style, and that the whole Chateau was full of examples of it, the Duchess' petulant complaint was completely illogical and inconsistent.

"I'll tell you what the veil is for, Your Grace. It's to hide these." He whipped the cloth away. "Probably the finest set of genitals ever sculpted," he announced proudly. "I used my own as a model!"

The Duchess flinched, averted her eyes from the figure and stared at Benvenuto with a look that combined disgust and hatred.

"You loathsome beast! How dare you!"

"My next piece will be Juno. I shall enjoy looking for a model for her!" Benvenuto retorted, but Madame D'Etampes was already stalking out of the Gallery, her pale face flushing in anger and humiliation, while the onlookers broke into laughter.

"Benvenuto, my boy," said the King, "I do believe that you're going to live to regret that little scene."

He grinned, and putting his arm round Cardinal d'Este's shoulder, he led the others out after his mistress, leaving Benvenuto and his helpers alone.

As Francis reached the far end of the Gallery, he called out over his shoulder, "In fact, I think we both might!"

—✤—

Benvenuto had received a satisfactory but not over generous settlement from the King for the salt cellar and the Jupiter. The polite fiction was that commercial matters were of no concern to artists and their patrons, so the price had been negotiated by de Villurois, the King's Chamberlain, and by Cardinal d'Este on behalf of Benvenuto.

I'm sure you deserved more,' d'Este said as he handed over a fat bag of gold, "but His Majesty pointed out that he never really ordered the salt cellar." Benvenuto bristled. "And he did give you the gold to make it with," the Cardinal added hastily.

"He doesn't deny ordering the Jupiter I suppose?"

"No. But he said your labour costs were so high only because you took so long to make it. He, or rather de Villurois also... no never mind, it made no difference."

"De Villurois also what?"

"Well, um, de Villurois said that as you had to carry out experiments while you were making the piece, the King shouldn't have to pay you to learn how to do your work."

"WHAT!" Benvenuto shouted. "I'll murder him!" He turned and started to rush out of the door.

"Stop!" the Cardinal commanded. "At once, do you hear me? Now calm down. I said it made no difference. He was only joking. I shouldn't have told you. I forgot you've got no sense of humour. You've already agreed you got a fair price, haven't you?"

"You said I deserved more," Benvenuto grumbled.

"Of course it could have been more, and I suspect that Madame D'Etampes' influence was at work. And the King is still very hard up. The war, you know. He's only just settled with Charles, and he's still fighting the English."

"I'll tell you something, Your Eminence. The next candlestick is going to cost him a great deal more, or he can get Primaticcio to do it. I won't!"

"You'd better give him that message yourself then," said the Cardinal. "He's already told your friend Provost de Marmagna that he'd let him hang you if he found an artist to replace you."

Benvenuto went pale.

"It's alright," said the Cardinal soothingly. "He was only joking too. At least, I think he was."

-45-

The plans for the Juno candlestick were submitted to Francis, but were not returned approved and no other commissions were received from the Palace.

However, orders did come in from members of the Court, but not enough to keep Benvenuto's large staff of craftsmen busy, so one by one, as they finished whatever they were working on, unless they brought in new jobs of their own, they were dismissed.

Finally he was again only left with Ascanio, Busbacca and Bartolomeo.

The money he had been paid by the King for the salt cellar and the Jupiter was more than he had had in his hand at one time for longer than he could remember.

He sent some to his sister, Cosa, who lived in Florence with her husband and two children. After she left the convent he had made her an allowance despite his irritation at his brother-in-law always being too busy planning to make a fortune on what Benvenuto contemptuously called "get poor quick" schemes, to earn a living for his family.

He still had quite a reasonable amount left, but his plans for it did not include frittering it away on paying non-productive workmen.

———

Benvenuto asked for, and was granted a private audience with Francis, surprisingly quickly because the King was still inconsolable in his grief over the death from the Plague the previous September of his youngest son, Charles. At the age of twenty three he was the fifth of his seven children to have died. Now only the Dauphin, Prince Henry, and Princess Marguerite survived.

The war with England was in its closing stages, and the King was also heavily involved in delicate and seemingly never-ending negotiations to try to bring it to an end.

As if all that was not enough, Francis was seriously ill. In 1539 the King had developed an abscess below his stomach which nearly killed him. After that, at least once a year, it flared up again. It was probably tubercular, but stories began to circulate that it was venereal, and that the husband of one of the King's mistresses, had deliberately got himself infected in a brothel so as to pass the disease on to the King via his wife.

Several months before Benvenuto's audience, Francis had burst a blood vessel in the groin which had turned septic. The doctors again feared for his life, but his remarkable constitution enabled him to recover. His physicians also suspected that his bladder was ulcerated and he was constantly fainting.

—⚋—

When Benvenuto was received by the King, Francis looked pale and haggard. His eyes were bloodshot and his voice, usually deep and resonant, was thin and quivery.

"How are you, Monsieur Cellini? And what have you been doing these past months - apart from wenching. ?"

"I am very well, Sire, and I am glad to see that Your Majesty is recovering his health. If you please, I have brought these to show you."

He produced two objects wrapped in strips of black velvet, and handed them to the King. They were matching silver vases, each with six panels depicting scenes copied from twelve of Primaticcio's frescoes in the Great Gallery. Benvenuto had designed them with Francis in mind as the buyer and as a test of the King's intentions. Francis only gave them a cursory examination before handing them back.

"Quite nice, Monsieur Cellini, but surely these aren't what you wanted to see me about in private. Was there something else?"

"Only a rather tiresome little matter, Your Majesty."

"What?" asked the King suspiciously.

Benvenuto took a deep breath. "Sire, I have come to ask your permission to return to Italy. Only on a short visit of course. I want to look at the sculptures and paintings to get fresh inspiration. There's nothing new here. I must see what the artists in Florence have been doing since I was last there."

His voice trailed off, but the King said nothing.

"You let Primaticcio go - to study sculpting," Benvenuto reminded the King.

Francis still did not reply and Benvenuto desperately played his last card.

"I would be pleased to defer payment of the last seven months' salary which Your Majesty still owes me - until I return, that is."

"Monsieur Cellini, you are a fool. What's worse you take me for one. No, you can't go to Italy - or anywhere else. Take these vases to Paris. I want them gilded."

Without another word, he stalked out of the room.

"Let me understand this," Cardinal d'Este said slowly, "you want me to persuade the King to let you go to Italy on a visit - a temporary visit ....," he stressed, "when I know perfectly well, and so does he, that you have no intention of coming back."

"I haven't said that I won't."

"No, and you'd better not, for the good of your neck as well as my conscience."

"Your Eminence," Benvenuto pleaded, "one day I'm going to die."

The Cardinal crossed himself. "Everyone dies, my son."

"Yes, but I've hardly done anything that I want to yet, and I can't afford to waste any more time."

D'Este seemed to be unconvinced so Benvenuto tried another tack.

"I want to see my sister again, and my nieces. They're the only family I've got left. Surely that's not too much to ask."

The Cardinal reached out to a bowl of fruit and selecting an apple, he polished it on the sleeve of his robe and took a big bite. This gave Benvenuto another idea.

"And to tell you the truth, Your Eminence, the food here is terrible. I want to get a decent meal for once. Some pollo cacciatore perhaps? Or some meat that's not smothered in glop!"

"Some pasta, properly cooked al dente," the Cardinal suggested.

"Yes," Benvenuto said enthusiastically "and some white wine that doesn't taste like dog's sweat or red that's not like vinegar."

"The sort that makes your ears go soft and furry after a few goblets."

"Cheese, Your Eminence. Straccino, Bel Paese, Tallegeo, Polenghi, Provelone. Not that muck that smells like the inside of a cow shed."

The Cardinal closed his eyes and licked his lips.

"You know, Your Eminence, I wouldn't even say no to a plate of polenta."

"Now you are definitely lying," said the Cardinal with a laugh. "Go on, get out. I'll see what I can do for you."

—⁂—

A week later Cardinal d'Este was seated in his usual place at the centre of the long dining table. There was a litter of papers strewn along it. He looked up from the quill pen he was sharpening as Benvenuto was shown into the room.

"I came as soon as I got your message. Your man said it was very urgent, so I didn't stop to clean myself up." Benvenuto looked at his fingers which were stained black from the silver he had been working on.

D'Este waved the apology aside. "It's not important. I wanted to see you right away because I've got some news from the King. Sit down."

The Cardinal rummaged amongst the documents in front of him and gave Benvenuto a piece of parchment folded into four. Benvenuto could feel a thick wax seal inside.

"His Majesty has consented to your going to Italy on a visit. A temporary visit, as you asked. That document is called a passe port, permitting you to leave. It will see you past the most powerful official you are likely to meet, just so long as you don't break any laws or do anything to upset anyone important."

Benvenuto held the document in his hand gingerly and started to open it, but the Cardinal said, "No, you can read it later. Did you hear what I said about 'temporary'?"

Benvenuto nodded.

"If you stay away too long and the King catches you back in France again, it will be treason." The Cardinal stared at Benvenuto for a moment and then his face broke into a smile. "Here, have some wine."

He pushed forwards a tray on which stood a glass decanter and several goblets.

"What are you going to do about your workmen, Benvenuto?"

"There are only three left. Bartolommeo's been here so long, he's more French than Italian. Ascanio's met a French girl - he told me last week he's fallen in love with her. He actually wants to get married, can you imagine?"

"What about his friend, that young lad of yours? The fat one. What's his name?"

"Busbacca?" Benvenuto pinched his nose for a moment before answering. "I'll leave him here with Ascanio. He's a problem."

"What sort of problem?"

"Nothing serious. He just irritates me, that's all. Everything he says or does. It's not really his fault. He's better off with Ascanio, because one day I'll do him an injury. Besides, if I don't take him with me, no one will suspect - um, no one will jump to the conclusion that I'm not coming back, will they?"

"And your house? Your furniture?"

"The house isn't mine. The King just lets me use it. I'll leave it with Ascanio. Anyway, he's just about ready to start up on his own." He gave a little snigger. "And if he's going to be a family man, he can have the furniture as a wedding present."

Benvenuto took a sip of his wine. "Do you know how many times I've had to pick myself up and start again?"

The Cardinal shook his head. Benvenuto held up five fingers.

"Once from Florence when I was a young man. Someone wanted to hang me. I don't even understand why. Once from Rome; once from here the first time when I came and the King ignored me. Rome for a second time all because of the Pope's bastard son Pier Luigi, and now from here again." He punched his hand with his fist. "It's just not fair - I didn't do anything."

"Perhaps the King's illness and the war ….." the Cardinal said.

"No, it's all the fault of that damn woman. All I wanted was to spend the rest of my life working for the King, and she's turned him against me. I'm right back where I started."

Benvenuto sat with his head lowered and biting the knuckle of his middle finger. The Cardinal came round the table and patted him on the shoulder.

"You have endured worse things. God grant an end to it."

D'Este picked up two more letters. They were both sealed and Benvenuto could see that each had a different wax impression.

"These are letters of recommendation. One is from me." He handed it over.

"Thank you, Your Eminence."

"And the other is from …." the Cardinal paused for effect. "The other is from the Dauphine. Catherine de' Medici," he said triumphantly.

"They are both for her cousin, the Duke of Florence. I suppose you are actually going back to Florence. What about somewhere new? A completely fresh start? Venice maybe?" the Cardinal suggested hopefully.

Benvenuto shook his head vigorously.

"Ah well, never mind. Just let me tell you, the King doesn't know about these letters, and he'd better not find out, or we'll all be in trouble. Especially you. Now then," the Cardinal said, "I don't have to remind you how much a Medici's word counts in Florence, do I? Getting the King's daughter-in-law to vouch for you was probably the last thing I'll be able to do for you - except to give you my blessing."

Benvenuto knelt, and he found himself staring with professional interest at the jewelled crucifix which swung forwards and backwards like a pendulum as d'Este leaned over him. He felt the Cardinal impatiently tugging his sleeve to get him to stand up again.

"Go on, you'd better be on your way. Goodbye, my son." He gave a loud sniff. "I don't know what I shall do for aggravation once you've gone."

As he left the room Benvenuto saw d'Este pulling out his handkerchief, and felt his own eyes get hot and moist. Angrily he brushed them with the sleeve of his robe.

"Sloppy sentimental old fool," he muttered.

But it was himself he meant.

—⚜—

"But why can't I come with you, Master?" Busbacca whined.

He and Ascanio were standing in the courtyard of the Petit Nesle watching Benvenuto checking the ropes holding down the load on his pack animal. The air was still fresh as the sun had only just risen, and its warmth had not yet had time to stir up the stench of the streets and of the cattle and the horses.

Benvenuto gave a little sigh and pinched the young man lightly on both flabby cheeks.

"I've already told you, my fat friend, Ascanio needs you here. Besides, I'm in a hurry, and I won't be gone forever."

He saw Ascanio staring at him knowingly over Busbacca's shoulder. Benvenuto stared back and Ascanio quickly looked away.

"I'll be back before you know it," he said, "and if I find you've been idle, I'll kick your backside to make up for every day I've missed." He turned to Ascanio and quickly changed the subject. "Have you got the stock inventory and list of work?"

"Yes."

Benvenuto's head jerked up at the insolent tone of Ascanio's voice and the absence of the courteous word, "master" or "sir". Ascanio flushed and quickly added, "I have them here safely, just as you gave them to me a few minutes ago." He flourished a couple of slim rolls of paper.

"Ah well," Benvenuto said, "It's time for me to be off. I can't waste any more of this daylight."

He solemnly shook hands, first with Ascanio, then with Busbacca and then impulsively embraced them both. Without another word, he jumped into the saddle of his horse; he started out of the courtyard, ducking his head under the arch as he went.

A little way up the street, he glanced backwards. Busbacca was standing in the centre of the roadway with Ascanio's arm round his shoulder.

"Go on, back inside," he shouted. "I haven't been gone a minute yet, and you're slacking already."

He waved his arm in the direction of the house, but he did not look round again to see if they had gone in. He blinked away the tears from his eyes, not daring to wipe them in case the two men were still there.

"That's funny, the sun's very bright for so early in the morning," he excused himself.

Benvenuto did not hurry on his way out of the city.

First he stopped to pay a small bill he owed to a Florentine exile who made his leather presentation boxes. When the man heard Benvenuto was going home he asked him to take some messages for him, and insisted that Benvenuto drank some wine with him while he wrote them out. Before the invention of the post, this was a normal courtesy that a traveller would willingly give.

Then Benvenuto took the slow route out of Paris, to have a last look at some of the places that had become his favourites during his five years there, and also stopping at one of the cuisines to buy his midday meal. It was a beef pie which he put in a shallow basket tied behind his saddle.

"It'll probably be smashed to bits before I get to eat it," he thought.

With all these delays, it was almost ten o'clock before he was a couple of miles along the road south.

There was very little traffic. The farmers had long since brought their produce in to the market and would have to sell it before going home, and most travellers had made an early start on their journeys.

Benvenuto was, therefore, surprised to hear the sound of galloping hooves behind him. Looking round he saw three horsemen and caught the flash of sunlight on metal breastplates and helmets.

"Oh God, no! Not again," he thought. Then with a feeling of relief, he made out the clothes worn by the third of the riders. It was the same burnt-orange tunic that Ascanio had been wearing that morning. The rider half stood in his saddle and waved his hat and Benvenuto caught the sound of his name.

"Messer Cellini! Alto! Stop!"

"What's the matter?" he said when the party caught up. "Who are these soldiers, and what are they doing here?"

Ascanio was panting. He paused for a moment or two to get his breath back.

"I'm so glad I found you. There's been a little mistake, and after I checked with Monsieur de Villurois, he positively insisted, that I brought these men with me in case I needed an escort back to the city."

"What the hell are you talking about? Benvenuto snapped.

"What sort of mistake? And why should you need an escort **back** to Paris? And what's more, what have you got to do with de Villurois?"

"The mistake is that you did not leave behind everything we were working on. I checked with Monsieur de Villurois because you left me in charge and said I was responsible. He confirmed what I thought, and sent me after you so that the King would not get upset." He added in French, "These two gentlemen are here to assist me to take His Majesty's things back to Paris, where they belong. Only as a protection against thieves, you understand."

"No, I don't understand," Benvenuto replied in Italian.

"You must be crazy. What things of the King am I supposed to have?"

"The two silver vases you're finishing."

Benvenuto clenched his fists. "Now I know you've gone mad! They're mine, not the King's. You bloody well know that it's my own silver and that the King didn't commission them."

"Monsieur de Villurois says the King told you to have them gilded for him."

"But he hasn't paid for them."

Ascanio gave a crooked smile. "Never mind, he can settle with you when you get back, can't he?" His voice assumed a brisk commanding air, without any trace of the polite respect of an employee to his master. Again he spoke in French.

"His Majesty's property, Monsieur. Hand it over and you can be on your way. Hurry, I haven't got all day!"

"Why are you doing this to me? How can you be such a bastard?"

"I had a good teacher. Do you think it was right just to abandon me and Busbacca here after all these years? If I am going to be left behind, I might as well be goldsmith to His Majesty instead of taking your place in one of his dungeons. Rescuing his vases ought to get me into his good books for a start, especially if he doesn't have to pay you for them!"

"You stinking, thieving pig," Benvenuto snarled through gritted teeth. Even though he again spoke in Italian, the two soldiers loosened their swords in their scabbards.

"It isn't me who's stealing anything," Ascanio answered insolently. He held out his hand. "The vases, if you please."

Benvenuto twisted in his saddle and undid one of the bags. In it there was the old flute his father had given him, his model see-saw, a velvet sack with the two vases and next to them a loaded pistol. For a moment he hesitated - tempted, but there were three of them and he had only one shot.

He flung the bag to Ascanio, who caught it neatly, one handed.

"May your wife give you the pox, you whore's son."

Ascanio swept his hat off in an ironic salute, wheeled his horse and without another word, galloped away, followed by the two soldiers.

Benvenuto sat watching until they disappeared. Gradually the dust they raised settled, and he got another sight of the rooftops of the city. As he set his two horses trotting off in the direction of Florence, he turned to take his last look at Paris.

He patted his purse which held some gold and gemstones which he had brought for easy transportation of his valuables. He sighed. It wasn't much to show for five years in France.

He had no family, no friends, and no work. At the age of forty-five, all he had accumulated so far in his life was years.

Part VI: The Man on the Pisa Road

-46-

It was late in the afternoon when Benvenuto topped the last rise on the road between Pisa and Florence. Reining in his horse, he looked down on his native city.

The gates had not yet been closed for the night in the walls that Michelangelo had designed and strengthened fifteen years earlier when, as the high-sounding "Governor-General of the Fortifications", and one of the **"Nove della Milizia"** - the Militia Nine - he had taken the wrong side against Pope Clement VII in the ill-fated revolution that was launched against the Medicis in the wake of the Sack of Rome.

Michelangelo saved his life by hiding in a cellar and in the bell tower of the church of San Niccolo by the River Arno until word reached him that he had been forgiven. His lapse was put down to "artistic temperament," although, in truth, the Pope simply did not want to stir up more trouble by punishing a local hero.

As he looked at the battlements, Benvenuto congratulated himself on having stayed out of that war by pretending that he had not received the Pope's command to join the artillery of the relief column, and by running off to work for the Duke of Mantua until the fighting was over.

Still thinking about the past, instead of riding into the city, he turned back towards an inn with the sign of a Bronze Horse that he had passed a little way along the road.

—⚜—

Benvenuto ducked his head as he went through the low doorway of the Inn, and stared disdainfully round the grimy main room with its three long battered tables running in parallel lines down its length and flanked with a mixture of odd, unmatched wooden chairs, benches and backless stools.

He wrinkled his nose at the smell coming from a black-encrusted iron pot which stood in a corner of the wide fireplace in which a huge log fire burned, both to heat the room and to cook the food.

In the corner of the fireplace a lump of charred meat was being turned on the spit by a scruffy girl aged about ten with vacant eyes and a lolling head. As Benvenuto watched, she wiped the dirty sleeve of her blouse across her running nose.

Benvenuto shuddered and looked at the other occupants of the room: three men playing dice at one end of the table near the door gave him the barest glance before resuming their game. One of them threw the dice and cursed loudly; the second laughed and took a gulp from an earthenware mug of ale, while the third gloomily added another cross to a long line of marks on a slate.

Benvenuto remembered that the inn had a very poor reputation. It was too close to Florence for travellers who were leaving the city. They would want to be miles on their way before stopping for rest or refreshment. As it was, the Inn only served those who arrived after the town gates were closed, so that they could not get in until the next morning, and who therefore had to accept whatever the innkeeper offered them.

Benvenuto stood in the doorway waiting for someone to pay him attention. Nobody did, so he slammed the door behind him with a crash that made one of the players drop the dice on the dirty floor, while the girl at the spit cowered in fright.

"Landlord!" he roared, "Where in God's name are you?"

A door opened and the innkeeper came out from a side room, followed by a serving girl. Short, bandy-legged with a flattened nose and a fringe of oily black hair that hung over a pimply forehead until it almost touched the bushy eyebrows framing his close set, small eyes. His belly bulged over the string of a greasy apron on which he wiped his hands before wringing them obsequiously, as he took in Benvenuto's expensive, if travel-stained clothes.

"I'm sorry, er - Your Excellency. It's so early that I wasn't expecting any visitors yet."

"Why not? You're supposed to be ready for guests at any hour of the day or night. This is an Inn, is it not?"

"Yes sir. Of course it is."

"Good. For one moment I thought it was the local pest house. I want my horses fed. I want my baggage brought in, and I want a room for the night - a room all to myself, do you hear?"

The landlord looked dubious. Roadside inns were few and far between, so however many guests arrived had to be crammed in somehow, which meant that several strangers would be using the same room, and might even have to share the same bed.

Benvenuto stamped his foot. "I said, 'do you hear me?' my man. I'm not going to share with anyone - unless I choose to." He flicked a glance at the serving girl who dropped her eyes. Benvenuto pulled a small gold coin from his purse and stood rubbing it between his fingers while the landlord eyed it greedily.

"Why yes. Anything Your Lordship wishes. Naturally I wouldn't expect a gentleman like you to share with anybody." The man pocketed the coin and held out a chair for Benvenuto at the head of the centre table. "Your Excellency desires some refreshment?"

"What have you got?"

"Some soup from the stock pot, and then perhaps ...." He pointed in the direction of the spit.

"I'll have the soup, but I'm not eating that meat. What is it? Roast dog?"

"It's lamb, sir."

Benvenuto snorted with derision. "I've travelled all the way from the Court of the King of France himself. I'm certainly not having that muck for my first meal back in Florence."

"I've got some nice beef, sir"

"Fry it for me then." Benvenuto jerked his thumb at the serving girl. "Tell her to do it. I'm not having the other one slobbering into it. And wine. Have you got any wine?"

"Certainly."

"Trebbelino?" Benvenuto asked hopefully.

"Well no - not exactly."

Benvenuto slapped his forehead. He was now regretting not having gone into the city. "Oh just bring me the best that you've got." The innkeeper thought for a moment. "Now!" Benvenuto shouted. "What's the matter, aren't the grapes ripe yet or something?"

The innkeeper scuttled away, while the girl went to the pantry, picked out a thick steak, laid it on a griddle and put it on the fire, looking coyly at Benvenuto over her shoulder as she did so.

Only two other travellers arrived, obviously worn out from a long journey. They sat for a few minutes nibbling at pieces of the meat from the spit which they speared on the points of their daggers, drank down a mug of wine and then stumbled off in the direction of bed without a word to anyone.

Benvenuto also stood up, stretched his arms and yawned elaborately. "I'm tired. I think I'll go to my room."

The innkeeper clasped his pudgy hands in front of him and gave a little bow. "I'll show you the way, sir."

"Not you. Her."

Benvenuto caught the interplay of the girl's raised eyebrow and a barely perceptible answering nod from the landlord. "Good," he thought, "she's not his wife."

Whatever she got from customers supplemented her meagre wages - after she had given the innkeeper his share, while he, in common with many in his trade, also relied on this additional source of income.

She went over to the fireplace, took a taper and lit a two-branched candelabra. She smiled at Benvenuto archly, and shielding the flames of the candles with the palm of her hands, led the way up the stairs.

In the light of the candles and the glow of the moon through the landing window, Benvenuto could see the girl's figure outlined through her dress.

Somehow it reminded him of something in the past. Something that strangely excited him.

—⚋—

It was just getting light when the sound of the girl getting out of bed and furtively creeping about the room woke Benvenuto up. Through half closed eyes, he saw she was dressing.

He squinted in the direction of the window seat where his belongings were piled. His sword and dagger and belt were arranged in the same pattern as he had set them down the night before, and the feather in his hat was still pointing at the same angle into the bedroom. This was his tried and tested system, developed from long experience on his travels, for checking that his things were not tampered with while he slept.

Benvenuto jumped out of bed and pulled on his drawers, stockings and breeches. He opened his purse. "Look, I don't know when I'll pass this way again, but I'd like you to buy a little remembrance of me. Here, take this."

He pressed a couple of silver coins into her hand. She gave them a disappointed look. Benvenuto was not impressed - she would have put on the same look no matter how much he had given her.

"I'll have to share this with my uncle."

"Your uncle, so that's who he is. Well, I'll tell you what. Here's another two soldi. Don't tell him. Keep them and buy yourself something." Benvenuto continued with the pretence that he and the girl were not bargaining.

"He'll find out," she said petulantly. "He always does."

"Not from me he won't. It'll be our secret." Benvenuto knew what the going rate was and he had no intention of paying more. "Go on," he said, propelling the girl out of the door, "tell your - um, uncle, that I'll be down in a minute, and I'll want my breakfast so I can be on my way."

—⚏—

Benvenuto stood in the courtyard of the inn, leaning against the doorpost, watching the ostler saddling his horses. He held a cold mutton chop in one hand and a mug of beer and an apricot in the other. He sniffed the fresh morning air appreciatively and bit the meat out of the centre of the chop.

The groom straightened his back and touched his forehead with two fingers.

"There you are, sir. They're both ready."

Benvenuto flung the meat bone into the corner of the yard. A thin mongrel came bounding out from behind a heap of rubbish where it had been rooting around, fighting the bluebottles for something to eat, and ran off with it.

Benvenuto mounted his lead horse, and quickly rode off, tossing a copper coin to the groom on his way out of the gate.

When he came into sight of the **Duomo** and the **Campinile,** the River Arno was sparkling bright in the sunlight, with no indication of its normal yellow colour that it showed close up.

He spat out the apricot pip that he had been sucking and then, untying the flap of his saddlebag, he pulled out his flute and experimentally tried a few notes.

He waved the instrument skywards.

"Papa! Can you hear me? I'm on my way home. And yes, I have been practising on my flute while I've been gone. Listen."

He wiped a tear from his eye and rode in through the city gates playing a little tune.

-47-

During his long, solitary journey back from France, Benvenuto had day-dreamed about which city gate he was going to use to make his re-entry into Florence. Despite his flute-playing, he was totally unnoticed by the early morning travellers pushing past each other as two streams of traffic struggled in opposite directions through the same gate, and along the same narrow street.

The **Porta di Giustizia,** the "Gate of Justice", across the Ponte St Niccolo, would have been his best route to his first destination the Santa Croce area. This was the most crowded section of the city, the birthplace of Michelangelo, and the area where the dyers and weavers produced the rich, uniquely coloured cloths that he longed to see again, hanging in the huge drying sheds on the river bank.

But the Porta di Giustizia got its name from being the site of the town scaffold, and Benvenuto had an aversion even to the thought of the gallows, especially as he had had to leave Florence as a young man to avoid being hanged at this very spot.

He conjured up a picture of the many executions he had seen: the condemned man being led from the grim **Bargello** prison, through the Via Proconsolo and up the Via de' Neri, named after the black robed priests who comforted the prisoners on their last journey. Some would be walking as slowly as possible to spin out their final few minutes of life, and some being dragged, screaming and struggling, by a halter around their necks. The procession would continue down the Borgo Santa Croce, through the "Street of the Malcontents" and on to the executioner's noose.

Benvenuto shuddered.

Instead of the Porta Giustizia, he made his way to the Porta Romana, with its view of the Belvedere Fort across a desolate stretch of land. When he drew level with the Pitti Palace, he stopped to stare at the enormous blocks of rough stone, hewn from the quarry behind the building, from which it was constructed.

A hundred years earlier when Luca Pitti, a rich cloth merchant, decided to build a house, he picked a spot outside the crowded, smelly and disease-ridden centre of Florence where the other noblemen lived. It was also away from the Via de' Serragli, the Via Maggio and the Via Guicciardini, which were the fashionable avenues outside the walls.

He deliberately used the giant blocks of stone to impress the local citizens with his importance as a member of the **Signoria** - the Government - and a close confidant of Cosimo de' Medici. The house was financed largely by the bribes he greedily exacted in return for favours done in the Signoria.

"The power! This is where the power is, right here in Florence. And the money too. Benvenuto my boy, this is your last chance. This time you're going to make your fortune, and the sooner you get started, the better."

He dug his heels into his horse's flanks, and rode past the villas and palazzos on the Via Guicciardini, over the Ponte Veccio, and into the city.

—⚜—

Immediately after crossing the river, Benvenuto turned left into the Borgo SS Apostoli, which followed the original twelfth century walls. He was looking for a livery stable and found one close by a tavern curiously called **Purgatorio** - Purgatory.

The stable had a badge outside showing that its owner was a member of the Guild of Carters. This was no guarantee of his absolute honesty, but Benvenuto could be sure that his horses and gear would not be stolen while in the man's care.

The owner was sitting under an awning outside the stable, perched on the edge of a table, with his feet resting on a stool repairing a bridle with saddlers' twine. His tongue jutted from the corner of his mouth as he concentrated on pushing a thick needle part way through the tough leather strap with the aid of a lump of leather tied to the palm of his hand, and then pulling it out the rest of the way with a pair of pliers.

He put the work aside, and rubbing his sweating hands on his shirt, took the reins of Benvenuto's two horses. He gave Benvenuto's expensive clothes a casual glance.

"I want you to take care of my horses."

The stableman walked slowly round the two animals and stood holding the pack horse and stroking the nose of the other.

"You haven't taken much care of them yourself, if I may say so sir. They're both worn out bags of bones."

Benvenuto scratched his ear. "You know, you're right. Do you want to buy them?"

"I'll take them off your hands if you like, but it will take me months of feeding and grooming to get them fit again."

"I don't care if you cut them up for shoe leather. If you want them you'll pay for them. Twenty florins."

The stableman nodded and Benvenuto realised he had not asked enough.

"Each," he added.

"Twenty five the two."

"Thirty," Benvenuto insisted.

Without another word the man went into the building and came out with a bag from which he slowly counted the coins into Benvenuto's hand. He paused at twenty five.

"Thirty," Benvenuto repeated.

Reluctantly the last five crowns were handed over.

"You can look after my luggage and saddle for me. I'll send for them when I find somewhere to stay."

"What name is it then?" The man pulled out a stump of charcoal and a piece of paper.

"Benvenuto Cellini."

"Benvenuto, eh? Well stranger, then you're......"

"Don't say it," Benvenuto warned. "I'll cut the tongue out of the next one who makes that stupid joke."

"What's the surname again?"

"Cellini. Don't you know who I am?"

"Never heard of you. How do you spell it?"

Benvenuto told him over his shoulder as he stamped out of the yard in disgust.

Benvenuto crossed the square in front of the Strozzi Palace and stopped to see what progress had been made in the building. It had been begun in August 1489 - on a precise date selected by an astrologer - and was built in return for forty years of tax exemption and to help to patch up a long standing quarrel with the Medicis.

Fillipo Strozzi the Elder died before the palace reached above the first storey, so did his architect, Benedetto da Maiano. Fillipo's son, Fillipo the Younger, did not live long enough to enjoy the almost completed palace either, for a different reason. When Alessandro de' Medici was murdered in 1537 by his unstable kinsman, Lorenzaccio, Fillipo decided to attack Cosimo, the Duke of Florence, but he was captured and publicly beheaded.

From 1507 to 1533, during the whole of Benvenuto's entire youth and exile, the work came to a complete halt, but then, in the following three years in a burst of activity, it was all but completed.

As a skilled worker in metals Benvenuto nodded in approval of the fine wrought iron and stared upwards at the hooks from which on feast days ornamental drapes or live caged birds hung. On the corners of the building there were lamps which were only allowed by permission of the Government as a sign of honour or rank. The man who had made the lamps, Niccolo Grosso, was nicknamed "Il Caparra". A caparra is a down payment or a deposit and Grosso always refused to work without one.

"That's how I'm going to be too. I'm fed up with having to beg for what's owing to me and always being in debt!" Benvenuto told a pair of startled passers-by, one of whom tapped himself on the temple with his finger as they scuttled out of his path.

―⚭―

Continuing on his way, Benvenuto skirted the edge of the Mercato Veccio - the Old Market, which was the main food market - superstitiously avoiding even looking at the south east corner which housed the **Tabernacolo della Tromba** before which condemned criminals were forced to kneel on their way to execution.

"The whole country is obsessed with hanging!" Benvenuto fingered his throat as he threaded his way past the stalls of onions and garlic and vegetables, past arcades of shops selling spices, meat and cooked dishes and barrows with charcoal braziers from where you could buy hot pies, tarts and herbs fried in butter.

The market place was crowded with farmers, housewives and tradesmen. Everyone was on foot except the more affluent women who were carried in litters for their own safety, since there was also a fair sprinkling of beggars, pick-pockets and snatch-purses.

As usual, there was a deafening hubbub from the haggling between the customers and the shopkeepers, from criers advertising anything from lost property to "help wanted" as well as the news, and from the stall holders themselves with their strange street cries. Sellers of baked pears, for example, which were believed to have medicinal properties, shouted "**Ecco il vero medico**" – "here's the real doctor." Radishes were "devils tears," and the local water melons, "Pistora's fire."

Donatello's **Dovizia**, a running nymph with a cornucopia representing abundance overlooked the square, an act of defiance by the irreverent Florentines, since the custom was that a Saint or Madonna should stand guard over an Italian market.

With a final glance around the square, Benvenuto pushed through the side streets until he found the building he was looking for, his father's old house.

—⁂—

Unlike on his last sight of the house, the stucco was repaired, the walls shutters and doors were neatly painted, the windows clean, the pavement around two sides of the building neatly swept clear of mud and refuse, and there were even little baskets of bright flowers hanging from the eaves. To the side of the door was a blue ceramic tile surmounted by a wrought-iron quill pen. The tile, lettered in white, said "Santino Moraglia - Notary."

"So father, you've got your wish. There's a professional man living in the house at last. Sorry it wasn't Cecchino."

Someone tapped his elbow and Benvenuto looked down to see a little girl in a neat, clean dress, with her hair held tidily in place under a close fitting embroidered linen cap.

Are you looking for the Notary, sir?"

"Why? Are you one? Is that you?" he pointed at the sign.

"Of course not, silly! It's my father. Why are you looking at our house?"

"I knew the people who used to live here."

"That must have been a long time ago. It's been our house for ages. Ever since I was very young."

"And of course you're quite old now."

The girl giggled. "I'm nearly eight Are you a merchant or something?"

"I'm a goldsmith."

"My father says that the goldsmiths are all moving into the New Market. Have you come from there?"

"The New Market, where's that?"

"At the top of the Via Por Santa Maria, right next to the Old Market, where all the building is going on."

"Ah yes, I think I saw it on my way here. Thank you, young lady. Tell me something else, is your father a good Notary?"

"Oh yes, he's very good. My mummy says so."

"Well, tell him he's got a new client. Benvenuto Cellini. I'll have some important work for him to do soon. You can tell him it's because he's got such a polite daughter."... because someone who once lived here would have liked it."

He patted the child's head and made his way back towards the New Market.

Benvenuto did not know what he was going to find when he went to look at the New Market the Duke of Florence was just building for the jewellers and silk merchants. It had been the talk of the goldsmiths in France and those he had met on his way home. A district where they could work near to each other; one place where their customers could easily find them instead of their being scattered about the artists' quarter or mixed up with other trades.

Benvenuto was disappointed. The site was still in the hands of the builders. Only a few of the shops had been finished and they were still unoccupied. The whole area was littered with scaffolding, timber, sand and all kinds of building materials, while the ground was rutted, and treacherous with mud and pot-holes.

"Customers won't come here for ages, but it might be nice to have a brand new workshop, and this is where the business will all be once it's finished," Benvenuto thought.

He walked back across the Via Por Santa Maria towards the cluster of little streets lying between the river, and the end of the Ponte Veccio and the Davazanti Palace. That was where, traditionally, the largest concentration of goldsmiths was to be found.

"At least there'll be a few people round here who I'll remember."

But there weren't. He looked carefully at all the names over the shops without seeing anyone he knew.

He also looked with professional interest at some of the goods on display in windows and waved away the proprietors of a few shops who hurried out to try to persuade him to go inside.

"No wonder they have to go out hunting for business if that's the sort of stuff they're turning out now."

It was not really so much disapproval of the craftsmanship that upset him, but that no one had recognised him.

He shrugged. "Still, how long has it been? Twenty years? It must be more. I expect all the old fellows are dead or retired. Besides, I was only a kid when I left," he consoled himself.

Just then he thought glimpsed a familiar face at a workbench in a shop window opposite. The man lifted his head to speak to someone behind him and Benvenuto got a proper look at him.

He was right! He hurried across the road, pulling his hat down over his eyes and turning up the collar of his cloak He stepped into the shop with his head turned away from the proprietor but the man did not look up.

"Excuse me for just a moment, sir. I must finish this very tricky bit of soldering before the iron gets cold. My assistant will show you anything in the cabinet while you're waiting."

He waved his hand, still without looking up, in the direction of a glass fronted cupboard standing against the wall. In it, was a collection of crucifixes goblets and small pieces of jewellery, the sort of thing that every goldsmith would make during slack periods or while waiting for some time consuming process to finish - for molten metal in a mould to cool for example.

"I'm not interested in them," Benvenuto said disguising his voice. "I came in to find out why, when I scratched the gold shoe buckles you made me, I found lead underneath."

"What's that!" the goldsmith shouted. He jumped up, knocking over his tall stool. "Lead! Who dares say such a thing?"

He stepped across the room to face Benvenuto.

"Who says so?" His voice trailed off as recognition dawned on him. He snatched off Benvenuto's hat and flung it on the floor.

"Benvenuto! It's really you! I don't believe it!"

"Yes, Rafaello, it's me, in person."

The two men began hugging and pummelling each other to the amazement of del Moro's workman.

Del Moro caught his breath again.

"Benvenuto, what are you doing here in Florence? I thought you were settled in Paris for good. How long will you be staying? How did you find me? What's the French court like?"

Benvenuto held up his hand to halt the stream of questions.

"Whoa! All in good time. The answer to the most important question you haven't asked me yet is, 'yes'."

"What question's that?"

"Will I have some wine with you? Yes, I will."

Del Moro lightly hit his forehead in mock despair. "Of course, please excuse me. What must you think?"

He turned to his assistant. "Ignazio! Some wine and glasses. No, my best silver goblets. No, two gold ones from the showcase." He sniffed. "What can I smell? What have we got for lunch?"

"Lasagna verde," Ignazio said.

Del Moro did not live over his shop, but his young assistant did, to guard the stock. The brazier used to melt the metal also served to cook his food, or rather to warm it up, because in this bachelor establishment, del Moro bought their midday meals ready-cooked from one of the many pastry shops, similar to those in Paris.

Lasagna was made then, as now, with minced meat and cheese between layers of pasta. In the sixteenth century it was highly spiced and sweetened to disguise the fact that the meat was quite often "high."

"You know what, Ignazio, you can take charge of the shop. I'm going to spend the afternoon talking to my dear friend"

"A good idea," said Benvenuto. "We don't want to be interrupted by customers, especially ones complaining that their shoe buckles are made from gilded lead."

It was nearly evening by the time that Benvenuto had finished telling del Moro his highly coloured stories of his adventures at the court of Francis I, and del Moro had explained why he had left Rome.

"It's quite simple, really. Gina got married to some cloth merchant who came from Florence. I'm really sorry, but she couldn't wait for you forever."

"I hope she's happy. At least you'll stop nagging me about her from now on."

"Anyway, I sold all my properties and came to Florence.

It's just as easy to be a landlord here as anywhere else, and I do a bit of goldsmithing to keep my hand in. Now, tell me about that salt cellar of yours. That was something we heard about here and I saw some sketches."

Benvenuto stood up and stretched himself. "We'll have to talk about it another time. I must be off. If I don't go now, I won't find my sister's house."

"When will you be back?"

Benvenuto fluttered his hand. "I don't know. Tomorrow or perhaps the day after. As soon as I can. I've got to settle in, make a few contacts, find somewhere to live and work."

"You can share my workshop if you like. I expect you'll want one of the new ones when they're ready, but there's plenty of room here. I spend most of my time making rubbish for other shopkeepers."

Benvenuto nodded. It would be useful to get himself a base in case he had to do some work in a hurry - like making models or samples. Besides it would give him time to look round.

"Thanks. I won't impose on you for too long. Anyway, I wouldn't feel right opening a new workshop if you weren't there to go rushing around buying my furniture for me. I'll see you as soon as I know what I'm doing."

He stepped out of the shop and into the gloom of the late afternoon and set off to look for Cosa's house.

Benvenuto's sister lived with her husband and two daughters in one of the narrow streets running parallel with the south bank of the river.

Nearby the Palazzo Coverelli, the home of one of the Duke of Florence's cavalry officers stood on the corner of the road called Via dei Pizzicotti – "Pincher's Alley," which was named after the habit of some of the residents of playfully pinching any stranger who was foolish enough to venture down there.

"I'd like to see them trying it on me," Benvenuto thought grimly as he walked along the road. He gripped the hilt of his dagger under his cloak, but the street was deserted.

He went down the dark side turning where his sister lived. The roadway had sunk in the middle all along its length like a shallow "V". The depression was filled with refuse and filthy water, so Benvenuto had to walk down one side instead of down the centre and he could only read the names on the houses nearest to him. He hoped he had picked the correct side and that he would not have to make a double journey.

He was lucky. On the fourth house he saw a crude hand-painted sign with his brother-in-law's name. In the centre of the door was a large black ring knocker hanging from the mouth of an iron lion's head. There was a gleam of light from a crack in the door, and another showing from the single ground floor window which was set high above the pavement level so that passers-by could not look in.

Benvenuto rapped on the knocker twice. There was no reply. He knocked again, louder, and this time there was the sound of approaching footsteps.

Benvenuto ducked to one side of the door post and pulled his flute out from the pocket of his cloak.

A small square panel in the door behind a metal grille opened, and a girl peered out of the peep-hole but could not see Benvenuto, who was out of her line of sight.

"Who's there? Is anyone there?"

In reply, Benvenuto played a few notes of an old familiar piece that his father had made him practice every night as a child. A voice came from inside the house.

"Who is it, 'Seppina?"

"It's just a beggar playing on the flute."

"Tell him to go away. No, wait! A flute did you say? Let me see."

Cosa came to the door and called through the grille, "Who is it? What do you want?"

Benvenuto repeated the first few bars of the little tune.

Cosa let out a shriek, "Benvenuto, it's you! Why don't you say something? Quick 'Seppina, undo the bolts. Hurry!"

The door flew open, and his sister rushed forward and enveloped her brother in her arms, alternately kissing him and crying. Benvenuto, did not know what to do except to pat her on the back saying, "There, there, there," whilst he knuckled away the tears from his own eyes with his free hand.

Cosa dried her eyes on her apron, and sniffing loudly, dragged Benvenuto into the house where her husband and other daughter were standing, wondering what all the commotion was about.

"It's him," Cosa shouted. "He's here at last. It's my baby brother, Benvenuto!"

"At forty-six, I'm not such a baby," Benvenuto said gruffly.

Still clutching Benvenuto's arm, Cosa made the introductions. "This is my husband."

A slender grey haired man with watery eyes and a bald patch on the back of his head covered with a grubby skull cap, stepped forward and held out a bony hand.

"My dear brother-in-law. After all these years. I'm glad to meet you."

Benvenuto shook his hand enthusiastically. "Ugo. It is Ugo, isn't it?"

The man nodded. "Brother-in-law, I must tell you how grateful we are for all your help over the years, for all you've done for us...."

Benvenuto silenced him with a wave of his hand. "It would have been my father's wish. It was a pity I couldn't have managed more." He changed the subject. "Tell me, who are these beautiful young ladies?"

The two girls giggled.

"This is my oldest, 'Seppina."

"'Seppina? That's short for Guiseppina, isn't it?" Benvenuto asked.

Cosa nodded. "Yes, after our father. And this is Elisabetta. Named for Mama, may she rest with the angels," said Cosa.

The eight year old 'Seppina had curly hair, round dark brown eyes and dimpled cheeks who gave a little curtsey when Benvenuto playfully pinched her cheek.

"No boys? What's the matter, Ugo? Don't you know the recipe?"

"There were two, but they … they both…. they were only babies. Neither of us was very young when we got married, so we couldn't have any more," Ugo added.

"I'm sorry," Benvenuto said. "It was a foolish joke. I should have remembered from your letters. What's that I can smell?"

Cosa gave a little yelp. "The supper! It'll be burning.

Come on everyone, sit down. It's not what you've been used to, living with Popes and Kings and all," she said, apologetically, "but there's plenty, just like in Mama's house. And you look as if you could do with a good meal. You're so thin. You haven't been back in pris…" Cosa glanced at the children. "You haven't been back in one of those places have you?"

"Certainly not!" Benvenuto was indignant. "A thousand miles on horseback and you'd also be thin."

He playfully poked Cosa in her well padded ribs.

Now I've been looking forward to this for years. A home meal. What are we going to start with? Is that soup I can see?"

—ϖ—

The two girls were washing the supper plates in a wooden bucket of greasy water. It had been used for all sorts of cleaning jobs during the day. In the morning it would be 'Seppina's job to throw it into the street and with Elisabetta draw a fresh bucketful from a nearby public fountain, while Cosa fetched one for drinking.

While Cosa was clearing the table, Ugo fitted stumps of candles into holders in preparation for bed time. Lighting was expensive and inefficient and in any case there were few books, and only limited ways of amusement. Life was also hard and tiring and within three or four hours after dark, any town would be silent and deserted with its population asleep.

Benvenuto was playing with the six year old Elisabetta who was sitting on his knee.

"Please." he begged, I'm still hungry. Can I have a bite of your nose?" He began chomping his teeth together and pushed his face towards the child. "Um Um.Um."

Elisabetta squealed, and pushed him away with her pudgy hands. "If you bite my nose, I'll give yours a bang like this."

Benvenuto's eyes watered as a baby fist cracked the bridge of his nose. "Hum, well I think you'd better get down now. I want to talk to your Mama and Papa. We'll play some more tomorrow."

"Tomorrow?" Ugo asked anxiously. "Er - how long are you planning on staying? We've only got two rooms upstairs and this one down."

"Ugo!" Cosa protested.

Benvenuto held up his hand. "Shush now, Ugo's right. I'm not going to stay - at least not more than one night. I'll sleep on a couple of chairs tonight. Tomorrow I have to start looking for a place of my own. Raffaello del Moro asked me to share with him until I'm settled."

"Settled? Are you staying in Florence long then?"

"Yes, Ugo. I'm staying here for good - or until I've made enough money to retire to my farm."

"What farm?" Cosa asked. "I didn't know you had a farm."

"I didn't, until last week. I've just bought one outside Pisa. I saw it on the way here. I used most of the money I saved in

France. It'll give me an income for a few years, and with what I earn here will keep me for the rest of my life. Then I can spend the rest of my time making what I want for my own pleasure, and not for damn customers with no taste. Even another salt cellar. Or maybe the most magnificent chalice ever seen."

"How are you going to find new customers here in Florence? Who is there left who knows you."

Benvenuto laughed. "You don't know how famous your brother is. Let me show you something." He pulled two letters from his wallet and laid them on the table. "Do you see who they're addressed to?"

Cosa peered over his shoulder and shook her head. She could not read. Education was not wasted on girls.

"The seals are very impressive. What does the writing say, Ugo?"

"They're addressed to His Grace, Cosimo de' Medici, the Duke of Florence."

Cosa was impressed. "Who are they from?"

"That one is from Cardinal d'Este. I made that seal for him. The other is from the next Queen of France, Catherine de' Medici."

Cosa's hand flew to her mouth. "They've both written to the Duke for you?"

"Yes, asking him to take me into his service."

"What about the money you'll need to start up your new studio?" Ugo asked.

"I've got some money I sent to Chigi the banker, which is quite funny really. Did I ever tell you what happened to me with Madonna Porzia when I was a young man?"

"Yes you did," Cosa said firmly, "and I don't want to hear it again, especially in front of my daughters."

"Also," Benvenuto continued, "there's the money I sent ahead for you to hold for me so I didn't have to carry it with me while I was travelling."

This would have been by a "Letter of Credit," an invention of the Florentine bankers, which helped to found the city's wealth.

Benvenuto caught an exchange of worried glances between his sister and her husband.

"What's the matter? Didn't it arrive? It was a thousand ducats." Benvenuto's voice began to rise.

"Ugo's got most of it for you."

"Most of it? What does that mean? How much is 'most of it,' and what's the matter with Ugo? Has he suddenly gone dumb?"

"There's eight hundred left," Ugo said.

Not good, but not as bad as he had feared. Benvenuto raised an eyebrow and waited for an explanation.

"After the money came, I told the Banker to invest it, just like you said. Then I got the chance to use some of it myself for a share in a business deal. It was to finance buying a load of French silk. It would have made a lot of money. I'd have given you your share, of course."

"Of course." Again Benvenuto waited.

"It was a swindle. I lost my money."

"My money, you mean."

"No, mine. I put back two hundred ducats. I sold all the jewellery you gave to Cosa and everything else I could, but I couldn't raise the last two hundred. I still will if you give me time, but I suppose you'll put me in jail," Ugo finished miserably.

Benvenuto shook his head. "No, I won't put you in jail. You're not a thief; you're just a fool."

"I was unlucky," Ugo protested.

"No, someone who's always failing and blaming bad luck instead of himself is a fool, and the worst kind of fool is one who thinks he's a really a genius - with bad luck."

Ugo looked despondent and Benvenuto relented. "Ugo, you're an honest man. You put back as much as you could, and I'm proud of you." He turned to Cosa. "Look, if he'd asked me for a loan I'd have given him one for your sake, and as to paying the rest back, I only hope your Ugo lives as long as it will take him. Don't let's talk about it anymore."

Cosa flung her arms round him and began to cry. Benvenuto pushed her away. "That's enough of that. Let's have another drop of wine while I tell you what I'm going to do next."

He sat down facing Cosa. "Since I went to France, I've been sending you an allowance of four gold crowns a month, haven't I?"

Cosa and Ugo both nodded silently.

"Well, I'll keep on with that until Ugo finally gets lucky." He rolled his eyes upwards. "But there'll be no more lump sums of cash, except I will find some for each of the girls to have a halfway decent dowry, so that they won't …." He stopped.

"So they won't have to marry someone like me," Ugo said.

"I didn't say that. It's so that they'll get a decent start. In any case, isn't it time that an old lady like 'Seppina was married? Who are you waiting for, Madame? The Emperor of China?"

The child simpered. She had not understood what had been going on, but she did have a question that had been bothering her since Benvenuto arrived.

"Uncle, where are our presents? Mama says that you are very rich and would bring us all a lovely present when you got here."

"'Seppina!" her mother expostulated. "Benvenuto," she said apologetically, "I'm sorry. She's only a child. She doesn't mean anything."

"No, she's quite right. I didn't mean to come here empty handed after all these years. I left all my things at the livery stable and I'll collect them tomorrow. I've brought something for everyone from France. But Elisabetta can only have hers if she lets me bite her nose. What about it?"

The girl shook her head.

"Well, I'll have a kiss then." He crouched down and Elisabetta quickly pecked his cheek and then ran and hid behind her mother's skirt.

-48-

Benvenuto had two important tasks to do while waiting to be received by the Duke of Florence.

The first was to find some lodgings, which was easily accomplished since Benvenuto's wants were simple and he expected that he would soon set up his own home again.

The second was to find out something about his intended employer. News and stories were carried around Europe by travellers and usually became garbled as they passed from one mouth to another. Benvenuto decided to get this essential information at first hand from a permanent long term resident of Florence; and who better than one of the officers at Chigi's bank?

What he found out was not very reassuring. Cosimo de' Medici, Cosimo I, Duke of Florence was the great-grandson on his mother's side of Lorenzo the Magnificent.

The senior branch of the House of Medici became extinct when Duke Alessandro, who was the son of Pope Clement VII was murdered by his father's cousin, Lorenzaccio de' Medici. Lorenzaccio had been expelled from Rome because of his drunken habits, which included slashing the heads off antique statues.

In Alessandro, three years his junior, he found a companion who shared his taste for drink, women and transvestism. Nevertheless Lorenzaccio was bitterly jealous of Alessandro's prestige and status, and decided that his own way to power would be to assassinate him and to lead another uprising against the Medici.

Lorenzaccio had a beautiful and impeccably virtuous cousin, Caterina Soderini Ginori, who was totally faithful to her elderly husband. Lorenzaccio persuaded Alessandro that if he could get her to bed, his reputation in Florence as a seducer would be unsurpassable. Then he convinced Alessandro that he had arranged an assignation for him at Lorenzaccio's house on Twelfth Night, which fell on a Saturday, when all the population would be out celebrating and no one would notice where just one lady was going.

Alessandro, believing that even La Ginori could not resist the chance of an affair with the city's ruler, left his bodyguard outside Lorenzaccio's villa soon after dusk on the night of the festival, undressed, and lay on a bed, waiting. But instead of Caterina Ginori, it was Lorenzaccio and a hired assassin named Scoroncolo who came into the darkened room.

Lorenzaccio struck the first blow with a stiletto into Alessandro's belly. When his victim began to scream for his bodyguard, Lorenzaccio thrust his hand into his mouth and had one of his fingers bitten right through to the bone. Then Scoroncolo dashed forward and slashed the Duke's throat. Blood sprayed from his severed jugular vein, spraying both of the murderers who fled from Florence after locking the bedroom door so that the crime was not discovered until the following evening, and then only because the bodyguard complained about having not been released from duty for nearly forty-eight hours.

The Medicis managed to keep the news of the Duke's assassination a secret until the next day, by which time their troops were in control of all strategic positions. Francesco Vettori, the most prominent member of the anti-Medici party, the "Republicans," realising there was no hope of a successful revolution, because other potential leaders were either unprepared or in exile, gave his support to the pro-Medici mayor.

On the Monday, the Inner Council of the Senate met at the Palazzio della Signoria to elect a new Duke.

One group wanted Alessandro's four year old illegitimate son, Guilio, with Cardinal Cibo as Regent. The others, led by the Mayor wanted Cosimo, who, although young - he was only seventeen - and politically inexperienced, was a direct and legitimate descendant of Lorenzo the Magnificent, and with no moral taint.

The Mayor had hopes of using Cosimo as his puppet, and securing his own position by marrying him to one of his daughters.

The argument continued long into the next day until the military forced the issue by throwing their lot in with Cosimo, and that settled the issue, but if the Mayor or Cardinal Cibo or the Captain of the Palace Guard thought that they would be able to manipulate the new Duke to their advantage, they soon discovered that they were mistaken.

He trusted no one except his mother and his Secretary, and not even either of them too much. He generally kept his own counsel and rarely sought outside advice.

Cosimo began his reign by securing the support of the lower classes, and of the many citizens who respected his late father, and last but not least of the Militia.

In July, seven months after his election, and with the help of the Spanish troops of Charles, the Holy Roman Emperor, he defeated the forces of the rebellious Florentine exiles led by Filippo Strozzi the Younger at a skirmish - it could not be called a battle - at Montemurio.

The Republican leaders fell into Cosimo's hands and at once he demonstrated the utter ruthlessness and cruelty with which, throughout his reign, he would deal with his enemies.

The prisoners were first humiliated by being paraded through the streets of Florence in front of jeering crowds. Then he had four of them beheaded each morning in the Piazza della Signoria until, after four days and sixteen executions, even the most blood-thirsty citizens were sickened, and Cosimo, showing an early appreciation of the need not to offend public opinion, "reprieved" the rest by imprisoning them in the dungeons of Volterra and Pisa prisons where most of them died from disease or slow poisoning, or were tortured to death.

Hired murderers were often used by Cosimo to dispose of dissidents, rivals and enemies including leaders of the Republicans who had taken refuge in distant or even foreign cities.

Lorenzaccio, the indirect cause of Cosimo becoming Duke, was relentlessly hunted down and eventually caught in Venice, where he was stabbed to death with a poisoned stiletto.

Cosimo's agents constantly spied on the citizenry and it was not until he had ruled for seventeen years that he gave an amnesty to the surviving Republican supporters, and then only to put an end to the continual festering danger of a new rebellion.

He levied forced loans from the wealthy, but unlike his namesake, the original Duke Cosimo, he actually repaid them, and paid interest on them too.

Cosimo, early in his reign, consolidated his position in Florence by disenfranchising the population and abolishing the Signoria and the influential post of Gonfalioniere. Although he retained some of the city's governing councils, Cosimo, by making himself chairman of them all, ensured that they did not dare to make a decision of which he did not approve.

On the other hand, justice, except for his opponents, was fair. He established a University at Pisa and increased Florence's prosperity by boosting the woollen and silk trades.

As soon as the upheaval of Alessandro's assassination and his own accession to the Dukedom was over, Cosimo set about diminishing the influence of Spain. Despite it having been the principal supporter of the Medicis ever since the war with Francis, he was not prepared to continue to pay the price of making Tuscany nothing more than a satellite of the Holy Roman Empire.

The culmination of Cosimo's career in 1557 would be the conquest of the Republic of Sienna after a bitterly fought war in which three out of four of the inhabitants of the capital city - thirty thousand men women and children - would die. In this war he would defeat Piero Strozzi, the son of his old enemy Filippo who had died in Volterra prison. Piero was by then a

Marshal of France in the service of Francis' son, Henry II, and the fact that Henry was married to his cousin Catherine de' Medici made no difference to Cosimo in the tangled politics of the sixteenth century.

Cosimo's final reward would come when Pope Pius V appointed him to be "Grand Duke of Tuscany" in return for his cynical acquiescence in the torture and execution of one of his protégées by the Roman Inquisition.

―⚏―

This was the man whom Benvenuto had come back to Florence to serve.

His character presented the same paradox as Francis I and many other rulers of the time - on the one hand, despotic and savagely cruel and often merciless to his enemies, while on the other hand he was a generous supporter of the arts. In this respect he was following the traditions of the Medici family. It was as if the many works of art and architecture that they and their contemporaries have given to posterity were to expiate the wrongs they were doing in their lifetimes.

Cosimo moved into the Palazzo della Signoria in 1540. Originally it was called the Palazzo del Popolo - the People's Palace - and was the town hall and the centre of government. At first, the State was ruled by representatives of the craftsmens' guilds, but gradually they were replaced by bankers and members of the newly forming aristocracy - Signori - gentlemen. Thus the building became known as the "Palazzo dei Signori," or "Palazzo della Signoria."

It was not only his home, but also, in common with the practice of every other ruler, it was his administrative office too. The machinery of government was uncomplicated in those days and a ruler would expect to have it closely under his hand at all times, both for reasons of prudence as well as practical convenience.

The Council Chamber had been built by the direction of Savonarola, the religious and political reformer after he expelled Piero de Medici in 1494. It was intended to accommodate five hundred Councillors Two battle scenes were to have been painted on the eastern walls, facing the entrance, the subject of a famous and uncompleted competition between Michelangelo and Leonardo da Vinci.

The Medicis returned to power in 1512 and had no use for such democratic frills as Council Chambers, so they divided the room into two and used part as a barracks and the other half as a tax office.

As a result of the second revolt after the Sack of Rome, the Medicis were briefly expelled - for three years - and the Council Chamber was again used for its original purpose.

When Cosimo came to power, he converted it into an audience chamber. As an impressive and intentionally overawing background against which Cosimo could receive his official visitors, a large podium was specially built at the northern end and in niches there were four statues: Pope Leo X, the murdered Duke Alessandro, Cosimo's father, and one of Cosimo himself.

It was into this room that Benvenuto was ushered when, a week after his return to Florence, he was granted an interview by the Duke.

As he came through the doors, Benvenuto glanced briefly at the scaffolding round the wall fountain that the Architect, Bartolommeo Ammanati was building on the south wall, and then stopped, nonplussed.

He was used to the courts of the Popes and the King of France where there would be throngs of people waiting for a brief word with the ruler, but the room was completely empty except for Cosimo, seated on a high backed chair and his Secretary at a table a few feet away. The usher nudged him with his elbow and hissed, "Go on! Don't keep him waiting."

Benvenuto approached the Duke, uncertain how to greet him. He decided, as he had in the past, that humility was the best tack. He knelt on one knee with head bowed and murmured,

"Your Grace."

Cosimo motioned him to his feet and Benvenuto heard the doors slammed shut behind him, while out of the corner of his eye, he saw the usher standing in front of them with arms folded.

The Duke was a broad, well built man with a long thin neck. The heart shape of his head was accentuated by a short, pointed, curly beard and closely cut hair. Beetling eyebrows and wide bulging eyes gave him a naturally fierce expression. As he turned those almost lidless eyes on him, Benvenuto gave a little inward shiver. He had seen that look before, and the wearers of it had never done him any good.

"So," the Duke growled, "one of Florence's wandering sons has decided to bring his talents back home. I wonder what made you leave in the first place." The Duke glanced again at the letters of introduction that Benvenuto had sent ahead.

"So you are the famous Messer Cellini. Benvenuto Cellini. Well ….."

"Holy Mother!" Benvenuto thought. "Here it comes again."

"….. Benvenuto. Welcome back to Florence."

The Duke gave a loud guffaw. Benvenuto, never an actor, let out an explosive "Ha!" and assumed an open mouthed expression which he hoped resembled amusement.

"Your Grace has made a pun on my name! You will permit me to repeat what you have said to my friends?"

The Duke smoothed down his mustachios and stared at Benvenuto suspiciously for any trace of sarcasm, but all he saw was a guileless, wide-eyed look of seeming innocence.

"I suppose you've had it said to you before."

"I believe my father was responsible for this little joke a few minutes after I was born, but I have not heard it since I was a child." Only a small untruth.

"Hum." The Duke tossed the letters in the direction of his Secretary. One went sliding across the desk and the Secretary slapped it down with the palm of his hand. The other hit the edge of the table and fell to the floor. Cosimo waited until the man had scurried round to retrieve it.

"You are well recommended by our cousin, Catherine de' Medici and by His Eminence Cardinal d'Este of Ferrara."

"They are too kind."

"They probably are," the Duke grunted. "You were in the service of my cousin Giulio - Pope Clement?"

Benvenuto nodded.

"He wasn't too pleased with you I hear."

"He was misled by jealous rivals of mine. We were reconciled before he died."

"And Pope Paul had you in jail for two years, didn't he?"

"Same reason. His son, Pier Luigi, was the cause. When I was in Piacenza on my way home, I met him and he begged my forgiveness."

"Did he now? That doesn't seem like him," Cosimo said disbelievingly. "I'd have thought the Pope was too busy grabbing control of Parma to worry about you, but I'll ask him about it some time."[2]

The Duke continued his interrogation. "Then you went to work for the King of France?"

Benvenuto realised that he could not use the same excuse for a third time, so he remained silent.

"What do you want from me, Messer Cellini?"

"Only one thing. To work for Your Grace for the rest of my days." Benvenuto thought that the speech he had made to Francis would serve him just as well again.

---

[2] Cosimo would never get the chance. The strategic corridor of land from Parma to Piacenza, lying between Lombardy and Emilia had changed hands between the State of Milan and the Holy Roman Empire. In 1545 Pope Paul persuaded the Emperor, Charles V, to give the territory to his son, Pier Luigi and to create a new Duchy for him, but Pier Luigi showed himself to be so unreliable and potentially treacherous to the cause of the Holy Roman Empire that the Spaniards had him assassinated in September 1547. Benvenuto, when he heard of the killing ascribed it to, 'God inflicting punishment on a great Lord who made a mockery of justice by wronging the innocent.' Himself in particular.

"You want me to employ you as a goldsmith? Are you going to make me a salt cellar, like the one you made for Francis?"

"If it pleases you to employ me as a goldsmith, then that is how I shall serve you, but I also hope to be allowed to work as a sculptor. I made some pieces for Francis in bronze too, you know. But no, Your Grace, I won't make a salt cellar for you."

The Duke's eyebrows shot upwards.

"No, Your Grace, I am thinking of a Chalice."

"What sort of Chalice?"

"If you will excuse me, I've only recently begun to think about it. I spent two years planning the Salt Cellar before I even put pen to paper." Benvenuto neglected to mention that he had designed the salt cellar in his mind in his cell in Sant' Angelo to preserve his sanity. The Duke was impressed.

"Well, let's hope you won't take as long with my chalice."

"My chalice," Benvenuto thought. "He's commissioned it already."

"Messer Grifoni," Cosimo turned to his secretary. Ugolini Grifoni was no mere clerk. He was a nobleman and a Knight Commander of the charitable order of the Altopascio whose headquarters were in his Palazzo home. "Messer Grifoni," Cosimo said again, "make a note of this: Messer Cellini is to be paid a yearly allowance of ...." he thought for a moment, ".....six hundred crowns."

"If you please, Your Grace, King Francis paid me seven hundred."

"Six hundred," the Duke repeated, "and the rent of a studio. He will be paid a fair price for all work he does for me."

The Duke shook his forefinger at Benvenuto. "Now look Messer Cellini, I know all about your habits. Messer Grifoni, write this down too. You will have a fixed date to finish every commission and you'll pay a forfeit for every day's delay. If you take too long, you'll owe me money. What's more, you will not take any work from anyone without my permission, and if I give it, it will be on condition that my work comes first. Is that clear?"

Benvenuto nodded.

"And agreed?"

"Does Your Grace really mean that I have to trouble you when someone just wants me to make a bangle?"

"Of course not me personally. I decided to employ you as soon as I read your letters of recommendation. I've arranged for someone to represent me in dealing with you. He made this for me."

The Duke swept his arm in an arc, pointing to the elaborate podium behind him. "I'll introduce you to him."

The Duke pointed snapped his fingers at the usher who went out, returning after a minute followed by a tall, slightly stooped man with short curly hair, whose long nose with backward flaring nostrils and deep set almond shaped eyes and double forked beard gave him an almost satanic appearance.

He was wearing a plain dark blue robe with a wide collar and a simple belt. His only piece of jewellery was a heavy red gold chain from which was suspended a flat gold scallop shell superimposed with a crucifix enamelled in orange.

The man bowed to the Duke and then turned to Benvenuto with a mocking smile.

Benvenuto felt a surge of horror and dismay when he saw who it was.

"God! I wanted to start with a clean sheet and the swine has put me in the hands of a ready-made enemy. I'm in trouble before I even start!"

"Messer Cellini," the Duke said, "I believe that you and Baccio Bandinelli know each other already. Was he not chief architect and an artistic adviser to my cousin Pope Clement when you were in his service?"

"In fact, I met Benvenuto when he was apprenticed tomy father," Bandinelli said patronisingly "I was already a fully fledged craftsman myself."

"You gave up goldsmithing because it is harder than painting and sculpting," Benvenuto retorted tartly.

"I say, do you remember when you made those overweight doubloons for Pope Clement?" Bandinelli asked sweetly, as if recalling some boyhood prank.

"I remember there were thieves at the mint who used all sorts of tricks to steal gold and to blame anyone they could - especially me. I caught one of them myself. Caesari Macherone. He got hanged, but they never found out who put him up to it, did they?"

Bandinelli flushed angrily, and the Duke's eyes flashed at the prospect of a long running clash of temperament.

"Gentlemen! Gentlemen! Enough of your reminiscences. You can chat over old times later. What we're here to discuss is Messer Cellini's first commission. What is it to be?"

"Your Grace," Benvenuto interjected quickly, "as I've said, I will gladly do whatever goldsmiths' or jewellers' work you command, but I hope I may be offered some sculpting in bronze too."

"What have you got in mind?"

"Your Grace earned the reputation as a warrior by your victory over the Strozzis at Montemurio." Some of the information that Benvenuto had got from his banker had come in useful already.

"And in the tradition of your illustrious family, you are a benefactor of all the arts and sciences."

"So?" The Duke turned his head, and unseen by Benvenuto, and winked at Bandinelli.

"For someone as great as Your Grace, I have in mind a truly great statue - a giant Mars surrounded by four life-size figures representing the ...."

"That sounds like the Colossus you tried to sell to King Francis," Bandinelli interrupted.

Benvenuto looked puzzled.

"Primaticcio came here on a visit from France, remember?" the Duke explained. "He told us everything that was going on in the French court. Now just you listen, if it wasn't good enough for Francis, it damn well isn't god enough for me either. I don't want a colossus, not now, not ever."

"If Your Grace says so."

"I do." The Duke tapped his teeth with his finger tips. "I'll tell you what, though. When you're well settled in, I'll sit for you to do a bust. Meantime, I expect we'll also find you some small jobs to get you started."

"What about the chalice?"

"It's just as well you didn't suggest another salt cellar, or you'd have been on your way back to Paris. You can design a chalice if you want to, but in your own time. If I like it, I might - I say 'might' - commission it, but I don't even want you to mention it to me for at least another two years. Bandinelli has told me all about your habit of nagging."

Benvenuto shrugged and waited. Obviously there was more to come. The Duke got out of his chair and began pacing up and down, with one upraised finger making little circles in the air above his head.

"I'll tell you something. I do have an idea about a large - um, a largish - statue which I may tell you about one day. On a mythological theme."

"Capricorn? Your Grace's personal symbol?"

"I said I'll tell you in my own good time."

The Duke's Secretary gave a little cough. "The agreement, Your Grace. It will be ready in a week."

"Is that satisfactory, Messer Cellini?"

"Yes, Your Grace. Perhaps Messer Grifoni will send it direct to my notary."

"Your notary? Since when does an artist need a lawyer when dealing with his Prince?"

Benvenuto laid both hands flat on his chest, fingers spread out.

"I don't need a lawyer when dealing with Your Grace, but you have just told me that I will be dealing with others acting on your behalf. I am sure that Messer Grifoni will write everything down properly," Benvenuto gave a little bow in his direction. "Now if my notary confirms that everything is as you and I both understand it, there will be no chance for - er, some people with bad motives to cause problems."

"Who is your notary?"

"Santino Moraglia."

"I know him," Grifoni said. "He's very good."

"He was very well recommended to me." Benvenuto thought about Moraglia's little daughter.

Bandinelli stepped forward and whispered in Cosimo's ear.

"Oh yes, apart from your annual retainer, I'm supposed to pay you for each piece of work."

Benvenuto flinched at the word, "supposed."

The Duke pointed at Bandinelli. "Bandinelli here will represent me. He will do the valuations."

Benvenuto bit back the protest that came to his lips. If it was not Bandinelli, it might be someone equally objectionable. Grudgingly, he said, "Messer Bandinelli is very knowledgeable. His father taught him, and I believe he is an honourable man."

"And anyway," he thought, "I can always find someone to argue with the Duke on my behalf if he tries to cheat me."

Bandinelli gave a little smile. He was going to enjoy having Benvenuto under his thumb.

-49-

"Get yourself settled in as quickly as you can," was the Duke's advice to Benvenuto, but it proved to be far from easy.

The problem began with a quarrel with the Duke's Chief of Staff, a nobleman named Pier Francesco Rizzio who was a relative of Mary Queen of Scots' Foreign Secretary, David Rizzio.

Pier Francesco Rizzio's influence over Duke Cosimo did not come from his famous relation, but from his having been the Duke's boyhood tutor.

Benvenuto's argument with him was about his new house. Being dissatisfied with the contractor whom Rizzio had selected to build his studio and workshop, he simply threw him out, got in his own materials, and finished the job himself with the help of his boyhood friend, Tasso, who was a carpenter and general handyman.

Rizzio did not take a sympathetic view about Benvenuto's self help. "You ordered all this without my authority. I won't allow the Duke's money to be thrown about in this way."

"Is that your last word?"

Rizzio nodded. "It certainly is."

"Good. Then I won't have to hear anything more from you. What a pleasant thought! Tell His Grace I want to see him."

Rizzio did no such thing, and Benvenuto sulked for several days until it became clear that he was not going to get an audience, so, reluctantly, he paid the extra cost himself.

Remembering the trouble that Rizzio's counterpart, Tommaso da Prato, had caused him in Rome, Benvenuto had half a mind to leave Florence. He even went so far as to write a friendly, newsy letter to King Francis, but instead of even a hint that he would be welcome to return, all he got in reply some months later, was a curt note written by Robert de Villurois, demanding an account of all the money that had been paid to him.

That was another door permanently closed.

—⚒—

As well as his argument with Rizzio, there was the endless bickering with Bandinelli, starting with Benvenuto trying to poach builders working on the new Cathedral under Bandinelli's supervision, to help him build his new studio.

Bandinelli had won a commission to sculpt a fine block of marble which had previously been reserved for Michelangelo who had intended to use it for a **"Sampson"** since 1508. Pope Leo X took it away from him, and in 1525 Pope Clement VII gave it to Bandinelli, who did nothing for five years, and then spent the next four on producing the grotesque, muscle-bound pair of figures, **"Hercules and Cacus"** which was set up in the Piazza della Signoria next to Michelangelo's **"David"**. Bandinelli's statue received almost universal criticism from the Florentines - particularly the artists' colony, who, instead of decorating the new piece with sonnets of praise, festooned it with highly critical notes.

Soon after Benvenuto returned to Florence, the Duke asked him for his opinion. Cosimo was looking for some reassurance that all the criticism was unfounded, especially as Hercules was a symbol of Medici rule. He got no comfort from Benvenuto.

"Starting from the top, if you shaved all of Hercules' hair off, there wouldn't be enough head to hold his brain; the face looks more like a lion - or perhaps an ox, and I've never seen a head so badly joined to a neck. He's got shoulders like a packmule's saddle, breasts like a sack of melons, loins like marrows and it's impossible to understand how the legs are joined to the trunk, let alone which one he's standing on. Shall I continue?" Benvenuto asked with relish.

The Duke shook his head. "I can see you're not very keen on it," he said and mischievously went off to tell Bandinelli that Benvenuto had attacked the statue with what he described as "a stream of abuse."

—⁂—

The Duke kept his promise to Benvenuto to employ him as soon as he had fitted out his studio. Nothing of very great importance, but there was a steady flow of minor commissions, coupled with his annual retainer. The rule about taking outside jobs was soon largely ignored. He simply wrote to Grifoni to say:

> "I propose to accept an order from Messer Falconi and will assume this is in order unless I hear from you to the contrary."

Eventually he finally wrote referring to **"various minor orders which will not interfere with my duties to His Grace"**, and accepted whatever work he was offered from members of Cosimo's court, including the Duchess, and rich merchants wanting to be in fashion.

All of this provided Benvenuto with a comfortable income which enabled him to live reasonably, employ a small staff, make an allowance to his sister, and put aside something for his nieces' dowries as well as paying off the mortgage on his farm.

However Benvenuto was far from satisfied because he was not given anything that could enhance his prestige, and particularly no great work in bronze. All the plans and ideas that he submitted to the Duke were totally ignored.

—⁂—

After he had been back in Florence for two years, he fell out with Cosimo's wife, Duchess Eleanora. It was really not his fault, but it happened because he attempted to be on two sides - the Duke's and the Duchess' - at the same time.

When it came to jewellery, the Duchess' acquisitive nature was not always discouraged by her husband, so she became one of Benvenuto's best customers.

The Duchess had set her heart on a string of large pearls that Bernardo Baldini, Cosimo's chief jeweller, had for sale. Benvenuto had early in his new career in Florence given a very low valuation of a diamond that Baldini was offering to the Duke. Cosimo bought it just the same, but relations between Benvenuto and Baldini were poor, to say the least.

Benvenuto was working in the palace when the Duchess showed him the necklace.

"My lady, I don't like pearls at the best of times, but I really don't believe these are worth the price. Six thousand crowns is far too much. They aren't even perfect."

"But I want them," the Duchess said petulantly. "All I ask you to do is to take them to my husband and praise them, even if you have to pretend just a little. I've done enough for you, and I promise it will be worth your while."

Reluctantly, Benvenuto agreed, but the Duke was far from impressed with Benvenuto's obviously half-hearted salesmanship.

"Look here, if you value your reputation as an honest man, you'll tell me the truth."

"If I do, will Your Excellency protect me?"

"Trust me," said the Duke. "Everything you tell me will be in confidence."

"The pearls aren't worth the money. I wouldn't value them at more than a couple of thousand. They're not perfect and they're badly shaped and the colours don't match."

"Then why did you ....?"

"Her Grace made me."

At that moment the Duchess came into the room. "My Lord, I hope you will buy me the pearls. Messer Cellini says they're very beautiful."

"Waste of money," the Duke said.

"What do you mean? Benvenuto says they're a bargain."

"No he doesn't. He says they're too dear and they're faulty. Look, this one's not round, nor is this, and this one's cracked. Even I can see they're no good now that it's been pointed out to me. No, they're not for you."

The Duchess flounced out of the room shooting Benvenuto a malevolent look that even the Duke noticed.

"Don't worry, old chap. She's not like Madame d'Etampes.

She'll forgive you as soon as she wants something. I only wish I'd listened to you over that diamond of Baldini's, too."

Cosimo clapped Benvenuto on the shoulder. "You can never go wrong picking the strongest side, and to show my appreciation, I'll try to find a way to let you spend some of the money you've just saved me."

―❦―

Soon after, Cosimo gave Benvenuto his chance to prove himself as a sculptor. He had been invited to the Palace with other guests to celebrate Shrove Tuesday. Lord Stefano of Palestrina had sent Cosimo a mysterious crate as a gift. A servant levered open the lid, watched by the Duke. He beckoned Benvenuto to join him.

"What do you think it is, Messer Cellini?"

Benvenuto heaved the heavy object upright.

"It's a piece of ancient Greek sculpture. It's really beautiful. I don't ever remember seeing such a perfect statue of a boy. Your Grace, I've got an idea. Let me restore it. I can replace the hands and feet, although it's not really my job to repair statues - there are plenty of botchers here in Florence who can do that, Bandinelli, for example." Benvenuto could not resist a dig in at his rival. "But after that Excellency, I can put a bronze eagle on the same plinth, and you can call it '**Ganymede**'. You know, the cup-bearer to Zeus."

The Duke frowned and scratched his ear for a moment or two, and then nodded slowly.

"Very well, Benvenuto."

"And if Your Grace is pleased with the result, as I know you will be, will you let me ....?"

Cosimo put his fingers to his lips. "Patience," he said. "I suggest you concentrate all your attention on not ruining that statue. But, if it comes out alright, well we shall see."

At a time when famous artists frequently received fabulous sums for a painting or a piece of sculpture, the amount Benvenuto was paid for the Ganymede' was derisory. It was fixed by Bandinelli in revenge for Benvenuto's attack on his "Hercules".

"As Messer Cellini admits, the repairs to the hands and feet of the marble could have been done by any botcher," he said. Obviously the Duke enjoyed stirring up trouble between his artists. "The bronze eagle is quite nice, I suppose, but small. It couldn't have taken long to knock it off. It doesn't do much for the statue though. Now if the whole group had been an original composition and larger ...."

Benvenuto's real reward for his work on restoring the little marble was the long awaited commission to make a bust of Duke Cosimo.

"I won't sit for any sketches," said the Duke. "I'm far too busy. You can come here and do your drawings when I'm working. You can take the measurements in private and you can have three - no, four sittings at the most for your model."

"I regret that Your Grace will have to come to my studio for those. A clay model has to be kept damp and cool, especially as our local clay can be difficult to handle. Donatello had trouble with it a hundred years ago. Did you know that?"

"I'm not interested in technicalities - or history either. Cosimo said testily, "Just tell me how I'll be dressed. Greek? Roman? Modern?"

"It will be Your Excellency's head and torso." Benvenuto chopped his stomach with the edge of his hand. "I will have you in a Roman General's armour."

"Like the Bandinelli statue." The Duke pointed to the statue standing in its niche in the audience chamber.

"Nothing like that thing!" Benvenuto snorted.

The Duke smiled. "We'll have to wait and see, won't we?"

With the help of four burly labourers and two of his own staff, the finished bust had been manhandled from the handcart that had brought it from his studio to the Palazzo della Signoria and then, on a canvas stretcher, up the stairway to the audience chamber on the first floor.

He set the bust on its pedestal in the centre of the room, draped it with a white sheet and waited for Cosimo to return from Mass. It was Sunday, the one day when the Hall would be empty and Benvenuto could have the privacy he had begged the Duke for.

The Duke acknowledged Benvenuto's bow with a curt nod, and without a word, indicated that Benvenuto should remove the cover.

Cosimo stood, arms folded, leaning to his right, his weight all on one leg, and stared at the twice life-size bust for a full minute that, to Benvenuto, seemed endless. Then as the Duke began slowly to walk round the figure, he clumsily tried to fold up the sheet, but finally gave up and rolled it into a ball, crept over to the nearest wall and dropped it to the floor.

When he turned back, the Duke was half crouched down peering up into the rough interior, looking at the discoloured patches of oxide and sniffing the still strong smell of the smelting. The bust was held in place by a thick iron bar, running vertically through it from the pedestal to an octagonal hole in the crown of the head.

The Duke straightened took several steps backwards to get a view from a distance and then came forward again, staring closely.

The head was half turned to its right, and every tendon and crease in the neck was clearly shown. The Roman armour was richly decorated with a winged "Perseus", while the links of the shoulder straps ended in small bearded masks. From under the folds of the cloak peeped some links of chain mail, and the whole of the breast plate was covered with a fine, muslin like-pattern.

The Duke, however, concentrated his attention on the head and face, from the lines between the frowning eyebrows, to the little wisps of hair creeping down the back of the neck.

Cosimo gently ran the back of his hand over the bust's curly beard and touched the wart on his own left cheek that was mirrored in the figure's and then he reached up with his thumb to feel the eyes which, instead of being blank, had been finely moulded to show the iris and pupil.

"There never was a bust like it," he breathed, breaking his silence. He turned to Benvenuto and held out his hand.

"My dear Benvenuto, congratulations! A masterpiece. He's so real."

He bowed deeply to his portrait. "Please excuse us Your Grace, Messer Cellini and I are going to take a glass of wine together."

Cosimo put his arm round Benvenuto's shoulder and led him up the broad, winding staircase to his study.

The Duke's Secretary rose to his feet, but Cosimo waved him down, and crossing to a sideboard poured one goblet of wine for himself and another for Benvenuto. He raised his in a toast.

"To the Maestro."

"To a great Prince," Benvenuto responded. "And let's hope a generous one," he added mentally.

As if he had read Benvenuto's thoughts, Cosimo poured himself another drink and said, "We'll have to find some way to show our appreciation."

"To serve Your Grace is honour enough," Benvenuto replied with conventional politeness, but not convincingly.

"Tsk, tsk, We can't have that. You'll starve to death, or run off to work for someone else. No, we'll have the bust valued and Messer Grifoni here will pay you right away. Bandinelli shall do the valuation." Seeing Benvenuto's crestfallen expression, the Duke patted him on the arm. "Don't worry. I'll tell him to be generous and if you're not satisfied, you can ask Messer Grifoni to get a second opinion. I'll see that Bandinelli knows that too."

Benvenuto would have preferred a valuation by a jury of artists, but this procedure was reserved for major works of art that might had taken years to complete. He spread his hands,

"I trust myself entirely to Your Grace's generosity."

The Duke took Benvenuto over to the window looking down on the square. Immediately beneath them were Michelangelo's "David" and Bandinelli's despised "Hercules and Cacus".

Cosimo pointed to his left to the Loggia dei Lanzi - the open sided Arcade that had got its nickname from Cosimo's bodyguard of Swiss lancers whose barracks were round the corner in the via Lambertesca.

"You know, although everyone now calls this the Palazzo della Signoria, its real name is the Palazzo Vecchio - the Old Palace - it's been standing here so long," the Duke said.

"About two hundred years," Benvenuto said.

"All that time, and the most important square in the city is still an architectural hotchpotch. No one has found a solution. I even asked Michelangelo's opinion."

"What did he suggest?" Benvenuto asked.

"He wanted to knock down all the other buildings and to carry the arches of the Loggia right round the square."

"Wouldn't that have been far too expensive?"

"Prohibitive," the Duke agreed, "and impractical. That's why I'm putting all the statues in the square and in the Loggia into lines. Maybe they will draw attention away from the buildings."

Benvenuto wondered why the Duke was repeating what was common knowledge. As if in answer to the question Cosimo pointed to the most prominent gap in the statues in the Loggia, at the front left hand end.

"I have had it in mind for a very long time to set a large bronze piece just there. Large, but not a Colossus. The roof's not high enough!"

Benvenuto's eyes glistened greedily as the Duke continued, "It's funny you should have put Perseus on the breast-plate of my bust. Do you know the legend about him?"

"Naturally, Your Grace. Any artist worth his salt knows Greek and Roman Mythology by heart. As a matter of fact it was Bandinelli's father who started to teach it to me when I was apprenticed to him, and many a beating I got when I couldn't repeat the stories, word perfect."

"Messer Grifoni, you did not have the advantage of learning about such things, did you?"

The Secretary dutifully shook his head.

"So Benvenuto, tell him the story, but keep it as short as you can."

"Perseus was the son of Jupiter or Jove, the chief of all the Gods. The Greeks called him Zeus. Perseus' mother was Danae, daughter of the King of Argos."

"Go on," said the Duke.

"A soothsayer told Danae's father, that his daughter's son would kill him, so to prevent her from marrying, he locked her in a tower. Jupiter changed himself into a shower of gold and got into the tower. Perseus was the result."

"Then what happened?" Grifoni asked.

"The King tried to kill his daughter and grandson by throwing them into the sea in a chest, but Jupiter rescued them, and the boy was brought up by King Polydectes." Benvenuto paused for effect. "The prophesy came true when Perseus accidentally killed his grandfather with a discus at the Games at Larissa."

"Tell him the most important bit about Perseus," Cosimo said irascibly.

"King Polydectes thought he would improve his chances with Danae if he could get rid of her son, so he sent him off to kill the Gorgon - Medusa."

"What's a Gorgon?" Grifoni asked.

"She was one of three hideous sisters whose hair was made of snakes. If anyone looked into their eyes they turned into stone." said the Duke. "Do stop interrupting, and let him get on with the story."

"Minerva, the Goddess of Wisdom, lent Perseus a polished shield that he used as a mirror so that he didn't have to look at Medusa, so he was able to chop her head off. Does Your Grace know what he did with the head?"

"Oh do get on with it!"

"First of all he rescued Andromeda who was chained to a rock and guarded by a sea monster, and then he used it to turn Polydectes and all his guests at a feast into stone."

"Very good indeed," said the Duke. "I'm impressed. So what do you think of Perseus as a subject?"

Benvenuto began to pace up and down the room, first with one hand clasped in the other behind his back, his head bent forward, and then beating time in the air with both forefingers.

"I see Your Excellency as Perseus, trampling the dead body of Medusa under your feet, just as you have trampled the Strozzis and all your other enemies. Your sword will be in your right hand, ready to defend Florence, while in your left hand you will hold the Medusa's head up high, still dripping with blood, daring any rebels to defy you and suffer the same fate."

The Duke sucked his upper lip. "How can you make dripping blood in bronze?"

"Leave it to me Your Grace, I'll have to think it out. Hanging strips of metal, I suppose."

"I had thought about having the rescue of Andromeda depicted." said the Duke. "What do you think of that?"

"It would be too wide for the space, what with rocks and sea serpents and all. Of course, I would make whatever Your Grace commands," he added hastily, "but you want a tall, slender statue. Perseus at the moment of slaying Medusa is how I see it. The plinth could be so wide." He held his hands about a yard apart. "And say six feet high. Then the statue would be about ten feet high on top, running straight up, like this." He flung one hand up in the air above his head. "I'll tell you what though, we can have a plaque on the base in low relief showing that story."

The Duke nodded which encouraged Benvenuto to continue.

"Then we could have a niche on each side of the pedestal, with a different figure in each. I have plans already for some Greek mythological figures."

The Duke looked at him sharply.

"I assure Your Grace, these are new designs I have been working on since I came back to Florence. Nothing that I prepared for - for anyone else. Your Excellency hinted to me that you were thinking of one of the Fables for a theme."

Benvenuto was lying. What he had in mind were Jupiter, Minerva, Mercury and Danae which he had planned for Francis' candlesticks. So as not to upset Cosimo, he could alter the Jupiter, and add a cherubic infant Perseus to Danae, who was in any case an unidentifiable nondescript female who might have been anyone.

The Duke toyed with a medallion hanging from his neck on a gold chain. On one side was Cosimo's sign of the Zodiac, Capricorn; on the other was the Medici coat of arms. Benvenuto had made it for him.

"Alright, I'm satisfied. The job's yours so long as I approve of the designs." He rubbed his hands together briskly. "Now, let's see. Shall we say that you will produce drawings within a month?"

"Easily, Excellency."

"And a wax model?"

"Another six weeks. A month if it can be a rough one."

"And how long to finish?"

"Oh Your Grace, I can't tell you that until we know exactly what I'm going to make."

"But roughly?" the Duke persisted.

".... and how much money Your Grace allows me for assistants and labourers."

"I'm not going to feed an army of pensioners forever," the Duke grumbled.

Benvenuto shook his head mutely.

"Three or four years, that's all you're going to get." Cosimo turned to the Secretary. "Did you hear all that? Good. Well Messer Grifoni, you can draw up the contract and send it to Cellini's notary. What's his name - Moraglia."

The Duke refilled the goblets and handed one to Grifoni.

"Come on, my friends. It's time for another toast. To Perseus, slaying Medusa. You're sure it won't be him rescuing Andromeda? No? Ah well, poor bitch! **Salute!**"

-50-

The first part of the statue to be finished was the headless, naked corpse of Medusa, sprawled on her back on a deep cushion, horribly contorted in her death agonies, and with twists of metal representing the blood gushing from her neck.

Cosimo, accompanied by the Duchess, and, to Benvenuto's annoyance, Bandinelli, came to see the piece lying on the ground of the work-yard, newly broken out of its mould. It was still stained with burnt clay and the chemicals generated in the casting and pitted with the usual little marks and flaws that would need patient weeks of polishing.

The Duke's party barely glanced at the marble plinth standing in the corner of the yard. It had half-relief female figures crowned and garlanded with fruit and surmounted with ram's heads on each corner, and a skull over each of the domed niches that had been prepared for the supporting statuettes.

Benvenuto had done a token amount of the carving on the marble so as to be able to claim it was his work, but most of it had been done, not by a sculptor, but by a local stone mason.

Cosimo gently prodded the bronze with his toe, and then walked round it slowly. Bandinelli merely stood back, disdainfully looking through half-closed eyes.

"What do you think, Messer Bandinelli?" the Duke asked.

"Ridiculous!"

Benvenuto took an angry step forward, but the Duke pushed him back.

"Explain yourself," Cosimo ordered.

"She's twisted into an impossible position, that's what I mean. Her right arm is flung outwards and hanging down;

that's alright. Her left leg is twisted over her right thigh; I agree that's possible. But look at her left leg: it's bent back at almost a hundred and eighty degrees so that she's clutching her ankle in her left hand. No, It's not ridiculous. It's impossible!"

By now Benvenuto was hopping from one foot to another, almost gibbering with rage.

"Your turn," the Duke invited.

"Your Grace, why did you bring this ignoramus here to torture me? He doesn't know any more about composition than my left shoe. Go and have another look at his 'Hercules' if it hasn't fallen over in the night, if you don't believe me. It's even got muscles in its teeth!"

"Messer Cellini, it's your work we are talking about," the Duke reminded him, mildly.

"The reason she's lying like that is to fit her on top of the plinth. She's convulsing in the throes of death, not lying back waiting to be screwed! And apart from that, if I had her all spread-eagled like this buffoon undoubtedly wants," he pointed at Bandinelli, "anyone passing by in the dark would be just as likely to brain themselves, or poke their eye out on an arm or a leg." He turned to Bandinelli. "You bloody know-nothing fool. If I was as stupid as you are, I wouldn't go parading myself around in front of real artists - I'd hide. Do you hear me?"

"Why not? You're shouting loud enough for them to hear you in the next street."

The Duchess interjected, "I think what Messer Bandinelli is suggesting is that it would be impossible for a woman to lie in that position."

"Oh no?" Benvenuto said rudely. "Well, you'd never know until you tried, would you?"

The Duchess flushed bright red.

"Fabbiana!" Benvenuto called, and a tall, well built girl came out of the kitchen. Benvenuto grabbed her by the wrist.

"This is my housemaid. She was the model for the Medusa. Fabbiana, show them how you posed for me."

"Now?" Fabbiana said.

"No, next Christmas," Benvenuto snapped. "Come on, their Excellencies are waiting."

Reluctantly she began to unlace her blouse.

"Dear God, girl," Benvenuto said wearily, "you don't have to undress. We only want you to show us the position."

"There's no cushion. The ground's hard."

"So is the back of my hand. Just hurry up, will you?"

Fabbiana got down on to the stone flagged floor of the yard, and, with a practised movement of her supple body, adopted the same pose as the statue.

"See, she can stay like that for five or ten minutes at a time. It's not an impossible position, and the only thing that's ridiculous round here is that tombstone chiseller." Benvenuto jerked his thumb in Bandinelli's direction.

The Duke gave a little cough. "I think we'd better be going. We've taken up enough of your time for now. I'll come by in a day or two. Alone."

Benvenuto bowed politely to the Duke and Duchess as, with their escort, they rode out of his yard. Bandinelli was the last to leave. Benvenuto turned his back on him and, half crouching down with his hands on his thighs, waggled his buttocks vulgarly.

The Duke's private visit to Benvenuto's workshop a week later did not begin too well. Leaving his bodyguard outside in the street, he strode across the yard and perfunctorily acknowledged Benvenuto's greeting.

He looked at the two workmen who were engaged in the painstaking work of cleaning the Medusa's torso and filling the tiny pits in the surface before it was polished. It seemed to Cosimo that no progress had been made since he had last been there. He stood slapping his thigh with the palm of his hand.

"Your Grace?"

"I want to know why this job is taking so long."

"Respectfully, Your Excellency, it's not taking long at all. We're doing very well."

"Why can't you go any quicker then?"

"Money Your Grace."

"Money? What money?"

"The money I don't get from Your Grace. You instructed Messer Grifoni to draw up a contract that I would get all the staff and resources I need."

"I know. So?"

"You left it to your Chief of Staff, Pier Francesco Rizzio, to interpret what that means. Do you know how he does it? 'Why do you need another labourer, Messer Cellini? Can't you manage with those you've got?' and 'Isn't building the furnace your job?' 'More money for tools? How quickly you wear them out.' 'Did you really need all that timber? It's so expensive'." Benvenuto mimicked Rizzio's hoarse voice and country accent.

"Is that what he says?" the Duke asked.

"Yes, and Bandinelli's no better."

"What's it got to do with Bandinelli?"

"He's in charge of the Cathedral building. Several times I've asked him to lend me a couple of men for a short time. He always refuses."

"Quite right too. What makes you think that you've got the right to borrow staff from the *Opera del Duomo*, may I ask?"

"No right, Your Excellency, but it's the biggest building company in Florence, and it's often used for other municipal work."

"And you think your sculpture is 'municipal work,' and that you can hold up the construction of the Cathedral?"

"I'm making a statue to beautify the square in front of the Palace of the Ruler. Isn't that municipal? And as to holding up the construction of the Cathedral, they've been building it for nearly two hundred and fifty years, so what difference would it have made? May Your Excellency live forever, but it won't be finished in your lifetime." Benvenuto held up two fingers. "All I asked him for was for two men for half a day to dig that."

He pointed to a pit about twelve feet deep at one side of the yard under a tall, lean-to building.

"What's that for?"

"We're going to lower the mould of the 'Perseus' into it so we can pour the metal. We don't want to lug molten metal up in the air; we pour it down, you know." Benvenuto's tone was far from polite.

The Duke scowled at him.

"Your Grace, we're craftsmen here: sculptors, goldsmiths, metal workers, not labourers. It took us three full days to do what two navvies could have done in as many hours, and we were so stiff afterwards, we couldn't work properly for a week. If Bandinelli had lent me the two men I asked for when he was slack - God alone knows how much time they spend over there doing nothing - I could have got it done for the price of a couple of bottles of wine."

"Alright! You've made your point. I'll speak to Rizzio myself, and Bandinelli too. Now tell me about that thing over there."

"That thing" was the clay model of the "Perseus", in its protective canvas coat. The legs were covered to the knees with about half an inch of wax.

"It looks a little smaller than I thought," the Duke observed.

" Less than an inch. This is the inside of the mould. I've got to allow for the thickness of the metal. You can't tell exactly how much the clay will shrink when you bake it, even though it's strengthened with rags, so I make sure that I get the right dimensions with the wax."

Cosimo had only one question: "How long?"

"Weeks. I can't just slap the wax on. If I'm not careful, I'll have one leg thicker than the other. Then, when the wax is hard, I've got to carve in all the fine details. After that there's the plaster cover for the wax. You've no idea how delicate that bit is. I make the plaster a piece at a time and reinforce it to make sure it doesn't twist as it dries, and I have to check each of those pieces when they are dry to make sure they will make a proper impression on the outer mould and no join marks between each one. The outside clay mould actually needs two separate coats of clay each nearly an inch thick."

"How do you get rid of the wax between the inner and outer moulds?"

"There will be vent holes in the outside wall, and I'll draw it off with a slow fire. If you try to do it too quickly the wax boils and you get lumps left in the mould. Even then, the hollow mould needs baking to get out every drop of moisture. There's no way I can hurry without ruining the whole job."

"Benvenuto, I'll be frank with you...."

Benvenuto was startled. The Duke hardly ever referred to him by his first name.

"..You've said you will make this great statue - nearly six cubits high - all in one piece. I'm told it can't be done."

"By whom? Bandinelli, I suppose. I agree that he couldn't do it. No one else can. Only me."

"Perhaps you'll explain how you'll get this whole twisted mould filled. Other people - not just Bandinelli - have said that it's against all the rules of art, and what's more, you've Medusa's head hanging by the hair from Perseus' upraised left hand. How on earth will you make the metal run up his arm and then down again? The head will never come out."

"Oh yes it will. Perfectly. However, I am making a spare head and hand from the same metal - just in case. But I'll tell you what, if you understood anything about casting bronze, you wouldn't worry about the heads. You'd be anxious about Perseus' right foot - the lowest bit of the statue, seeing that his left leg's bent."

"Don't be insolent. Just explain."

"Excuse me for a moment, Your Grace."

Benvenuto went across the yard and came back in a few moments with a grimy, tattered working drawing. "These are all vent holes." He pointed with a crayon and circled the spots. "When you pour in molten metal, the air inside the mould mixes with the gas coming off the metal and gets trapped in bubbles. I've made a vent everywhere there's a danger of that happening. We'll pour metal until it starts running out of the vents. It won't run far, so the vents will stop themselves up."

"Also," he continued, "metal cools as it falls, and the further it falls, the cooler it becomes." He drew some vertical arrows on the plan. "But because heat rises, the metal is the hottest near the top of the mould, so the top will fill the easiest of all. We will simply keep pouring till it has to run up the arm and then down into Medusa's head."

"Very clever," said the Duke.

"I've just put in more vents and channels than usual, and I've made the vents from earthenware water pipes because they will stand the heat without cracking.

By now the Duke had relaxed. "Fascinating," he said. "When you're ready to pour the metal I'll come and watch."

"I'm sorry, that won't be possible."

"Why not?"

"Because melting the metal takes a long time - days actually - and we won't know exactly when it's going to be ready. It's dangerous too."

"How so?"

"The whole furnace could explode. I'm even making the bricks myself with that special white clay they use in the glass-works, and I'm fitting each one personally and filling in the cracks with more clay. That's another of my secrets."

"You still haven't told me what happens if the mould doesn't fill properly the first time."

"I'll have to do it again - this time in pieces. You won't have to pay me though, because straight after, I'll die of shame!"

"Well, if I can't watch, is there anything I can do to help?"

"Why yes, Your Grace. I could use the two most skilled workers from the bell foundry. They won't come unless you order them to."

"They'll be here," promised the Duke. "Just you say when."

The final steps in casting the "Perseus" began in an atmosphere of almost unbearable tension, and continued through blind panic into near disaster.

The delicate double-shelled clay mould from which the wax had been melted was taken out of the brick drying kiln and suspended by two thick ropes from pulleys set in the roof of the lean-to shed. Slowly and gingerly, little by little, it was winched down into the pit that had been prepared for it.

"Watch it! Watch it!" Benvenuto kept shouting at the two men from the bell foundry who were operating the windlass. "One bump and you'll knock the whole core out of place, and months of work will be wasted. For Christ's sake, be careful!"

The foundrymen looked at each other resignedly. This was their trade, and they did not need what they regarded as an amateur to keep telling them what to do.

Benvenuto peered down and flung up his hand. "Stop! That's far enough."

The mould hung about a foot from the bottom. He leaned over the edge of the hole and manoeuvred the tubes sticking out of the lowest vent holes into the outlet drain pipes that had been laid in the pit.

"That's it. Tie it down."

The figure was counterweighted with blocks of stone weighing over a ton. When Benvenuto was satisfied that everything was secure, he clapped his hands at a pair of labourers from the Cathedral that Bandinelli had reluctantly lent him.

"Right you men. You see that pile of earth there? It goes back down the hole. Put it through the sieve and mix it with that sand. Use the dry earth from near the kiln first - we don't want the clay to get damp again."

Every few inches of earth that went into the hole was rammed down carefully so as not to damage the mould, and every vent hole was joined by a pipe to a drain.

While all that was going on, the fire was lit under the pre-warmed furnace in which blocks of copper and scrap bronze and a little tin had been laid in such a way as to let the flames play through them to melt the metal as quickly as possible.

As soon as the mould had been covered with earth, Benvenuto and the foundrymen frantically set about building brick channels from the mouth of the furnace to the top of the mould. The joints between the bricks were filled with wet clay instead of mortar, and hot coals were spread along the channels to fuse the bricks together so that no metal would escape.

These channels then had to be blown clear of ash with bellows so that the flow of metal would not be impeded and the hemp plugs at the top of the mould were made ready to be removed the instant the metal was poured.

—⚁—

To fire the furnace, Benvenuto used slow-burning logs of pine but the pine's greasy resin began to throw off fumes which mixed with those from the melting metal. What with this, and the intense heat of the fire, and the rushing from one part of the job to another, and the weeks of hard physical labour, Benvenuto suddenly began to feel desperately ill.

His head ached, his eyes smarted, his throat was sore. He hurt everywhere and he was giddy and nauseous, and to cap it all, he began to shake and shiver uncontrollably with a recurrence of the fever that attacked him from time to time. He tried to fight the symptoms but it was no good. One moment he was standing up issuing a stream of orders, and the next he was on his hands and knees, shaking his head, trying to clear it.

"My work's finished. There's nothing more I can do," he groaned to Tasso to whom he had given the job of building foreman. Tasso and del Moro helped him to his feet. "God's taking me off. Why couldn't he let me have just a few more days so that I could see how it came out?"

His eyes glazed, his knees buckled and he pitched forwards. He would have dropped right on top of the mould if Tasso had not grabbed his belt and stopped him. Tasso hoisted Benvenuto across his shoulders, carried him into the house and unceremoniously dumped him on the bed.

"Hey! Fabbiana! Madame Fiore!" he called to the maid and the housekeeper. "Your master's sick. Come and cool him off."

—⚘—

He lay on his bed, semi-conscious for almost four hours. He did not hear a sudden burst of excitement in the work yard outside his window, but it seemed to Benvenuto that someone or something was in the darkened room with him. He looked towards the door through eyes that were bloodshot and sore from the smoke and fumes, and into which drops of sooty sweat were trickling from his forehead because he felt too weak and lethargic to brush them away.

> Then, silhouetted against the light from the door, he made out what it was. It was a gigantic serpent - one that had escaped from Medusa's head! No it wasn't. It was the great snake that he had fought in his delirium when he had had the Plague. It had come back to life to get its revenge. He tried to call for help, but all he could manage from his parched throat was a croak. He groped around for his knife, but it was out of reach.
>
> "No! Tommaso da Prato, not you! You're dead and gone to Hell years ago! Oh God! I'm dying and he's come to carry me off!"
>
> The figure reached out and Benvenuto saw a hand with ink-stained fingers. As he looked, it changed into a skeleton's bony claw.
>
> "Mercy! Mercy! God, kill me if you must, but don't make me spend eternity with him!"
>
> The man grabbed his shoulder and Benvenuto gave another shriek and tried to wriggle out of his grip.
>
> "No! No! Let me go! Please let me go," he sobbed.

Still struggling feebly, he heard the man's voice faintly above the roaring noise in his ears.

"Benvenuto, stop it! It's me, del Moro. You're just having a dream."

Benvenuto relaxed and lay still, panting. "Rafaello? You? For Christ's sake, open the shutters. You look like the Angel of Death in the dark. How long have I been here? What's the matter?"

"You've been asleep for about four hours and what's wrong is that the metal's not melting properly. It's curdling and forming a crust. The smelters say that they've never used a furnace like yours with the fire high up, instead of underneath. They want to put the fire out and break it up."

"What! They'll damage the mould. Quick, help me up. I've got to get out there and see what's happening."

Benvenuto staggered into the yard and shouted at the foundry men,

"What the hell's going on here?"

"*Migliaccio*. The metal's caking."

"You bloody fools! Of course it's caking. You've let the fire die down. It's not hot enough. Are you both mad?"

"The roof was beginning to smoulder," one of the men said sullenly.

The lean-to did not have a proper roof - just strips of thin wood loosely tied together to keep the sun off the workers.

"We tried putting water on it." the other man said.

"And damn near put the fire out, I suppose," Benvenuto snarled.

"We're metal founders not stokers."

"Metal founders? When I tell your master what you've done here, the nearest you'll get to metal working will be shovelling horse shit in the smithy."

Benvenuto turned to Tasso. "Quick! Chuck some more logs on the fire."

"There's hardly any left."

Benvenuto tore at his beard. "Jesus! They've wasted it all. It's never ending!" He snapped his fingers. "I know. Capretta the butcher over the road has got a whole load of seasoned oak he uses for smoking those salamis of his. Tasso, take some men and bring it back. Tell him I'm taking it - don't stand for any argument - just grab it. Rafaello, you go with - I don't want him calling the soldiers. Pay him for it. Find out what he says it's worth and give him double. Go on, all of you. Hurry!"

As the men started through the gate, he shouted, "Stop! Wait! Are you going to bring it back one twig at a time, you loonies? Take the hand cart with you."

—⚏—

Oak burns much more quickly and fiercely than pine or elder or willow which are the soft timbers normally favoured for smelting, so the heat rapidly built up and the metal soon began to move in the furnace again.

"Now you idiots," Benvenuto said to the thoroughly discomfited foundry men, "perhaps you'll take those iron rods and stir the metal, and see if you can avoid falling in. No, on second thoughts, I don't care if you do. It'll serve you right!"

Benvenuto had more and more wood piled on to the furnace until it was roaring with flames. The heat was tremendous, and suddenly Fabbiana came running into the yard screaming,

"The roof! The roof! It's on fire!"

So it was. It had been so hot in the shed that nobody had noticed. Everyone ran outside and some of the workmen started to draw buckets of water from the well to throw over the roof.

"No! No!" Benvenuto shouted. "Use your heads, God blast you! You'll put the furnace out! Get back inside with those long poles some of you, and the rest, jump on the back wall and push that burning stuff off into the yard. Quickly! Before the whole lot caves in"

Spurred on by a series of kicks and blows interlaced with threats and curses it took the men less than five minutes to clear the burning debris.

"Alright, don't just stand there scratching yourselves. Get back to work! Start stirring again, you two. *Dio!* The furnace is nearly out. It's the wind. Put on more wood. How many times have I got to tell you to shift yourselves?"

Suddenly one of the metal workers called to him, "Sir, come and see. It still doesn't seem right."

As an expert, the foundry man could judge the quality of an alloy by its colour. Benvenuto looked at the glowing metal through his fingers to protect him from the heat and the bright glow of the liquid bronze.

"It just needs the rest of the tin. Pick up those sheets of pewter and drop them in. And keep that metal moving."

As he stepped down, Benvenuto felt something small gently hit his face. And then again and again. He stopped in midstride, puzzled. There it was again.

"Oh no! That's all I needed. Now it's beginning to rain. It couldn't have done that before the roof caught fire. If it doesn't put the furnace out, it'll cool the metal. Worse! The crucible can crack!"

He turned his face upwards and shook his fist.

"What are you trying to do to me now? You didn't kill me and I won't let you ruin me! You can't win! I'll beat you yet!"

The onlookers hurriedly crossed themselves at this blasphemy.

"You women, go into the house and bring some carpets. Tasso, get some planks and see if you can rig up some sort of roof."

There was another rush of frenzied activity to cope with this new crisis, but no sooner was it resolved than another one happened.

There was a tremendous flash and crash and for a moment everyone stood transfixed, thinking they had been struck by lightning, but then one of the labourers began rolling on the floor, screaming in agony, his clothes smouldering. He had been splashed with molten metal. The cover of the furnace had blown off.

"It's ready! It's ready!" Benvenuto shouted excitedly, ignoring the injured man who was helped away by the two women.

"Clear the stopper from the mouth of the mould. You, fellow!" He pointed to one of the foundrymen, "I suppose you know how to crack the plugs of the crucible."

"Of course."

"Well here, you and your friend, hold these **mandriani** - iron hooks - in front of the outlets to begin with, only until the metal's running at full flow, otherwise it will spurt out."

When the bronze began to flow into the channels, the older of the two men called out, "Look! I don't think it's running properly."

Benvenuto, who had been anxiously watching the outlets himself had already seen it.

"You're right. The heat must have done something to the tin. Let's have some more pewter."

"It's all gone, and anyway it wouldn't melt quickly enough to do any good."

Without a word, Benvenuto grabbed Tasso and del Moro and hustled them into the house. They came out a few seconds later, followed by Fabbiana and Madame Fiore, all carrying armfuls of pewter plates, dishes and goblets.

Benvenuto tossed the largest pieces into the furnace, and then, picking out a few very thin plates, he threw them into the channels themselves where the heat of the running metal quickly melted them down and the bronze began to flow in a smooth, bubble-free stream.

At last the level of the metal reached the top of the mould, and when the foundry man closed the plug there was only a small amount left in the crucible.

Benvenuto was elated. His calculations had been almost exactly correct. He had carefully weighed the wax used to cover the form and worked out the equivalent weight of bronze needed to fill the same volume.

The two foundry men were the first to jump down to congratulate him, shaking his hand and slapping his back, soon joined by del Moro and Tasso who dragged him round the yard in a wild jig. Benvenuto leaned, exhausted, against the upright posts which held up the pulley beam, clutching his sides and panting.

"Look, it's nearly daylight. We've been at it almost a whole day, non-stop." He ignored his own involuntary four hours rest. "Get some food all of you, and Fabbiana, some cool wine for everyone - me especially."

"I thought you were dying," Tasso jeered.

"No, I was just giving birth. My baby's down there." He pointed to the pit.

His legs felt weak again, and he stumbled back to bed and slept right through until the late afternoon.

-51-

Benvenuto spent the next three days waiting in anxious frustration, first for the bronze to cool completely, and then for the mould to be dug out of the pit.

This in itself was a difficult job because there was only a one foot wide gap between the edge of the mould and the side if the hole. When it got too deep for the labourers to reach down with their long handled shovels, two small boys were employed to squeeze themselves into opposite corners and to scoop the earth-and-sand mixture into buckets which were pulled up to the surface and their contents dumped.

Every time the boys reached another of the drain pipes, they had to stop and climb out while Benvenuto lay on the ground and looked over the edge to see how much metal had run out of the holes. There was surprisingly little.

"Is that good or bad?" Tasso asked.

"Either. The mould could be filled just right, or there could be a blockage or a big air bubble. If there was no spillage at all, then it would be a disaster.

Benvenuto took time off to go to the bell foundry to take a look at the cooling moulds of the five figures that were to fill the niches in the pedestal. These had been cast on the day after the main statue had been poured. Being only a little over two feet high each, they presented no difficulty despite all the intricate detail Benvenuto had put in, even on the backs of the pieces which would not be visible from the front.

He had gone to the foundry only to take his mind off the "Perseus" for a while. A messenger called him back to his workshop just as the bottom of the legs were going to be uncovered. By now the whole massive mould was again held in place by the same two thick ropes which had once more been rigged to the winch and pulleys.

No metal had run out of the bottom-most drain hole. Benvenuto sucked his teeth and shook his head with disappointment.

"I knew it! I knew that lousy foot wouldn't come out. Ah well, it could have been worse. It won't be too hard to make a new piece and solder it on."

Del Moro gave a sympathetic smile and said, "That's fine then."

Benvenuto made a twirling movement in the air with his forefinger to signal the men to haul the piece up, but before they could start, he changed his mind.

"No, leave it where it is. It's too late today; we'll make an early start tomorrow."

He caught the two foundrymen exchanging knowing looks. Puzzled, he shrugged his shoulders and went in for his supper.

—⚒—

Early next morning Tasso went out and brought back four husky porters from among the men waiting to hire themselves out at the Old Market. Benvenuto rubbed his hands together and said, "Good, let's get started."

One of the porters, the biggest, had obviously appointed himself their leader.

"What do you want us to do?"

"You see that windlass and rope? Two of you on one handle, and two on the other. Haul up that thing in there."

"You needed four of us to pull that up? Well, it's your money."

He strolled over to the handle, spat on his hands, and flexing his muscles, made as if to turn it by himself. He gave one heave and went sprawling on the ground as his feet slipped from under him without his having budged the statue even a fraction.

"Christ! What have you got down there?"

"Not as tough as you thought you were, are you?" Benvenuto helped the man to his feet. "There's over two thousand pounds of metal in there. Now, if you'll stop larking about …."

Sand was sprinkled around the winch and the four men bent to the handles and grunted in unison as they started to heave.

The moulding came up as slowly as it had gone down. The two ropes were taut and iron-hard with the weight, and Benvenuto slapped his thigh with his hand in rhythm with the clank of the ratchets while he anxiously watched the large bolts with which the blacksmith had riveted the pulleys to the beam, fearful in case they should give way and send everything crashing back down into the hole again.

As soon as the foot of the mould was clear of the lip of the pit, the two foundrymen lassoed it with a thin strap and guided it over to the side of the hole, while the four men on the winch, in response to Benvenuto's silent hand signal, slackened off the ropes and laid the piece face down on the trestles that the carpenter had made while the bronze was cooling. The new wood groaned with the strain, but held firm.

Benvenuto let out a little sigh of relief. "Fabbiana!" he called, "a little ale for our friends." He turned to the four sweating men. "You can wait over there in case I need you again."

Without being asked, Tasso cut the iron bands that clamped the mould shut.

Benvenuto dramatically picked up some tools and held them up and addressed his helpers.

"This, gentlemen, is a mallet and this is a chisel. Soon we shall be the first to see if His Illustrious Excellency is going to get his money's worth."

A voice boomed out from behind his back. "Well, what are you waiting for? A fanfare of trumpets?"

Benvenuto swung round. It was Duke Cosimo and the Duchess. Behind them was the Duke's Chief of Staff, Rizzio.

They had come in through the gate of the yard while he had been clowning around.

Benvenuto gave a deep bow. "Your Graces. What a pleasant surprise." His tone of voice made it clear that it was anything but.

"Thank you Messer Cellini. I believe you were saying something about seeing if I was going to get my money's worth. Do carry on then. I can't wait to find out either."

Benvenuto placed his chisel at the head of the mould and took aim with his mallet.

"I heard you had some trouble here," the Duke said.

Benvenuto halted the blow in mid-air. "I beg your Excellency's pardon?"

"Trouble. I hear you had some trouble."

The Duke jerked his head in the direction of the burnt wreckage of the shed. "That trouble."

"Oh that. There wasn't any trouble. The roof started to smoulder, that's all. Your Grace is doubtless thinking, couldn't the statue have been damaged?' It could have been. And then you are thinking 'how was it saved?' I'll tell you. It was saved by the extraordinary bravery of me and my men. And then you will...."

"I'd rather you didn't tell me what you think I'm thinking. Actually, there's only one question I've got: how did it happen?"

That was the one question Benvenuto had been trying to avoid. "Because Rizzio didn't give me enough money to build a proper furnace house like I wanted. It's the sort of thing that happens when you put a miserly bookkeeper in charge of anything - especially something he doesn't understand."

Benvenuto lifted the mallet again.

"I heard that the metal all curdled in the furnace," the Duke said.

Benvenuto slowly and deliberately laid his tools down. He glared at the two foundrymen until they wilted. Now he knew the meaning of the strange look that had passed between the two men the night before. Now he knew who the Duke's spies were.

"Your Grace is well informed. It happened while I was resting before the critical stage of the pouring. Unfortunately those two fellows over there couldn't follow my simple instructions.

Oh, I don't really blame them," he said magnanimously. "I suppose they did their best. It's only natural that their master at the bell foundry wouldn't send me his most skilled workers."

"You said you were 'resting'. I heard you thought you were dying," said the Duke.

"This time your Excellency's informants have let you down," Benvenuto lied, shooting a sideways glance at the two smelters who shuffled their feet sheepishly. "Do I look as if I've even been indisposed, let alone ill or dying? Is there anything else your Grace desires to know? If not, may I begin my work?"

"Please," said the Duke.

The chisel took its first bite into the hard baked clay. After a few blows, several large lumps fell away. Benvenuto placed a wooden stake on the exposed inner side of the mould, and struck it with his mallet and broke off the last piece covering the head.

With a besom whisk, he brushed away the remaining fragments of the mould and most of the flakes of white dusty material adhering to the metal. He took hold of the winged helmet and tugged. It held firm. Then he crouched down on his haunches and ran his hand over the face, finally tweaking its slim nose between his first two fingers.

"My! You are a handsome fellow!"

He straightened up and exuberantly signalled the Duke by making a circle with his thumb and finger. Cosimo stood at Benvenuto's side staring at the curly hair on the back of Perseus' head, then he too crouched down, his fine brocade cloak trailing on the ground.

"Yes, it's true. He is a handsome fellow. Now, what about Medusa's head? Do you think you managed to make the metal run upwards?"

"If Perseus' head came out, then so did Medusa's," Benvenuto said confidently.

"Perhaps you'll show me."

The piece was designed so that when it was standing upright, Perseus would have his left arm raised high, holding Medusa's severed head by the hair. With the figure lying face down on the trestles, the arm stuck out almost parallel with the ground.

Benvenuto cut a circle round where he judged the middle of the forearm to be, and split the mould down to the wrist. A few more blows, and there was Medusa's head, eyes closed, thick sensuous lips turned down and spirals of blood dripping from her neck.

"Perfect, my dear fellow. Perfect."

"Messer Cellini," the Duchess spoke for the first time, "aren't the arm and head very heavy?"

"Yes, Madame, they are."

"Then won't the arm bend?"

"I see we shall make a sculptor of your ladyship yet," Benvenuto replied condescendingly. "The metal nearest to the shoulder is a lot thicker than at the hand end. Not only does it make it stronger, but I don't have to worry about the statue overbalancing either."

"Why that's very clever, isn't it, my Lord?" she asked the Duke.

"It's his job to think of these things," Cosimo replied peevishly. "Now are we going to see how the right leg came out?"

"It didn't, Your Grace"

"How can you tell until you've looked? Come on, set to. I want to see for myself."

"It will take longer to break the mould. A lot longer. Both legs are in one solid thick skin of clay to the knees."

"In that case," said the Duke, "send for a couple of chairs. Her Grace and I will sit."

Cosimo saw the housekeeper standing watching with the rest of the staff. "Ah, Madame Fiore, I don't suppose you've got any of those delicious almond macaroons you used to make for me when I was sitting for the bust?"

The woman curtsied and rushed towards the kitchen door.

"And some white wine would be nice," he added.

"Ready," Benvenuto called, and the Duke and Duchess came to look. The whole of the right calf, ankle and heel were all there, but the toes and the front of the foot were missing.

"Not too bad, Your Grace. In fact it's much better than I thought it would be."

"How so?"

"The alloy was of an exceptionally high quality and slipping some pewter into the channels must have helped it to run more smoothly. In fact, it's quite likely that I've invented a whole new process, thanks to that pair of incompetents over there."

The Duke carefully brushed some crumbs from his tunic.

"I believe it's time for us to go. Messer Cellini," he said briskly. "I wish you good fortune in uncovering the rest of the piece."

"I pray it will be worthy of a great Prince." Benvenuto gave an elaborate bow.

"We shall visit you again very soon." Arm in arm with the Duchess, and followed by Rizzio, Cosimo left the work yard. The Duchess gracefully inclined her head at Benvenuto and smiled at him as she passed.

He was obviously forgiven for the incident of the pearls.

Even before the "Perseus" was publicly unveiled it attracted a great deal of attention and praise. Tradesmen and visitors to the studio got glimpses of it in spite of the boards covering the gates of the work yard. Also, Benvenuto could not avoid inviting members of the Florentine artists' colony to private previews - even if he had wanted to. And then the Duke got into the habit of bringing distinguished visitors in to watch – "hold up", Benvenuto used to complain - the work on the statue during the long months that it took to clean and finish it.

Even Michelangelo, who had seen some drawings and heard descriptions of the bronze, took time from working simultaneously on St. Peter's and the Farnese Palace and the Capitol to write to him from Rome.

> "My dear Benvenuto,
> I have always thought you were the greatest goldsmith ever, but now you have proved you are a master sculptor also …."

This gave Benvenuto an idea. In 1500, the year Benvenuto was born, Michelangelo had carved into the band crossing the bosom of the Virgin in his newly finished **Pieta** the words:

> "Michaelangelvs Bonarotvs Florent Faciebat"
> *("Michelangelo Buonarroti of Florence made this").*

If Michelangelo could, then why should he not indulge in the same sort of self advertisement? So on the leather strap crossing Perseus' naked body supporting the scabbard of his drawn sword, he embossed a similar message:

> "Benvenuto Cellini, Sculptor, of Florence made this."

The Perseus and its plinth were taken in secret to the Loggia dei Lanzi and hidden behind screens while they were set in place in the front row, and on the day that the hoardings were taken down, the Piazza della Signoria was thronged with people as if it was a feast day.

When the canvases were pulled aside, there was a second or two of silence, followed by a roar of cheering, and then a surge as everyone pressed forward to get a closer look.

It was Benvenuto's greatest ever triumph, and he enjoyed every moment of it as he stood with Cosimo at the second floor window of the Palazzo Vecchio, acknowledging the shouts of the crowd until Cosimo pulled him back inside to share some wine.

Overnight, little notes and the customary sonnets of praise appeared in all the available niches and crevices of the statue, some in Latin and Greek from scholars from the nearby University of Pisa.

Even Bandinelli was forced to find some grudging words of approval.

"It's certainly not to my taste, and artistically, well, I'm not so sure either. But as a technical feat of bronze casting, I must agree that it's a remarkable achievement. Perhaps that is what he should be doing: executing the work for real artists."

-52-

A few days after the unveiling of the "Perseus' – "my Perseus" as Benvenuto ever afterwards proudly called it - and as soon as the Duke had been able to gauge the views of both public and artists, Cosimo very properly started the arrangements to have the statue valued.

He realised that it would be unfair to Benvenuto to allow Bandinelli to do it, so he instructed his Chief of Staff, Rizzio, to go and ask Benvenuto to suggest an impartial expert. If Cosimo and Benvenuto could not agree upon a single valuer, then, since this was a major work of art, they would each appoint one, and those two would select a third, a so-called "Jury of Artists".

Rizzio arrived unannounced at Benvenuto's studio one afternoon, just as they were finishing the midday meal. He was relaxing with del Moro and Tasso, and still basking in the enjoyment of the complimentary letters that were still arriving daily.

Fabbiana put her head round the door. "Master, Messer Rizzio's here to see you."

"Rizzio? What in hell's name does he want? The last thing I need right now is to see that pen-pusher. You know," he said waving his goblet in the air, "these bookkeepers are all alike. This one reminds me of that swine da Prato, although he's not quite as ugly."

Rizzio followed Fabbiana into the room without waiting to be asked. "I heard that."

"So now you're here, perhaps you'll tell me what I can do for you. If you've come to see how much bronze I've got left over, it's about a bucket full. I'll make you a chamber pot with it if you like, decorated with your coat of arms."

"I'm here with an important message from His Grace, Duke Cosimo," Rizzio said pompously.

Benvenuto who was a little drunk lurched unsteadily to his feet.

"In that case I'll take back everything I've just said about you. Anyone who brings important messages from the Duke must be a very important man himself." He gave a deep bow. "Pray proceed, Your Magnificence."

"Messer Cellini, I am His Grace's representative. In future you will speak to me with proper respect."

"Is that the Duke's important message?" Benvenuto asked scornfully. "Thanks very much. Excuse me if I don't show you out!"

"He sent me to ask you how much you want for the Perseus."

"WHAT!" Benvenuto exploded. "What's that he said?"

The Duke, of course had said nothing of the sort. All Rizzio was supposed to do was to discuss the choice of a valuer, with both patron and artist standing aloof from such mundane matters as money, avoiding any unseemly haggling about price, but Rizzio had endured so much abuse and so many insults from Benvenuto over the years, culminating in this latest display in front of his two cronies that in his rage he deliberately altered the Duke's message into the most objectionable terms that he could think of.

Benvenuto duly took the bait and advanced on Rizzio, reaching for his throat. Rizzio retreated a step or two until he backed against the table before Benvenuto realised just in time what the Duke would do to him if he so much as laid hands on his Chief of Staff.

He slightly changed his stance and held out his ten extended fingers.

"Ten thousand crowns. Tell his Illustrious Excellency that it's not for sale. Not even for ten thousand crowns. Great works of art aren't bought and sold like cabbages in the market. They are **given** by the artist to a patron who doesn't pay for them. He generously **shows his appreciation**. The Duke shall not have my Perseus. I'll remove it as soon as I find someone worthy of it. He can keep the plinth with my compliments as a souvenir."

Rizzio realised that he had gone too far.

"You wouldn't refuse to let the Duke have the statue, would you?"

"You're watching me do it"

"Benvenuto," del Moro intervened "you can't! I don't believe it!"

Benvenuto rounded on him. "You can believe it more than you believe in your immortal soul. Now shut up and don't interfere."

Rizzio was aghast. He clapped his hand to his mouth.

"What shall I tell His Grace?"

"Anything you damn well like. Now, piss off, I'm getting bored with this conversation."

Rizzio stopped at the door.

"I rather think, Messer Cellini," he said brightly, "that the next severed head to be exhibited in Florence might be yours."

—⚜—

Rizzio wasted no time in making mischief with the Duke.

"Cellini says he doesn't need a valuer. He says he knows what it's worth. He wants - no he actually demands - ten thousand crowns."

"Ten thousand crowns?" the Duke scoffed. "I could build a new palace for ten thousand crowns - a whole city," he exaggerated.

"He says the statue is his, and if you won't pay him what he wants, then he'll take it back and sell it to someone else."

"Are you sure you didn't say something to provoke him, Messer Rizzio?" asked the Duchess. She knew only too well what went on between him and Benvenuto.

Rizzio shook his head.

The Duke frowned. "You may well be right, Madame. With wild talk like that, something must have happened...." Rizzio tried to avoid Cosimo's accusing eye. "…. but I'm not going to demean myself by asking Cellini what his version is. You say that there were other people present and heard all this? Well, that settles it, Bandinelli can value it," he decided, "and Cellini will just have to accept his figure."

Bandinelli fixed the price at three thousand five hundred crowns - a carefully calculated sum. Not so low that the Florentines would regard it as unreasonable and obviously inadequate, but certainly far from generous, and much less than could have been justified by the universal acclaim the piece had received.

The Duchess Eleanora sent Benvenuto an urgent private message via Cosimo's Secretary, Ugolini Grifoni.

"Her Grace advises you not to accept the valuation. She will plead your cause with her husband and will persuade him to give you five thousand crowns."

Benvenuto was too indignant and upset, first by Rizzio's insult, which he now also blamed on the Duke who had not tried to put matters right, and then by what he regarded as Bandinelli's vindictive valuation, to take advantage of the Duchess' offer.

"Please thank Her Grace. She is very kind - kinder than I deserve. I don't care what the Duke pays. I don't care who hears that the Duke has robbed me. The whole world should know how he treats artists. No one will ever work for him again."

Benvenuto was near to tears with mortification. "I refuse to accept anything from him. No amount is enough if he pays it with a bad heart. I've already said that my Perseus is not for sale."

Now the Duke was in a real dilemma: how to get this temperamental artist to accept any payment at all, and at the same time avoiding it being thought that he had forced an unfair settlement on him, especially as the news of the quarrel was spreading, with public sentiment being on Benvenuto's side.

It was Grifoni who tactfully found the solution which preserved the dignity of both sides: Benvenuto would accept the three thousand five hundred crowns that had been grudgingly assessed by Bandinelli, but this was not to be regarded as payment for the Perseus. It was an "honorarium" and a "contribution towards Messer Benvenuto Cellini's upkeep while he had been creating his great artistic achievement."

Letters were duly exchanged to this effect, but Cosimo was still smarting from having been put in an uncomfortable position without having done anything to deserve the storm that burst around his head.

The inevitable result was that no more commissions were forthcoming from the Palace.

Benvenuto's studio worked on quite well on staple bread-and-butter pieces in gold and silver ordered by customers for whom he barely concealed his contempt, realising that they were coming to him only to boast that they had something by Benvenuto Cellini, but at the minimum possible outlay.

In his own time he made, entirely in bronze his own version of "Ganymede" mounted on a fierce eagle, which was one of the many shapes that Zeus changed himself into.

He also made a superb bust of the Roman banker, Bindo Altovini, which irritated the Duke even further. Not only was it inevitably compared with Benvenuto's bust of Cosimo, but also Cosimo also discovered that Altovini had invested Benvenuto's money for him by lending it to Cosimo at interest, which for some reason the Duke irrationally regarded as some sort of trick.

"I pay him handsomely for his work so that he can lend it back to me and charge me interest on my own money," the Duke grumbled. "Don't talk to me about 'unworldly artists.' This one's missed his vocation. He should have been a moneylender. 'Benvenuto' he calls himself? 'Malvenuto' is more like it." After all these years the Duke had invented a new joke about Benvenuto's name. "I wish I'd never heard of him."

Benvenuto also tried his hand at sculpting in marble.

He finished off his "**Apollo and Giacinto**" and "**Narcissus**" that he had started after his return from Paris and had worked at in his spare time, on and off, as the mood took him, but the slim and graceful, boyish figures in the Greek style that he carved were not to the liking of the Florentines who preferred the muscular, voluptuous figures that Michelangelo had made fashionable.

In a period of melancholy and depression, he also made a crucifix in the brittle black Carrara marble on which he fixed a life-sized Christ in starkly contrasting white marble also from Carrara, whose face bore a resemblance to himself at the age when Jesus was crucified - thirty three years.

He morbidly designed this crucifix as his own tombstone and then had the humiliation of it being rejected by the monks of Santa Maria Novella which he had chosen as his last resting place, and instead had to offer it to the Church of the Annunciation where his ailing enemy Bandinelli was racing against time to complete his own tomb in the Pazzi chapel.

During these bitter, empty, frustrating years, Benvenuto became more and more quarrelsome, He fought with everybody.

He also became even more intensely preoccupied over money. He added to his farm at Pisa by purchasing an adjoining property, and becoming violently ill soon afterwards, convinced himself that he had been poisoned by his tenant, so he then tried to get the transaction cancelled by beginning a long and acrimonious piece of litigation which took up a most of his time and sapped his remaining creative energy.

His physical strength was also failing him. Never in the best of health as a result of his privations in jail and his recurring bouts of fever, he found that his hands were losing their suppleness and power, while his eyes, from years of straining, often in poor light, over fine engraving and etching, were becoming watery and his vision blurred.

—⁂—

Almost without thinking about it, Benvenuto came to a decision. Before there could be any possibility of changing his mind he hurried to tell his sister, Cosa.

"I've decided to retire. I'm going to Pisa to live on my farm, and I'm never going to come back to Florence again if I can help it."

Cosa took hold of his hands and ran her thumbs over his long calloused fingers.

"You're going to stop working? I don't believe it. And what will you live on?"

"Cosa, I'm sixty two years old. What with the money I brought from France and what I've earned here in the last seventeen years, the rent from my farm and the investments banker Altovini has been making for me, I've got enough to keep me comfortably for the rest of my life. You're my only responsibility, and I can still give you an allowance until Ugo finally earns that fortune he keeps trying for."

"You shouldn't laugh at him like that."

"Why not?" said Benvenuto with a broad smile, "For what he's cost me over the years, I'm at least entitled to a bit of amusement for my money!" Seeing that Cosa was upset with him he reminded her, "At least 'Seppina and Elisabetta are well settled with good husbands."

"Thanks to the dowries you gave them. And with families of their own too. You should be a grandfather yourself by now," Cosa said accusingly.

"I might be, for all I know." Benvenuto replied. "Alright. I know, none of that sort of talk in your house," he added as Cosa started to get angry again. "And the answer to your other question is that I never said I was going to stop working."

"But you said you were retiring."

"That means that I'm going to stop making things for customers. I'm going to make the things I want to for my own satisfaction, not what someone else orders. You know," he said, nibbling on a little biscuit that Cosa offered him, "I've come to the conclusion that in one way, Father was right."

"I never thought I'd live long enough ever to hear you say that. Go on, tell me."

"Don't you remember that routine of his about how a goldsmith was only a shopkeeper and 'you do my humble establishment too much honour by allowing me to work for you'? Then there was the one about 'Does Your Excellency want to kick my'...."

"Benvenuto! I've told you before I won't stand for your swearing in my house."

"Well anyway that's exactly how these know-nothings do expect you to behave, and I've had enough of it - and of them. It's worse than that. I spend months making something, and no sooner is it finished than they have it melted down again because they can't afford it. That's why I've turned my hand to sculpting. They can't melt marble and let's hope they'll never need my bronze to make cannon with."

Cosa began to cry. "But why have you got to go away? Can't you retire here in Florence?"

"Pisa's only a day's ride away. You can come and see me whenever you like. There's plenty of room. You can bring Ugo too," Benvenuto added generously.

"But you'll be coming back to Florence sometimes on business, won't you?"

"Not if I can help it. To tell you the truth, as much as I used to love it, now I hate it. Everywhere I look I see magnificent works of art, but none of them mine - except the Perseus and a couple of marbles in the Boboli Gardens that nobody likes, and some bronzes locked away out of sight in private houses."

"But your friends are here."

"What friends? Poor old del Moro's gone. So are most of the others. If you live long enough, you finish up knowing more dead people than live ones."

"What will you do for workers out there in Pisa?"

"Tasso's just lost his wife. He doesn't want to stay here either. He says he'll come and work for me as soon as he finishes the contracts he's got. I'll get a couple of apprentices - there's no shortage of goldsmiths who would like to be trained by me and I can always hire any craftsmen I need. In any case, the first thing I'm going to do isn't either goldsmithing or sculpting."

"What is it then?" Cosa asked.

"I'm going to write my life story. Everyone tells me that I've done so much and known so many famous people, I ought to write it all down."

Cosa nodded her agreement.

"I'll also be able to tell my side of the story about how these so-called noblemen treat great artists. I'm going to write another book too: a treatise on the art of goldsmithing. If I can't leave any of my work behind because the bastards - I beg your pardon - because the customers keep melting them down, at least I should tell future generations how to do it properly!"

"But why you?"

"Because who is there better qualified than the greatest goldsmith the world has ever known? You know who called me that? Michelangelo himself!" he said triumphantly.

—⁂—

Benvenuto sold up what his belongings as he did not want and sent the rest ahead on a carrier's cart.

He rode along the banks of the River Arno and turned down the **Borgo Ognissanti** - the Street of All Saints. His birthday was on All Saints' Day.

From there he continued along the Borgo Prato, and out of the city by the Prato Gate and on to the road to Pisa.

Forty-five years before, when he had followed exactly the same route on his first journey to Pisa, he had been a young man with his head full of ambitions, plans and dreams. Now here he was, old, ill and embittered, with those ambitions unfulfilled.

He had money, but he was not wealthy; he was well known, but not as famous as he wished; respected, but not popular.

As he rode through the Prato Gate, he suddenly remembered his old foe, Tommaso da Prato and a montage of names began to pass through his mind. A lifetime of friends and enemies, lovers, patrons and fellow artists - all mixed together:

Two Popes, Clement VII and Paul III; two Kings, Charles V and Francis I; two Queens of France; Cardinal d'Este, Cardinal de' Medici, the Bishop of Salamanca, Duke Cosimo, Madonna Porzia, Madame d' Etampes, Pier Luigi Farnese, Gabriello Ceserino, Rafaello del Moro and Gina, Lucagnolo, Pompeo, Bandinelli, Primaticcio, Caterina and Pagolo, Pantasilea, Busbacca and Ascanio and a host of others.

He had gone about two miles along the road.

On past occasions that he had left a city that had been his home - Florence that first time, Rome, and then Paris - he had always stopped to take a final look back.

This time he kept his eyes firmly looking forward between his horse's ears.

Then, for no reason he could think of, he reached behind him into his saddle bag. He touched the wooden box holding his toy see-saw and felt around until he found his flute.

He put it to his lips and began to play.

- FINITO -

Afterword

Benvenuto's fears were well founded. Hardly any of his work has survived, although some collections boast items "attributed to Cellini."

Of the pieces mentioned in this book, the most important, the Francis I Salt Cellar (completed in 1543), is in the Kunsthistorisches Museum, Vienna. It was stolen from the museum on 11th May 2003 by thieves who smashed through a window after climbing up some scaffolding to the first floor. It was recovered on January 21st 2006 having been buried in a lead box in a forest about 50 miles from Vienna. The culprit was identified having been photographed by a security camera purchasing a mobile phone which he then used to send text messages in order to secure a ransom.

Pope Clement's Cope button was broken up for its gems and melted down in 1797, but a detailed drawing of it by Francesco Bartoli is in the British Museum, London. The bust of Duke Cosimo is in the dreaded Bargello Prison, which now houses the Museo Nazionale, Florence and so is "Narcissus". The "Nymph of Fontainebleau" is in the Louvre, Paris.

The bust of the banker, Bindo Altoviti, is in the Isabella Stewart Gardner Museum, Boston, Massachusetts. Paradoxically, to the right of this bust is a self-portrait of Baccio Bandinelli from which his description in this book is taken. "Perseus" stands in his original place of honour in the front left-hand corner of the Loggia dei Lanzi in the Piazza della Signoria, just a few yards from Bandinelli's despised statue of "Hercules and Cacus".

With equal irony, Benvenuto is buried in the Church of the Annunciation close to Bandinelli who died in 1560.

Benvenuto Cellini died in Florence on February 13th 1571, aged 70.

Acknowledgements

I would like to express my special thanks to Dr. Manfred Leithe-Jasper of the Kunsthistorisches Museum, Vienna for sparing the time to talk to me extensively about the Francis I Salt Cellar.

I am also grateful to the museum for their permission to use their copyright photograph of the Salt Cellar on the cover of this book.

Also the staffs of the British Museum, London; the Metropolitan Museum of Art, New York; the Isabella Stewart Gardner Museum, Boston and the Museo Nazionale, Florence for their courtesy and help. I regret that I cannot extend similar thanks to the Louvre, Paris.

I am also grateful to several friends who read one or other of the drafts (they know who they are) and for their helpful comments and advice, some of which I took!

Last, but not least, my secretaries for their sterling work in translating into typescript, the hundreds of pages of the original manuscript, written with a blunt pencil (really!) in handwriting that **"some people"** pretend to find difficult to read.

Author's note and Bibliography

This book is an historical novel – "faction" – a work of mixed fact and fiction.

The historical narrative is accurate within the bounds of interpretation of sometimes conflicting recorded "facts" and the confines of the space available to me.

On the fiction side, I have taken the novelist's privilege of inventing conversations, of sometimes combining several characters into one and of giving my own explanation for otherwise inexplicable occurrences. After all, the distinguished historian Procacci did describe Cellini's own account of his life as "adventure fiction."

Since this is a novel and not a thesis for a Doctorate, it may be presumptuous to include a detailed bibliography incorporating many of the books that I have referred to in many years of research. However, those readers who have borne with me so far may be assumed to have some interest in the period, and the following is an abbreviated list of some of the reference material.

First and foremost and above all, Benvenuto's own brash, rambling and sometimes contradictory autobiography, "La Vita" of which there are superb translations into English going back as far as 1822 (Roscoe), 1887 (J.A. Symonds), 1903 (A.MacDonell), 1910 (Cust) and more recently in 1956 by George Bull.

Then there is Cellini's **"Trattati dell' Oreficeria, della Scultura e Discorsi Sopra l'Arte"**, "Treatises on Goldsmithing and Sculpture." There is a translation into English by C. R. Ashbee (1888).

Other books covering the period are:
Art & Architecture in France (1500-1700). Anthony Blunt (1953)
Four Centuries of European Jewellery. E. Bradford (1953)
Cesare Borgia Sarah Bradford. (1976)
Civilisation of the Renaissance in Italy. Jacob Burckhardt (1960)
Culture & Society in Renaissance Italy. Peter Burke (1972)
The Fall of the House of Borgia. E. R. Chamberlin (1974)
Florence in the Time of the Medici. E. R. Chamberlin (1979)
The Flowering of the Renaissance. Vincent Cronin (1969)
Army Royal. An Account of Henry VIII's Invasion of France, 1513. C. G. Cruickshank (1969)
The Counter Reformation. A. G. Dickens (1968)
Imperial Spain. J. H. Elliot (1963)
Reformation Europe. G. R. Elton (1963)
Heresy and Obedience in Tridentine Italy.
Cardinal Pole & the Counter-Reformation. Dermot Fenton (1972)
A History of Europe. H. A. L. Fisher (1936)
Life in Italy at the Time of the Medici. John Gage (1968)
Battle of Pavia. Jean Giono (1963)
Renaissance and Reformation. V. H. H. Green (1952)
Numismatics. Philip Grierson (1975)
Essays on French Humanism (1470-1600). Ed. Werner Gundersheimer (1969)
Florence and the Medici. J. R. Hale (1977)
Introduction to Italian Sculpture. John Hope Hennessy (1967)
Catherine de Medicis. Jean Hertier (1963) Translated by Charlotte Haldane
The Rise and Fall of the House of Medici. Christopher Hibbert (1974)
Goldsmiths and Silversmiths. Hugh Honour (1971)
The Sack of Rome (1527). Judith Hook (1972)
Jarbuch der Kunsthistorisches Museum (1966)
Louis XI. P. M. Kendall (1971)
Goldschmiedarbeiten des Mittelalters der Renaissance und das Barok. Dr. Ernest Kris

Armour and Weapons. Paul Martin (1967)
Power and Imagination (City States in Renaissance Italy). Lauro Martines (1979)
Man and the Renaissance. Andrew Martindale
Concise History of Warfare. Earl Montgomery of Alemain (1968)
The Hapsburg-Valois Wars and the Blaise de Monluc (1592)
French Wars of Religion. Edited Ian Roy (1971)
The Late Renaissance and Mannerism. Linda Murray (1967)
The History of the Italian People. Guiliano Procacci (1970)
Henry VIII. Jasper Ridley (1984)
Lorenzo the Magnificent. Maurice Rowdon (1974)
A Concise History of Bronzes. George Savage (1968)
Henry VIII. J. J. Scarisbrick (1968)
Prince of the Renaissance, Francis I. Desmond Seward (1973)
The Medici Ferdinand. Schevill (1949)
Oxford Companion to Music. Percy N. Scholes
Gold. C. H. V. Sutherland (1959)
History of Fortification. Sidney Toy (1953)
Short History of the Italian People. J. P. Trevelyan (1956)
Catherine de' Medici. Hugh Ross Williamson (1973)
Lorenzo the Magnificent. Hugh Ross Williamson (1974)

Lightning Source UK Ltd.
Milton Keynes UK
UKOW051440170512

192765UK00002B/10/P